KILL RED

KILL RED

MAX O'HARA

PINNACLE BOOKS
Kensington Publishing Corp.
www.kensingtonbooks.com

PINNACLE BOOKS are published by

Kensington Publishing Corp.
119 West 40th Street
New York, NY 10018

All Kensington titles, imprints, and distributed lines are available at special quantity discounts for bulk purchases for sales promotion, premiums, fund-raising, educational, or institutional use.

Special book excerpts or customized printings can also be created to fit specific needs. For details, write or phone the office of the Kensington Sales Manager: Attn.: Sales Department. Kensington Publishing Corp., 119 West 40th Street, New York, NY 10018. Phone: 1-800-221-2647.

PINNACLE BOOKS and the Pinnacle logo are Reg. U.S. Pat. & TM Off.

First Printing: June 2022
ISBN-13: 978-0-7860-4712-3
ISBN-13: 978-0-7860-4716-1 (eBook)

10 9 8 7 6 5 4 3 2 1

Printed in the United States of America

CHAPTER 1

"*Help!* The railroad dick Wolf Stockburn's gone madder'n a bull buff with a snoot full of cockleburs! Somebody rassle him down before he kills the lot of us and rips the saloon to *smithereens!*"

Stockburn had heard the plea, which an old graybeard had shouted into the street, a half second before a large clenched red fist came arcing toward Wolf from behind a stout shoulder clad in green plaid wool. The clenched fingers were broad and white, pink at the tips, and with dirt showing beneath the thick, shell-like nails.

That fist slammed against Wolf's left cheek. It was a hammering, brain-numbing blow. Having just thrown a punch of his own, this one came before Stockburn could prepare for it. It was obviously delivered by a big man who'd thrown a few punches before. Stockburn flew back onto a table, his six-foot-four-inch frame clad in hard muscle breaking the table right down the middle.

The railroad detective smashed through the table to the floor, both halves of the table dropping toward him at steep slants, spilling onto him several shot glasses and their contents, a whiskey bottle and its contents, a couple of ashtrays, playing cards, coins, and greenbacks.

Wolf sat up, shook his head, then scrambled to his feet, brushing the whiskey and cards and ashes and half-smoked cigarettes off his chest and belly, and looked around for the man who'd thrown the punch. Through a fog of senseless fury, he saw the green plaid shirt before him. The shirt was crowned with a big, square head and a cap of thinning dark red hair behind a bulging forehead, and a thick beard of the same color. The big man, a muleskinner named Whip Larimore, was crouching, waving his fists, smiling at Stockburn in challenge.

His brown eyes glinted with inebriation and open mockery.

"If you liked that one, Stockburn, get up! I got plenty more where that one came from! I'll turn you inside out and beat your head flatter'n a pancake grill!"

Bellowing like a poleaxed bull, Stockburn leaped to his feet then dropped to a crouch in time to avoid another savage blow from Larimore's swollen fist. He heard the whoosh of displaced air over his head. Larimore gave a startled grunt when his punch missed its mark by a good foot. Staying low and still bellowing, Stockburn leaped forward and bulled into the muleskinner's broad, lumpy chest, driving him up off his feet and backward.

Now adding his own yells to Stockburn's as he and Wolf went airborne, flying backward toward a large plate-glass window over which the words THE ATHENAEUM SALOON were written in large green-leaf letters in a broad arc. Those letters separated, shattered, blew outward, and fell along with the rest of the window as the two men, locked together like two rogue grizzlies in a battle-to-the-death over the same sow, flew through it.

They landed together on the boardwalk fronting the saloon, still locked together, raging, lips stretched back from gritted teeth, broken glass peppering them both.

"You four-flushin', double-dealin', fat, ugly poker cheat!" Stockburn raged, rising to his knees, glass tumbling off his head and shoulders. He slammed his right fist across Larimore's heavy jaw.

The man's head was so large and solid it was like punching a side of fresh beef. Larimore shook off the blow, grinning, then rose up sharply to slam his big head against Stockburn's own.

Ears ringing, vision swimming, Wolf sagged backward.

Larimore slammed his meaty fist into Stockburn's left cheek.

That drove Wolf farther backward. Somehow, he managed to lift himself to his feet. He'd seen Larimore gain his own stout legs and knew that if he was low when Larimore was high, that would be the end of him.

Vaguely, beneath the yells of the crowd that had followed him and Larimore out of the saloon and onto the boardwalk, he heard someone shouting his name. The shouts grew louder as the shouter drew closer, but Stockburn gave the shouts no more notice than he would a fly buzzing several feet away.

He was ready when the big bearded muleskinner bolted toward him, bringing a hamlike fist up from his heels. Again, Stockburn ducked. Again, he heard the whoosh and the grunt. He stepped forward, hips and shoulders squared, raised fists clenched, and smashed the right one against Larimore's hard, meaty face.

He followed the right with a left and then another right.
Another left.

Right.

Left.

"Wolf!" a man's pleading voice yelled, closer now than
before.

Ignoring the yells, Wolf kept moving forward, crouching,
working his feet like a well-trained pugilist, hammering the
muleskinner's face with a blur of jabs and uppercuts as
Larimore grunted and groaned and staggered backward
along the boardwalk fronting the saloon. As the Red Sea
parted for Moses, the yelling crowd made way for the two
warring bruins.

Smack! Smack!

Smack-Smack-Smack!

Smackkk!

Each blow so dazed and weakened Larimore, his face
turning redder and redder with fresh blood oozing from
his eyes, nose, and smashed lips, that he was no longer
able to raise his hands to defend himself. Each punishing
blow so tormented him that he was at the mercy of the big
man before him clad in a black three-piece suit with white
silk shirt and ribbon tie, broken glass still raining down
from his head distinguished by a thick mane of roached,
prematurely gray hair that stood out in sharp contrast to
the brick red of his broad, chiseled face further singular-
ized by a pair of deep-set, coal-dark eyes.

"Wolf!" came the pleading voice again from behind
Stockburn.

Again, Stockburn smashed the muleskinner's face.

"Wolf—stop, galldangit! I ain't gonna say it again!"

Though Stockburn knew the shouter was close behind

him, to his enraged mind the man's pleas seemed to come from the bottom of a distant well.

Again, he slammed his left fist against Larimore's jaw.

"All right—you asked for it. I'm sorry, old pard!"

Stockburn had started to thrust his left clenched fist forward once more when something hard slammed against the back of his head and everything went as black as night and as quiet as a mountain lake at midnight.

When Wolf opened his eyes again, a poison-tipped Apache arrow of raw misery pierced his pupils to drive deep into his brain. The fiery poison spread like acid, instantly corroding the tender nerves.

"*Ayyy!*" he cried, gritting his teeth.

He lay very still on a cot, a sour wool blanket beneath him. He squeezed his eyes closed, waiting for that arrow to give a little ground. Every muscle in his strapping, forty-year-old body was drawn taut as razor wire.

The arrow slid back a little, giving some ground, the pain abating if only slightly.

Wolf opened his eyes. He wasn't sure where he was. He had no idea how long he'd been out like a blown lamp. It could have been a few minutes, several hours, or, hell, even a few days. His mouth felt stuffed with soiled cotton.

Lying there on the cot, he found himself staring at a small hole at the base of a mud brick wall. Something moved inside the hole. Light glinted off two tiny eyes and then the small, arrow-shaped head took shape as the rat moved closer and stuck its long-whiskered, pink-tipped snout into the room, the sides of the narrow hole pressing the rat's ears back flat against its head.

As the rodent slid its head into the room, the hole slid back to release its ears. The ears sprang straight up in the air. They resembled a mule's ears—albeit those of a rat-sized mule. They were stiff and triangular, a dirty gray color on the outside, pale pink on the inside.

The pointed snout worked, sniffing.

The rat looked around. It looked up at Stockburn.

The pair exchanged stares for stretched seconds. If the rat felt any fear of the man, it gave no indication. It peeped faintly, still working its nose, and pushed its body, roughly the size of a small man's fist, out of the hole and into the stone-floored room. It swung to its right and scuttled along the floor against the wall, head down, sniffing, pausing to nibble what appeared to be tiny bread crumbs, maybe some bits of bacon from a bacon sandwich.

It paused to investigate a very small, shriveled, dried brown apple core, which had to be well over a week old. After giving the core a thorough sniffing, and apparently finding nothing desirable about it, the rat took two steps forward before its vaguely oval-shaped, gray-brown body erupted in blood and torn bits of skin and fur spraying onto the floor and the wall behind it.

The shredded beast lay shivering, little spidery feet quivering, before the mangled carcass lay still.

Blood dribbled down the wall above it.

Stockburn sucked a sharp breath and squeezed his eyes closed as the concussive report of the gun exploded inside his head, threatening to do to his skull what the bullet had just done to the rat.

A man guffawed as the echoes of the blast gradually stopped rocketing off the adobe brick walls surrounding Stockburn. "Sorry to wake ya, Wolf! I been after that rat for a week now!"

More laughter.

Stockburn opened his eyes. The rotten egg odor of gun smoke fouled his nostrils as he turned his head to gaze through the iron straps of a cell door. A tall, skinny man in a worn, sweat-stained white shirt and black leather vest and patch-kneed black denim trousers crouched forward, thin shoulders jerking as he laughed. Waylon Wallace, marshal of Ruidoso, held his smoking Smith & Wesson Russian .44 straight down along his right leg, smoke still curling from the barrel.

That was probably the barrel that had caused the goose egg Stockburn could feel still rising, throbbing, on the back of his head, near the crown. Probing with his fingers, he felt a short cut on the swollen area, crusted with semi-dry blood, which meant he'd been out only an hour or so though it felt like days.

"Thanks a lot, Waylon."

"Don't mention it, Wolf." Still chuckling, his craggy, gray-bearded, sixty-year-old face mottled red with wry humor, the lawman pulled a ladderback chair out from the wall by the door. He dragged it over in front of Stockburn's cell and plopped into it, swinging his arms up and groaning against the creaks in his arthritic hips. "Rats carry rabies, don't you know."

"So do town marshals, apparently. A good dose of rabies must be what made you kiss the back of my head with that old Russian of yours."

"Nope, nope." Waylon crossed his long legs, skinny as broom handles, and wagged his head. "You caused that your ownself. You wouldn't pull your horns in. Not for anything. I gave you fair warning."

"I reckon I didn't hear you," Stockburn lied.

"You would have killed Larimore if I hadn't introduced

you to my trusty Smith & Wesson. Not that killing an underhanded varmint like that would have been any real loss, but I'd have had to arrest you for murder. Neither of us would have wanted that, Wolf."

"Small price to pay."

"What caused the foofaraw?"

"He and Fritz Carlson were cheating. They'd been cheating the whole damn game, since six o'clock this morning. I warned 'em twice but I still saw another creased card on the table."

"That's when you went off half-cocked and slammed Carlson's face down on the table? The sawbones is with him now, tryin' to straighten out his nose. Larimore's over there, too, waiting for stitches."

Stockburn looked at him with a question in his eyes.

"Nils Taylor filled me in." Taylor was the barman on duty at the Athenaeum. "Says you exploded like a Napoleon cannon, just reached across the table, grabbed a handful of Carlson's hair, and slammed his face straight down against his shot glass. Then you went for ol' Whip and he went for you, and now you got a forty-six-dollar repair bill due over to the Athenaeum before I can let you out of here."

"They were cheating."

"You started the fight."

"They started the fight when they started cheating."

"You know their cheating ain't what started the fight, Wolf."

Stockburn opened his eyes, squinting against the pain in his head, scowling at his old friend Waylon who'd managed a Pony Express station back when Wolf, only sixteen years old, had been a hell-for-leather pony rider recently orphaned in western Kansas by a pack of rampaging Cheyenne.

"What?"

Waylon narrowed his copper-brown eyes at the younger man. "You've played stud poker with both those jaspers before. Everybody knows they cheat but nobody cares because they're so bad they still lose!"

"Oh, go to hell, Waylon!" Wolf rested his head back against his pillow, which smelled as sour as the blanket. "My head hurts."

"You exploded because of what happened to Billy."

"Oh, go to hell!" Stockburn fumed again then instantly pressed the heels of his hands to his head, sucking sharp breaths through gritted teeth.

CHAPTER 2

The railroad detective was trying to suppress the raking agony inside his head as well as trying to obliterate the image of the young man, Billy Blythe, lying dead outside the Sierra Blanca Railroad's express car, which robbers had blown off the tracks then peppered with lead before absconding with seventy thousand dollars in payroll money en route to the Pegasus Mining Company in Ruidoso.

"He was so damn young," Stockburn said, grief rolling through him in hot waves.

"Had his whole life ahead of him," Waylon said. "It's not fair."

"I assigned him to that train."

"I know you did, Wolf. But you didn't know Red Miller's bunch was gonna hit it."

"I didn't even know Miller and his kill-crazy bunch of owlhoots was operating in this neck of the woods." Stockburn dropped his feet to the floor, rising, and leaned forward over his knees. "If I had . . ."

"I know—you never would have assigned a kid so green to that payroll shipment."

"Hell, I would have taken it myself!" Stockburn wrung his hands together, seeing in his mind's eye the freckle-faced young man he'd pulled out of an outlaw gang around Las Cruces, befriended, rehabilitated, and recommended for a messenger job with Wells Fargo, lying dead with his head resting against a blasted-off iron wheel of the express car.

Blood dribbling down one corner of his mouth, glistening in the sun.

The kid must have come out of the express car, flames from the explosion wreathing him, Winchester blasting. There'd been a half-dozen empty casings lying around Billy's charred, bullet-riddled body.

"He just got married," Wolf said. "I walked Sofia down the aisle myself on account of her father had passed."

Billy had met Sofia Ortega, the shy young brown-haired, brown-eyed daughter of a Mexican seamstress, in the post office one day in Mesilla. He'd stumbled into her, knocking several parcels out of her arms.

By the time he'd collected them for her, he'd fallen in love with her. Sofia had returned the sentiment. Before they'd officially hitched their stars to each other's wagons, Billy, with Wolf's help, had put a down payment on a little frame house between Las Cruces and Mesilla.

"Ah, Christ!" Wolf said, raking a big hand down his face, pressing his fingers deep into his skin as though trying to plunder his brain of his grief.

"Here—have a cup of this." Stockburn looked to his left. Waylon was extending a stone mug of steaming black coffee through the bars while holding a second mug in his other hand. "Make you feel better."

Stockburn rose with a wince, his head feeling like a

sadistic gnome was inside it, whacking at his brain with a miniature but very hard hammer.

Stockburn took the mug in his hand then leaned his right shoulder against the cell's right, barred partition. "I'll feel better when I pick up Miller's trail." He blew on the coffee and narrowed his eyes through the steam, angrily. "I can't do that in here."

"You couldn't do it when you were gambling in the Athenaeum, either."

"Yeah, well, I'm waiting for Sofia to ride up here from Las Cruces to claim Billy's body. I can't go anywhere, I can't go after Miller's bunch, till I've seen Sofia." Stockburn winced at the bleak prospect of having to show Billy's bride her young husband's charred, bullet-riddled body. He shook his head and sipped the hot, black brew.

He'd gotten himself entangled in the stud game to distract himself from his misery. He'd drunk too much firewater for the same reason. Waylon was right. He'd started the ruckus with Whip Larimore and Fritz Carlson for the same reason.

He'd had to take out his fury over Billy's brutal murder some damn way. Leave it to him to cut off his nose to spite his face. Someday his Scottish fury was going to get the better of him.

Waylon had been right. He would have killed Larimore if Waylon hadn't intervened. Then where would he be except headed for a gallows?

He was glad he'd been in the area when the Miller gang had struck. In fact, he'd been on the work train one hour behind the express Billy had been on, guarding the payroll money. Wolf had just been finishing up another job investigating illegal whiskey shipments on the Sierra Blanca and was heading back to Kansas City. Instead of heading straight north from Las Cruces to Denver, he'd decided to take the Sierra Blanca to Ruidoso to meet up with Billy for one last meal before they parted. Afterward, he'd take a leisurely horseback ride, astride his smoky gray stallion appropriately if unimaginatively named Smoke, north through the mountains and back to his home base in Kansas City.

As a railroad detective, he spent a lot of time on trains. Sometimes he liked to get away into the wild on his horse—just him and Smoke and the streams and woods, curling up in his bedroll every night after several cups of mud laced with whiskey, stars trimming the sky like Christmas candles, coyotes yammering from distant crags, the heady tang of pine smoke lingering in his nostrils.

He was a loner, Wolf Stockburn was. Always had been, always would be. Whenever he could, he sought the quiet sanctuary of the high and rocky.

He'd be doing that again soon. Only, he wouldn't be seeking sanctuary. He'd be running down the gang that had murdered Billy Blythe and taken the payroll money they'd blown from the Wells Fargo strongbox.

But not until he got out of this cell.

Stockburn frowned at the lawman gazing in at him reprovingly. "Come on, Waylon. Let me out of here!"

"Forget it." The craggy-faced marshal shook his head. "You sit an' stew for a while. If I let you out right away, you won't have learned a damn thing."

"Come on—I'm not an eighteen-year-old firebrand!"

"No, you're a forty-year-old firebrand!" Waylon chuckled without mirth then sipped his coffee. He swallowed, turned, and started walking over to his cluttered desk. "I'll let you out tomorrow. First thing. And then you'll go over to the Athenaeum and pay for the damages."

"I'll pay for them now!"

"No, you'll pay tomo—"

The lawman stopped and turned as the office door latch clicked and the door opened. A matronly, gray-haired lady clad in a green felt hat with a half-veil poked her head into the door. "Waylon, dear, I brought the dinner you asked . . . for . . ."

She let her voice trail off as she turned her gaze toward Stockburn, a surprised, puzzled frown cutting deep lines across the age-wrinkled, Southwestern-sun-seasoned skin of her forehead. She had an oilcloth-covered wicker basket hooked over her left forearm. "I certainly didn't know it was for Wolf!"

Waylon's wife, Ivy, walked into the office, the pleated skirt of her lime-green velvet gown buffeting around her legs and black ankle boots. She clucked in both amusement and curiosity as she strode toward where Stockburn stood just behind his cell door, flushing sheepishly. "Wolf, what on earth are you doing in there?"

"Drunk and disorderly," Waylon said. "Stay away from him, honey. He's as dangerous as a stick-teased rattlesnake!"

"What did you do, Wolf?"

"Ivy, do me a favor, will you?" Wolf said. "Grab those keys over there and unlock this door. Waylon won't stop you. We both know who's been wearin' the pants in the Wallace house for the past—what is it?—thirty, thirty-five years . . . ?"

"Forty-two," said Ivy, shifting her eyes to her husband with mock disdain. "Though it sometimes feels like sixty."

"She might wear the pants at home," Waylon said. "But if my lovely bride touches those keys, I'll lock you two up together."

"Hmmm," Ivy said, flouncing on her stout hips and arching her brows at Stockburn, playing the coquette. "I might not mind being locked up with such a tall, handsome drink of water as the storied Wolf of the Rails." That was what the newspapers and magazines had dubbed Stockburn several years ago, after his reputation as a dogged rail detective had grown into legend. That was *after* he'd been known as the Wolf of Wichita, having once been town marshal of that fair, hoot cow town.

"I don't know, Ivy," Wolf said, grinning at his lawman friend, "you might not know how to handle a real man after all those years living with that sissy over there."

Waylon had just taken a sip of coffee; with a loud chuff, he blew it into the air before him.

Ivy smiled sidelong at her husband. "He may not look like much, but believe it or not, Wolf, the old boy can still curl this gal's toes from time to time." She flounced over to her husband and rose up on the tips of her shoes to plant a peck on her blushing husband's leathery left cheek. "Can't you, my wild stallion?"

"Wild stallion," Stockburn laughed. "Hah!"

"Oh, hell," Waylon said, his flush deepening as he turned to his desk. "Just feed that damned criminal over there, will ya, honey? I have enough trouble with him alone without you two throwin' in together against me!"

"I have to tell you I'm not exactly hungry, Ivy," Wolf said. "I hurt too bad thanks to that old bruin and the barrel of his Smith & Wesson, not to mention a few lucky licks from Whip Larimore."

"You just wait till you see what I—"

Ivy stopped abruptly as a gun blasted out in the street beyond the office door. "Oh, my gosh!" she said, raising a hand to her mouth.

The first blast was followed by another . . . another . . . and another. Ivy's shoulders jerked with each loud report. Men shouted. A horse neighed shrilly.

"What in the hell . . . ?" Waylon hurried to the door, grabbing his hat off a wall peg and saying, "Ivy, you stay here!"

"Waylon!" Wolf said as more guns blasted in the street. "Let me out of here, dammit!"

But the marshal had already opened the door and run into the street, leaving the door half open behind him. The shooting continued, a veritable fusillade growing more and more heated with every shot. More men shouted, a woman screamed, horses whinnied, hooves pounded.

"Oh, my God!" Ivy said behind the hand over her mouth, staring in shock through the half-open door.

"What's going on, Ivy?" Wolf asked, his heart racing. He walked to the cell's far side and peered through the door but all he could see was dust being kicked up by the running horses, and gun smoke.

Waylon's voice muffled by distance and gunfire, shouted, "Hold it right there, you devils!"

More guns blasted. A man screamed.

"Waylon!" Ivy cried, dropping the wicker basket and hurrying toward the door.

Stockburn shoved his right hand through the door to try to stop her. "Hold on, Ivy! Don't go out there!"

But then she, too, ran through the door and was gone.

Stockburn stared in frustration and horror through the half-open door. The din continued—shooting, shouting, screaming, the thunder of maybe a half-dozen horses.

A horse and rider appeared in the street beyond the half-open door. The pair was galloping from Wolf's left to his right, heading north. As the rider, clad in a cream hat and a black duster, passed the jail office, he cast a glance over his right shoulder and triggered a pistol shot behind him.

He gave a savage, coyote-like howl and then he was gone, galloping off to the north.

"Oh, Waylon!" Ivy Wallace's voice wailed beneath the din. "Wayon! Oh, Waylon!"

Her cries were cut off by an agonized scream.

"Ivy!" Wolf shouted, stretching his right arm helplessly through the strap-iron bands of his cell. "*Ivyyyyy—come back!*"

But something told him she wasn't coming back.

His heart a runaway train inside him, Stockburn grabbed the bars of his cell door and shook them wildly, cursing. He looked at the keys hanging from a peg by Waylon's cluttered desk—from the same peg on which hung Stockburn's cartridge belt and two holstered, ivory-gripped Colt Peacemakers as well as his sheathed bowie knife.

Only ten feet away, but they might as well have been a hundred.

Amidst the din of crackling guns and running horses,

thumping sounds rose from the boardwalk fronting the
jailhouse. A man appeared, crawling on the boardwalk
from Stockburn's left to his right. Waylon stopped just
outside the open door and turned a craggy-faced, gray-
bearded, agonized look toward Wolf.

"Waylon!"

The man's face was drawn and pale. His hat was gone.
He was dusty and sweaty. Blood dribbled onto the boardwalk from his bullet-torn belly as he remained there on
his hands and knees, face turned toward Stockburn, the
poor man's cheeks sunken, his eyes sharp with pain.

Thumps rose from behind the lawman—the heavy,
regular thuds of someone walking toward him. Waylon
lifted his right hand from the boardwalk. He was holding
his Russian .44. He winced, as though the gun weighed a
hundred pounds. Stretching his lips back from his teeth,
he tossed the revolver underhanded into the jailhouse. It
landed only a few feet away from the lawman then slid up
to within three feet of Stockburn's cell.

As the Russian came to a stop, a gun popped in front
of the marshal's office. Stockburn stared in horror as a
bullet slammed into Waylon's head from behind, pluming
his hair then exiting his forehead while blowing out a
fist-sized chunk of bone, brains, and blood.

Waylon dropped belly down and lay quivering as he
died.

As the foot thuds resounded on the boardwalk, Stockburn dropped to his knees, reached through the bars,
stretched his right arm straight out before him, and closed
his hand over the Russian .44. Before he could bring
the revolver back toward him, a tall, broad-shouldered,

long-haired man with a patch over one eye turned through the jailhouse door, kicking it wide.

Wolf pulled the Russian into his cell.

He was too late.

The pistol in the hand of the long-haired, one-eyed man leaped and roared, flames lapping from the barrel. The bullet ricocheted off an iron bar directly in front of Wolf and thudded into Waylon's desk, blowing up papers and toppling an ashtray.

Ears ringing from the ricochet's deafening clang, Stockburn poked the Russian through the bars, thumbed the hammer back, and lined up the sights on the big man before him.

The killer's eyes widened suddenly with the recognition of his own imminent demise. The man's lower jaw sagged in shock.

The Russian spoke.

"Choke on that, you devil!" Stockburn shouted.

CHAPTER 3

The Russian thundered twice more as Stockburn punched two bullets into the cell door's lock plate.

The bolt broke after the second bullet struck it, and the door whined and sagged in its frame.

Wolf dropped to his knees and clamped his hands over his ears, trying to quell the renewed pounding in his head. When those bullets had struck the lock plate, he'd felt he were inside a steel barrel being assaulted with large rocks. He suppressed the thunder still rocketing around inside his tender head—as much as he could—and heaved himself to his feet. He grabbed his hat off a stool near the cot, gingerly set it on his head, shoved the door wide, and stepped into the office.

As he hurried toward his guns hanging from a peg in the front wall, to the right of the door, he glanced down at the dead man, frowning. He grabbed his guns and knife off the wall peg, strapped and buckled the weapons around his waist, and continued to study the man with a patch over his left eye.

"Sheldon Crane?" Wolf muttered, puzzled.

He tied the thong of his right-hand Colt's holster to his

thigh and hurried out the door, looking around as he dropped to a knee beside his old friend, Waylon Wallace, placing a tender hand on the dead man's back then looking along the street to his left.

The din had dwindled to the screams of a single woman. She knelt in the street in front of the bank, beside a man lying belly down and not moving. A pink parasol lay in the street beside her.

"Eddie!" she screamed. "Eddie! Eddie! Oh, dear God—Eddie!"

Obviously, the gunmen had robbed the Territorial Bank of Ruidoso, for several men and one woman lay dead on the street and boardwalk in front of the adobe brick building. Dust and smoke fogged the high-mountain, sunlit air.

Townsmen moved sleepily out from where they'd taken cover when the shooting had started, looking around warily, as though half-expecting the gunmen to return. Two moved slowly, sorrowfully toward the woman still screaming for Eddie near the boardwalk on the street's other side.

A man stepped out of the bank, through the smoke lingering in front of the building. He looked as though he'd just woken from a nap. His round, steel-framed spectacles glinted in the sunlight as he looked up and down the street, blinking against the dust and wafting smoke.

He was a middle-aged, balding gent with a soft belly bulging out of the shirt and vest of his suit. He wasn't wearing a coat; sleeve garters encircled his arms.

"Dead!" he said, stepping uncertainly into the street and glancing over his shoulder at the single-story bank building behind him. "*Dead!* They shot them all! I hid behind my desk! They shot . . . they shot . . . *everybody*. Just shot them all down . . . *laughing* . . . !"

The killers had fled after killing anyone they saw moving in the street. They'd made a party of it. Judging by the whoops and yells and raucous laughter that Stockburn had heard from inside his cell, they'd had one hell of a good time.

They could have just robbed the bank and fled. But that hadn't been enough for them. They'd taken the time to kill as they'd shot their way out of town.

There was only one gang that savage.

And it was led by Red Miller. Which meant the same gang that had robbed the Sierra Blanca Express and murdered Billy Blythe had robbed the bank right here in Ruidoso one day later. Corroborating that theory was Sheldon Crane lying dead in the town marshal's office.

Crane was one of the worst of Red Miller's bunch, almost as savage as Miller himself.

The other three with the worst reputations were Pike Brennan, Flipper Harris, and Gopher Montez.

Stockburn had stopped in the street about ten feet out from the jail office. Now his gaze settled on a lumpy, gray-haired form lying in the street to his left.

"Ah, for Heaven sakes!" He strode over and knelt down beside Ivy Wallace.

She lay on one side, legs twisted, eyes squeezed shut as though still in pain, though the bullet through her chest had likely shredded her heart and killed her outright. Her veiled felt hat lay smashed in the street beside her, where a horse had likely trampled it. Her white-gray hair had spilled down from its bun to lie over her left ear. Dirt streaked one of her soft, porcelain-pale, wrinkled cheeks.

"I'm so sorry, Ivy," Stockburn said, a wave of tangled emotions rocketing through him.

Grief. Sorrow. Fury.

Yesterday, it had been Billy. Today, Waylon Wallace and his lovely wife, Ivy.

All killed by the same bunch while Stockburn had been supine in that damned jail cell because he couldn't control his anger.

He looked up to see a woman standing in the doorway of a lady's dress shop. She stared in glassy-eyed shock down at Ivy Wallace, her face ashen.

"Ma'am, fetch a blanket for Mrs. Wallace, will you?" Stockburn said, his voice trembling with emotion.

The woman rolled her eyes up from Ivy to Stockburn. They remained flat and expressionless, as though she hadn't heard him.

"Ma'am, fetch a blanket for this poor woman!"

"*Yes!*" The woman screeched, tears glazing her eyes. She turned and stumbled back into the shop, shoes clacking on floorboards.

Stockburn rose. Fury and grief roiling through him, he strode south through the growing crowd in the street. He walked one block, angling toward the Sierra Blanca Hotel, a tall, narrow, three-story, wood-frame building on the street's west side.

The man who ran the place, Norman Snodgrass, stood near the hitchrack fronting the hotel, his own shocked eyes taking in the bloody scene before him. The tall, thin man with a pencil-line mustache locked eyes with Stockburn, and shook his head. "What a brazen bunch of killers!"

Stockburn brushed past the man, climbed three steps,

and entered the small lobby with a potted palm on his left and the front desk on his right.

"I thought you was in jail," Snodgrass called behind him. "I seen three fellas hauling you like dead freight to the town marshal's office!"

Stockburn climbed the stairs to his room, returning one minute later wielding his brass-breeched 1866 Winchester "Yellowboy" rifle. "There ain't a jail ever been made that can hold Wolf Stockburn, Norman," the detective said, pausing to light a three-penny cheroot. "Don't you know that?"

"Where you goin', Wolf?"

"Where do you think?"

"You'd best form a posse. There was a good dozen of them killers, Wolf, and I think I seen Red Miller and Pike Brennan amongst 'em!"

"No time, Norman."

Stockburn dropped the match in the street and cut down a side street to the east. At the Federated Livery & Feed Barn, he roped and saddled his smoky-gray horse and shoved the Yellowboy into the sheath. He led the horse out of the barn, mounted up, and galloped north.

Fifteen minutes later, he sat Smoke on a high, bald promontory overlooking Ruidoso and the fir-clad mountains around it. Holding his brass spyglass up to his right eye, he surveyed the country in all directions. He slid the glass with its circle of magnified vision across a narrow valley to the west. He started to slide his magnified gaze up a fir-clad slope when he abruptly slid the glass back to the valley.

He'd glimpsed a flicker movement.

He trained the glass on the movement, twisted the brass

casing slightly to the left, removing some of the blur. In that sphere of magnified vision, several men and horses milled, dust rising around them. Wolf could see only three or four men and horses, and the arched tail of one more horse, for the group appeared to be riding down a rise, heading away from Stockburn's position.

A second later, the riders were gone, only their dust lingering in the air behind them.

It was the dust of more than only four riders. Likely close to a dozen riders.

Stockburn might have seen only part of Red Miller's gang, but the rest were there in the valley, all right. They'd left town in separate directions to make them harder to track, but, according to a previously conceived plan, they'd converged in that western valley. Now they were riding as a group to the south.

With loot they'd plundered from the Sierra Blanca Express and the bank in Ruidoso . . . and with blood on their hands . . .

"Let's go, Smoke!"

Stockburn neck-reined the stallion around and booted him on down the slope and into the forest that started a hundred feet down from the top of the ridge. Having hunted this country several times with Waylon Wallace, he knew it well enough to know that Miller's bunch, heading south, would have to pass through Eagle Canyon. That meant they'd have to follow the canyon to the east for a couple of miles before swinging south again.

Waylon had once shone Wolf a little-known shortcut from Ruidoso to Eagle Canyon. If he could make it to the canyon ahead of the killers, he'd have a good chance—to do what?

There was a good dozen of them.

The Wolf of the Rails was not a man to bog himself down in too much consideration of the odds. He knew where the gang was heading and he matter-of-factly intended to get there ahead of them and to gain the high ground, which might give him a fighting chance even against twelve cold-blooded killers of the Red Miller gang's caliber.

When he and Smoke gained the base of the ridge, Stockburn reined the horse to the southeast and gave him the proverbial spurs. He wore no actual spurs, being a good enough horseman—and riding a mount trained well enough—that he didn't need them. Spurs jangled. A detective who often found the need for silence didn't need the aggravation of jangling spurs.

Wolf and Smoke thundered through two valleys, crested a pass, and raced down the other side.

Here they entered another valley. Wolf steered Smoke into an intersecting valley that wandered straight south, the valley floor gradually dropping between high, bald, rocky walls that thrust their craggy peaks straight up toward the faultless blue New Mexico sky.

This was Navajo Canyon, the rocks to Wolf's right and left brightly painted with ancient hieroglyphics depicting hunting and feasting scenes.

Navajo Canyon dropped into Eagle Canyon, which lay slightly lower on the sierra than Navajo, and had a wild and rushing river—Eagle River—thundering down its rugged, rocky heart.

Halfway down the sloping, boulder-strewn canyon wall, Wolf stopped Smoke and swung down from the saddle. He dropped his reins, shucked his rifle from its sheath, and levered a live round into the action. He off-cocked the hammer, patted the sweat-lathered neck of the horse, said, "Stay here till I whistle, Smoke," then hurried off down the ridge, wending his way between rocks and boulders and the slash of fallen pines.

He'd taken only a dozen or so long strides before the sudden, echoing thunder of many shod hooves rose from below and to Stockburn's right. The riders had just entered the canyon.

He quickened his pace, crouching so he wouldn't be seen from below. The gang was moving fast, at hard gallops, likely pushing their mounts from an imagined posse. Stockburn had to hurry or all he'd be confronting was their dust.

He pulled up behind a boulder roughly two-thirds of the way down from the ridge crest. He edged a look around the boulder and down the slope. His heartbeat picked up when he saw Red Miller riding out in front of the pack of eight riders, maybe seventy yards away from him now but coming fast along the canyon floor. He and the others would be directly below his position in less than thirty seconds.

Eight men, not twelve. The reduced number was encouraging.

Stockburn rose, took two more long strides then leaped onto a large, table-flat rock, and dropped to a knee. He raised the Yellowboy, ratcheted back the hammer, and took aim at Red Miller's jostling, large-framed figure, the man's long, womanishly pretty, copper-red hair blowing back behind him in the wind.

Stockburn drew a bead on the man's bespectacled face—inched it up past Miller's big walrus mustache and broad nose to his high forehead shaded by the crown of his big, tan Stetson. Wolf paused with the bead on the man's forehead, caressing the trigger, gritting his teeth.

He wanted to kill him right then and there—just blow the killer out of his saddle.

Something wouldn't let him do it. Not a concern for the man's constitutional rights. No, it wasn't that. As far as Stockburn was concerned, the man had given up those rights long ago, even before he'd murdered young Billy Blythe. Miller and his bunch were reputed to be responsible for the murder of over thirty innocent people during their train- and bank-robbing depredations both north and south of the border.

No, it wasn't Miller's constitutional rights Stockburn was concerned for.

Wolf wanted to see the man hang right along with all the others in his savage bunch. He wanted them to hear and watch their own gallows being built, and then drop through the trapdoors to hang and strangle, doing the good ol' midair two-step, soiling themselves.

Stockburn raised the rifle barrel a half inch, squeezed the trigger, and smiled as the bullet blew the man's hat off his head and tossed it high and bounced it off the shoulder of a man riding behind him.

"What the *hell*!" yelled the rider whose shoulder Miller's hat had bounced off of.

Ejecting the spent cartridge casing, Stockburn rose to his full height and slammed another round into the Yellowboy's breech. Miller had jerked back on his cream horse's bridle reins, looking around wildly, in wide-eyed exasperation. His horse whinnied and reared steeply as the other riders behind him followed suit, checking their own mounts down to skidding, whinnying halts.

"*There!*" one of the gang shouted, holding his reins up high against his chest and jerking his chin toward the tall railroad detective standing on the flat-topped boulder roughly thirty feet up from the canyon floor, grinning toothily beneath his neatly trimmed gray mustache.

CHAPTER 4

"Hold it right there, Red," Stockburn yelled from his stony perch. "Your trail ends here!"

Red Miller blinked behind his round, steel-framed spectacles that gave his otherwise raw-boned, walrus-mustached features a bizarrely bookish look. The hoot lenses flashed in the sunshine.

He and all seven of the other killers had closed their hands over their holstered six-shooters but none had slid their guns from the leather, instinctively knowing that doing so would get them shot out of their saddles.

They were as nasty and villainous-looking bunch as Stockburn had ever seen, and he'd seen a few. Long-haired, dusty, sweaty, clad in combinations of wool, leather, and buckskin, they had the seedy, sun-cured, rancid look of the dodgiest border desperado. The breeze wafting over the canyon toward Stockburn brought the nose-curling stench of horses, sweaty wool, and unwashed men.

Pike Brennan rode just behind Miller. Flipper Harris sat a white-socked black gelding to Brennan's left. Harris was known as "Flipper" due to his underdeveloped right arm concealed by the sewn-up sleeve of his dark green duster.

Gopher Montez rode near the end of the group, beside a tall, rangy fellow with a long, shaggy, colorless beard hanging to his chest, and a black opera hat with the feather of a red-tailed hawk poking up from its band. The opera-hatted man flared his nostrils at Stockburn and angrily spat a long stream of coal-black chaw on a rock to his left, making a wet plopping sound.

To a man, their flat, angry, squalid eyes were riveted on the detective bearing down on them. They were embarrassed to not only have been followed out of Ruidoso, but cut off, as well. The humiliation filled them with even more rancor than usual. They looked as choleric as stick-teased rattlesnakes.

"What the hell are you doin', Stockburn!" Red Miller said in his wheezing, nasal voice, glasses glinting. "There's eight of us, only one of you." He waved a gloved hand out before him. "Less'n you got some square heads from town hunkered down in them rocks, likely squirtin' down their legs!"

He laughed harshly and without humor.

"It's just me, Red." Stockburn held out his rifle. "I got one bullet in this Yellowboy for each of you. The first one's special, though. That's one just for you. I'm gonna blow your muckin' head off."

He was imagining Billy Blythe lying dead against that coach wheel, and Waylon and Ivy Wallace lying dead on the main street of Ruidoso.

Miller smiled and jutted his chin with mocking belligerence. "Yeah, I heard you was fast with that purty Winchester. But you ain't *that* fast. Not fast enough to get all of us!"

"I'm fast enough to blow you out of that saddle right

here and now, you worthless piece of privy slime, unless you throw your weapons down and order your men to do likewise."

"If I tell my boys to open up on you, Wolf, you're gonna die bloody, an' you know it!"

Stockburn pressed his cheek up against the Yellowboy's stock, and narrowed his shooting eye. "So are you, Red." He glanced at the others behind Miller. "And I think I can empty at least half of those other saddles. Maybe more. Hell, given I got the high ground and you fellas are all still mounted, I might just take you all down. Old Scratch is gonna have him some fresh coal shovelers real soon!"

Stockburn smiled confidently down the Winchester's barrel at Red Miller. His head still ached but adrenaline had taken over, and a strange but welcome calm that nearly always visited him in such situations had fallen over him.

With that calm came confidence.

Some men had it even when the odds were stacked against them. Some didn't. Stockburn had it. He'd realized it when he'd still been a young pony rider and had been confronted with war-painted Indians out for his scalp or by outlaws just as mean and low-down though of the non-Indian variety. You had to be calm and clear-headed in such situations or you simply didn't make it through.

"Unbuckle your gun belt and drop it to the ground, Red," Wolf said. "Tell your men to do the same."

Miller stared at him, his eyes unreadable behind his glinting spectacles. He drew a deep, fateful breath and glanced at the seven behind him. "Looks like we got us a dilemma here, boys."

"What do you want to do, Red?" Flipper Harris asked

behind Miller, shuttling his nervous gaze from Stockburn to Miller then back to the detective again.

Miller smiled. "Only thing we can do, I reckon." He kept that smiling, glinting gaze on Stockburn for a full five seconds. "*Slap iron and shoot that son of a bitch!*" he bellowed, at the same time ramming his heels against his dun's loins and drawing back savagely on the reins.

Stockburn squeezed the Yellowboy's trigger. Red Miller's head jerked back as his horse reared, front feet bounding nearly straight up in the air. Wolf's .44 slug cleaved off the tip of the gang leader's nose before slamming into the neck of the man to Miller's right and slightly behind him.

"*Ohhhh, you low-down dirty devil!*" Miller wailed as he kicked free of his stirrups, leaped over the arched tail of his mount, and somehow landed, catlike, on both feet without even stumbling.

Stockburn cursed as he ejected the spent shell casing and levered a live one into the Yellowboy's action. He triggered another round at Miller but his bullet merely plumed dust a half inch behind Miller's right boot spur as the bespectacled, redheaded outlaw grabbed his pitching horse's reins and then pulled the fiercely whinnying mount into the rocks on the far side of the trail.

Only two and a half seconds having passed since Miller had leaped from his horse, the other seven outlaws were just now making their own moves, some leaping from their horses while others grabbed six-shooters from holsters or rifles from saddle sheaths and returned fire, bellowing furiously.

As the lead curled the air around his head, Stockburn aimed the Yellowboy and fired.

Again, he cocked, aimed, and fired.

Cocked, aimed, and fired . . .

In two seconds, he blew two men off their saddles and a second later wounded another man who'd just leaped to the ground clawing a pair of Remingtons from the holsters thonged on his thighs. Stockburn shot the man in the chest as a bullet from one of the others burned a line across Wolf's left cheek.

Stockburn peered through his own wafting powder smoke as he levered another round into the Winchester's action. The man who'd creased his cheek was blinking and coughing against the dust that had been kicked up by the scrambling horses. As the man raised both Remys toward Stockburn, Wolf blew a .44 caliber hole through the dead-center of his forehead, painting the rock behind him with blood and brains.

The man hadn't fallen before Stockburn, aware he'd just capped his last rifle round, leaped off the boulder and into the trail, bending his knees to distribute the impact evenly. Knowing he'd taken down only half of Miller's bunch, he threw himself forward and rolled off his right shoulder into the rocks on the trail's far side.

Rising to one knee, he looked around quickly, squinting against the powder smoke and the dust from the horses, most of whom he'd seen fleeing either straight up the trail or back in the direction from where they'd come. He was surprised to find no more lead screeching toward him, spanging off the rocks around him.

Where were the other four?

He leaned the empty Yellowboy against a boulder and palmed both of his pretty, ivory-gripped, silver-chased

Peacemakers. Staying low, he scuttled forward through the rocks, looking around carefully.

He'd seen Miller jerk his horse off the trail and into the rocks. Three of the others must have made the same play while Stockburn had been distracted by those slinging lead at him. He didn't think any of the dead, aside from Sheldon Crane in town, were the ones he wanted the most—Miller, Harris, Brennan, and Montez. Those four coyotes were not only the most savage of the bunch, they were the smartest and slipperiest, to boot. They'd let the others take the lead while they scuttled off into the rocks to hole up and make themselves extra hard to take down.

Damn . . .

Stockburn crabbed forward through a narrow cavity between two boulders. When he approached the rear of both boulders, he stopped, then removed his hat and edged a slow, careful look around and behind the boulder on his right.

Nothing but gravel and cactus.

He looked to his left.

Same there.

He cursed again, then slowly gained his feet. Crouching, he took one step forward before a bayonet blade of crushing, searing agony tore into his upper right arm, throwing him back against a boulder. He gritted his teeth as he looked down at his arm. Blood oozed through the four-inch tear in the sleeve of his black frock coat.

He groaned and, knees buckling from weakness, slid down the face of the rock just as another slug ripped into the boulder maybe a foot above his sinking head.

The shrill spang-kicked up an agonized ringing in his ears.

Numb from shock, he looked straight out ahead of him and up, seeing the smoke from that last shot tearing on the breeze. Just below and to the left of the quickly disintegrating smoke, stood a man holding a rifle in one hand, the reins of a cream horse in his other hand.

The man was maybe a hundred yards away, not too far that he couldn't see the frigid glower on Red Miller's ugly face. Miller stood on the canyon's south wall, about halfway up from the bottom. The other three men—Flipper Harris, Pike Brennan, and Gopher Montez—were climbing the ridge above Miller, leading their horses by their bridle reins.

No, not all three were leading horses.

The tall, slender, black-hatted figure between the two men leading horses was not leading a horse. That was likely Flipper Harris. Having only one good hand, he'd probably been unable to grab his horse's reins before the mount had fled, spooked by the gunfire.

Miller lowered his rifle and, still glowering, no doubt in a good bit of pain himself—Wolf could see the white line of the man's teeth beneath his big mustache and the bloody tip of his nose—raised his left arm in a broad, mocking wave. Then Stockburn slid down until he was sitting on the ground, and a rock in front of him rose to block Miller and the other three men climbing the ridge from his view.

"Ah, hell!" he spat through gritted teeth.

He reached back with his left hand to fish a red handkerchief from his back pocket. Still gritting his teeth against the raging agony in his arm, he gingerly rested the handkerchief over the wound. He wrapped it around his arm then sucked a sharp breath, and, cursing a blue streak, jerked it tight and knotted it.

His vision dimmed, his heart raced. He fought off a faint, then drew a deep breath. He leaned forward and crawled, putting most of his weight on his right arm. He crawled through a natural corridor between rocks and into the open.

Here, he had a better view of the ridge.

As he'd expected, the four killers were nearly to the top of the ridge, all four leaning down, pushing off the steep incline with their hands, three jerking their horses along behind them. Sweating and dizzy from blood loss and pain, Stockburn rolled onto his left shoulder and watched all four killers move to the top of the far ridge. Red Miller, following the other three, gained it last.

The redheaded outlaw leader stepped up onto the lip and turned, leaning back and pulling his cream mount up behind him. When the horse was settled, shaking so hard it nearly threw the saddle from its back, Miller stepped up to the edge of the canyon. He canted his head to stare down toward Stockburn.

Wolf saw the glistening red smear of blood dribbling down his ruined nose to cover his mustached mouth.

He was too far away for the detective to see the expression on the man's face, but Wolf knew it was there. A bright, greasy, devil-eyed stare of profound fury and self-righteous indignation.

Gritting his teeth with rage, Wolf slid one of his Peacemakers from its holster with his left hand, clicked the hammer back, thrust the big .45 straight out from his shoulder and up toward the ridge crest. He emptied the entire wheel, bellowing, "We'll meet again, Red! You can bet the bull on that!"

All six rounds plumed dust well down the ridge from the crest.

Miller cupped hands to his mouth. "*I'm gonna hold you to that, Stockburn!*"

The words echoed around the canyon.

Miller turned and walked away with his horse.

CHAPTER 5

The cool water of the springs pushed softly against Sofia Ortega's naked body.

She scrubbed herself with a cake of her mother's home-made soap scented with rosemary then tossed the cake onto the grassy bank studded with mesquites and ocotillos. She stepped backward into the deep, dark water that pooled here in this hollow in the rocks, then bled off into a stream that wended its way through an arroyo all the way to Mexico. Bending her knees, she let the water come up and wrap its cool arms around her.

She straightened her legs and spread her arms, her body weightless now as she floated. She stared up at the leaves of the cottonwoods arching over this little canyon, which lay behind her and her mother's thatch-roofed adobe shack at the edge of Mesilla. The spring oozed, singing softly out of a stone wall painted many colors by the Ancient Ones.

Sofia closed her eyes and smiled as she floated dreamily on the gently rippling water of the spring. She was a lucky girl. Her mother had given her the afternoon off from the sewing and laundering they did for the people in and around Mesilla and the nearby smaller settlement of Las Cruces.

The area was growing after the arrival of the Santa Fe Railroad two years ago, bringing more people to both Mesilla and Las Cruces—people with money to pay to have their clothes repaired and laundered. Sofia and her mother were busier than they'd ever been, but, still, her mother had given her a few hours off this afternoon, so that Sofia could go off and *mirar a las musarañas,* or "moon around" about her boy with the promise that she would return to work the next day without distraction.

Sofia felt her smile stretch her lips a little wider.

Her boy . . .

Something bounced off her big toe and plopped into the water.

Frowning, Sofia opened her eyes and looked around. She looked up at the branches arching over the spring. Something must have tumbled down from the trees.

She lay her head back again and lolled dreamily once more.

Something plopped into the water to her right.

She dropped her feet to the spring's sandy bottom, standing, the water covering her nearly to her neck, and looked around curiously. To her left, the water was still rippling from whatever had displaced it. As she looked up at the branches again, something plopped into the water to her right.

This time, out of the corner of her right eye, she'd seen the pebble arc toward her from the bank near where she'd left her dress and underclothes.

She gasped, fear chilling her, and folded her arms across her breasts.

"Who's there?" she called in Spanish. "Who's there?"

A singsong voice replied, calling her name in a playful, lilting rhythm: "Soo-fee-ahhh . . ."

"Billy?" she said, looking around, frowning. "Is that you, Billy?"

In the same lilting, singsong rhythm: "I gotta see-crett, Soo-fee-ahhh . . ."

"Billy?" Keeping her arms over her breasts, she looked around, trying to follow the voice to its source. "Where are you?"

"You have to guess my secret," came the young man's voice without the lilting rhythm this time.

Sofia smiled in relief. "Billy, you shouldn't be here. I'm naked!"

"I know."

"Did you *see?*" she asked, suddenly horrified.

"Nah, I didn't see. I mean, I could have, but I didn't look."

"You did, too!"

"How do you know?"

"Because you're a bad boy, Billy Blythe—spying on a girl while she's bathing!"

"I'm sorry, Sofia. I just couldn't help myself. You're too purty not to look at! But enough of that—guess my secret, doggoneit!"

Sofia felt her cheeks and ears warm, not so much with embarrassment but with the knowledge that her young man had seen her—that he hadn't been able to resist the temptation of her—and he'd obviously approved of what he'd seen.

"What secret?" she said with feigned disgust.

"Guess!"

"No!" Sofia turned to face the stone wall of the spring.

"Billy, you have to leave. If *mi madre* found you here—
like this!—she'd take a cane pole to both of us!"

For several seconds, there was only the tinny murmur
of the spring dribbling fresh water into the pool, and the
piping of desert birds.

In a quiet, intimate tone, Billy's voice came again: "I
love you, Sofia." Behind her there was the light tread and
crunch of a foot on gravel. His voice came more clearly
now: "That's my secret."

Sofia glanced over her shoulder. Billy Blythe stepped
away from the tree behind which he'd been hiding. He
stood there tall and straight, looking so young and handsome in his new three-piece suit, smiling at her lovingly.
His longish sandy hair curling down behind his ears from
beneath the brim of his flat-brimmed hat. His eyes were a
soft, gentle blue green—the color of the desert sky at dusk.
The mustache he was trying to grow was a pale shadow
across his upper lip.

He held a small, gift-wrapped package the size of a ring
box out in the palm of his right hand.

"This is for you."

Sofia turned her face sharply forward so he couldn't
see the broad smile blossoming across her Mexican-dark
features. "Billy, this is very bad," she forced herself to say,
again faking the steely, reprimanding tone of an old
schoolmarm. "You have to leave now. It's not proper. I'm
bathing, Billy!"

But as soon as the last word had spilled from her mouth,
her lips were smiling again. The warmth of love . . . of
being loved . . . filled her to the brim until she thought she
might cry or throw her head back and scream in raw delight.

"All right, honey," Billy said behind her, to her chagrin. "I know it ain't right. I know your mother wouldn't approve. So I'm gonna set this right here . . . on the ground by your dress . . . and I'm gonna leave. I'll come to your casa tonight after dark. I'll tap on your window so you can give me your answer."

Sofia closed her hands over her face in a rush of shock and delight. Her heart fluttered like a nervous little bird's. She didn't dare say anything; she knew if she tried, she'd only sob like an idiot and make a wailing fool of herself.

"Good-bye, now, honey," Billy said gently behind her. She heard his footfalls as he walked away through the trees. "I love you, Sofia!"

She stood there in the water, sobbing joyfully into her hands. Behind her, a horse blew. There was the squeaking of leather as Billy climbed into the saddle of his paint horse—the one he'd bought after his friend Wolf Stockburn had helped him get a job as express messenger for Wells Fargo. A clack of a bridle bit against the horse's teeth. Billy clucked. Galloping hooves thudded, dwindling into the distance until there was only the sound of the rippling spring and the birds.

And of Sofia Ortega sobbing quietly into her hands. "I love you, Billy," she whispered.

"What's that, honey?"

The unfamiliar voice plucked Sofia out of a deep sleep. She opened her eyes and jerked her head away from the train window she'd been resting it against. A long-faced man in a wool work shirt and cracked leather vest and with too-blue, glassy eyes smiled at her and said, "Who you in love with, sweetheart? Billy, you say? I bet Billy don't have nothin' on me."

The man reached over and set his large, rough hand against Sofia's left cheek. He slid her dark brown hair back from her face, tucking it behind her ear. He wore a battered Stetson hat and leather chaps, marking him as a ranch hand.

The stench of his breath marked him as a drunk one. Drunk in the middle of the day, on a train heading north toward Ruidoso, and letting his heavy-lidded, too-blue, glassy eyes roam across Sofia in a most ungentlemanly manner while he kept his hand on her cheek.

"There, there, sweetheart. Don't cry for Billy. I'm here. My name's Wat. Wat Wade. What's your name an' where you headed? You all by your lonesome, are you?"

Sofia glowered at the man and swatted his hand away from her face.

"Easy now, easy now," he said. "I'm just bein' friendly. You travelin' alone, are you? I am, too. Now, ain't that a coincidence! Say, you're a pretty girl. I like the senoritas. A purty senorita like you shouldn't be travelin' alone. Why, somethin' bad might—*hey, hey, hey! Stop, there! What you doin'—oh, dear Lord!*"

Before Sofia had boarded the train in Las Cruces, her mother had slipped a stiletto into her food sack. Her mother had called the six-inch, obsidian-handled blade a *chaperona*. Pilar Ortega had winked, pecked Sofia on the cheek, then trundled away in her heavy-hipped fashion, confident her daughter would use the knife if needed.

Well, now it was needed.

Sofia pressed the savage blade, tapering to a needle tip, against the man's shirt, just above his cartridge belt. The man leaned back away from it, looking down at it in horror. "Oh, dear Lord," he said again, panting, stretching his lips back from his teeth as Sofia slipped the blade through his shirt and snugged it up taut against his skin. "Don't do that, now, honey! I was just . . . I was just bein' friendly's all!"

He screeched out his pleas, but the train was clicking, clacking, and squawking along the tracks loudly enough that no one else in the sparsely populated passenger coach appeared to have heard. The other ten or eleven passengers were reading, sleeping, or engaged in desultory conversations.

Sofia pressed her face up close to the cowboy's, narrowed her dark brown eyes, and hardened her jaws, feeling the heat of an angry flush rising in her cheeks. "If you ever touch me again, you gutless *pendejo*, I'll gut you like a pig!"

She shoved the sharp point of the blade into the man far enough to take away any question about the threat's sincerity.

"*Si, si, si,*" the cowboy screeched, stretching lips back from tobacco-stained teeth. "I hear ya, sweetheart. Pl-please . . . please . . . take the blade away!"

"I will on one condition," Sofia hissed, her face only inches from the cowboy's, a bead of blood bubbling up around the tip of the blade, staining his shirt. "That you find another seat—one that is as far from me as you can get. *Comprende, pendejo?*"

"*Si, si*—I undersand! *Comprende! Comprende!*"

Sofia pulled the blade away from Wat Wade's belly but kept her savagely snarling face pressed up close to his, her eyes glazed like those of an angry she-lion. Pulling his head back away from hers, Wade sort of wriggled off the seat, holding one hand against his side, over the little bloodstain on his shirt. Glaring at her with deep indignance he looked her over again brashly, and said, "Hot little chili pepper!"

He jerked around and stomped down the middle aisle toward the rear of the coach car. Sofia had been wrong about none of the other passengers having witnessed her "encounter" with Wade. It appeared that at least one had.

That man sat near the rear of the coach, on the opposite side of the aisle from the side Sofia was on. This man was dressed similarly to Wade. Long, stringy blond hair hung down from his sweat-stained funnel-brimmed Stetson. He had little eyes and a little mouth, and he was showing his two little upper front rat teeth now as he hissed mocking laughter at Wade, pointing at him.

Flushing and scowling, Wade plopped into the seat beside the man, and whacked his hat across his mocking friend's shoulder.

Sofia sat back in her seat beside the window and returned the stiletto to her food sack. As she did, she realized that the train was slowing—probably for water and wood. According to the battered old timepiece, which she'd inherited from her dead father and wore on a gold chain around her neck, they were still an hour's ride from Ruidoso.

Now as she turned to look out the soot-streaked window, at a pine-covered slope bathed in high-mountain sunshine, she spied three horseback riders moving toward her along the rails. No. There were four men. Two rode double on a rangy paint horse.

They were moving slowly up along the rail bed. They

were haggard, savage-looking men with grim sets to their eyes and jaws. The man riding out front of the other two horses, including the horse carrying double, had a bandage over his nose. He was a big man with long, flowing red hair and dusty spectacles that glinted in the sunshine, hiding his eyes.

He wore buckskin pants with whang strings, and suspenders over a collarless cotton tunic with red piping on the shoulders and down the sleeves. The shirt was badly sweat-streaked, and trail dust was ground into the sweat.

As he and the other three men approached Sofia's window, she saw that the tip of the bandage on the red-haired man's nose was dotted with blood.

She found herself staring at the man, fixated. As she did, a chill of apprehension climbed her spine. Her heart hiccupped and quickened.

Why?

She had no idea.

But for some reason, she could not remove her gaze from this man, though keeping it on him caused panic to grow in her. Her heart kicked like a horse, and her palms grew sweaty. There was something about this man that held her rapt, though her body sang with panic.

As he rode up beside Sofia's window, just ten feet from the rails, straight out away from her, he stopped his horse suddenly. The other two riders rode around him, to each side of him and, all three casting him vaguely puzzled gazes, continued riding along the rails to the south. The redheaded man stared straight ahead for several beats then, as though feeling the hot brand of Sofia's gaze on him, turned his head to stare directly at her through the sooty window.

His return stare came as a shock to her.

His broad, almost inhuman-looking face with the bandaged nose framed by those flowing locks of red curls made her insides writhe. She couldn't see his eyes. His glasses flashed in the sunlight, a trick of the changing light making them appear to spin and change reflected shapes, like a kaleidoscope she'd looked through once in a circus booth outside Mesilla.

Staring at this man staring back at her, expressionless, she felt as though she were looking through an open door to Hell and right into the face of the Devil himself.

Her heart pounded. Her skin crawled. Sweat trickled down her back.

Still, she couldn't look away.

Finally, the ogre—for that's how she saw him; an ogre straight from the bowels of Hell—lifted the corners of his mouth mantled by a thick, dusty, sweaty mustache that drooped down over both corners of his mouth. He raised two fingers to his hat brim. Lenses glinting and shifting various reflected sunbursts, he turned his head forward, clucked to his horse, and continued riding along the rails to the south.

Sofia absently noticed, beneath her continuing panic, that two sets of swollen saddlebags were draped over the hindquarters of his horse.

Sofia turned her head forward and sank back into her seat.

Slowly, her heart slowed.

After a time, she was able to draw a full breath.

Yet a cold knowing remained in her still-writhing belly.

CHAPTER 6

"Pull it out, Doc! Stop horsin' around an' pull the damn thing out!"

"If you'd hold still, I'll do just that!"

"Hell, as long as it's takin' you to do it, I could've done it twice by now myself!"

"Hold still, dammit, Stockburn!" the old medico said as he worked the pincers around in the wound in the railroad detective's upper right arm.

Lying on a table in the doctor's second-story office in Ruidoso, Stockburn took a slug from the bottle he'd acquired upon returning to town with the bullet in his arm. His next stop had been Dr. Leonard Larsen's office here above a furniture store/undertaking parlor. After all the blood that had oozed out onto the towels the doctor had wrapped around the arm, Wolf was thinking that his *next* stop would be the undertaking parlor directly below him.

"Ah, hell," Stockburn said, tipping the bottle up yet again, trying to quell the misery in his arm, "just pull the damn thing out!"

"I'm tryin'! It's snugged up against the backside of the bone!"

"*Christ!*"

Crouched over Stockburn's arm, the medico pulled the pincer out of the wound. A small, bloody slug was clamped between the pincer's bloody jaws. "Here it is!"

"Damn!" Stockburn sagged back against the table, the doctor's small operating room pitching and swirling around him, his head growing light, his vision dimming. "Don't pass out," he told himself, sweating and breathless. "Don't pass out, Wolf. You don't got time to sleep!"

"That's exactly what you should do," the doctor said as he dropped the bullet with a clink onto a metal tray. "You should go over to your hotel and go to bed. Sleep the rest of the day and through the night. I'll check that wound in the morning."

"No, no," Stockburn said. "Miller's on the run. I gotta get after 'em. Hell, he and those other three devils are likely halfway to Mexico by now."

He tried sitting up but the doctor shoved him back down on the table. "Lay down there, dammit. I have to wash out that wound so you don't develop gangrene. Christ, you've lost a lot of blood!" He clucked and shook his head.

He grabbed the bottle out of Wolf's hand and tipped it over the arm. The firewater gurgled out of the lip. When it hit the bloody hole in Stockburn's arm, halfway between his elbow and his shoulder, it felt like the long, razor-edged teeth of a raging grizzly.

Wolf sat halfway up and gritted his teeth and tensed every muscle in his body against the agony. "*Bloody hell, that burns!*"

The doctor chuckled as he used a sponge to swab the wound. "That means it's killing germs."

Stockburn drew two quick, shallow breaths as though to cool the flames in his arm. "It's about to kill *me*!"

The doctor chuckled again as he continued cleaning the wound.

Stockburn glowered at the old, potbellied, gray-headed man. "Doc, I think you got a sadistic streak."

The doctor only shook his head and chuckled again.

When he finished cleaning and bandaging the wound, Stockburn sat up and looked at the old sawbones' handiwork. "Good as new," he said, dropping his feet to the floor and rising. "Thanks, Doc. What do I—*whoah!*" He sagged back against the operating table, the room spinning faster around him.

"You're drunk and anemic, you damn fool," the sawbones said. "You better lay there till you get your strength back. Then get on over to your hotel for some food and a good, long sleep."

Wolf shook his head. "No time." By sheer force of will, he forced the room to stop spinning. At least, he forced it to slow down a little so he could gain his balance. When he did, he walked over and grabbed his shirt with its torn and bloody right sleeve off a wall peg. "I have to get after those killers before their trail goes cold."

"You can't track 'em dead, Stockburn," the doctor said as he sponged the blood off his operating table.

Wolf shrugged into his shirt and fumbled drunkenly with the buttons, seeing a whole lot more than were actually there. "Don't worry, Doc—I'm too mad to die. Those devils killed a young man I'd taken under my wing. It was on account of me Billy was on that express car.

I convinced him to stop his outlaw ways and join Wells Fargo. I pretty much got him killed."

"That's one way of looking at it, I suppose." The doctor tossed several rags into a corrugated tin pail then leaned back against a cabinet cluttered with medicine bottles, glass jars, and all manner of instruments. "You could also look at it like you saved him from a life of crime that probably would have gotten him killed even sooner."

"Just not how I see it, Doc."

Wolf gave up on the shirt after securing three buttons. The shirt was a goner, anyway. "What do I owe you?"

"Bullet removal is a buck fifty."

Stockburn reached into his pants then shoved a two-dollar gold piece into the doctor's hand. "Buy yourself somethin' nice with the extra fifty cents."

He winked at the old man who merely stared at him disgustedly.

He grabbed the nearly empty whiskey bottle, snatched his hat off the tree near the door, and grabbed the door-knob. His dizziness returned so suddenly that he wasn't able to get out of the way before he opened the door in his face, almost knocking himself off his feet.

He cursed and stumbled backward, closing his left hand over his chin, which had taken the brunt of the door's punishment. He pulled the cork out of the bottle and took another deep pull, nearly finishing it.

"Good God, man!"

Stockburn raised the bottle in salute. "See ya, Doc!"

"Not if I see you first!"

Stockburn chuckled then staggered out onto the medico's small, second-story stoop. He stood there, swaying, warily pondering the long stretch of wooden stairs angling sharply toward the ground.

Damn, they looked steep!

"Hell's bells." Stockburn raised the bottle and drained it. He dropped it over the rail to his right, heard the thud when it hit the ground, then stepped off the stoop and started down the stairs.

He'd descended only three steps before his right boot slipped off a riser. "*Ah, hell!*" he wailed, trying to grab the rail. His left hand merely grazed it. He fell hard on his left hip and the vile hand of gravity took him as though by the back of his shirt collar and fairly hurled him down the steps.

He grunted and groaned and cursed with every nasty, pain-aggravating roll.

He finally landed belly-down at the bottom of the stairs, which abutted a boardwalk running along the side street on which sat the furniture store/undertaking parlor and doctor's office. He lay with his left cheek pressed up against the rough boards, shivering in pain.

"Good God, man—are you *trying* to kill yourself?" the sawbones cried from the top of the steps.

Stockburn lifted his head to inspect the wounded arm. A little blood shone through the bandage. Not a lot, but some.

Burned like the unholy fires of Hell, though!

"Wolf?"

The girl's voice had come from above, on the heels of the soft taps of light feet.

With a groan, Stockburn rolled onto his back. He squinted against the harsh, midafternoon light.

A pretty, brown-eyed girl stared down at him, long hair slanting out from her slender shoulders. She wore a gray wool skirt, a red-and-black calico blouse, and a hand-sewn, deerskin vest that hung down over her nicely curved hips. A canvas satchel hung from her neck and left shoulder. A shapeless black hat sat on her head. Its scruffiness was in sharp contrast to her almost doll-like beauty, her facial bones carefully crafted for a distinctive, heady attraction.

It was that beauty, along with the girl's seeming obliviousness to it, that had first attracted his young friend, Billy Blythe.

"Sofia . . ."

She dropped to a knee beside him. "Wolf, what are you doing? Are you hurt?"

"Yes."

"Where?"

"Everywhere."

Sofia sucked a sharp breath through her teeth and placed her hand on his right arm, near the wound. "That looks nasty. What did you do?"

"Took a bullet." Wolf raised his left hand and regarded the girl with silent urging. "Would you mind? I know you can't pull me up alone, but I'll try to do what I can from down here."

"Oof! Maybe you should lay there. You don't look so good, Wolf."

Stockburn shook his head from side to side. "Too much to do. I was supposed to meet you at the train station. I'm sorry, darlin'. I forgot . . . what with that damn bullet in my arm. How'd you find me?"

"I asked around on the street and a man said he saw you climbing the steps of the doctor's office around an hour ago." Sofia straightened then took his hand in both of her own. "Who shot you?"

While Sofia set her feet close together and leaned back,

pulling on his hand, Stockburn gained a knee uncertainly. Just as uncertainly, he heaved himself to his feet then staggered back to steady himself against the front of the furniture store. He drew a deep breath. "Same bunch that killed Billy."

Just hearing her dead lover's name brought tears to her eyes. She rushed to Stockburn, wrapped her arms around him, and pressed her cheek to his chest, sobbing.

He wrapped his good arm around her, squeezing, and lowered his left cheek to the crown of her hat, flattening it against her head.

"I'm so sorry, Sofia." Stockburn choked on a sob of his own. "I'm just so damn sorry I helped him get that job!"

She sniffed, and, keeping her cheek pressed taut against his chest, said in a small, emotion-choked voice, "It's not your fault, Wolf. It's the fault of the man who killed him."

"Ah, hell—I just—"

"Don't!" She looked up at him, her eyes grave, worried. "He loved you like an older brother. You loved him like a young brother. It's not good for his soul or yours to hold yourself responsible for his death. It is not only a waste of time; it is a desecration."

She reached up and cupped his chin in her hand, squeezing, staring into his eyes. "Do you understand? Only the men who killed him—they are the only ones responsible."

Stockburn blinked a tear from his eye and gave a weak smile to the beautiful little Spanish princess gazing up at him with such concern. "You're wiser than your years, darlin'."

"Where is he?"

Stockburn canted his head at the building holding him upright. "Around back. Follow me"—he placed his hands on her shoulders—"if you're ready . . ."

"I have had the train ride to prepare for it."

"You didn't need to ride up here, you know, Sofia. I could have brought him home."

She shook her head quickly. "No. You don't understand, Wolf. It is important that I see him, that I pray for him quickly, to free his soul. When a man is murdered . . ." She let her words trail to silence, and shook her head. "Never mind. It is a hard thing for others to understand."

She glanced away, vaguely sheepish.

"All right."

Stockburn took her hand and led her around the building's front corner. Hand in hand, they walked beneath the stairs rising to the sawbones' office and around the rear corner to the back.

Two large doors stood open, revealing the undertaking parlor in which a big-bellied, bearded man in a long, green, bloodstained apron was running a plane across a pine coffin propped on sawhorses. A short-haired, long-legged dog lay near the undertaker, Jim MacDonald, against the far wall, chewing on a beef bone.

Scattered across the large, open, wooden-floored room, several dead men and two dead women lay on planks also propped across sawhorses, apparently awaiting coffins and their eventual burial. More victims of Red Miller's bunch. All of the bodies were liberally stained with blood. Just workaday men and women who'd been innocently going about their daily business until Red Miller had burst out of the bank and shot up the town out of pure meanness.

As he entered the parlor's open doors, Stockburn stopped and looked down at two of the dead. Waylon and Ivy Wallace lay side by side, on two separate planks, close enough that they could have held hands if they'd been able to. Waylon's brown eyes stared blindly up over Stockburn's right shoulder, reflecting the brassy light of the sun angling through the open doors—the lens-clear, high-mountain New Mexican sunlight he would never see again.

"Hell, Waylon," Stockburn said, choking back a sob.

Wolf raked his fingers across the lawman's eyes, closing them. As he did, a wave of bitter fury and sadness churned inside him, momentarily drowning his other sundry miseries of various degrees of severity.

His Wells Fargo work often took him through Ruidoso, usually on his way to Las Cruces and Tucson farther west. But never again would he stop and have a beer and a shot of whiskey with his old pal, Waylon Wallace. Never again, would Waylon badger him into following him home to one of Ivy's delicious suppers punctuated by her trademark cobbler.

Never again.

Death was so damned nonnegotiable. An argument lost before it even began.

"Sorry, Wolf," the bearded undertaker said. He'd stopped planing the coffin and stood holding the plane from which sawdust curled, regarding Stockburn grimly from over the coffin he'd been finishing. "I'm gonna fix 'em up nice and get 'em into my best boxes here soon."

"I know you will, Jim," Stockburn said. He glanced down at Sofia smiling sympathetically at him then turned to the undertaker once more. "Where's Billy? His wife is here to say good-bye."

CHAPTER 7

Deputy U.S. Marshal "Lonesome" Charlie Murdock rode his buckskin gelding into Ruidoso, swinging his gaze from one side of the street to the other, scowling curiously beneath the brim of his tan Stetson trimmed with a single gray owl feather jutting up from the rawhide band.

As he continued down the main drag, the middle-aged lawman's curious scowl wrinkled his grizzled brows even more severely and cut a washboard of deep lines across his ruddy, age-freckled forehead.

There wasn't nearly enough traffic on the street for this time of day, which was midafternoon. Those folks who were out—and there were damn few—looked as long-faced as boys whose houses Santa skipped at Christmastime. There were a few men drinking out in front of the saloons here and there, but Lonesome Charlie heard none of the usual, easy, bawdy laughter he'd heard last time he'd drifted through this burgeoning mountain mining and lumber town. Most of the shops looked deserted.

If Charlie hadn't known better, he'd have sworn it was Sunday.

"Howdy, Marshal!"

Lonesome Charlie drew back on his reins, stopping the buckskin he called Bill for no other reason than he was tired of hearing buckskins called Buck, and cast his gaze toward a pretty young lady smiling down at him from the second-floor balcony of a two-story, wood-frame clapboard house painted purple with white trim around the window and on the porch and balcony directly above it.

The old lawman's craggy face, so weather-scarred that it resembled a relief map of Arizona, crumpled into a slanty-eyed grin, mustached lips stretching back from his tobacco-brown teeth—those remaining in his head, that was. "Well, well, well . . . Miss Kansas City Jane, if you ain't a sight to these lonesome old eyes! I was wondering not ten minutes ago, back on he trail down from ol' Albukirk, if I'd find you here."

"Awww, now you've gone and made me sad, Lonesome," the pretty redhead said, leaning far enough forward against the balcony rail that the purple corset she wore— the same color as the parlor house she worked in—sagged down far enough that the view nearly knocked Lonesome from his saddle. "I thought maybe you'd come all this way just to see me!"

She pooched out her pretty red lips in a feigned pout.

"Jane, honey—you know ol' Lonesome Charlie would love nothin' more than to, um, *see* you if ol' Lonesome wasn't such a busy man runnin' down ring-tailed owlhoots of every stripe an' color! That there is a full-time job—especially now with me gettin' on in my gray-beard years . . ." He grimaced as he ran a gloved hand over his long, reddish gray-streaked beard as thin as a baby's hair.

That seemed to cheer the girl. A radiant smile returned

to her dimpled cheeks; the left one bore the short, hooked scar of an old knife wound. "You would?"

"Of course, I would. No workin' girl ever curled the toes of this old catamount like Kansas City Jane has, an' that's a natural fact!"

Lonesome and the girl shared a bawdy laugh. Lonesome enjoyed the view of her laughing—or what her laughing did to her corset, rather.

Lonesome looked around at the sluggish street traffic then tipped his face with its puzzled expression up to Jane and said, "Jane, honey, why all the long faces here in Ruidoso? I swear it looks like the whole town was gettin' ready for one big funeral."

"Well, we are," Jane said, drawing her mouth corners down in a genuine expression of sadness.

"Huh?"

"I suppose you haven't heard since you were on the trail an' all, but the bank got robbed by the same bunch that robbed the train and killed the express agent and the young man guarding the Wells Fargo car!"

"Red Miller's bunch?"

"Them's the ones. How'd you know, Lonesome?"

The lawman looked around, scowling and scratching the back of his head, nudging his hat down onto his forehead. "'Cause they're the ones the Chief Marshal sent me down here from Albukirk to run to ground since he didn't have no one else—younger marshals, I mean—to send down here, so he—oh, hell, never mind about that!"

The oldster ran a hand sheepishly down his face, inwardly cursing his old age and fading reputation. Returning his attention to the topic at hand, he deepened his scowl and narrowed one eye, giving his incredulous gaze to the pretty doxie once more. "You're tellin' me that Red Miller had gall enough to rob the Sierra Blanca Express and *then* to ride into Ruidoso and rob the *bank*?"

"That's right. Happened just this morning—four or five hours ago."

"Did Waylon Wallace form a posse and go out after 'em?"

"Nope." The girl shook her head darkly. "They killed Marshal Wallace. And his wife."

"No!"

"Sure enough."

"Those devils! Did *anybody* go after 'em?"

"Wolf Stockburn did. You know—that handsome railroad detective for Wells Fargo?" Kansas City Jane flushed and her bosom heaved. Her creamy exposed cleavage turned crimson. "He went out after 'em all by his lonesome. I heard tell he got half of 'em, but, him bein' only one man against eight, he took a bullet. Four got away, including Red Miller."

"Stockburn, huh?" Lonesome grimaced distastefully and fingered his beard again.

"He's about as handsome a man as I ever laid eyes on," the doxie said, fairly swooning. "I hear he don't frequent the parlor houses, but if he ever came over here, I'd want to be the one to—"

"Jane, honey, if you'll forgive me, I'm gonna go rest my horse a spell and tend a powerful thirst that's been buildin' ever since I left Albukirk. Then, if it ain't too late and I'm still sober, I reckon I'll do some sniffin' of my own on the trail of Red Miller."

Jane gasped and splayed her fingers across her breasts.

"You be careful, Lonesome Charlie! Promise? If Wolf Stockburn couldn't take them down—"

"Listen here, young lady," Charlie said, pointing an arthritis-crooked, gloved finger up at the girl. "I got me a purty good reputation as a man tracker my ownself." Well, at least he *once* did. "Some might even say *legendary*. Forty damn years' worth. At least among them in the know. While I may not have had all the ink spilled over me that Stockburn has, it's mostly because I don't go around fawning for attention and gilding my own lily the way Mister Wolf of the Rails his own fancy self tends to do!"

Jane placed a hand on her hip and pooched out her pretty lips in bewilderment. "Hmm. I always heard he was more the tight-lipped sort."

"Hah—tight-lipped sort, my buttooskie!" Lonesome Charlie reined Bill around and threw an annoyed arm up in parting. "I'll be seein' you, Jane."

"Come by any time you feel a hankerin' for a romp, Lonesome!"

"All righty—I will, honey!"

As Charlie turned Bill toward a little hole-in-the-wall saloon called Pistol Pete's, he grumbled under his breath. Why did Stockburn have to be in town?

Charlie didn't like the man. One, Stockburn was a Wells Fargo detective. Wells Fargo detectives were known to be thorns in the sides of *bona fide lawmen* like Lonesome Charlie. In Lonesome's experience, Wells Fargo men—not unlike the Pinkertons—only stomped and preened and wagged their fancy credentials around and got in the way of the *bona fide lawmen* like Lonesome Charlie doing the heavy lifting. Another reason Lonesome didn't like Stockburn was because in Charlie's albeit limited experience with the man, Charlie had found him cocky.

Lonesome Charlie didn't like cocky men. Especially when they were younger and better-looking than he was, and especially when they had such oversized reputations. If Stockburn was around, he'd likely only get in Charlie's way while the *bona fide federal lawman* tried to perform his customary expert job of running down career criminals.

Oh, well. Charlie would just find a way to work around Stockburn—that's all. Usually those dandified high-hatted Wells Fargo boys were easy to bluff and misdirect. Once he got on Red Miller's trail, he'd leave Stockburn in his dust with his thumb up his behind wondering what day it was.

Charlie cackled a laugh as he swung down from Bill's back.

He tied Bill's reins around the worn hitchrack. Turning toward the three steps leading up to the saloon's front porch, he stopped suddenly. Bunching his lips with pain, he staggered back against the hitchrack and, as a bayonet of poison-soaked misery pierced his brisket, he pressed the end of his right fist against his chest.

"Ah, hell—not now, dammit!" he choked out, lowering his chin in pain.

He pressed his gloved fist harder against his chest, trying to quell the lurching of his old ticker and ease the pain of a steel claw in his chest closing around his heart. As he did, what felt like two sharp bayonets gouged his left arm from shoulder to wrist. He flexed the arm and tried to make a fist with that hand.

No doing. The bayonets had skewered him good.

Damn . . .

He drew several slow, deep breaths. By the fifth one, the pain was easing. He drew two more breaths despite his feeling that a four-hundred-pound woman was sitting on his chest and bouncing up and down like a demented, overfed whore. By the time he'd exhaled the second breath, the whore had eased her lard butt off him a bit. He raised his left hand and made a fist, clenched it tight.

The bayonets in his arm pulled back.

So far, so good.

Lonesome Charlie drew a couple of more breaths. When the ground had stopped moving around him, as though he were walking drunk, he drew one last breath then pushed himself away from the hitchrack.

Here we go. Let's see how we do on the steps . . .

Lonesome Charlie stepped forward. His legs felt weak, especially in the knees, but that always happened when he had one of his "spells." Like the rest, it would go away in a few minutes.

Whiskey. He needed whiskey and a smoke. He always felt better after a couple of shots of tangleleg and a cigarette. The elixirs of life.

When he'd made it up the steps without dropping to his knees and making a fool of himself, he drew one more deep breath, held it, let it out, then walked forward, spurs chiming, and pushed through the batwings and into the saloon.

"Hello, my dear friend, McDougal," he greeted, grinning as he headed for the bar that ran along the rear of the plainly furnished room with several deer and elk trophies on the walls and sawdust on the floor. "Why don't you set your old pal Lonesome Charlie up with a bottle that won't blind him?"

Apparently, the bartender, McDougal, didn't find the joke funny. A tall, skinny man with thinning hair starting well back from his bulging forehead, merely flared a nostril, grimaced at his new customer, and reached under the bar without looking.

He set a bottle on the bar, popped the cork, set a shot glass beside the bottle, and slid both toward where Charlie walked up to the time-worn, bullet-pocked mahogany. He stood to the left of five young men in saddle tramp attire already lined up there, palavering and sipping beers.

They were drifters. Likely out of work cow punchers. Lonesome Charlie had seen their broomtail cayuses at the hitchrail out front.

"Thank you kindly, McDougal." Lonesome Charlie removed his owl-plumed, weather-stained hat, set it on the bar, and ran a hand through his own, thinning, red-brown, silver-streaked hair. "You, sir, are a gentleman and a scholar."

Charlie lifted the shot to his lips, closed his eyes, and took half of the who-hit-John down in one swallow.

One of the men to Charlie's right turned to him, slapped the bar, and said, "Hey, there, Lonesome Charlie—you old drunken sidewinder! You still kickin'? Hell, I heard you was dead years ago!"

He elbowed the two men standing to each side of him. "Did you fellas know old Lonesome Charlie Murdock was still *alive?* Imagine that! Charlie, you must be older'n Jehosophat's cat!"

The short, badger-faced speaker and the others laughed.

Lonesome Charlie felt the burn of anger in his logy ticker. The uncertain organ hiccupped and churned.

Ignoring the badger-faced brigand, whom he could see in the backbar mirror—little bulging blue eyes gleaming in mockery at the deputy U.S. marshal—Lonesome Charlie threw down the rest of his whiskey then refilled his glass from the unlabeled bottle.

"You still kickin', Lonesome Charlie?" Badger Face asked again, broadening his jeering grin. "I bet not very high." He elbowed his friends again and hiccupped a laugh.

Lonesome Charlie took another sip of his whiskey then set his glass down on the bar. Calmly, he walked around the man standing to his right and stopped before the badger-faced devil, a few inches taller than he, who'd been hoorahing him.

Badger Face turned to face Charlie, squaring his shoulders, dropping one hand down over the worn walnut grips of his old Smith & Wesson. Lonesome Charlie recognized him now—a seedy little stock thief known as Little Dave Bingham.

"Well, well, Little Dave," said Lonesome Charlie. "You've inquired as to how high I can kick . . ."

Bingham grinned, making his pale, unshaven cheeks bulge like two ovals of fresh bun dough. "Yeah, how high *can* you kick, Charlie?"

Lonesome Charlie grabbed the bar with his left hand for support and thrust his right boot straight up. It made a satisfying crunching sound when the pointed toe buried itself up high between Little Dave's thighs.

"There," Charlie said, lowering his foot and releasing the bar. "That's how high I can kick, you little satan spawn!"

Little Dave's face crumpled in misery as he jackknifed

forward over the buckle of his cartridge belt, releasing a loud half-wail, half-chuff of displaced air.

His ratty hat tumbled forward from his head.

"*Ohhh!*" Little Dave cried, his round face swollen and even paler than before as he dropped both knees to the floor, clutching his privates with both hands.

Charlie scowled down at the brigand, shaking an admonishing finger at him. "Next time you feel like badgering a respected servant of the federal government, recall this day!"

CHAPTER 8

"Jesus, Dave!" said the man standing to Little Dave's right. "You gonna be all right?"

Dave's four friends gathered in a ragged circle around the ailing, badger-faced man, who knelt on the floor clutching his privates, his face a swollen, pale, bug-eyed mask of near-silent agony. Tears glazed Dave's horrified eyes as he shook his head slowly, saying in a sobbing, strangling little girl's voice, "He hurt me. He hurt me real bad."

He raised his arms slightly and looked around imploringly. "He hurt me real bad, Tuttle. Chris, he hurt me real bad. Fetch me over to the sawbones. Oh, Lordy—I'm hurt down there *real bad*!"

He screeched out those last two words as tears dribbled down his cheeks like a hard summer rain over a window.

Little Dave's friends looked at each other. They looked at Lonesome Charlie, who chuckled and said, "He's right. You better get him over to the medico. Apparently, this old lawdog can kick a lot higher than he thought I could. Hell, *I* didn't even know I could kick that high! Made a fairly solid connection, yessir."

He placed a hand over the .44 Colt Dragoon conversion pistol holstered low on his right thigh and added with steely, mocking menace, "Less'n, of course, you wanna see how fast this old man can still draw this old horse pistol . . ."

Little Dave's friends looked at each other again, then, apparently wanting no part of a lead swap, and believing that Little Dave might have had the punishment coming, removed their hands from their guns. Two stepped forward, each grabbing one of Dave's half-raised arms.

They half-dragged, half-carried the wailing man across the floor, Dave's boot toes scraping across the puncheons, clicking across the seams, and out the batwings.

The batwings clattered back into place behind them.

Dave's two remaining friends cast Lonesome Charlie bitter looks then turned back to the bar and resumed drinking.

Charlie turned back to his own drink and grinned at McDougal who stood regarding him without expression, slowly drying a beer schooner with a towel. The dead-eyed barman had seen far bigger dustups than the one he'd just witnessed, and the bullet-pocked bar, stained here and there with ground-in blood, attested to that grim note of historical fact.

"I still got it, McDougal," Charlie said. "Don't ever say I don't." He picked up his half-empty glass and his bottle and turned toward the room. "I do believe I'm gonna sit down and put my feet up. Been a long ride from Albukirk." He winced, adding, "And I think that kick might've dislocated my hip a little . . ."

"Pay up first."

Charlie turned back to the bar, one brow arched. "What's that?"

McDougal tapped the bar with his index finger. "Pay up first. I ain't gonna let you go skippin' out on me again, Charlie. Pay up. That bottle is a buck fifty."

Grumbling and cursing under his breath, Charlie tossed a few coins onto the bar. While they were still rattling around, he limped off to a near table, favoring his right hip. He had his pick of tables, for only three others of the dozen or so were occupied.

Those occupants were regarding him warily, muttering secretively amongst themselves. At least, he took their expressions to be ones of wariness.

What else could it be?

Hadn't he just proven the old dog still had some bite? That this cat did not take to teasing?

He chuffed with satisfaction as he kicked a chair out and sank into it. He set the bottle and the shot glass down on the table and leaned forward on his elbows. He grimaced as his heart beat erratically, sending out small daggers of pain. He drew a breath, tossed back the whiskey, and refilled his glass.

The whiskey sent a warm glow through him, soothing his worn-out old ticker. Remembering the pills a doctor in Albuquerque had given him, he reached into a pocket of his vest and removed the small tin box. He opened the velvet-lined box, plucked out one of the small gelatin tablets little larger than a shotgun pellet, and slipped it under his tongue.

He returned the box to his pocket and almost immediately noted a loosening of that steel claw in his chest. The claw loosened a little more and then he was smiling, encouraged that he was not about to croak right here in Pistol Pete's squalid watering hole and make a damn fool of himself.

He wanted to go out either in a hail of hot lead or in bed with a pretty young doxie and a big grin on his face.

He chuckled at the thought, took another couple of soothing sips of the whiskey then dug his makings out and rolled a cigarette. He did so in a dreamy haze now, the alcohol and the tablet taking full affect, knocking off about ten years from his age.

Well, five, anyway. He hadn't felt as good as he felt now in at least five years, before that crab had spawned in his chest, growing from a weakling to a berserker.

The wonders of whiskey and modern medicine.

And Bull Durham . . .

Charlie dragged a lucifer match across the scarred table. The flame flared into a long pyramid, the top of which he touched to the end of the tightly twisted quirley. He drew the smoke deep into his lungs and flipped the match onto the floor.

"Ahhh . . ."

Slitting his eyes, he blew the smoke into a heavy wreath around him and took another deep drag.

"There," he said, smiling and studying the burning end of the cigarette. "That there's the cream on the pie . . ."

Glancing over the cigarette, he noticed a man sitting near the front of the room staring at him. No, two men were staring at him. As he lowered the quirley to stare back at them—both sitting at the same table—they quickly turned away, one flushing a little, the other leaning forward on his elbows and feigning a casual throat clearing.

They sat directly in front of Lonesome Charlie, against

the large front window, facing each other. They were playing poker, smoking, and drinking beer. The one on the left was a bull-like fellow with black hair combed straight back across his scalp. He was blue-eyed and black-mustached. He wore two pistols on his hips.

The man on Charlie's right was tall and slender. He had thin ginger hair on his bullet-shaped head, and freckles on his long horse face. He wore his hair long over the ear facing Charlie, but it was too thin to conceal the fact that he had only half of that ear. The top half of the ear was missing, leaving a pale, jagged-edged scar.

Bit off, no doubt, during a savage fight. Or by a whore. The ginger-haired man with only half of his left ear wore one pistol that Charlie could see, tied down on his right thigh. A Winchester carbine leaned against the window to his right.

He and the other man were roughly fifteen feet away from Charlie.

They were trying to resume their casual game of cards, but now that they knew that Lonesome Charlie, for whom this wasn't his first rodeo, had spotted them both, giving them the wooly eyeball, they were nervous.

Why?

Charlie puffed his quirley and stared through the smoke webbing a blue haze around him. He scrutinized each man in turn. The big, black-haired, granite-faced gent looked familiar but Charlie couldn't place him.

He reached into his shirt pocket and pulled out a small notepad with a badly wrinkled pasteboard cover. In fact, the entire small book, having ridden many miles for several years with Lonesome Charlie, looked like a scrap of ancient leather. It was swollen, its pages curled and yellowed, from having been soaked with rain and sweat and then dried over and over again by remote campfires, scorched by stray cinders. It had coffee and whiskey stains on it, and the back cover was half torn away.

The pad contained fifty lined pages. The bulk of those pages had writing on them, mostly in pencil but some in smeared ink. Those pages contained the names of men, some accompanied by brief, scrawled descriptions. Most of those names, comprising a list of wanted men and even a few wanted women, had been crossed out over the years.

There was still a dozen or so names that had not been crossed out, representing wolves still running off their leashes.

Avery Willis, for instance. Curly Hodges. Louis del Torro. Luther Carter Brown. Snake Margolies, May "Big Mama" Brandon, Hoodoo Carlton, H. G. Rutherford . . .

Red Miller and his seven associates were on that list, as well. They'd been added a little over a year ago, when they'd started their killing and robbing spree in the Arizona and Utah territories and the federal wanted posters had started circulating their names and likenesses. Lonesome Charlie had dutifully added them and their brief descriptions (Red: glasess, sissy voyce and purty red hare) to the notebook. Red and his associates occupied one of the pad's last few pages.

But these two men before Charlie now were not Red or any of Red's associates, half of whom, if Kansas City Jane had it right, were dead at the hand of Stockburn. The Wolf of the Rails had probably dry-gulched or backshot them.

Charlie chuffed with amusement at the thought then took another pull from the quirley and continued to give the thrice-over to the two men sitting directly ahead of him. As he did, he slowly flipped the notebook pages, surveying the outstanding names and the accompanying descriptions.

The men before him had resumed their card game, flipping cards and coins onto the table. But they did so with a definite tenseness, faces flushed with self-consciousness. They were not talking. Their eyes were pinched up at the corners. A few times one or the other turned his head toward Charlie slightly, casting him a quick, furtive glance.

Charlie did not turn away when they looked at him. He continued to brand each man with his scrutinizing gaze. He didn't care that they knew he was looking at them. He liked it that they were self-conscious. Self-conscious men were nervous men. Nervous men got jumpy and made mistakes.

Holding the notebook out away from his far-sighted eyes, the quirley clamped in a corner of his mouth, Lonesome Charlie flipped another page, perused the names on it, then flipped another . . .

He squinted down at the name scribbled there. His old ticker quickened.

He cast his suspicious gaze from the name on the page to the black-haired, granite-faced gent sitting at the table before him. He felt a smile tug at his mouth corners.

"Junior Dunleavy, eh?" he muttered. *Black Irish, blu eyes—face like a buldog. Stinx like a dog with the liver farts.*

That last bit of description must have been a direct quote from someone who'd shared the same air space as Dunleavy.

Charlie flipped two more pages until he came to a torn one with a cigarette burn on the bottom right corner. The only name on the page not crossed out was on the bottom, just above the burn.

Wilburn "Mad Dog" O'Neil. Hore chewed lft ear off in Glendive.

Again, Lonesome Charlie cast his gaze from the notepad to the table before him, this time focusing on the ginger-haired man with half his left ear missing. Again having to fight the grin threatening to blossom on his craggy face, Charlie closed the ragged pad and returned it to his shirt pocket. As he did, he saw that the two men before him had broken their silence.

They were both still holding their cards, but they were leaning forward across their table, exchanging words in low, pinched voices. As they did, Mad Dog O'Neil glanced directly at Charlie, keeping his gaze on Charlie for a whole two seconds before turning his head forward again.

Charlie took another deep drag off his quirley and blew the smoke out toward the two men before him. They were still in bitter conference.

Charlie refilled his shot glass, threw back the entire shot, then slammed the glass down on the table so hard the glass nearly broke. The sound resonated around the saloon like the report of a .44 revolver, making everyone in the room jump, including Mad Dog and Junior Dunleavy.

They turned their heads sharply toward Charlie. Their eyes blazed. Their taut jaws bulged.

Charlie let that wolfish grin go ahead and do what it wanted with his lips and his eyes as he leaned forward, jutted his chin toward the pair of long-wanted brigands, and said, "What do you say, boys—ready to do-si-do? Or you gonna come willin'-like to palaver with the federal judge in Albukirk . . . and the hangman, no doubt?"

Both men held their darkly shimmering gazes on Charlie.

They turned to face each other.

Like two rattlesnakes coiled and striking, both leaped from their chairs, Dunleavy turning to face Lonesome Charlie while clawing both of his hoglegs from his hips. Mad Dog O'Neil first reached for the carbine behind him, then, rising, turned toward Charlie and jacked a round into the Winchester's chamber.

Charlie gave a wild rebel yell as he closed his hand over the edge of the table and lifted it sharply before him. As he raised the table, he raised himself from his chair then dropped to his knees as the deafening thunder of two pistols and a Winchester rifle rose before him.

Several slugs plowed into the table now standing on its side before him, a wooden shield, and hammering it back against Charlie's head and shoulders.

One slug clipped the edge and peppered Charlie's face with wood slivers.

Charlie slid the old Colt Dragoon from its holster and thumbed back the hammer.

As more rounds pounded the table, one pushing through far enough that Charlie could see the angry lead nose, Charlie thrust his head and right hand around the table's right side, and fired.

Giving another shrill rebel yell, he fired again and again, laughing in satisfaction as first Mad Dog O'Neil and then Junior Dunleavy raised their arms and threw away their guns as Charlie's .44 slugs blew them both back through the large, plate-glass window behind them, screaming.

Lonesome Charlie whooped and hollered like the town drunk on the Fourth of July.

He gained his feet heavily, winced, and pressed the end of his fist to his chest again, trying to quell another couple of kicks from his crab-bit heart, then looked around, beaming. The others had all dropped belly-down to the floor or were cowering behind chairs and tables.

"Did you see that?" Charlie bellowed. "*Did-you-see-that*? Don't you ever let anyone say Lonesome Charlie ain't still got some bite in him! No, sir. Don't you ever stand for it. Charlie's gonna stomp with his tail up till a purty whore does me in on a feather-stuffed mattress, an' Ol' Scratch throws me a shovel!"

He threw his head back and cast another rebel yell at the rafters.

CHAPTER 9

As Jim McDougal removed the lid from the coffin near the rear of the cluttered undertaking parlor, Sofia Ortega gasped and slowly lifted a hand to her mouth. She stared down in sorrow at her beloved Billy Blythe.

Wolf Stockburn placed his hand on her back, lending comfort.

"Oh, Billy," the girl said softly, her voice trembling. She placed the back of her hand against the dead young man's pale left cheek, caressed it softly. "Oh, my darling . . . Billy . . ." She shook her head. "I thought we were going to have such a long life together. I thought we would raise a family . . . have many kids . . . a couple of dogs . . . a cat . . . then grandchildren later on . . ."

She sniffed, shook her head again. Tears trickled down her cheeks. "We didn't even make it a year."

Stockburn's own throat swelled.

Sofia removed a chain and a small silver crucifix from around her neck. She slipped the cross in Billy's right hand resting with the other one on his belly then leaned down and gently pressed her lips to the cold, blue lips of her dead husband. She lifted her head slightly and said something in Spanish. Stockburn couldn't make it out though he had a rudimentary understanding of the language. It sounded to him like Spanish mixed with some other language—possibly Apache or Yaqui.

She spoke to Billy in that tongue for over a minute and then she kissed his lips again, lifted her hand to his forehead, and drew a cross. She added a box around the cross, which Stockburn found puzzling. He'd never seen that sign before.

Usually, it was just the sign of the cross.

"Good-bye, my love." Sofia straightened. "Till we meet again."

She looked at Jim McDougal who stood nearby, his head bowed. When McDougal looked up at her, Sofia nodded. As McDougal set the lid on the coffin once more, Sofia turned to Stockburn. Her eyes were dry now, though tear trails remained on her cheeks.

"I must ride along with you when you ride after Billy's killer."

The girl's words had been so unexpected, her tone so oddly certain and matter-of-fact that Stockburn blinked and frowned in surprise. "What? Why?"

"Because I've seen his killer. I have to be there when the man is killed."

"Why?"

"Because I'm his wife. Only his closest relative—a sister, a brother . . . a wife . . . can set his soul free . . . after I've seen the demon who killed him brought to justice or killed."

"What do you mean you've seen . . ." Wolf stopped, shook his head. This could wait. The poor girl was in shock.

She didn't know what she was saying. Sometimes deep grief caused delirium.

He took her arm and turned her toward the open doors. "Come on, honey. Let's go sit down somewhere . . . get some coffee an' food in both our bellies."

"I don't want either."

"Well, I have to have both or I'm liable to pass out. Humor me, will you, kid? Then we'll get you a hotel room. I was going to get after those killers today but it's getting late and I won't be worth a damn without some food and a night's sleep."

"I would just like to go to my room, but I will join you, Wolf. You should eat. You don't look so good."

"You don't, either. We should both eat."

"I can't eat." As Sofia walked along beside Stockburn, her satchel dangling over her left hip, her dark brown hair winging back behind her, she added in a strained voice, "I don't think I will ever be able to eat again." She brushed a fresh tear from her cheek.

She gasped and stopped in her tracks, as did Stockburn, when loud gunfire exploded in a building just ahead on their right. It came on the heels of a wild rebel yell and the thunder of what sounded like a trapdoor being dropped— or a heavy table overturned.

The gunfire continued. Wolf felt the reverberations through the boardwalk beneath his boots. Another, even louder rebel yell accompanied the gunfire. The shooting increased and then, one second later, a man came crashing backward, arms thrown high, through a window of Pistol Pete's Saloon.

He gave a loud yell and then a fierce grunt when he struck the boardwalk not ten feet in front of Stockburn and Sofia, glass raining down around him and flashing in the late afternoon sunshine. The man was still shivering in death spasms when a second man came crashing out the same window, a little farther along the boardwalk from the first one.

This man also struck the boardwalk on his back.

He lay spread-eagle, grunting, then heaved himself up onto his knees.

Stockburn released Sofia's hand and used his right hand to slide one of his Colt Peacemakers from its cross-draw holster on his left hip, aiming it out in front of him at the man who was trying desperately to climb to his feet.

Finally, the man said, "Ah, hell!" and dropped back down to his knees.

Kneeling there, swaying, frothy blood oozing from a wound in his chest, he stared at Stockburn and Sofia, or maybe between them, not seeing much of anything anymore. He blinked twice and then, with a slack expression on his glass-peppered face, said, "I'm d-deader'n a damn post!"

He fell facedown on the glass-littered boardwalk.

Raucous, wheezing laughter rose inside the broken window. Boots pounded and spurs rang. The pounding and ringing grew louder until they stopped and a weathered old man with a long, thin, red-gray beard stood in the busted-out window, smiling broadly, eyes narrowed to slits and tilted upward at the corners, at the two dead men on the boardwalk before him.

He held an old-model Colt Dragoon down low in his right hand. A thin sliver of smoke curled from the barrel. The oldster nodded, chuckled, and said, "Deader'n last year's Christmas goose!"

The old gun-toter must have spied Stockburn in the corner of his left eye; he turned his head suddenly toward the railroad detective and the girl, and his eyes turned cold and mean. "Stockburn," he said, flaring a nostril.

Wolf glanced at the deputy U.S. marshal's moon-and-star badge on the man's wool shirt, partly hidden by his cowhide vest, then returned his gaze to the old codger's face.

He frowned, curious.

The old-timer looked a little indignant. He punched his thumb against his chest. "Lonesome Charlie Murdock. *Deputy U.S. Marshal* Charlie Murdock." He swung a leg, wincing with the effort, over the bottom of the window and stepped down onto the boardwalk.

He spat to one side as he looked down at the two dead men once more, grinning, then swiped the back of his left hand across his mouth. He chuckled again with satisfaction. "They even got the drop. Drew iron first. But I still shot 'em cold, all right."

Stockburn scowled curiously at the wizened old man before him. "Wait a minute," he said. "You're Lonesome Charlie Murdock?"

The federal badge-toter regarded him again with deep indignation. "That's right. *Lonesome Charlie Murdock.* You hard o' hearin', Wells Fargo?"

Stockburn gave a surprised chuckle. "I'll be hanged if I didn't think you were dead."

Right away, he realized his mistake.

The old man snapped another hard look at him, his eyes turning bright with rage. "Dead? Hell, I ain't dead! Hell, I ain't never been more alive!" He kicked one of the dead men. "See this one here? This here is Mad Dog O'Neil.

That one there is Junior Dunleavy. Both been on the run for years now, runnin' off their leashes from federal warrants."

He holstered his pistol then plucked a tattered notebook from a shirt pocket hidden by his vest. He slapped the pad against his hand and said, "Had 'em wrote down here in my notebook for the past fifteen, twenty years. I call this my Murder Book. I only write down them wanted, dead or alive, for murder. I started keeping this book when I first started workin' for Chief Marshal Brennan Quinn, God rest his soul, goin' on twenty years ago now. I've damn near crossed out the name of every curly wolf I ever wrote down, and that's a fact!"

He slapped the pad against his hand again, grinning.

"Ah, Charlie," Stockburn said, taking two steps forward and glancing down at the dead, black-haired man lying on his back before him. "You should have crossed this one off your list about twelve years ago."

"Huh?"

"Junior Dunleavy done did his time in Leavenworth. He'd been given a ten-year sentence because he'd cooperated in the hunt for the rest of his gang. He got out two years ago, as I recall."

Stockburn took two more steps forward and looked down at the ginger-haired man lying facedown on the glass-peppered boards. "As for ol' Mad Dog, he's been out of the pen for six, seven years now. He was part of a new program called *parole*."

"Parole?"

"That's right."

Lonesome Charlie gazed down in wide-eyed exasperation at Mad Dog O'Neil. "Mad Dog was on *parole*?"

"That's right."

"Well, I'll be damned," said Lonesome Charlie, his craggy face darkening with chagrin. "Imagine that." He brushed his fist across his nose.

"What I wanna know is who's gonna pay for Pistol Pete's window?" This from a tall, lean, apron-clad fellow standing inside the saloon, looking out the empty window frame, hands on his hips, head canted to one side. "He's gonna wanna know his ownself when he wakes up from his hangover, and I better have a good answer or he'll take it out of my hide!"

Lonesome Charlie swung around to face the barman, face swelling and turning red again. "Oh, go to hell about Pistol Pete's window, McDougal! *Christ!*" Charlie stepped through the window and into the saloon, bellowing, "As if bein' a federal lawdog ain't bedevilin' enough, I gotta put up with bartenders caterwauling about their damn windows!"

He disappeared into the saloon's shadows then reappeared a moment later, a dirty brown Stetson adorned with an owl feather on his head, carrying a corked bottle in the crook of his arm, like a baby. He turned to the barman, snarling, and said, "I'm gonna take this cheap gunpowder concoction you call whiskey and find me a little better—not to mention purtier!—company."

He stepped through the window, cast Stockburn one more angry scowl, then swung around, ripped the reins of a beefy buckskin from one of the hitchrails fronting Pistol Pete's, and led the horse along the street to the north. He paused to kick a horse apple and nearly lost his balance and fell for his trouble.

McDougal looked through his broken window at Stockburn. "Who's gonna pay for this window?"

"Don't look at me," Wolf said. "I didn't shoot 'em."

He extended his hand to Sofia standing behind him. She walked forward, took his hand, and together they continued on up the street until they came to a little Chinese restaurant roughly two blocks from Pistol Pete's Saloon. Stockburn led Sofia through the door and into cool shadows scented with the smell of wood smoke, pork spiced in the Oriental style, salted cabbage, and chili.

Stockburn was craving a bowl of chili and some fried oysters, and he knew from experience that a little Chinaman named Li Po made the best chili and oysters he'd ever encountered anywhere on the western frontier.

He and Sofia took seats at a table in the room's rear shadows. Stockburn had made enough enemies over the years that he usually chose saloon or restaurant tables concealed by support posts or shadows and at which he could sit facing the room at large. That was especially true when he was in the company of an innocent bystander, as he was now.

Once they'd given their orders to Li Po's shy daughter clad in black slippers, deerskin leggings, and a red silk smock, her coal-black hair secured in a queue with a red ribbon, Stockburn glanced across the table at Sofia.

The senorita was staring out the window with a forlorn expression. She'd tucked her upper lip under her bottom lip and was biting down on it hard, trying to control her emotions.

Stockburn knew she was still seeing Billy Blythe lying dead in the coffin. Stockburn had seen a lot of dead men, but seeing Billy like that would haunt his sleep for many years, as he knew it would the young man's wife, as well.

Stockburn knew no words could comfort the poor girl, for none could comfort him, so he merely reached across the table and wrapped his hand around her wrist. Sometimes merely expressing shared sorrow was all the comfort one could lend or find.

Keeping her face to the window, Sofia lowered her head and closed her eyes. Tears oozed out from behind the closed lids to dribble down her cheeks, following the tracks remaining there from her previous sorrow in the undertaking parlor.

CHAPTER 10

When the food came—or his food, rather, for Sofia didn't order anything except coffee—she turned to Stockburn and said, "When are we going after them, Wolf? Red Miller and the others."

Stockburn scowled as he pulled his whiskey bottle out of his coat pocket and added a healthy amount to his black coffee steaming in a stout stone mug. "What's this we business?" he complained. "Sofia, don't you know there's no way in hell I'm going to let you tag along with me when I hunt those killers?"

Sofia leaned forward and widened her eyes pleadingly. "You have to, Wolf!"

"That's just crazy, girl!" He extended the bottle and poured a few drops of the whiskey into Sofia's coffee. "Here—have a little busthead. Maybe it'll settle you down a little, clear your head. You're not making sense."

"Wolf, I saw him!"

Stockburn set the bottle down beside his chili, fried oysters, and a bowl of noodles seasoned with pork and water chestnuts. "Who'd you see?"

"Them, rather. I saw them all. I saw Red Miller and the other three men riding with him."

"You did not!"

She thrust her chin at him and bobbed her head, making her hair dance. "Wolf, I did! About an hour out from Ruidoso. I saw them when the train stopped for water. Two were riding double."

Stockburn stared at her through the steam rising from the food and coffee before him. "Darlin', you don't even know what they look like."

"Does Miller have red hair and wear glasses?"

"Well, yeah . . ."

"Does he have a bandage over his nose?" She touched her pretty, olive nose.

Stockburn sank back in his chair in astonishment. "I think I blew the tip of his nose off, so . . ."

"He would probably have a bandage over it." She went on to describe Pike Brennan, Gopher Montez, and Flipper Harris. Harris had been the one she'd seen riding double with another one of the bunch, which would make sense. Harris had been the only one who had made it out of the canyon without a horse.

When she was finished, she sat as before, head thrust over the table, eyes wide, eyebrows arched.

"That there is just too damn much of a coincidence, darlin' . . ." he said finally.

"I don't think it was a coincidence at all."

"Of course, it was. I reckon that's where they'd be, though, since they're heading south. They're probably heading for the old Las Cruces trading trail. If they rode hard enough, they might even make it to Alamagordo by tonight, on the west side of the San Francisco Mountains.

But they can't ride that hard. They don't have fresh horses, and unless they've found a fourth horse by now, two are still riding double. They could make it to Tularosa, though. Good to know, darlin'! I'll send a telegram down to Hamm Sanchez, the lawman down there. Maybe he can deputize a few men and throw a loop around them, end their trail right then and there!"

Suddenly starving, Stockburn dug into his chili.

"He won't."

"What's that?" the rail detective asked, shoveling food into his mouth.

"I am meant to be there when he's captured. Or killed. That would be my preference. Kill him." She pronounced it "keel him." She glowered angrily, curling her upper lip and flaring a nostril. "That way Billy's soul would not only be free, but it would rest easier. I would rest easier, too."

"What's all this crazy talk, darlin'? I know you're grieving, but—"

"It is not crazy talk, Wolf. I looked into the eyes of the man who killed my Billy. Red Miller is a demon straight from Hell. Some people are. When they kill, they must be killed or the souls of those they murdered will never be at peace. It is best if they are avenged by a family member. If that is not possible, that family member must at least be present when the killer dies or is somehow brought to justice. That family member must mark the killer and say a prayer over him, setting free the soul of the one he murdered."

Stockburn chewed a mouthful of fried oysters and noodles. The food was making him feel better but there was still a rat inside his arm, trying to chew its way out.

The girl's crazy talk about demons and souls and prayers and such was aggravating his misery.

He knew she couldn't help it. She really believed this stuff.

"What religion is this?" he asked after he'd swallowed his food. "It sure ain't Catholic."

"It is the ancient belief of my mother's people, the Yaqui."

"Ah."

"I have the same, rare gift as my mother. Being able to identify demons. Red Miller is a demon. He must be stopped. When a demon kills and the person he kills is unavenged, the murdered person's soul spends eternity tormented. Bound to the demonic soul of his killer."

"Yeah, that's an old religion, all right. I've heard similar versions in Old Mexico. I didn't realize you believed that stuff, Sofia. You and Billy were married in the Catholic church!"

"My mother turned Catholic when she married my father, because my father wanted her to. But she has always, privately, followed the beliefs she was raised with. Because she believes them. As do I. She raised me to believe them because she recognized soon after I was born that I had the same gift—some would say a curse—as she. I attend the Catholic church, because there is much to believe there, as well. I follow both religions. In some ways, they are similar, especially when it comes to last rites and penance and purgatory. That is where Billy is now. I must set him free."

Stockburn scooped more chili into his mouth, chewed, and swallowed. He winced and said with genuine sadness, "I'm sorry, honey. You can't tag along with me. I'm going after killers."

"Wolf, I have to. There is no other way."

"We could be on the trail for days. On a hot, dry, desert trail. You're not prepared for that."

"I can ride as well as any man. As you know, my father captured and broke horses for a living. I helped him until he died. Then my mother wanted me to work with her repairing and laundering clothes. I've never been happy doing that work. I much prefer riding horses in the desert." Sofia wrapped both of her hands around his wrist. "Please, Wolf. You must let me ride along with you. I can take it. If I can't, I will turn back to Mesilla. I will not be extra work for you."

Stockburn stared into her eyes. He couldn't believe he was really considering what he was considering, but she was just so damned sad and sure in her beliefs, and determined . . .

He studied her, wanting so much to find the words to turn her down.

He just didn't have the heart to do it. He was liable to get her killed, but what else could he do? She really believed she had to free Billy's soul!

Frustrated and angry by the position he was in, he pointed a stern finger at her. "When I catch up to those killers, you fall way back and keep your head way down— understand? I mean way down. Even then you might get killed. I hope you realize that!"

Sofia's pretty, brown-eyed face blossomed with a relieved smile. She rose, leaned forward, and wrapped her arms around his neck. "Wolf Stockburn, I love you!"

Stockburn hoped he wouldn't regret his decision to let Sofia ride along with him while he tracked Red Miller and Miller's three cohorts.

He partly rationalized it by believing that he'd ride down to find that Hamm Sanchez had already thrown a loop around those four and had turned the key on them. Or, if Miller and the others managed to slip away from Hamm and his deputies, which was entirely possible, and Stockburn was forced to track them for several days, possibly even into Texas or Old Mexico, Sofia would get tired enough and saddle sore enough to realize the error of her ways and go back to Mesilla and await word from Stockburn on Miller's fate.

The latter scenario was the more likely of the two. While Hamm Sanchez was an effective lawman for a town of Tularosa's size, neither he nor his deputies were really a match for Red Miller. Stockburn felt a little guilty sending the wire to alert the man of Miller's approach though he warned Sanchez not to try to take them down without a sizable bunch of deputized men backing his play.

Wolf knew he shouldn't feel guilty. Hamm Sanchez wore a badge; it was his job to run bad men to ground.

It was just that Red Miller was the baddest of the bad. One thing Sofia had right was that Miller was a demon. Maybe not a literal demon, the way she told it, but a human demon, sure enough.

Having sent the cable, his belly padded out, his hunger sated, badly in need of an early bed to heal his arm and all his other sundry complaints, and to prepare for an early trail in the morning, Stockburn led Sofia over to the hotel in which he'd rented a room.

As they went inside, he said, "I'll get this, Sofia. You hold onto your money. You're gonna need it in the—"

"Wolf?"

Sofia stopped by the door and tugged on his coat sleeve.

He stopped and turned to her. "What is it?"

"Would it, uh . . ." She wringed her hands together and looked down at her moccasins then back up at Stockburn, a strained, sheepish expression twisting her olive features. "Can I stay in your room? I know it's asking a lot, but . . ." Tears shone again in her eyes. "I really don't want to be alone." She sniffed. "Not yet."

"Honey," Stockburn said, glancing over his shoulder at the sack-dressed crone, Mrs. Chesterfield, manning the front desk beneath a tick-tocking grandfather clock. "That ain't proper!"

Blinking tears from her eyes, Sofia said, "I really don't care what's proper anymore, Wolf. I don't care what anyone thinks."

Stockburn sighed, smiled understandingly. "I understand, honey. Come with me." He took her hand and led the girl past Mrs. Chesterfield, saying, "Howdy, Mrs. Chesterfield. This is a friend of mine from Mesilla. She's just gonna come up and have a brief visit over a cup of tea . . ."

He and Sofia mounted the stairs rising at the back of the lobby.

Mrs. Chesterfield removed her reading glasses and rose from her chair, eyes wide and round, lower jaw hanging. "Without a *chaperone*?"

"Keep walkin', darlin'," Stockburn said tightly as they reached a landing.

Mrs. Chesterfield pounded her desk with her fist and trilled, "Mister Stockburn, this is not *that* kind of a place! My rules are written very plainly on . . ."

"She thinks I'm a puta," Sofia said with mild amusement. "She thinks we are going to make love."

Mrs. Chesterfield's words trailed off as Stockburn and Sofia reached the second-floor hall, Stockburn's boot thuds echoing. "Don't worry about that hen, darlin'. She's really more squawk than bite. Her memory's going. She won't remember even seeing you in the morning."

"Like I said, Wolf," Sofia said, sadly. "I don't care anymore."

"I know, honey. I know." Stockburn poked his key in the lock and opened his door.

Inside, they sat and talked about Billy.

Stockburn drank whiskey and smoked, sitting by an open window, hearing the late-day sounds of Ruidoso, smelling the burning pinyon of supper fires.

Finally, they each washed behind a room partition. Sofia undressed down to her underwear, sat on the bed and brushed out her long, dark brown hair. It caught the gloaming light angling through a window, and shone like copper. She crawled under the covers of the room's only bed. Stockburn remained clothed and lay atop the bed covers, both of his Colts nearby.

He held the sad girl in his arms until she'd cried herself to sleep.

Then he, too, slept. It was the sleep of a dead man. In fact, he dreamt that he died. The dream had the troubling cast of a premonition.

CHAPTER 11

Kansas City Jane rolled off of Lonesome Charlie, making the bed in her crib in the Purple Palace bounce.

She rolled onto her side, propped her head on the heel of her hand, hooked her bare feet around one of his, and pooched out her plump red lips in a pout. "Don't you like me anymore, Lonesome?"

"Ah, hell—I'm sorry, honey!" Charlie lifted the bedcovers and looked down at himself. "I don't know what in holy blazes happened. I was feelin' just fine an' then all of a sudden, kaput!"

"Am I too skinny? I know most men like more curves on a girl."

"It's got nothin' to do with you, sweetheart." Lonesome Charlie rose, grabbed his hat off a peg by the door, and set it on his head. He always felt more comfortable wearing his hat even when he had nothing else on. He even wore his hat when in the middle of the night he stumbled out to the old privy behind his cabin to evacuate his bladder.

Now he grabbed his bottle, his shot glass, the small tin pillbox, and his makings pouch off of Jane's cluttered dresser, and sat his skinny, pouch-bellied, fish belly–white carcass down in an ancient, brocade rocking chair. "I just need more whiskey is all. Whiskey and a smoke. And one of these here little lozenges the doc gave me for my ticker."

He pressed the heel of his hand against his chest and winced. "Been kickin' like a mule of late."

"What kind of a lozenge is it, Lonesome?"

"Doc says it's an elixir for the heart. A ticker elixir. Hah!" Charlie popped a pill into his mouth. He followed it up with a swig from the bottle. He swished the pill and the whiskey around in his mouth and swallowed.

"There—that's the ticket. That mule should settle his nasty self down in a minute." Charlie filled his shot glass, took one more pull straight from the bottle, sighed, and smacked his lips. "Yep—feelin' better already."

"What's in the elixir, Lonesome?"

Charlie plucked his makings pouch off the table then sat back in the rocking chair, rocking ever so slightly as he withdrew a cigarette paper from his canvas tobacco sack. "Doc said it was nitro . . . uh . . . nitro*glycerin*. Somethin' new they came up with to settle down that mule in my chest. It's the same thing that's in dynamite."

Chuckling, Charlie dribbled chopped Durham on the paper troughed between the first two fingers of his right hand. "Had me a wicked spell last winter. Woke up and I felt like a horse had sat down on my chest. Froze up my whole left side! It happened a few more times till I finally paid a visit to the doc."

"Oh, no!" The naked girl gazed at him with concern from the bed, her lovely red hair spilling down her slender back and pale shoulders. "Was it a heart stroke, Lonesome?"

"Nah, nah—I don't think so, honey. The doc said maybe

it was but I think it's just gas from eatin' too many beans! Me—I love beans more'n the chili-chompers, don't ya know!" Charlie cackled out a long, wheezing laugh then poked the quirley into his mouth and scratched a match to life on his thumbnail.

He drew the smoke deeply, luxuriously into his lungs then blew it out his nostrils.

The girl studied him sadly, wrinkling the skin above her long, freckled nose. "Don't die, Lonesome."

"Ah, hell, honey—I ain't gonna die." Charlie took a sip from his whiskey glass.

"You're one of the good guys, Lonesome."

Charlie blew the whiskey into the air before him, guffawing. He coughed then, chuckling, ran the back of his hand across his mouth. "Don't make me waste good whiskey like that, honey!"

"You are, Lonesome." She stretched a wan smile. "You're always gentle. You pay beforehand and give me a little extra when you leave. You never hit me or cuss me like most would under tonight's circumstances."

Charlie poked an admonishing finger at her. "I told you—that wasn't your fault."

"Most men would blame me. They'd be embarrassed and they'd tell me I was ugly or they didn't like my missing tooth or I wasn't fat enough to please them. They'd take their money back. Might even slap me. A man almost cut my throat once for that very thing."

"Jane, you should get out of this business."

"Would you marry me, Lonesome?" she asked with a frisky smile, her hazel eyes sparkling.

"Damn—you're gonna make me waste more good whiskey!" Again, Charlie chuckled. "Lady Jane, I am old enough to be your father. Make that your grandfather. Good Lord—is that true?" He looked at the ceiling, moving his lips as he counted under his breath. "I'm sixty-two. What are you—twenty?"

"Nineteen."

"Oh, good Lord—it's true!" Charlie closed his eyes, lowered his head, and sobbed.

He cried real tears for over a minute. His logy heart hiccupped and twisted around in his chest, threatening another rebellion. He stopped crying when he felt a hand on his bare left leg.

He lowered his head and saw Jane kneeling on the floor beside him, sitting back on her heels, smiling sympathetically up at him. "What's got you so sad tonight, Lonesome?"

"Ah, hell—I don't know. I just get hit with cryin' spells once in a while. I've always been like that. I reckon that's why they give me this nickname way back when I was in the army fightin' Injuns."

"Is it because you shot those two owlhoots in Pistol Pete's Saloon?"

"Heard about that, didja?"

Jane drew her mouth corners down and nodded.

"I suppose the whole damn town knows by now."

Jane squeezed his leg. "It wasn't your fault, Lonesome."

"Oh, hell—of course it was my fault." Charlie scrubbed his arm across his eyes, mopping up the tears. "I don't keep up with things like I should anymore. Made a blame fool out of myself. Of course, it had to be Wolf Stockburn who pointed it out. Damn him!"

"I'm sorry, Lonesome."

"I've outlived my usefulness, darlin'. Hell, I can't even pleasure a pretty woman anymore."

"You drink too much," Jane said quietly, tenderly. "You shouldn't smoke with your bad heart an' all."

"Drinkin' an' smokin' is a tonic."

"No, it's not."

"Sure enough it is! Hell, the old pill roller even said so!"

"He did not, Lonesome Charlie!" Jane slapped his thigh in mock outrage. "You stop tellin' fibs or I'll tan your naked behind!"

Charlie chuckled and took another pull from the bottle. He dragged on his cigarette and blew the smoke over Jane's red head. The girl rested her cheek on his thigh and caressed the inside of his leg very lightly with her fingers. "Have you ever been married, Charlie?"

"Few times. First one was long ago. When I joined the frontier army, she ran out on me. Ran off with another man. A friend of mine. Or so I thought he was."

"That's awful—doin' such a thing to a friend. It's got so you can't even trust your friends anymore."

"That's why I don't have no friends."

"Please don't say that, Lonesome," Jane said, keeping her cheek on his thigh. "I'm your friend. I count, too, even though I'm just a whore."

"Of course, you count. I'm sorry, honey. I'm just a drunk, stupid old man."

"Oh, Charlie."

"I killed the son of a bitch." Again, Charlie took a pull from the bottle. He stared straight across the room at a faded oil painting but he wasn't seeing the painting. He was looking far back in time.

Jane lifted her head from his thigh. "What'd you say, Lonesome?"

"I killed my friend."

"You really did?"

"Shot him and threw his body in the Eleven Point River. Then I headed West. Never went back. I don't know what became of Evelyn."

"Boy, don't go messin' with Lonesome Charlie's girl!"

"You got that right," Charlie said with a chuckle though for some reason he felt like crying again.

"The law never went after you?"

"Nope. I got away with it. Leastways, as far as the law is concerned."

"How else is there?"

"In here." Charlie tapped his finger to the side of his head. "It haunts me still. The thing of it is, Grover was a better man than me. He crossed me, sure, by takin' up with Evelyn behind my back, but he would have been a better man to her. And a better provider. His father owned the mercantile in our hometown.

"My father was a drunken circuit preacher who stopped to make water on his way between country churches one Sunday afternoon. He stood in front of his buckboard's front wheel. He was so drunk he passed out. The horse spooked and jerked forward. The wheel ran over my father's back and snapped his spine. Some kids fishin' in a nearby creek seen the whole thing."

"That's a sad story, Lonesome."

"It's been a sad life. A lonely life. That nickname fits me, it sure does." Charlie tipped his head back, drew a ragged breath. "Damn, I feel a black pall comin' over me."

"A black pall?"

"Like there's a black cloud over me and it just won't lift. Like a whole flock of yammering crows are flying around my head!"

"Come back to bed, Lonesome. You don't need to be lonely tonight. Jane's here."

"I'm sorry, honey. This old man is just a foul, nasty mess tonight."

"I can make you feel better," Jane said with a smile. "You leave it all to me."

She gave his leg another slow pleading squeeze. Charlie sat in the chair, staring at the painting again. He wasn't seeing the painting this time, either. He was looking into the future.

Sometimes, that was the only way to make those dark clouds lift when he felt one of his spells coming on. One of his dark and lonely spells that even whiskey didn't help. In fact, it seemed to make them worse.

"I'm gonna run down Red Miller, by God, honey."

"Are you, Lonesome?"

"Sure as hell I am. If it's the last damn thing I do, I'm gonna run him and them other devils of his to ground." Charlie pounded the chair arm. His heart was quickening but it did not kick. "I'll show 'em. I'll show 'em all. Including Stockburn. One more hunt for Lonesome Charlie before they kick me out with a cold shovel!"

Charlie took another pull from the bottle, another drag from his quirley, slapped both chair arms, thumped his bare feet on the floor, and wheezed out a phlegmy laugh. "Sure as hell!"

Jane smiled up at him brightly, glad to see his mood brightening.

"Come to bed, Lonesome."

Charlie looked down at her, cupped her cheek in the palm of his hand. "You know what, darlin'? I think ole Charlie's gonna get'er done this time."

He rose from his chair, feeling lighter. Even younger—by a few years, anyway.

He and Jane crawled back into bed, and he got her done, all right. It took a while, but when he rolled off the girl, he was sweating and trembling and cackling like an old witch in victory.

"Oh, Charlie," Jane said, rolling against him and placing her cheek against his sharply rising and falling chest. "I knew you could do it!"

"I did, too, by . . ." Charlie let his voice trail off.

Jane looked up at him. "What is it, Lonesome?"

Charlie stared at the red-painted door against which a low-turned lamp fluttered watery light against.

"Thought I heard somethin'," he whispered.

"What'd you—"

"Shhh!" Charlie placed a finger against his lips.

He stared at the door. He heard the sound again—the faint creak of a floorboard beneath a slow, stealthy tread. Beneath the door, a shadow moved. It moved again as another floorboard squawked.

The room filled with thunder as the door burst open to slam against the inside wall.

Jane screamed.

Glimpsing two men standing in the open doorway raising rifles, Charlie snaked his left arm around Jane's slender shoulders and rolled to his right, throwing himself and the girl out of the bed. As they hit the floor together, side by side, Jane loosing another shrill scream, a man shouted, "Here's a message from Little Dave, Charlie!"

The rifles thundered, the bullets tearing into the bed where Charlie and Jane had been lying only seconds before. As they did, Charlie reached up with his right hand

and pulled his old Colt Dragoon from the holster of his gun rig hanging from the front bedpost.

The rifles continued blasting, bullets ripping through the mattress and sending dried yellow corn shucks flying in all directions. While Jane lay belly-down beside him, cupping her hands over her ears, Charlie looked up to see one of the riflemen stride into the room and around the bed.

He was one of the men who'd been with Little Dave in Pistol Pete's Saloon earlier, when Charlie had sent Little Dave to the sawbones in misery south of his belt buckle. The rifleman stopped near the bottom of the bed, grinning demonically and jacking a fresh round into his Winchester's action.

As he pressed his cheek against the rifle's stock and slanted the barrel down toward Charlie and Jane, Charlie raised the cocked Dragoon, hardened his jaws, and sent a .44-caliber bullet punching through his assailant's heart, pulverizing a bone button on his hickory shirt.

The man screamed and stumbled backward, triggering his rifle into the wall behind Charlie and Jane. He hadn't hit the floor before Charlie lifted his head a little higher and swung the Dragoon to his left, aiming up and over the bed at the second rifleman who just then triggered a round into the bed six inches to the left of Charlie's left cheek, pluming more pulverized corn shucks.

The man saw Charlie's big horse pistol aimed at him and widened his eyes in shock. *"Noo!"*

"Oh, yeah," Charlie raked out, smiling as the Dragoon bucked and roared, spitting flames from the barrel.

The bullet painted a puckered blue hole in the rifleman's forehead, just beneath the flat brim of his weathered tan

Stetson. He flew back against the wall on the opposite side of the hall, dropping his rifle and sliding down the wall to the floor, leaving a long streak of blood and brains above him.

He slumped to one side, gave a ragged sigh, and died.

"Charlie!" Jane jerked her head up and stared at Charlie in horror. "Are you all right, Charlie?"

"I'm fine, darlin'. Just fine."

"Oh, Charlie!" Jane threw herself against him, burying her face in his chest, sobbing.

Charlie wrapped his arms around her, still holding the smoking Dragoon in his right hand. "Even better than fine," he added, grinning at the dead man lying in the room before him. "Ol' Charlie's found his pluck again, sure enough!"

CHAPTER 12

"Sipping cider under a crawdad moon,
   Under a crawdad moon,
   A crawdad moon . . .
   Hidin' the jug from Ma."

The gravelly-voiced singing, if you could call it singing, came to Wolf's ears as he sat on the loafer's bench fronting the Meade Hotel. He turned to gaze north along Ruidoso's still mostly deserted main street, muddy and steaming after a brief, hard rain just after midnight. A horse and rider drifted toward him out of the milky half-light and thick dawn shadows.

"Sippin' cider under a crawdad moon,
   Under a crawdad moon,
   A crawdad moon . . .
   Waitin' for my dear Em-ma!"

As horse and rider drew within a half a block of Stockburn, he could more clearly see the hunched figure atop the beefy horse as well as the plumed, high-crowned Stetson atop the rider's head.

> *"Gonna marry that girl, by gum!*
> *Gonna marry that girl, by gum!"*

Lonesome Charlie slapped his thigh with each refrain then threw his head back and wailed:

> *"Sippin' cider under a crawdad moon,*
> *Under a crawdad moon,*
> *A crawdad moon . . .*
> *Wonderin' where my true love could beee!"*

The words echoed around the otherwise silent street, Charlie's cracking, uncertain voice dwindling swiftly, replaced by the slow clomps and sucking sounds of the buckskin's shod hooves in the muddy street.

Lonesome Charlie angled the buckskin over to the hotel and reined up in front of Stockburn sitting on the porch, near where Stockburn's horse and the black-and-white pinto he'd rented for Sofia stood tied to a hitchrack. The old lawman spat to one side then sat regarding the Wells Fargo man with a sage smile crinkling his weathered, bearded features.

"I'll be hanged, Charlie, if you're not givin' voice to that song as if you could actually sing."

"Well, you know what they say, Wells Fargo—the worst singers always sing the loudest in church."

"That they do, that they do. What's got you in such a merry mood this morning? You must've had a successful visit to one of Ruidoso's hurdy-gurdy houses."

"Me—I ain't one to customarily visit parlor houses. A fella with my reputation has no problem attractin' *proper* ladies. As it so happens, though, I have a special friend over at the Purple Palace, and she gets all long in the face if I visit her fair city and don't make a call at her crib. She claims, don't ya know, that no man can satisfy her the way ol' Lonesome Charlie can!"

Charlie sat a little straighter in his saddle, grinning from ear to ear.

"Braggart."

"Well, hell," Charlie said. "The truth will stand when the world's on fire. That's a direct quote from my dearly departed old pap, Caleb Ezekiel Murdock."

"To coin a phrase."

"Come on—get mounted, Wells Fargo," Charlie said. "We're burnin' daylight."

Stockburn chuckled. "What're you talkin' about?"

"We're goin' after Red Miller. You're the last one to see him. I want you to take me to where you last seen him so's I can get after him myself. Well, you can ride along if you want, but you gotta promise to stay out of my way. Normally, I prefer to work alone, but since you seen Miller and the others an' all, I suppose I can make an exception. I hope you can keep up!"

"I don't think that's a good idea, Charlie."

"What ain't?"

"You goin' after Miller."

Lonesome Charlie's red-gray brows, thick as furry beetles, hooded his eyes. "What're you talkin' about? It's my job to go after Miller's bunch. That's what I was sent down here to do."

"Why don't you let me handle it?"

"What do you mean—why don't I let you handle it? You're Wells Fargo." Charlie rammed his thumb against the moon-and-star pinned to his shirt. "I'm a *federal lawman!* Now"—he drew the big Dragoon from its holster tied down on his right thigh, aimed the barrel at Stockburn, and clicked the hammer back, showing his teeth—"you're gonna show me where you last seen Red Miller, by God, or I'll throw the cuffs on you and lock you up in Waylon Wallace's jailhouse. Won't let you out till I get back, neither!"

"On what charge?" Stockburn said, scowling at the old lawman with deep indignance.

"For withholding information from a federal peace officer, that's what charge. For . . . for gettin' in the way of justice. By God, I'll do it, Mister Wells Fargo! Now you climb onto your horse and let's get movin' before them curly wolves get any farther away than they already are!"

Stockburn looked at the Dragoon. It trembled slightly in the old man's gloved hand. He switched his gaze to Lonesome Charlie's eyes beneath the brim of his weathered, tan Stetson. What he saw there was not so much anger as fear.

Fear of what?

His own incompetence, maybe.

Fear of death.

The old man could not ask for help, of course. But Lonesome Charlie knew he needed Stockburn to help him run Red Miller down. He knew he could not run him down on his own. He could not admit that even to himself. Admitting that his skills had diminished would be a fate worse than retirement for a man like Lonesome Charlie Murdock, who had nothing more than that horse and saddle . . . that old conversion pistol . . . and that badge pinned to his shirt.

Without them, what did he have?

A dingy room in a squalid rooming house on the

ragged outskirts of Albuquerque. The yawning void and a lonely death in a fetid room.

Stockburn understood. He and Lonesome Charlie were not all that different. In many ways he sensed they were similar. Solitary souls for whom the badges on their shirts meant everything. The only real ways they differed were in that Stockburn still had a few years left on his docket while Charlie had come to the end of his tether, and he knew it.

It scared holy hell out of him, as it would Wolf Stockburn, who here and there around the edges of his consciousness and usually late at night, had already started anticipating it.

"All right, Charlie," Stockburn said, raising his own gloved hands, palms out, wincing a little at the burn in his right arm. "I can see you're serious."

"I'm as serious as dog turd in a bucket! Now, climb up on that horse and show me where you last seen Miller."

"All right, all right," Wolf said, chuckling deviously. He walked over and grabbed his sheathed Winchester leaning against the hotel's front wall.

"What's so funny?" asked Lonesome Charlie, depressing his Dragoon's hammer but keeping the big pistol aimed at Stockburn.

Stockburn turned to the man, grinning like the cat that ate the canary. "Well, ya see, the joke's sorta on you, Charlie."

He stepped down off the porch and walked over to Smoke's right side.

Charlie scowled down at him. "What joke?"

Stockburn began lashing the Winchester's scabbard to his saddle so that the brass-plated walnut stock angled up over the right stirrup fender. "Ya see, I was sorta hopin' I'd catch you this mornin', Marshal."

Charlie's scowl deepened. "Ya were?"

"See, I got this injured wing here. It grieves me somethin' awful. The pain is a might distracting. I could use a partner. A good one. A man with some miles on him. I don't call that age. I call that seasoning."

Charlie's gaze turned skeptical as he turned his head slightly to one side. "You do?"

"Hell, I may be a Wells Fargo dandy, Charlie, but I'm not a total idiot. I know your reputation. Didn't you run down the Miles Silverhand bunch just after the war, in Sapinero in southern Colorado Territory, after they rode up here from the South to raise hell with the Yankee settlers?"

"Well, yes . . . yes, I did. That, uh . . . that was a few years ago . . ."

"Didn't you shoot down Carter Wilson in a fair fight in San Antonio?"

Charlie looked thoughtful. "Carter Wilson . . . Carter Wilson . . ." His eyes widened in recognition of the name. "That's right, I did! Been so long ago, I plum forgot. Took down Curly Calloway that day, too. Right after I shot Wilson. Blew him out of a window of the Hotel de Paris when he was fixin' to backshoot me with an old war-model Springfield!"

"That might have been a few years ago, but the man who brought down curly wolves of that caliber . . . and of Miles Silverhand's caliber . . ." Stockburn shook his head sagely. "That man's body might get old. But the mind of a man like that . . . the *sixth sense* of a man like that— those are the last things to go. I sense you still got a couple more rodeos left in you, Charlie. And truth to tell, I've never been much good . . . nor fond of . . . tracking. I've heard you can track a snake across a stone slab."

"Ah, you heard about that, too, didja?" Charlie said, grinning, slowly shaking his head. He was in a full crimson flush as he slowly returned the Dragoon to its holster, snickering.

He pointed at his eyes. "I still got the peepers of a falcon. In fact, before I was known mainly as Lonesome Charlie, they called me Falcon-Eye Charlie. That was when I was scoutin' Sioux for General Baxter and keepin' the red devils away from the fellas layin' tracks for the Transcontinental Railroad, don't ya know."

"Don't doubt it a bit."

"Let me tell ya about that time back when I . . ."

Charlie let his voice trail off when soft footsteps sounded from inside the hotel before the front door opened and Sofia stepped onto the porch, her satchel slung over one shoulder, a burlap sack slung over her other shoulder with a rope. "Sorry to keep you waiting, Wolf. I was preparing our grub sack . . ." She let the sentence dwindle as her gaze wandered to Lonesome Charlie sitting his beefy buckskin.

Charlie scowled back at the girl. "Who's that, Wells Fargo? What's she mean by *our* grub sack?"

"Lonesome Charlie, this is a close friend of mine, Senorita Sofia Ortega. I promised her she could tag along."

"What do you mean—'tag along'? She a whore?"

Sofia glared at the man.

Stockburn chuckled as he strode up onto the porch and took the food sack from the girl. "No, no—nothin' like that." He stepped down into the street, walking to his horse. "Red Miller murdered her husband. Billy Blythe was an express messenger on that Sierra Blanca Express those killers struck. She wants to see Red and the others run down with her very own eyes."

Charlie furled his brows at the girl then glanced at Stockburn, who was tying the food sack to his saddle horn. "You in a habit of lettin' girls ride along with you, Wells Fargo?"

"Not under normal circumstances, no." Stockburn extended his hand to the girl. "Come along, chiquita."

Sofia stepped down off the porch, dubiously regarding the old man straddling the buckskin. As Stockburn helped her up onto the pinto's back, using his aching right arm as little as possible, Lonesome Charlie said, "Well, I'm sorry, she can't ride with me. And since you're ridin' with me, Wells Fargo, she can't ride with you, neither."

Sofia swung her indignant gaze to the old lawman. "*Por que no?*"

Stockburn swung up onto Smoke's back. He reined the smoky gray stallion around to face Lonesome Charlie, frowning. "Look, I know she's young and, well, obviously, she's a girl. But in a weak moment—at least, I like to think that's what it was—I agreed to let her ride along. She has a special interest in the matter. A special *religious* interest, you might say."

"Si," Sofia said, turning her own horse to face the lawman.

"I don't care. She's not ridin' with me." Charlie shrugged a shoulder. "Ya see—I don't cotton to Mescins."

"What?" both Wolf and Sofia said at the same time.

Charlie glanced off. "I don't like Mescins. Won't drink

with 'em, play poker with 'em, or share a meal with 'em. I sure as hell won't *ride* with 'em!"

Flames almost literally shot from Sofia's eyes. "Why, you bigoted, used-up, old jackass!"

"Hey, now!" Charlie said, riled now himself.

"Easy, now, Sofia. Easy, honey." Stockburn chuckled and turned to Charlie. "You won't even ride with a *purty* Mexican, Charlie?"

"Especially a *purty* one," Charlie said, giving Sofia the woolly eyeball. "The purty ones are the most dangerous of all. You let your guard down, turn your back on 'em for even a second, they'll shove a stiletto between your ribs and rob you clean and be gone like a lightnin' flash!" He clapped his hands together as though to illustrate.

"I'll just bet you've lain with the putas, though, haven't you, you dried up bag of bones!" Sofia spat out with saucy sarcasm, one fist on her hip.

"Only the fat, ugly ones!"

Sofia heeled her pinto up close beside Charlie and leaned toward him, thrusting her chin at him and stretching her lips back from her teeth. "How would you like this pretty senorita to slip her stiletto in from the front, you old coyote?"

She closed her hand around the handle of the slender-bladed knife wedged behind her wide, black belt.

"Hold on, now, honey! Hold on!" Stockburn put Smoke up close to the buckskin and placed a placating hand on Sofia's shoulder. "It's way too early for this kind of shenanigans. Pull your horns in and let me talk to Charlie civilized-like."

Sofia removed her hand from the stiletto's handle and

pulled her head back a bit but kept her malevolent, lip-curled stare on the old man before her.

Wolf said, "Now, Charlie, it's like this. I made a promise to this young lady, and I have to keep it. If you don't see fit to ride with us—or, I mean to let us *ride with you*—on account of her bein' Mexican—well, all right, I can understand, but . . ."

"*What*?" Sofia snapped at Stockburn.

He held up a hand to quiet the senorita and continued to Charlie with, "It sure would be nice to ride with a man of your experience. If you could see fit to ride with—er, dammit, I mean, if you could see fit to let me and Sofia here ride along with you and take advantage of your prowess and experience—well, I'd sure appreciate it."

He glanced at Sofia. She was scowling at him with deep incredulity and exasperation. Ignoring her, he turned back to Charlie who glanced from the girl to Stockburn and brushed his fist across his nose, saying, "I don't know, I don't know . . ." He looked off, pondering, both hands on his saddle horn.

He spat a wad of chaw into the dust off his buckskin's left hoof, turned back to Stockburn, and said, "Are you sure we can trust her? I tell you, when there's a Mescin within a half-mile of me, I sleep with one eye open. That gets tiresome!"

"I can see how it would. Truth be told, don't trust most of the gallblamed chili chompers my ownself, but I'll keep a sharp watch on this one so you won't have to worry about her."

"All right," Charlie said, scowling in disgust at Sofia. "See that you do, Wells Fargo, or I'll quit the both of you and run down Miller and his pards my own damn self. I usually ride alone, anyway, dammit. Now I'm wet-nursin' a fancy-pants Wells Fargo man and a devious-eyed, chili-chompin' senorita!"

The exasperated old lawman reined his horse around and booted it south along the muddy main street. "What in the hell is my life comin' to?" Over his shoulder, he called, "Well, come along, you two. We ain't gettin' any closer to Miller sittin' here chinning in Ruidoso!"

Stockburn turned to Sofia. She was staring at him like he'd suddenly grown spots and a tail.

"I'll tell ya later," Wolf said with a chuckle. "Come along, you Mescin devil." He booted Smoke south. "You heard Lonesome Charlie. We ain't gettin' any closer to Miller sittin' here chinning in Ruidoso!"

He winked over his shoulder at her.

CHAPTER 13

At the same time but nearly fifty miles south of Ruidoso, Red Miller and his three partners were riding into the sleepy little mountain valley town of Tularosa and Miller was grinding his back teeth against the pain in his nose.

He felt like a dog trained to fight to the death had grabbed hold of the mangled sniffer and would not let go.

He turned his horse toward the first saloon he saw, The San Francisco Peak Inn, one of several in town, the other being the Busted Flush. His three partners, Pike Brennan, Gopher Montez, and Flipper Harris, followed suit. Flipper Harris was riding double with Montez. He'd been switching between Montez and Brennan ever since he'd had to cadge rides on his partners' mounts, having left his own horse in the canyon.

"About time we get somewhere," Miller growled as he crawled down from his cream's back, holding his hand over his burning nose. His raspy voice sounded hollow and nasal. "Can't make no time ridin' double, dammit, Flipper. You see that you get you a good hoss before we leave town. You hear me?"

The tall, gangly Flipper Harris who for all intents and

purposes had only one arm, the other hanging down only a few inches from his shoulder and resembling some pale, deformed, bottom-feeding river fish, slipped off the back of Montez's horse and turned a sheepish look to the redheaded, bespectacled outlaw leader. "I aim to, Red. I'm sorry, Red. Like I said, it wasn't my fault. I tried to grab the reins but, well, you know how it is . . ."

He gave the little appendage, hidden behind the cut-off and pinned-up sleeve of his duster a feeble little wag.

Miller snorted in disgust. He glanced over his cream to see three horses tied to the hitchrack roughly ten feet away from the one he and his pards were tying their own mounts to. He nodded at a tall, clean-lined, white-socked coyote dun and said, "There—take that one. That's a fine-lookin' mount."

"That one there?"

"Which one am I looking at? Yes, that one there! Fetch it over here. It's yours now."

Flipper chuckled. "All right."

He walked over, untied the mount, and started to turn it toward Miller and the other two men when one of the three men drinking beer on the boardwalk fronting the saloon to the south of the San Francisco Peak Inn jerked his head toward Flipper and said, "Hey, what in hell do you think you're doin' with my hoss?"

"We're takin' it," Miller said, stepping up onto the boardwalk and smiling at the man behind his dusty round spectacles.

The indignant man was tall and blond with blond goat whiskers and a hairlip, and he was dressed in the ragged, sweat-stained garb of your average thirty-a-month-and-found cow puncher. His eyes glistened from drink. He and the other two men with him, similarly attired, had probably been drinking and playing poker all night. Their eyes were red-rimmed and bloodshot.

Hairlip stepped forward, scowling, narrow eyes glinting exasperation. "What in the hell do you mean—you're takin' it? That's my hoss!" He rammed his thumb against his chest and closed his right hand around the Schofield .44 holstered on his right hip.

Miller took another step forward as Flipper continued leading the dun over to the hitchrack at which Miller, Brennan, and Montez had tied their mounts.

"It *was* yours," Miller said. "It's not anymore. We're takin' it. Savvy?"

"No, I don't savvy," said Hairlip, moving toward Miller.

He stopped as one of his friends hurried up to grab his arm. The man whispered into his ear then, looking at Miller as though he were regarding an escaped circus lion, walked backward, keeping his wary eyes on Miller and the other three outlaws, retreating to stand with the other cow puncher near the saloon's front door.

Hairlip stared at Miller, the anger shifting in his eyes, quickly transforming to a worried look. The taut muscles in his face slackened. "You, uh . . . you Red Miller?"

"Yes, I am."

"Oh . . . I, uh . . . I didn't realize that."

"Well, I am, so . . ."

Hairlip's frightened eyes were riveted on Miller. His right knee trembled perceptibly, as though the earth were quaking beneath that boot. "Oh. I didn't . . . I didn't realize, Mister Miller . . ."

"We all good then?"

"Sure, sure." Hairlip tried to smile but he appeared on

the verge of sobbing. "We're all good. He's all yours. A really good horse. He'll take you many miles!"

"Good. That's just the kind of hoss we need."

"All right, then." Hairlip walked back toward where his other two friends were snickering at him like schoolgirls with an embarrassing secret. He kept switching his gaze between Miller's holstered six-gun and Miller's eyes.

A small, wet stain shown near the buttoned fly of his wash-worn denim jeans over which he wore cracked bullhide chapaderos. "Thank you, Mister Miller. Have a good day, now!"

"Thank you," Miller said, smiling affably. "I will."

One of the friends laughing and snickering behind him stepped up, said with a mocking screech, "Thank you, now, Mister Miller! Have a good day now!" He swatted Hairlip's hat off his head then ran with the other one through the batwing doors and into the saloon, spurs chinging raucously.

"Damn you, Sandy!" Hairlip grunted out as he ran to fetch his hat.

When he'd snatched it off the street, he glanced once more at Miller, gave a weak smile, then set his hat on his head and hurried into the saloon behind the other two cow punchers.

Hoot Gibbons gritted his teeth, cheeks burning, as his two friends—though he doubted he could call them friends any longer, and he had nobody to blame for that but himself—squealed in mocking laughter over where they were sitting back down where they and Hoot had been sitting before they'd headed outside to drink a beer and get some air.

It had been a long night and come dawn they'd found themselves worn out and, worse, sober.

Now Gibbons needed a drink, something stronger than beer, very badly. He headed straight across the room to the bar on the room's left side. His "friends" were sitting on the room's right side, where the four townsmen they'd been playing poker with last night were still sitting, still playing, in a hazy cloud of tobacco smoke.

"What the hell's so funny?" one of the townsmen asked. "You two are cuttin' up like two Sunday school boys who'd just seen the preacher in the wood shed with the organist!"

"Listen to this," Woody Amos said.

Hoot saw him in the backbar mirror, grinning at Hoot's back.

Woody said, "The old outlaw devil Red Miller just stole Hoot's horse. You know what Hoot told him?"

"No, what'd Hoot tell him?" one of the other townsmen asked, blowing out a long plume of cigar smoke.

Woody slapped the table, making coins and playing cards bounce, and said, "'Thank you, Mister Miller. Have a good day!'"

"No!" said the townsman, shuttling his shocked expression to Hoot who was now bellied up tightly to the bar, pressing his splayed fingers into the scarred oak, his head bowed in humiliation. His hat fell off his head and landed crown down before him.

"Sure enough, he did! Didn't he, Ed?"

"That's exactly what he said, all right. Sure enough!"

howled Ed Waite, Hoot's other former friend and fellow hand out at the Box Bar B. "Thank you, Mister Miller!"

Hoot knew now he was finished at the Box Bar B. He could never return to the ranch. Not even to pick up what few possibles he'd left in the bunkhouse. Once Amos and Ed told the other hands what Hoot had done here in Tularosa when Red Miller had appropriated his horse, they'd ride him right into the ground.

He'd never be able to show his face anywhere in the San Francisco Mountains again. Maybe never even anywhere in southern New Mexico. Hell, maybe never *anywhere* in New Mexico!

All eight men in the room—at least, all eight customers in the room—were roaring. The barman, Herman Nettles, was only smiling as he scratched at a stubborn stain on the bar to Hoot's right. It wasn't so much a mocking smile as a smile of sympathy.

Which was even worse.

Keeping his head down, Hoot said through taut lips, "Whiskey, please, Herman. Leave the bottle. Please, hurry!"

He would have a drink—hell, he'd have several drinks—and then, when he was good and drunk, he'd leave town.

But how was he going to leave town when his horse, Ol' Rowdy, had been taken from him?

Now, he was shriveling with humiliation and left afoot, without a horse. But if he didn't get out of Tularosa soon, his head and heart were going to explode like shotgun-blasted cantaloupes.

Had he really said: "'Thank you, Mister Miller—have a good day'?"

Had he really said that? *Really?*

My God, what had gotten into him?

Fear—that's what got into you, you damn sissy! Hell, starin' into Red Miller's cold, dung-brown eyes that looked like fish eyes behind those round, dirty glasses, you even squirted down your leg!

Now you have no horse. He was a good horse. Way more loyal than you are, you yellow-livered chicken. You turned him over without so much as a fight. You even thanked the man who took him right out from under you, before your very eyes!

Worse, you dribbled down your leg!

Hoot picked up his shot glass in his trembling hand, and, grinding his molars against the jeering laughter behind him, threw back the entire shot, hating himself like no man had ever hated himself before.

When Hairlip had scuttled through the batwings and into the Busted Flush like a rat into its hole, Miller laughed despite the pain in his nose, and turned to his three partners.

"Gentlemen, I need a drink!"

"So do I," said Gopher Montez, who appeared nothing so much like a gopher in a ragged straw sombrero, with long mare's tail mustaches hanging down both sides of his thin-lipped mouth to dangle beneath his jaw.

"Not you, Gopher," Red said, placing his hand on the gopher-faced stringbean's chest. "First, you fetch me a sawbones. Bring him here and make it quick. I need to have him take a look at this beak of mine and make the pain go away. Tell him I need the pain to go away, and I need it to go away, now—*understand?*"

"What if Tularosa doesn't have a sawbones, Red?" Gopher said, glancing around stupidly, thinking more about a drink, Red knew, than the misery Red was enduring.

Red unsheathed his ivory-gripped Colt Army .44 and shoved the barrel up snug against Gopher's flat belly, and clicked the hammer back. He didn't say anything. He just stood glaring up at the rodent-faced half-Mex, who promptly got the message.

"All right, Red! All right! Pull your horns in!" Montez threw up his arms in supplication, his mustache jostling. "I'll bring you a sawbones, for Heaven's sakes!"

He trotted off, looking around as though for a lost dog.

Red said, "Yes, you will," as he depressed his Colt's hammer, sheathed the weapon, swung around, and pushed through the batwings into the San Francisco Peak Saloon. Flipper Harris and Pike Brennan had already entered. Flipper sat at a table on the room's left side, near the bar running along the left wall. Brennan stood at the bar, and the apron, a tall, gaunt Mexican with pomaded hair and black silk sleeve garters, was setting beers, a bottle of whiskey, and four shot glasses on a tray on the bar in front of Pike.

Miller walked over and sat down across the table from Flipper, who'd removed his Texas-creased Stetson and was running his hand through his short, curly, dark brown hair that was sweat-matted against his scalp and flecked with weed seeds. "Thanks for the hoss, Red. I think that was a wise choice."

"Shut up, Flipper, will you? Just shut up until I get a drink in me!"

"S-sorry, Red. Hurts some, does it?"

Miller drew a deep breath and crossed his eyes as he stared down his nose at the ragged tip. Rage thundered in him like Napoleon cannons. "What in blue blazes did I just tell you, Flipper?"

"Sorry, Red! Sorry about that!"

Brennan brought the tray and set it on the table.

Miller grabbed the bottle, popped the cork, and took a deep pull, his Adam's apple rising and falling three times before he finally set the bottle back down on the table.

"Jesus, Red!" Brennan said.

"Shut up." Miller grabbed one of the beers and took a deep pull of the malty suds, as well.

He'd just finished the beer fifteen minutes later when Gopher Montez pushed through the batwings and strode with a proud smile into the saloon.

"Found one, Red!" he said, stepping to one side and grinning at the little man walking in behind him, carrying a black leather kit.

The little man, who had greasy, longish red-blond hair and a weak chin and octagonal spectacles perched on his almost feminine nose, stopped just inside the doors that swung back into place behind him. His gaze quickly found Miller with his bandaged nose. He stepped forward tentatively, frowning, eyes apprehensive behind the queer spectacles.

"You're Red Miller?"

"See any other man in here with his damn nose shot off?"

As if to make sure, the little doctor, who appeared in his late twenties or early thirties and wore a mismatched, disheveled suit with bits of egg and toast crumbs on his faded foulard tie, looked around.

Returning his gaze to Miller, he swallowed and said, "I've heard your reputation, Miller. You're not going to shoot me, are you?"

"That depends on what you can do about this nose of mine." Miller waved a hand to indicate the ruined appendage. "If you can take the sting out of it, you'll be just fine. If not"—he glowered up at the little man—"you're buzzard bait!"

CHAPTER 14

The effeminate little doctor flushed.

He stepped forward, set the kit on the table, pulled a chair out, and sat down in it. "I'm Wilfred Teagarden, Doctor of Medicine. M-May I take a look?"

"I didn't call ya here to do-si-do, Doc!"

"All right."

The doctor flinched a little as he reached up with his right hand. He kept looking from Miller's nose to his eyes, as though he were tending a dog with a biting history, which, in a very real way, of course, he was.

He began to pull the bloodstained bandage, a strip of cambric, off of Miller's nose.

"Oh," Red said, half-closing his eyes, as pain burned through his nose and into his brain, like a rusty pig sticker.

"Hurt?"

Miller only chuffed and rolled his eyes at the man.

"I'm going to pull it off quickly," the doctor warned. "It will hurt, but—"

Miller wrapped his hand around the man's wrist and snarled like that quick-tempered dog the sawbones was worried about: "Dammit, just pull it off and tend it, you prissy fool!"

"All right, all right," the little man said, his voice crackling with fear.

He swallowed, drew a breath. His hand was shaking as he reached up, plucked an edge of the cambric bandage between his thumb and index finger.

"Here we go!" he said, and pulled the bandage off of Miller's nose.

Miller sat back in the chair, gritting his teeth against the raging wildfire burning between his ears. "Holy hellfire! When I meet up with Stockburn again . . . oh, I'm tellin' you . . . there's gonna be hell to pave an' no hot pitch!"

He picked up the bottle and took another couple of deep swallows.

The doctor laid his finger on Miller's cheek to steady the man's head. He looked at the ragged end of the outlaw's nose, and made a sour look. "My God," he said in hushed awe. "What happened to you?"

Miller slammed the bottle back down on the table. "Wolf Stockburn!"

"Who's Stockburn?" the doctor asked.

"Wolf of the Rails," Flipper Harris said.

Miller glared at him, then at the doctor. "Never mind. He ain't gonna be around much longer—I'll tell you that much. I hope I shot his damn arm off!" He slapped the table and laughed though there wasn't much mirth in it. "Is there anything you can do, Doc? Sew it up for me so it don't keep bleeding?"

Again, the doctor flinched. Keeping his cheeks balled up beneath his spectacles, he said, "There's really very little skin there to sew. About the best I can do is cauterize it, though it's going to hurt like hell."

"Then cauterize the damn thing!" Red said, again squeezing the man's wrist and glaring up at him with his wild, lunatic eyes behind the lenses that made them look three times larger than they were.

"I'm going to need a blade," Teagarden said.

Miller pulled his bowie knife from the sheath behind the holstered .44 revolver on his right hip. "Will that do?"

Teagarden looked at the broad, foot-long blade and widened his eyes. "That should do it." He turned to the barman who was stirring a pot of beans atop his range behind the bar. "Senor Huerta," he said, holding the knife in his hands as though it were a rattlesnake. He strode to the bar. "Please stick this under a stove lid. Keep it there for a minute."

"Ah, hell," Miller said at the end of a heavy sigh.

The barman turned his head to look at the knife in the little sawbones' beringed hand, and arched his brow. He took the knife, lifted a stove lid, and poked the knife down into the glowing coals inside the range. He turned his head to stare across the room at Miller, and one mouth corner rose with poorly concealed amusement. He took a puff from the cigarette poking out of a corner of his mouth, and ashes dropped from the quirley's glowing tip.

A minute later, Teagarden walked back to the table, holding the knife out before him, the hooked tip pointed at the ceiling. The long, broad blade glowed like molten lava. The doctor regarded it warily, wide eyes crossed behind his octagonal-framed spectacles.

Miller stared at the blade tensely, heart thudding slowly, heavily, like a war drum.

The doctor sat down beside him, holding the glowing, pulsating, smoking blade up between them. Wide-eyed with apprehension, Harris, Brennan, and Montez regarded the glowing blade.

"Are you ready?" the doctor asked Miller.

"No, but do it anyway."

"You . . . you won't shoot me—will you?"

"No, I won't shoot you! Just do it, by God!"

"You might pass out."

"No, I won't." Miller lifted his chin and the ragged tip of his nose, which now resembled a bloody pig's nose, and grabbed the sides of his chair to steady himself. "Just do it, Doc, or I *will* shoot you!"

"All right." Teagarden slowly shoved the blade toward Miller's face.

Miller closed his eyes and waited.

"For Chrissakes," he bellowed, "just get on with—"

He smelled the burning flesh and blood before he felt the blade.

Then what felt like a fireball unleashed by a raging wildfire smashed into his face. It seemed to consume his entire head and melt his teeth—a wailing, gnawing, agonizing heat that spread deep into his ear canals. Seven demented witches screamed into each ear from only inches away.

Beyond them, someone else in the room was screaming. A girl. But he hadn't seen a girl in the room.

One of his three trail partners, perhaps? A fragment of amused condescension touched Miller when he reflected that one of his partners must not have had the belly for what he was seeing.

No, that wasn't one of his men screaming, he realized.

Humiliation aggravated his misery as he realized that he himself was screaming the scream of a girl with her pigtails caught in the spokes of a moving wheel. He tried to stop the scream but could not do it. The pain was a demon in full possession of him.

When Teagarden pulled the blade away, Miller leaned forward, choking on the smell of his own burning flesh and blood. The room pitched and rotated around him. His three partners looked warily at him from across the table, lower jaws hanging. They, too, pitched and bucked while remaining in their chairs. Miller's own chair bucked him off. He hit the floor on his hands and knees, shaking his head, trying to quell the burning and the witches' screaming, fighting desperately to remain conscious.

He could not pass out. There was no telling what would happen to him if he passed out. One thing he knew would happen was that he would lose the respect of his partners. They would delight in his weakness. Like himself, they were savages. Savages rejoiced in the weakness of others. He knew this because he rejoiced in it himself.

Again, he shook his head. The room began to steady.

"Whiskey!" he yelled, glad not to hear that girl's scream again but a more manly bellowing wail. "*Whiskey!*"

He spied movement in the corner of his right eye. Teagarden had dropped to a knee beside him and held out a shot glass with a half-inch of some murky, green-brown substance in it. "Take this. It's better than whiskey."

Miller was in no position to argue. He grabbed the shot glass, threw back the substance in a single gulp, then, swallowing, threw the glass as hard as he could against the far wall. It was only then that he saw the ten or so other customers, all sitting at tables and regarding him warily, lowering their heads to avoid the hurling glass.

The glass shattered and dropped to the floor in pieces.

Miller made a face and smacked his lips as he rose to his knees and sat back against his heels. "Christalmighty— what in the hell did you give me? Tastes like horse water mixed with cow dung!" Again, he smacked his lips, trying to rid his mouth of the cloying taste.

The doctor grabbed a bottle off the table upon which his open medical kit sat. He showed Miller the square blue bottle. "Tilden's India Extract. It's faster and stronger than whiskey but you have to be careful with it."

"What's in it?"

"It's a powerful extract of the marijuana plant. Hemp. I use it for treating a man who was bit by a rabid coyote. It's the only thing that holds the rabies at bay. But, like I said, you have to be careful with it. It's so powerful that even in small doses it will drive you mad if you take it for too long. You can't take too much at any one time. And, for God sakes, don't take it, even in very small doses— just a small sip or two a day—for more than three days."

Miller was staring off across the room, past the faces of the other customers staring back at him in wide-eyed, albeit apprehensive fascination. He smacked his lips, frowning. "I'll be damned," he said.

"What is it?" Flipper Harris asked. He, Brennan, and Montez were behind Miller now as he knelt staring toward the far side of the room, past the other diners and drinkers regarding him warily, a slow smile shaping itself on Red's walrus-mustached mouth.

"I already feel some better."

"You do?" Brennan's mouth twisted a sour expression as he regarded Miller's smoking, fire-blackened nose.

"Hell, yeah."

"That's not surprising," Teagarden said. "It's a powerful medicine. Like I said, be careful with it. Respect that stuff or you'll rue the day I ever gave it to you."

"Rue, hell!" Miller lifted the bottle to his lips.

Teagarden widened his mouth and eyes in exasperation. "*No, no, no!*"

Too late. Miller had taken another good-sized pull.

"Good God, man!" Teagarden exclaimed. "Didn't you hear what I told you?"

Miller stared at the sawbones dreamily, as though at his life's one true love. "I'll be damned, Doc, if this ain't one powerful elixir. I feel no pain. None atall. In fact, I feel right spry." He chuckled and looked at the bottle in his hand. "Hell, I feel like I could go a-dancin'!"

"I'll be hanged!" said Gopher Montez, smiling at the bottle in Miller's hand and thrusting out his empty shot glass. "Pour me some!"

Miller heaved himself to his feet and wheeled, crouching, toward the table. He clawed his Colt from its holster faster than he'd ever pulled iron before in his life. The heavy pistol felt as light as a nickel. Miller clicked the hammer back and aimed at Gopher Montez's unshaven face.

"You stay away from this bottle, you greaser devil. Don't you ever come near it, or so help me, I'll blow your head clean off your shoulders!"

"Whoa, Red—whoa!" exclaimed Pike Brennan.

"Yeah—easy, easy, Red," added Gopher, throwing

his free hand in the air, palm out and leaning far back in his chair.

"That's better." Miller depressed his Colt's hammer and set the gun on the table.

He leaned forward to peer into Teagarden's medical kit. "You got any more of that stuff in there, Doc. Why, sure you do!" he said with a big, dreamy grin on his face, reaching into the bag and pulling out another square, blue, cork-stoppered bottle.

"That's for Senor Diaz," the doctor said, reaching for the second bottle. "I was just heading out to his ranch when your man summoned me. Diaz needs that bottle or the rabies will kill him but only after driving him stark-raving mad. Please, Mister Mil—"

He stopped when Miller clutched the second bottle against his belly, along with the first one, and lifted his Colt from the table. He cocked it again and this time aimed it at the sawbones.

"I'll be taking the second one, too. You can thank Senor Diaz for me." Miller laughed through his teeth, blowing out his thin, red mustache. "I'll toast him with it!"

He lifted the open bottle, and took another pull.

Teagarden stared at him in hang-jawed shock.

"Thanks, Doc," Miller said. "You can run along now." He lifted his chin to indicate the door.

Teagarden seemed unable to move. He just stood staring at Miller and the two bottles of the powerful elixir in mute exasperation.

"If you think I'm gonna pay you one thin dime," Miller spat out angrily, "you got another think comin', you prissy devil!"

"Hold it, Miller!" sounded a voice from the bar.

A sloppy, thick-set man with broad shoulders, a bulging belly, and a high-crowned black Stetson stood at the bar's right end, in front of a half-open back door. He wore a brown vest over a red-checked wool shirt, and black broadcloth trousers stuffed into high-topped, mule-eared boots. A five-pointed badge was pinned to his vest.

In both thick hands he held a Winchester repeating rifle aimed in the general direction of Miller and Miller's pards.

"Put the gun down, you damn killer!" the lawman ordered. He narrowed his brown eyes, dropping his chin just enough to show he meant business. With his right thumb he ratcheted back the Winchester's hammer to full cock. "We got you dead to rights!"

Miller grinned at the man while keeping his revolver aimed at the medico's belly. "Who's 'we'?" Red called.

"Right here," said two more men just then entering through the batwings.

They were both younger than the town marshal by a good many years. The bigger of the two, wearing bib-front overalls and a floppy-brimmed black hat, held a Henry repeating rifle on Miller. The other held a double-barreled shotgun aimed at Miller's pards. He was short, stocky, square-jawed, and with muscular, freckled forearms beneath the rolled-up sleeves of his worn blue cotton tunic.

"Dead to rights for sure, Hamm!" the stocky gent said, grinning devilishly at Miller. "We got him—Red Miller his ownself!" He chuckled through his nose.

"Take it easy, now, Peach," the town marshal, Hamm Sanchez, ordered from the end of the bar. "Don't get cocky, galldammit! You, neither, Alvin! These aren't just some drunk-an'-disorderly cow punchers we're dealin' with."

Miller smiled at the middle-aged lawman. "You got that right." He chuckled and blinked slowly behind his glinting spectacles. "You sure got *that* right!"

CHAPTER 15

"Set the gun on the table and step back away from it, hands in the air!" ordered the Tularosa town marshal, Hamm Sanchez.

"No," Miller said with quiet menace. He was looking at the sissified sawbones standing before him. He had his cocked pistol aimed at the little man's belly. "You put yours down and tell these two cork-headed fools before me to do likewise . . . or I'll drill your doctor a new belly button."

Pike Brennan chuckled. Pike always enjoyed a dustup, Pike did.

He and the other two outlaws, Gopher Montez and Flipper Harris, were still seated at the table. All three were grinning at Miller while sliding their devious eyes between the thick-set lawman standing at the end of the bar flanking them on their left and the two smiling younger men—Sanchez's deputies complete with shiny new tin stars pinned to their shirts, standing just inside the batwings.

The barman stood frozen behind the bar, his eyes wide and dark. The saloon's other customers sat at their tables with similar expressions, smoke curling lazily from cheroots and cigarettes.

None of them moved except to slowly blink their eyes.

Hell was coming. They knew it. They should have skinned out of the saloon the minute Red Miller had entered, but they hadn't and now they were stuck. There was a general, shared sense that any movement could detonate the bomb that was Red Miller as well as Miller's slip-triggered amigos.

The doctor stared up at Miller, shock and terror in his eyes. "For God sakes, I helped you. You can't kill me!" His voice was shrill with pleading.

"Don't want to," Miller said, smiling, slitting his fish eyes behind his glasses. "But if that fat javelina by the bar don't set that Winchester down . . . and if them two fools behind you don't do likewise . . . well, then, I reckon I got no choice."

"If you kill the doc, we'll kill you deader'n a butchered hog!" barked the short, stocky, freckled man called Peach, keeping his shotgun trained on Miller. His face was smudged with coal soot. That and the bulging forearms told Miller he was a blacksmith.

A blacksmith out for the reward money that had been issued for Miller's head. A quick glance told Red that the man had dollar signs emblazoned on his eyes. The other, bigger man in overalls did, too, but he looked a little more apprehensive than the overly eager Peach.

"Peach, will you please shut up and let me handle this?" called Hamm Sanchez from the end of the bar in deep frustration. Looking at Miller, he said, "You shoot the doc, Miller, and I'll blow your ugly head off!"

Miller swiveled his head to glare, fiery-eyed, at the

thick-set lawman. "Ugly, huh? *Ugly?* Did you just call me *ugly?*"

"Hold on, now, Miller!" Sanchez barked.

"Damn you!" Red raged, turning his head back toward the horrified doctor, hardening his jaws and grinding his back teeth. "You done just killed your sissy sawbones!"

"Miller, don't do it!"

Miller's revolver bucked and roared, drowning Sanchez's last two words. Teagarden screamed as the bullet tore into his worn fawn vest, the flames from Miller's revolver setting his shirt on fire. The doctor twisted around and staggered backward, screaming and swatting at the flames with his hands.

The sudden gunshot and the doctor's wails had stunned both Alvin and Peach for the eye blink of time Miller needed to whip his Colt in their direction. They stared at the burning sawbones slack-jawed and wide-eyed. Miller shot them both before they could tighten their fingers on the triggers of their respective weapons.

Miller's .44 slugs ripped through both men and punched them out the batwings together, locked in each other's arms as though two lovers waltzing. At the same time, guns exploded to Miller's right and he whipped his head in that direction to see flames leaping from Hamm Sanchez's Winchester as well as from the drawn and extended pistols of Pike Brennan and Flipper Harris.

Sanchez's round took Gopher Montez in the chest, lifting him up and throwing him onto the table in front of Miller, blood splashing across the table and grazing Miller's right shirtsleeve.

Gopher screamed and thrust his hand toward Miller as though desperate for help.

"Get your hands off me—damn you, Gopher!" Miller raged as he added his lead to that of Brennan and Harris firing at Hamm Sanchez. Sanchez lowered his rifle as the bullets punched into him, seemingly pinning him to the wall to the right of the bar.

He appeared to be dancing some bizarre two-step, jerking and bellowing and turning his head from side to side, blood oozing from his chest, belly, arms, and legs.

When Miller, Brennan, and Sanchez stopped shooting, Sanchez dropped his rifle and gave a deep groan and slid straight down the wall to the floor.

Miller gazed through the powder smoke, grinning at his and his pards' handiwork. The bartender stood to the right of Hamm Sanchez, staring wide-eyed at the dead or fast-dying town marshal, holding both hands to his ears, elbows jutting straight out to each side, like giant chicken wings.

Miller slid his smoking Colt toward the bartender and smiled.

The barman saw the gun aimed at him and whipped his head toward Miller, eyes widening in terror. He thrust his right hand over the bar, palm out, as though to shield himself from a bullet.

"*No!*"

Miller's Colt drowned the plea. It blew a .44-caliber round through the middle of the bartender's palm. It continued through the hand to drill a similar-sized hole through the man's left cheek, punching him back against the shelves behind him, knocking bottles to the floor.

The barman stumbled forward, reached for the bar but missed and fell down behind the bar and out of sight.

Miller looked at Gopher Montez. The gopher-faced

man lay on the table before Red, on his back, staring sightlessly up at the ceiling, blood matting his shirt over his shredded heart.

Brennan and Harris stared toward where the barman had been standing a moment before. They looked at each other, smiled, then, after a passing glance at their dead brethren, Gopher, they turned to Miller.

Red smiled back at them, his eyes heavy-lidded behind his glasses. He was feeling fine. Better than fine. He was feeling powerful, otherworldly. God-like. If God were a devil, that was.

He turned to gaze over his shoulder at the innocent bystanders cowering behind tables and chairs. A few had lifted their heads and were staring at the killers in wide-eyed shock, frozen in place as though too afraid to move.

Miller turned that death's head grin on Brennan and Harris again. They shifted their gazes toward the nervous bystanders. Their own smiles broadened, eyes glittering maniacally.

Chuckling, Miller flicked open the loading gate of his empty Colt and began emptying the wheel onto the floor.

Brennan and Miller followed suit, quickly plucking the spent shells from their own empty cylinders and reloading from their cartridge belts.

The bystanders didn't make so much as a peep. They were too afraid to try a run for the door, as though afraid to hurry the deaths they knew were coming for them.

Over in the Busted Flush, Hoot Gibbons stood staring over the top of his raised shot glass at his own reflection in the backbar mirror.

He was not seeing his own cowardly eyes, however. Not this time. He'd been staring into his own cowardly eyes for a long time, wondering at the depths of his cowardliness.

Where had it come from? Had he always been cowardly? Did it run in his family? But those thoughts had faded when the shooting had started in the saloon just south of the Busted Flush.

All customers in the Flush appeared to sit holding their breaths behind Hoot. He could see them in the mirror, staring toward the saloon's front doors. Occasionally, they'd glance at each other, exchanging wary looks, but mostly they just stared at the batwings while the thunder of angry gunfire rose from next door. Hoot's former friends, Woody Amos and Ed Waite, did likewise.

Bang! Bang! Bang-Bang-Bang-Bang! Bang!

Hoot could feel the reverberation of each shot through the floorboards beneath his boots.

The Busted Flush's bartender, Herman Nettles, stood sweating to Hoot's right, where the man was washing glasses in a corrugated tin washtub filled with steaming, soapy water. *Had been* washing glasses, rather. Now he just stood over the tub, his arms buried to his elbows in the suds, staring at the Flush's southern wall beyond which what sounded like a massacre was taking place. A loosely rolled quirley dangled from one corner of his mouth.

Men's shouts and cries and yowls and curses rose, muffled by adobe walls and distance. So, too, did the victorious whooping and hollering of those men doing the killing.

Red Miller's men. No doubt about it. The three men everyone in the Busted Flush by now knew Miller had ridden into town with nearly an hour ago, Miller's nose sorely missing its tip.

Roughly fifteen minutes ago, one of the other customers had seen Town Marshal Hamm Sanchez walk toward the San Francisco Peak Saloon from the direction of Sanchez's office, just up the street and around the corner. Sanchez had been flanked by the two townsmen, odd-jobber Alvin Parker and the blacksmith Peach Fitzsimmons, who Sanchez usually deputized when he needed a couple of men to help him turn the key on particularly contrary miscreants tearing up a saloon or brothel here in Tularosa.

Everyone in the saloon had watched through the front window as Sanchez and his deputies had palavered for a time, then split up, Parker and Fitzsimmons remaining on the street while Sanchez headed down the break between the Busted Flush and the San Francisco Peak, apparently fixing to enter the Peak from the rear.

A couple of minutes later, Parker and Fitzsimmons had entered the Peak through the front door. Several men had gathered at the Flush's front window (and they were still there now), leaning toward the glass, staring up the street to the north.

Everything had been quiet, maybe too quiet, for about four minutes. Then, maybe another four minutes ago, all hell had broken loose with the angry pops of large-caliber six-shooters. There'd been a short lull in the shooting.

Then the barrage had resumed, sounding even louder than before. It continued now, the blasts of the guns and the screams of the dying men and the jackal-like yowling of the killers causing Hoot Gibbons's blood to again run cold in his veins and his heart to race.

He was bathed in sweat as chill as winter snowmelt. He

could feel it bathing the bottoms of his feet inside his boots, soaking his socks.

"We gonna just sit here and do nothing?" asked one of the five men standing near the front window.

He'd directed the question at the men sitting at tables scattered around the room and who sat their chairs as though in a trance.

One of the other men standing at the window turned to the man who'd just spoken, and said, "Go on over and help out, Walter. Just keep in mind that's Red Miller's bunch!"

"Oh, for Christsakes!"

Walter, dressed in ragged cowboy garb, unsheathed his old, rust-mottled Confederate-model George Todd .36 revolver, and strode toward the batwings, his fringed chaps buffeting around his long, lean, denim-clad legs. He pushed through the batwings and strode north toward the San Francisco Peak.

The shooting over there was dwindling, growing sporadic. One man was howling shrilly. He sounded like a dog that had been run over by a wagon.

Suddenly, the shooting stopped.

Everyone in the Busted Flush stood staring toward the front or, in the case of the men standing at the front window, craning their necks to peer north along the boardwalk.

Hoot Gibbons stood staring into his own eyes but he was not seeing the coward staring back at him. He was imagining the carnage inside the San Francisco Peak.

He jumped violently as a man laughed in the San Francisco Peak, and two more loud pops followed. Hoot saw several of the other men behind him lurch in their chairs at the explosive reports. His two former friends sat frozen in their chairs, staring in stony-faced shock toward the saloon's large front window.

Outside, a man screamed.

Hoot stood staring into the mirror over the shaking glass in his hand, focusing now on the front window behind him. Foot scuffs sounded. With each scuff came the jangle of a spur being dragged across wood. A man appeared in the window, moving from north to south along the board-walk fronting the saloon.

He was stiff-backed, tight, moving heavily, dragging his heels. He had both hands clamped over his belly. When the light struck his face beneath his hat, Hoot saw that the awkwardly moving man was Walter.

Walter turned to the batwings, sort of heaved himself through the swinging doors and into the saloon. His face was taut, pale as flour, and bathed in sweat.

He took three shuffling steps into the room. He stopped. Sunlight angling in around him glistened on the blood matting his shirt over his belly. He sobbed, lifted his chin, and bellowed, "*You cowards, they kilt me!*"

He fell to his knees. As he slanted forward, toppling like a windmill, a shadow moved in the window behind him, to his right. Then there were two shadows . . . then three . . . moving fast, one behind the other . . .

Dark specters heading for the Busted Flush's swing doors.

There was a deep intake of breath. Maybe Hoot only imagined it. Real or not, Hoot heard one, all right, as though all the men in the room were collectively gasping.

He probably added to the sound but he wasn't aware of anything then except the fact that they were all about to die, and that they were all too frozen in fear to do a lick about it—even his former friends who'd mocked him for turning over his horse without objection.

Red Miller entered first, grinning, his red pig nose fairly glowing, fishy eyes shiny behind his dusty, glinting spectacles. The other two followed him into the Busted Flush and stood beside him, and for about two seconds, all three stood there grinning like boys awaiting the horn to signal the start of a rodeo.

A few of the seated men leaped to their feet—but not Hoot's former trail partners—and tried to raise their revolvers. But it was too little too late.

Miller yowled like a coyote as he raised his big Colt Army and started shooting. The other two killers followed suit, yammering and barking and laughing while they filled the room with the din of powder kegs exploding, with the screams of the dying, splashing blood, and powder smoke.

Somebody must have run up behind Hoot and, seeing him frozen there in front of the bar like a cowardly damn fool, waiting for a bullet in his back, grabbed him by the back of his shirt collar and the seat of his pants, and hurled him up and over the bar.

He hit the floor on the other side and didn't even feel the impact.

He waited for the man who'd thrown him over the bar to come sailing over it himself. But the man did not come. Hoot realized that no one had hurled him over the bar. He'd thrown himself over it. He'd been struck by some unconscious impulse for self-preservation though his life wasn't worth anything anymore. It was worth less than an empty airtight tin.

The shooting didn't last long.

Less than a minute.

When the shooting died, Hoot heard his former friend, Woody Amos, sobbing and yelling, "Don't kill me! Please don't kill me!"

A gun barked. Silence.

Hoot lifted his head from the floor. Above the shrill ringing in his ears, he heard the thumps of men moving around, muttering amongst themselves. One man laughed.

Boots thumped, footsteps growing louder. Hoot realized that someone was walking toward the bar. There was a grunt and a creak of wood. He smelled the sour, unwashed, sweaty smell of Red Miller before he saw the man standing atop the bar, staring down at him—a red-haired death angel with dusty spectacles through which large blue fish eyes peered, and only half a nose.

The flat tip of the nose was as black as charred meat.

Miller smiled that death angel's smile. He raised the Colt. Hoot closed his eyes. He opened them when someone screamed "No!" to his left. He turned to see Herman Nettles cowering about five feet away from him, also on the floor behind the bar.

Nettles buried his face in his hands.

Miller's Colt barked, and Hoot stared in numb shock as Nettles slumped to the floor with a hole in the crown of his head.

A shadow moved over Hoot. He looked up to see Miller smiling down at him, aiming his Colt at Hoot's face. The killer ratcheted the big pistol's hammer back.

Hoot stared at the Colt's yawning maw.

A strange calm passed over him. The icy grip of fear melted from his bones and muscles like spring snow in the sunshine.

He stared at the Colt's yawning maw and felt a smile

begin to tug at his mouth corners. Soon, his shame would be lifted from his shoulders. His soul would no longer feel the terrible burden of his cowardice.

At last, he could sleep.

Miller's finger tightened against the Colt's trigger. Hoot watched the hammer drop. The gun made a pinging sound.

Hoot frowned, befuddled.

No flames lapped from the barrel. There was only that benign tinny sound, echoing briefly. Miller stared down the Colt's barrel, arching his thick red brows in surprise.

He smiled again at Hoot and lowered the Colt to his side.

"Pilgrim," he said, "this is your lucky day."

He winked behind his spectacles, turned, leaped down from the bar, and said, "Boys, come on—we got some sage to fog!"

Hoot stared up at where Miller and the Colt had been only seconds ago—death's shadow enshrouding him with the promise of peace.

A deep longing filled him. His shame returned.

"No!" he cried. "You kill me, damn you!"

The only response were the whoops and hollers and the hoof thuds of the killers leaving town.

CHAPTER 16

"Hold on—I gotta see a man about a horse!" Lonesome Charlie Murdock reined his buckskin off the trail and into some ponderosa pines, the boughs of which were jostled by the building breeze.

Wolf and Sofia halted their own mounts and glanced after the old lawman, both wearing skeptical expressions.

Sofia turned to Stockburn. "That's the fifth time he's bought a horse in the past hour."

"I heard that, chili pepper!" Charlie called as he climbed down from his saddle. "Just drank too much coffee this mornin' is all. Go on ahead—I'll catch up to ya'll fastern' the devil can dance in the Long Branch Saloon in Dodge City on a Saturday night at the end of roundup!"

He wheezed a laugh that quickly turned into a strangled cough, and spat into the short grass and sage. Hacking phlegm from his lungs, he strode deeper into the pines and twisted cedars.

"How are we going to catch up to Miller with that old coyote slowing us down?" Sofia asked Stockburn in bitter disgust.

Wolf held up his gloved hand, not wanting Charlie to

overhear. He jerked his chin forward then rode a dozen yards ahead along the trail before reining Smoke in again. Sofia rode up beside him, looking at him curiously. The building breeze blew her hair around her face, beneath the brim of her floppy-brimmed felt hat.

Keeping his voice low, Wolf said, "I think we can shake free of the graybeard in Tularosa. I know a whorehouse madam there with a gaggle of the prettiest doves and best liquor around."

"You think he'll take the bait?"

"I'm gonna slip Miss Sylvia Winters—that's the madam—a few extra eagles to take his mind off the trail. With her ammunition, she'll be able to do it or I miss my guess." Wolf smiled and winked at his pretty trail partner. "Especially with a fella of Charlie's notorious, uh . . . distractibility."

"We could just ride off now at full gallops. On that fat, old cayuse of his . . . and in his condition . . . he'd never catch up."

"Now, darlin . . ." Stockburn's tone was gently reproachful.

"What?"

Wolf offered a tolerant smile. "That wouldn't be nice."

Sofia pulled her mouth corners down. "He's not nice."

"You mean the Mexican thing?"

"Si, of course I mean the Mexican thing."

"Lonesome Charlie's from a different time, darlin'. A wilder, harder time. I know it's no defense, but it does explain a few things. Besides, I think he's pretty damn near . . ."

Stockburn let his voice trail off as hoof thuds rose behind him and Sofia. He turned to see Charlie booting his buckskin into a lope, lifting dust and making his saddlebags flap like wings over his blanket roll. "Never mind," the old man said as he swerved to pass Wolf and Sofia on their left side, and beat it on up the trail to the south. "False alarm!"

He spat and cackled another witchlike laugh.

Wolf looked at Sofia and chuckled. Sofia rolled her eyes.

"I don't understand that soft spot you have for that old reprobate, Wolf," she said.

"Someday you will, darlin'." Stockburn clucked his horse on up the trail. "Someday you will."

They rode into Tularosa late that afternoon, crouched forward in their saddles, a cold rain spitting at their backs.

Stockburn felt worms writhe in his belly as he and his two trail companions crossed Tularosa Creek at the town's north edge, heading for the plaza at the heart of the old Spanish town. Cottonwoods lined the dusty main street, offering shade on sunny days. Behind the trees, the adobe brick, tile-roofed shops and houses sat sullen and vacant.

As it had in Ruidoso after Miller's gang had robbed the bank, a pall hung over Tularosa. The street was mostly vacant save a priest and several nuns gathered in front of the big, white adobe church on the square's west side, behind a low stone wall boasting a wrought-iron gate.

The gate was open. A buckboard wagon sat just inside it, backed up to the bottom of the church's stone steps. Stockburn saw that three or four coffins lay inside the wagon. Two beefy Mexican men in peon pajamas, striped serapes, and low-crowned straw sombreros were just then carrying a plain pine coffin up the stone steps and through the church's oak doors, each of which was held open by a nun, their black habits blowing in the wind.

As Stockburn rode on past the church, those worms in his belly gathered themselves in a tight, writhing ball. He suspected that Lonesome Charlie and Sofia were suffering from a similar case of worm infestation, for they, both riding to his right, turned toward him, brows raised in dark speculation.

They rode on out of the virtually vacant plaza, almond blossoms blowing across the cracked flagstones beneath their horses' hooves. Stockburn angled toward Chavez's undertaking parlor on the street's left side—a long, low, pink building with a living area on the left and a large open shed on the right, two large wooden crucifixes standing to each side of the shed's open doorway.

A man inside the shed was whistling while he worked. Stockburn couldn't see him very well because there was little light in there, but he could sure hear the man, hammering and whistling to beat the band. At least one man in Tularosa was having a red-letter day—thanks, Stockburn had a dreadful feeling, to Red Miller.

No one could put a pall over a town, and put as many of the town's citizens under it, the way Miller could.

Stockburn stopped his horse outside the shed and leaned forward to peer inside, saying, "Senor Chavez?"

The whistling and hammering stopped abruptly.

"You got another one?" came a Spanish-accented voice pitched with hope.

Stockburn shared a grim glance with Lonesome Charlie, then shuttled his gaze back to the shed. "No, Senor Chavez, I don't have another one."

"Oh." The shadowy figure inside the shed moved toward the opening, the misty, gray-blue light of the approaching storm illuminating his pudgy, pockmarked, coffee-skinned face. He was a slight man in his fifties or sixties clad in a calico shirt, baggy deerskin trousers, and sandals. He held a hammer in one hand, a handful of nails in the other hand.

He had a sheepish expression on his face as he stopped just inside the shed, raked his gaze across his three visitors, then looked at Stockburn and said, "A bad day in Tularosa. A very bad day." He shook his head and crossed himself with the hammer.

"I see that." Wolf had already seen around ten dead men lying on pine planks inside the shed, most propped on sawhorses or, in one case, on a wooden wheelbarrow. "What happened?"

"A very bad hombre named Red Miller. He rode into town—him and three others. Only two others rode out with Miller, but they left hell behind them." Chavez widened his eyes, raked his right index finger across his throat, and stuck out his tongue for dramatic effect.

"When'd they leave?" Lonesome Charlie asked.

"Hours ago now. Maybe four. I've been so busy, I've lost track."

Charlie spat a wad of chaw to one side, looked at the dead men distastefully, then ran the back of his hand across his mouth. "Where's Hamm Sanchez?" He glanced at Stockburn. "An old pard of mine. We fought the Injuns together, Hamm an' me." He cast a quick, wry glance at Sofia. "Despite him bein' half bean-eater, an' all . . ."

Sofia looked at Wolf and rolled her eyes.

Chavez stepped forward and pointed his right index finger out from the end of his right arm. Stockburn turned to follow the man's finger to a two-story wood-and-adobe building on the street's other side and south about fifty yards.

A sign over the boardwalk awning announced in gaudy red letters: THE SAN FRANCISCO PEAK SALOON. Just beyond it to the south lay THE BUSTED FLUSH SALOON. That was the Anglo part of town, as Stockburn remembered, so there were mostly only gringo-owned shops and saloons on that side of the plaza.

Stockburn turned to Chavez with a questioning frown.

Chavez shook his head grimly. "Very bad, senor. Very bad."

Wolf shared another darkly speculative look with Lonesome Charlie. He reined Smoke back away from the undertaking parlor, and with Charlie and Sofia flanking him, rode across the dusty street at a slant, large, cold raindrops now beginning to dimple the street's deep, finely ground dirt, straw, and horse apples.

Stockburn swung down from Smoke's back. He glanced at the sky and cursed. Swollen purple storm clouds were rolling in from the Sierra Blancas to the north, which he'd ridden down out of an hour ago, to the Sacramentos to the south.

He turned his gaze to the low-slung, brown Coyote Hills, which served as the foothills to the Sacramentos south of Tularosa.

If Miller had left town four hours ago, he was likely beyond the Coyote Hills by now and heading into the Sacramentos.

That son of a bitch!

Worse, this storm was going to pin Stockburn down for at least an hour. Probably two. Actually, with as much

water as those clouds appeared to have in their bellies, he
might be pinned down here for the rest of the day and
night. When that rain came, it would fill every canyon and
arroyo splicing the Coyote Hills, cutting off access to the
Sacramentos.

That lucky son of a bitch!

Lonesome Charlie swung down from his buckskin's
back. Squinting one eye, he followed Stockburn's gaze to
the Sacramentos hunched beneath the plum-colored sky
in which lightning now flashed and thunder rumbled like
war drums. He was thinking the same thing Wolf was.
He cursed then tied his horse and strode on into the San
Francisco Peak Saloon, spurs ringing, louvre doors swinging into place behind him.

As Stockburn stepped up onto the covered boardwalk
and pushed through the doors, he paused. Blood streaked
the inside slats of both doors. More blood—a lot more
blood—stained the saloon floor beyond him and which
Lonesome Charlie was just then crossing, also looking at
the blood.

Stockburn turned to Sofia who'd just stepped up onto
the boardwalk behind him. "You'd best wait here, girl."

She stopped and looked at him gravely.

Stockburn continued into the saloon.

Obviously, there'd been another massacre. There was
blood everywhere—splashed on the floor and on the bar
and walls and on the tables and chairs, most of which were
overturned. Glasses, bottles, spilled liquor, gold dust, men's
bloodstained hats and even a few boots were on the floor,
as well.

Stockburn saw a pair of cracked eyeglasses in a particularly large dried blood pool on the floor to his right.

Lonesome Charlie stopped a few feet ahead of Stockburn. He looked around then turned back to the railroad detective, raked a hand down his craggy, bearded face, and said, "Christ."

"Yeah."

Hearing the squawking of floorboards in the ceiling above his head, Stockburn made his way to the stairs near the back of the room. He climbed the stairs, Charlie following a few feet behind him, the old man's shallow breaths raking and wheezing in and out of his lungs as he climbed.

Wolf stepped onto the second-floor hall and followed unidentifiable sounds and the slow shuffling of footsteps to a door on the hall's right side.

The door stood a few inches open.

Stockburn reached out and nudged it wide. The squawk of the hinges caused a man in a suit without a jacket and standing by the room's only bed to turn a surprised look toward Wolf and Lonesome Charlie. As he turned, Stockburn saw a man lying on the bed—a big man who almost filled the double bed and made it sag low to the floor.

The man standing by the bed was old and gray-haired with a red-brown face, Spanish-brown eyes, and bushy gray brows. The sleeves of his white cotton shirt were rolled to his elbows.

"Doctor?" Stockburn asked.

"Retired," the man said. "I'm Doctor Vega. Vincente Vega. I sold my practice to Wilfred Teagarden, recently deceased." He added those words grimly and in a very faint Spanish accent. He wore a red necktie, the knot pulled loose, and he had a stethoscope hooked around his neck. His hands were crusted with dried blood. "I returned to the job because there was no one else."

"Is that . . . ?"

"Marshal Sanchez." Vega lifted his hand to indicate the black-mustached man on the bed, and took a step back.

"How bad?" This from Lonesome Charlie brushing past Stockburn as he stepped up to the bed and looked down at the thick-set, brown-skinned man before him.

"Bad," said Vega, taking a deep breath and pursing his lips. "He took nine bullets."

"*Nine?*" Stockburn said in shock.

"Nine," Vega said. "Don't ask me how he's still alive, but he is. Most men would have bled dry by now. I took out five of the nine. The other four I had to leave."

He shook his head.

The man on the bed coughed, making his whole body jump and the bed pitch. "You done a good job, Doc," Sanchez wheezed, opening one eye to peer up at the doctor. "I always trusted you over that fancy-Dan Teagarden, anyway . . . God rest his poor soul."

"Hamm, you old devil," said Lonesome Charlie, stepping up close to the bed and crouching low to smile down at his wounded friend. "Who takes nine bullets and lives to tell about it?"

"I do, you old polecat!" Sanchez grinned and chuckled. "Wish I had some grandkids to tell it to." He coughed and, gazing up at Charlie, said, "I thought you was dead—shot by a jealous husband in Albukirk!"

"Oh, he missed! I skinned out that window without a scratch."

The two geezers had a good laugh at that, then Sanchez turned to Stockburn, squinting. He lifted his head a little, then, apparently identifying the big man flanking Charlie, said, "Sorry, Wolf. You warned me. I should have been prepared. But I mucked it up. I wasn't countin' on Teagarden gettin' caught in the whipsaw. That threw me off."

Tears came to the lawman's light brown eyes above his broad, sun-seasoned nose and thick mustache. He blinked quickly to clear them. "My dunderheaded stupidity got a good many townsmen killed . . . includin' myself, it appears."

CHAPTER 17

Wolf stepped forward, doffed his hat, and squeezed the Tularosa town marshal's hand.

He gave it a very slight, gentle squeeze, for the man's body, most of his clothes having been cut off, was nearly entirely covered in bloodstained bandages, including one around his bulging and sharply rising and falling belly. Another stretched up from his left armpit and over his chest and around his neck. His left leg wore three bandages, the right one just one.

He'd taken a lot of lead. Amazing he was still conscious let alone still breathing. He was bathed in cold sweat, and shivering.

"It wasn't your fault, Hamm." Stockburn wished like hell he hadn't sent that telegram warning Sanchez that Miller had been on the way to Tularosa. He'd known the man wasn't up to the task of corralling Red Miller. At least, he should have known.

On the other hand, he'd have been negligent to have *not* warned him. He could have told him Miller would be pulling through Tularosa but to steer clear of him, but that only would have offended the proud lawman, who'd been one to ride the river with in earlier days.

Aging was damned hard on some men. Most men. Take Lonesome Charlie for instance. It wasn't going to be any easier for Stockburn himself. He knew that, and he was staring down the barrel of it. It wasn't all that far away.

"Oh, of course it was my fault!"

"Easy, now, Hamm," said Lonesome Charlie, placing his hand on the man's thick chest. "You just lie back and rest easy."

The dying lawman drew a ragged breath and stared up at the federal badge-toter. "You goin' after 'em, Charlie?"

"Of course, I am."

"Don't do it." Sanchez shook his head.

"You go to hell, you old chili chomper!"

"You, me—we're too old," Sanchez said. "Leave him to the younger man."

"Who—this one here?" Charlie said, thrusting up an incredulous hand to indicate the Wells Fargo man standing beside him, dwarfing his own scrawny frame. "Hell, he can't find his way out of a privy and back to a saloon if I don't tie a rope around him! How in hell is he gonna track Red Miller?"

"Ah, hell—don't make me laugh." Sanchez squeezed his eyes closed as mirth made his shoulders shake.

Keeping his hand on his old friend's chest, Lonesome Charlie cackled out a laugh of his own.

Opening his eyes, Sanchez gazed up at Charlie again and said, "You talk to a sawbones about your ticker?"

"Yeah, I finally did. He charged me double for a point-less visit. Turns out I got a heart like a Tennessee plow horse. If ever there was gonna be a man to live to a hundred an' ten, that was me. The sawbones' words exactly."

"You old liar."

Charlie raised up his palm. "I swear on a stack of Bibles."

"Do me one last favor, will you, you old devil?"

"Anything—you know that, Hamm."

"Get the hell out of here and go over to Dona Delores's place on the Mex side of town, buy a bottle and a senorita. Hell, buy two senoritas. Have a few drinks, dance, an' curl them li'l chili peppers' toes for 'em." He winked. "Have 'em curl yours." He paused then said with quiet gravity, "You never know when you'll get 'em curled again."

Tears flooded Charlie's eyes. He smiled and he said, "You know I don't lay with Mescins—damn you, Hamm! You can't trust a Mescin girl. The purtier they are, the more likely you'll wake to havin' your throat cut and your pockets emptied."

"Mierda," Sanchez said, smiling knowingly up at Charlie. "What about Antonia?" He blinked once, slowly.

Charlie swept his sleeve across his cheek. "That was a long time ago. Me—I'm a reformed man."

"She loved you, you old *pendejo*."

"I know. I didn't deserve it."

"Get out of here, dammit," Sanchez said, raising his voice as much as he could, shivering violently now.

Stockburn could tell he was weakening. He was pale, his cheeks sinking even as Wolf watched with his hat in his hands.

"Get him out of here, Wolf," Sanchez said. "He don't need to see this. Make him go over and stomp with his tail up for his old chili-chompin' amigo. You do it, Charlie! The way we used to!"

Charlie scrubbed tears from his face with his forearm. "Ah, hell!" He swung around and walked out of the room, spurs chinging.

When Charlie was gone, Sanchez looked at Stockburn. "Look after him. He's stubborn, Charlie is."

"Don't I know it."

"How bad is he?"

"Bad."

"Will he make it? I mean . . . is he, unlike myself . . . any kind of a match for Miller?"

"It's hard to know what a man has left in his game until he has to show his cards."

"Don't I know that!"

"I didn't mean it that way, Hamm."

"I know you didn't." Sanchez pinned Stockburn with a grave look. "We were both better men once."

"We all were."

"You got this to look forward to."

Stockburn nodded.

"Take the smart way out and quit before it's too late. Before the job . . . the badge . . . is all you got left. Then you can't quit."

Stockburn pondered on that, nodded. Good advice. He hoped he'd remember it and take it. He doubted he would. He was too much like this man before him, and like Charlie. He had nothing else but the job . . . his badge. He had his sister but she had more than he did. She had a son and a ranch to run. The memory of a dead husband to tend.

She didn't need him.

"Who was Antonia?" he asked.

Sanchez smiled. "Charlie's last wife. Former puta from Tucson. They met in a dance hall in Socorro. A good lady, a kind soul. I seen Charlie with a lot of women, but he never felt about them the way he did about Antonia. It about killed him when she died . . . how she died. Ten, eleven years ago now."

"How'd she die?"

"She took a bullet meant for him, fired by a man who'd just got out of prison and set his hat for revenge for the man who'd put him there."

"I didn't know."

"Charlie changed after that. Was never quite the same. Started to live up to his nickname." Sanchez twisted his mouth in a painful grimace. He glanced at the door and said, "Leave me now, Wolf. I'm about to go. Just as . . . just as soon . . . do it . . . alone . . ."

He didn't make it.

Stockburn had only started to turn away when the man's breath rattled in his throat. Sanchez looked up at the ceiling, and his chest stopped rising and falling. The light of life left his eyes. His eyes were suddenly two windows behind which there was nothing.

Just like that, he was gone.

Just like that, one day Stockburn himself would be gone.

He looked at the doctor who'd been standing near the bed, leaning back against the wall. Vega sighed, opened his timepiece to note the time for the death certificate, then snapped it closed.

"Just like that."

The doctor arched his brow at him. "Pardon?"

Stockburn hadn't realized he'd said the words aloud.

He fished in his pocket for two gold eagles, flipped them to the sawbones who caught them one at a time out of the air.

"Take good care of him for me an' Charlie—will you, Doc?"

He left the room feeling hollow.

Stockburn hadn't realized the storm's severity until he started down the stairs. Sanchez's room hadn't had a window in it, but now he could see the bright lightning flashes in the main drinking hall's windows. They contrasted sharply with the storm's nightlike darkness.

The thunder crashed so loudly it made the whole building shudder.

Remembering that he'd left Smoke in the street, he hurried down the stairs and over to the batwings. He'd just started to push through them when a slender, skirted figure ran up onto the boardwalk fronting the saloon. A lightning flash limned the pretty, olive-skinned face and nice curves of Sofia as, soaking wet, she ran across the boardwalk. Her wet hair clung to her shoulders.

Stockburn stepped back as she pushed through the batwings, doffing her wet hat and batting it against her leg, making water spray.

"Good Lord, girl—that's a helluva gully washer!"

"I waited it out as long as I could in the livery barn." Sofia crossed her arms over her wet blouse drawn revealingly taut across her chest. She was chilled as well as self-conscious, wet and revealed as she was.

"I boarded the horses at the north end of town," she

said. "There's a randy hostler over there. I thought I'd better brave the storm and head back here before I stuck my knife in him and *destripado como un cerdo*!" Gutted him like a pig!

Chuckling, Stockburn removed his black frock coat and wrapped it around her shoulders. "Thanks for tending the mounts, darlin'. Sorry about the hostler."

"Foolish men are everywhere."

"Yes, they are."

Shivering, she looked up at Wolf. "Speaking of foolish men, where was Lonesome Charlie going? I saw him leave the saloon and walk up the street, paying no mind to the storm."

"Charlie's feelin' extra lonesome this afternoon."

"His marshal friend?"

"He didn't make it."

"I'm sorry. He was your friend, too."

"He was. I got him killed."

Stockburn turned and walked around behind the bar. As he pulled a labeled bottle off a shelf and grabbed a shot glass off a pyramid, footsteps sounded on the stairs. He turned to see the doctor, Vincente Vega, striding slowly down the steps. The man looked old and worn out. So much work resulting in death had cost him.

"I'll send a couple of men over for the marshal once the storm breaks," he said as he reached the bottom of the stairs.

"Better wait here, Doc," Stockburn said. "Rainin' cats and dogs outside. I'll buy you a drink."

"No, no." Vega smiled, shaking his head. "I live behind the saloon. My wife will be worried after hearing all the shooting earlier. I'd best assure her I'm still on this side of the sod, as they say. Unlike poor Hamm."

"Unlike poor Hamm," Stockburn said, raising his freshly filled glass in salute.

Vega stopped and looked at Sofia sitting at a table, huddled down in Stockburn's coat, soaked and shivering. In Spanish, he said (as well as Stockburn could translate it): "There's a fire in the stove back in Nettles' kitchen, Senorita. I lit it to heat water for surgery. You might as well take advantage of it and boil some water for a bath. You'll find a washtub back there, too."

Shivering, Sofia thanked the man in Spanish and then Vega glanced through the windows at the sky, lifted his coat collar, hunched down in his coat, and strode through the batwings and outside.

Stockburn stood behind the bar, leaning forward on it, his hat on the bar beside his drink. He slowly turned the glass in his hand, trying to ward off the sour mood he was in.

"We will never find him now." Sofia's voice sounded small and forlorn beneath the low roar of the storm.

She was staring out at the street, which had become a flooded arroyo pocked by the bullet-sized raindrops.

She turned to Stockburn, frowning, the lightning's reflections flashing in her eyes. "He will lose himself in Mexico. My Billy will never be avenged!"

Stockburn studied her grimly. He threw his whiskey back, set the glass on the bar, then swung around and walked through a curtained doorway behind the bar. He returned a few minutes later. He came around the front of the bar, grabbed his bottle and glass off of it, and walked to Sofia's table.

"I set water to heat for a bath. You'll feel better after you've soaked in hot suds for a while. I'm sure there's some soap back there somewhere. I hope you don't frighten at a rat or two." He gave a mirthless chuff and sipped his whiskey.

Sofia sat sobbing, staring into the storm. "It's his soul I'm worried about. My loved one's soul."

"Listen." Stockburn wrapped his hand around the girl's wrist, squeezed it. "I'm not going to give up until Red Miller is either in chains or dead." He raised his shot glass to Sofia and nodded sincerely. "That's bond, senorita."

Sofia placed her hand atop his. "That makes me feel better, Wolf. A little, anyway."

"I know what you mean." Stockburn splashed more whiskey into his glass and pulled his makings sack out of his pocket. "It's gonna be a long, lonely damn night."

Maybe for us but not for Charlie, though, he thought with a smile.

CHAPTER 18

Lightning slashed across the purple sky and thunder sounded like large boulders tumbling down a stony mountain ridge, making the ground tremble beneath Hoot Gibbons's horse's galloping hooves.

The rain slashed down at an angle from behind him. He gasped when the first wave hit him so hard it nearly knocked him off the horse. The storm felt like a large cold hand wrapping itself around him in a death grip.

Instantly, the out-of-work cow puncher was soaked. Rain sluiced off the middle crease in his battered Stetson to pour straight down over his saddle horn. Well, not *his* saddle horn. He'd found the saddled horse standing at the hitchrack when he'd finally surfaced from the shot-up Busted Flush Saloon in Tularosa.

He'd figured the horse must have belonged to the man with Red Miller whom the Tularosa town marshal had shot before he himself had been pinned to a wall with hot lead. Hoot had hoped that since Miller and his other two men who'd survived the saloon shoot-out now needed only three horses they'd have left Rowdy at the hitchrack and taken the dead man's horse instead.

Nope.

With deep disappointment, Hoot had stepped out onto the blood-washed boardwalk to find Rowdy gone and the steel-dust gelding standing there instead. He'd figured Miller's men had chosen Rowdy over the steel because Rowdy had been fresher and because one look at Rowdy would tell any man who knew anything about horse flesh that the coyote dun, with his clean lines, broad barrel, and long, finely turned legs, was the better horse.

Likely more loyal, too. Hoot had never known a horse more loyal than Rowdy nor easier to train. He'd worked hard to save up enough money to buy the horse from Mrs. Shockley when he'd left the Circle C Ranch near Bisbee in Arizona two years ago. He'd found that his money had been well spent, though he'd known that even before he had actually owned the horse, with a signed paper to prove it.

He'd broken and trained the dun, after all—after he and his buddy Steve Underwood had caught the horse with a passel of others that had been running wild in the Chiricahua Mountains, likely owning Spanish and Apache-bred bloodlines.

Thank you, Mister Miller! Have a good day now!

Another flush of deep shame rose through the cold wind slashing at Hoot.

As soaked as though he'd just climbed out of a lake, the wind and rain beating him, Hoot reined the steel-dust to a stop. He'd glimpsed an unnatural object sitting off in the brush to the right of the trail he'd been following down out of the Sierra Blanca. Now he studied the object through the billowing gray curtain of rain.

A cabin!

Hoping that he'd soon be out of the storm and sitting by a hot fire, he reined the steel off the trail and into the mesquites, greasewood, and sage brush, heading for the cabin that appeared all but consumed by the desert. As he approached, he saw that it was a low-slung adobe brick shack with a roof constructed of tightly set ocotillo stems arranged over straw.

"Hello the cabin!" he yelled above the storm's roar.

Hoot looked around, spying no signs of recent occupation. The windows were dark behind flour sack curtains, and no smoke rose from the chimney pipe poking up out of the cabin's slightly pitched roof. He looked past the well on his right and saw a stable that resembled a smaller version of the cabin, with an attached ocotillo corral flanking it.

Like the cabin, the stable was enshrouded by desert scrub.

Hoot booted the horse over to the stable, the horse picking its own way through the brush. Hoot leaped out of the saddle and had to give the stable door a few hard tugs before it finally scraped free of its frame.

Obviously, it hadn't been opened in a while. More evidence the place hadn't been occupied for a good stretch of time.

Hoot led the horse inside and unsaddled him, setting the saddle over a saddle tree covered in dust, cobwebs, and dead flies. He found some parched corn in a bin, and set a dented tobacco can with a couple handfuls of the corn on the floor strewn with musty hay and straw, in front of the horse.

He set a water bucket under the stable eaves to catch the runoff. The rain was coming down so hard that the bucket was full in nearly a minute.

Hoot gave the horse a cursory rubdown, then set the water in front of it, grabbed the saddlebags and bedroll that had come with the horse, stepped out, closed the door, and jogged through the rain to the cabin.

The cabin's door was even harder to open than the stable's door had been. Hoot nearly pulled it off its top leather hinge before it finally scraped open, the bottoms of the swollen vertical boards comprising it gouging the earthen floor.

Hoot stepped inside and looked around, the intermittent lightning flashes offering the only light. In those brief shimmers he saw a sheet-iron stove sitting along the back wall, roughly ten feet away from the door. A cot lay against the wall to the right; another one lay against the wall to the left. One was bare and had holes chewed through it, likely by rodents. On the other one a wool trade blanket lay neatly folded but also dusty.

There was no table or even a chair. A few shelves on the cabin's rear wall, flanking the stove, had a few airtight tins on them and a burlap sack of maybe coffee, flour, or sugar.

The only wall hangings were what looked like a bleached coyote head peering bleakly into the room from over the door and an old gun rig hanging from a spike over the cot on the room's right side. The leather of the rig was dry and cracked and also coated in dust, spiderwebs, and dead flies.

The pistol residing in the holster was an old, cumbersome Walker cap-and-ball revolver, its walnut grips held together with baling twine. Hoot doubted it had been fired in the past fifteen years.

In one of the lightning flashes, Hoot spied a hurricane lantern residing on one of the shelves. He dropped the saddlebags and bedroll, and walked over to the shelves, leaving the door open for the intermittent flashes of light.

A small jar of lucifer matches sat beside the lamp, which appeared to have a few inches of coal oil in it. Good.

He was so wet and cold that it took him nearly five minutes to get the lamp burning. When he did, he set it on a shelf near the stove then inspected the stove itself, hoping for a fire. His hopes were fulfilled by a crate of ancient-looking but dried wood—cottonwood, cedar, and mesquite—on the floor behind the stove. Tinder and kindling was mixed in with the wood, and a mouse or squirrel had made a nest in the box from the pinecone tinder woven with bird feathers.

In his current desperate state, Hoot saw the fire makings as all the comforts of home.

He set to work building a fire in the stove. When he had one nursed into a growing blaze, albeit a smoky one—there was probably a nest in the chimney—he shucked out of his wet clothes and hung them to dry from shelves flanking the stove.

He found a coffeepot in the dead killer's sack as well as a small pouch of pre-ground Arbuckles. He filled the pot with rainwater tumbling down from the cabin's overhang and set it to boil.

While the coffee cooked, he rummaged through both saddlebag pouches, happy to find a fletch of bacon and a cast-iron skillet. On one of the cabin's shelves, he found a big can of pinto beans. Soon, he sat wrapped in the old trade blanket in front of the snapping fire, drinking hot black coffee and eating beans and bacon straight out of the pan.

He stared dreamily into the flames.

This was the best he'd felt in hours. He was as happy as a clam, as calm as he'd ever felt in his life. He was on the trail of Red Miller. He had no illusions that the trail would be short or easy. It would likely be long and hard. Red Miller had several hours' lead, and the storm would cover his trail.

But a man like Miller and the killers riding with him cut a broad swath. Hell, everybody in the Southwest had heard or read—if they *could* read, that was—about Miller's depredations and downright massacres that usually followed the robberies he pulled. The man was addicted to killing.

A kill-crazy lunatic.

Hoot had read plenty of newspaper and magazine articles about Miller's bunch. He'd taught himself to read when, as a boy with a facial scar due to his cleft lip and palate, he'd spent a lot of time alone. The botched surgical correction of the problem made his lip twist up in the middle—prime fodder for his jeering peers.

That feeling of estrangement had followed him into adulthood though the scar was less noticeable than before, his face having been seasoned for the past twenty-four years of his life by the hot western sun and winds. He'd been born to a whore in Leadville in the Colorado Territory.

Clara Gibbons had died when he was only six years old, so after a stint in a Catholic orphanage, he'd drifted from one cow punching job to another, mostly on remote western ranches where the owner/operators could rarely afford to keep men on the payroll throughout the entire year, usually cutting them loose after the fall roundups.

So he'd had plenty of time to wander and to read.

He'd read about Miller, all right. Maybe that's why when he'd encountered the man so suddenly, the raw, actual image—and sour smell!—of so many horrifying tales and nightmares, his knees had turned to mud and he'd squirted down his leg.

He was going to redeem himself, sure enough.

He was going to avenge his lost honor and retrieve his horse. Maybe he'd even kill Miller in the bargain.

Yeah, maybe he'd even kill Miller, he thought, staring into the flames with a heavy-lidded smile.

If he could keep this courage he'd found. Newfound, it was.

Would it last? Or, when seeing Miller again, would he again piss himself like a sissy encountering a snake in the grass?

Beneath the still-raging storm, a horse's whinny penetrated the shack's adobe walls and resonated in Backtrail's ears. A man shouted in what sounded like Spanish.

Hoot lifted his head, pricking his ears, listening.

The sound of wet hoof thuds grew louder.

Riders heading toward the cabin, likely seeking shelter from the storm.

Backtrail's heart quickened. Who would be out on a night like this? Surely cow punchers like himself would have sought shelter by now.

Who would be out on a night like this except desperadoes?

Horses made wet sucking sounds in the mud of the yard. There came the clatter of bit chains and the squawk of tack. Several shadows passed beyond the cabin's two front windows.

"Hola la casa! ¿Alguien en casa?" a man shouted, his voice obscured by the horses' heavy, wet thuds, the rain on the roof, and the near-perpetual thunder.

Hello the house! Anybody home?

The man laughed as he and the others rode on past the cabin, heading no doubt for the stable. In a few minutes, they would pound on the door.

Hoot thought about that then rose from his position in front of the stove. A minute later, he was back sitting on the floor in front of the stove, naked beneath the blanket wrapped around his shoulders.

Beyond the door came the wet thumps of men walking toward the cabin. Spur chings were muffled by the mud and the continuing thunder. Men were talking quietly in Spanish. One might even say secretively. One laughed a guttural laugh and then a heavy pounding sounded on the door.

"¿Hay alguien aquí?" Is anyone here?

Hoot wasn't fluent in Spanish, but like most cowpunchers in the West, he'd worked with plenty of Mexicans and through them had acquired a cow pen knowledge of the language. At least enough to butcher it.

"Come on in and sit a spell, pards!" Hoot yelled in a jovial tone. *"Mi casa es tu casa!"*

CHAPTER 19

"*Mi casa es tu casa!*" echoed the stranger on the other side of the door.

He and the others—there seemed to be three or four in total—laughed. The door scraped open with a grunt from outside, and a big man stood in the doorway. He was short but nearly as wide as the door. The flashing lightning silhouetted his thick, bulging frame.

He stepped inside, moving heavily, swaggering, removing his low-crowned sombrero and swiping it across his thigh. "Whoo-ee, it's a wet night out there, amigo! Thanks for letting us in, brother! We saw your light from the trail."

"Not a problem, amigo," Hoot said, smiling up from his position by the fire. "There's enough warm in here to go around. I even have some beans and bacon . . . if you don't mind eatin' out of the pan. Me, I've had my fill." He raised the pan and the fork to show his visitors then set both on the stove and scuttled back from the stove, making room for the others.

"Gracias, amigo," said one of the other two men lumbering through the door, smelling like sage and wet leather and wool. The storm blew in from behind them, making the flames in the smoky stove dance.

All three were Mexicans somewhere in their thirties, probably. They wore deerskin ponchos coated with bear grease over wool serapes. Two wore cowhide leggings, handsomely tooled and adorned, while the other, the third man who'd entered, wore orange charro slacks with gold embroidering on the outsides of the legs.

Those slacks probably looked right snazzy a few years ago, but now, wet and mud-stained, the embroidery unraveling, and worn nearly through in the knees, they made a pitiable impression. The knife-scarred face of the man wearing them, framed by long, wet hair, made Hoot silently opine that he might have taken the slacks off a dead man. He had a wayward left eye. Both eyes—a strange hazel color given the darkness of his long, craggy face—looked mean and cruel despite the smile twisting his mustachioed mouth.

The biggest of the three hooked a thumb at the man in the orange slacks and said, "Halcón's been hungry for miles. That's all we've heard from him—how hungry he is. I tell you, you never fill this one up!"

He and the other man laughed while Halcón eyed the pan on the stove like a wildcat eyeing a jackrabbit resting with its eyes closed in the shade of a rock. The man's wayward eye appeared to be staring at the scarred tip of his long, raptorial nose.

The big man lifted his rain slicker over his head and dropped it on the floor by the door. He walked up to Hoot and extended his small, fat brown hand. "I am Francisco. This is Lope," he added, canting his head to a thin, bearded man with a shy air. He said nothing and did not look at

Hoot but only walked up to the stove and held his hands out to warm them.

Halcón grabbed the beans and bacon off the stove then backed up to the front wall and sat down, leaning back against it, raising his knees, and hungrily forking the food into his mouth, eating loudly and with his mouth open.

"You save some for me an' Lope, damn you!" Francisco warned the man.

Halcón did not look up at him but continued forking the beans and bacon into his mouth, grunting.

Francisco gave a frustrated growl then swaggered over to Halcón and ripped the pan from his hand with one hand, taking the fork with the other. Halcón glared up at him, his savage face darkening. He closed one gloved hand over the ivory grips of the long-barreled Remington revolver holstered on his right side, in a worn leather holster.

Holding the pan in one hand, the fork in the other, Francisco stared down at the savage Mex, grinning. "*¿De verdad?*" Really? He said in Spanish that Hoot roughly translated as: "You want to try it again, amigo? You know I can blast you out of your boots before you even get that iron clear of your holster."

Halcón held his dead-eyed glare on Francisco for another couple of seconds, the wandering eye slanting toward the outside of its socket, as though looking over the man's left shoulder. Then Halcón curled his right nostril and lowered his hand from his pistol.

"Wise decision," Francisco said, sneering down at his opponent.

He scooped beans and bacon into his mouth as he stepped up to the stove and then sat heavily down in front of it, on the far side of Lope from Hoot. Lope still stood before the stove but had turned to warm his backside.

As he ate, Francisco cast a sheepish grin at Hoot. "Forgive our bad behavior. You are such a gracious host and we reward you with such a scene. We have been together too long, I think. Lope and Halcón and myself. We tend to get on each other's nerves."

He scooped another bite of food into his mouth then handed the pan up to Lope, who took it as well as the spoon. Wiping his hands on his leggings, Francisco glanced at Hoot again and said, "What is your name, amigo? If the question is impertinent, then please forgive me. I mean no disrespect."

"Hoot."

Francisco arched a surprised, black brow at him. "Say it again."

"Hoot."

"Hoot?"

"Hoot."

Francisco chuckled. He glanced behind him at the blank-faced Halcón, who still looked a little miffed from the recent foofarah. Then he glanced up at Lope, who was scraping the leftover beans and bacon from the bottom of the skillet and shoving the grub into his mouth. "Hoot," Francisco repeated, chuckling some more. Turning to Hoot, he asked, "you mean like the hoot of an owl? Hoot-Hoot-Hoot."

"A hoot owl," said Lope, still eating but now smiling.

"Yep, just like that." Hoot had raised his knees and draped the blanket over them. He leaned forward, hugging his knees, and rocked back and forth on his naked behind, grinning.

"Why did your mother give you such a curious name?" Francisco asked.

"She didn't give it to me. The name she gave me was George. My mother was a whore, you see. In Leadville. Mountain town in the Colorado Territory."

"Si, I have been to this Leadville," Francisco said.

"Oh, well, then you know about it," Hoot said. "The way she told it, one of her jakes started callin' me Hoot every time he came to see her because she said back then I sort of hooted when I breathed. See this scar here on my lip? That was open at the time, so I couldn't breathe right. Later on, a doctor fixed it—if you can call this fixed. But that's another matter. Back to my point—the name sort of stuck till everybody around the whorehouse called me Hoot."

"Hoot," Francisco said, beetling his thick black brows again, as though he were having a hard time believing the story.

"Exactly," Hoot said. "Just like the owl."

Francisco slapped his thigh and shook his head. "What brings you out here, then, Hoot? All by yourself."

"I'm chasing a damn horse thief."

"You are?"

"Sure enough I am."

"Who is this horse thief?"

"A no-account by the name of Red Miller."

"Red Miller?" Yet again he'd given cause for Francisco to exclaim his shock.

"Heard of him, have ya?"

"Of course, I have. Who has not? You are going after Red Miller? All by yourself, Hoot?"

"Don't have no choice. You see, he took away my honor. Every good thing I ever felt about myself evaporated in the course of a few seconds, when I let that bastard take my horse."

Real tears came to Hoot's eyes, and he dabbed at them with a corner of the blanket. "I'm sorry," he said. "It's just that Rowdy meant everything to me. I mean, he *means* everything to me. I'm gonna get him back or die tryin'. I just let him go and even thanked the son of Satan who took him before I wet myself down my damn trouser leg!"

Francisco stared at Hoot, smiling inside his beard, chuckling deep in his throat, his heavy shoulders jerking inside his serape. "I cannot blame you for wetting down your leg if you encountered Red Miller. Can you, mi compadres?"

He looked back at Halcón and then up at Lope, as though searching for a reaction but getting none. Halcón just stared over his knees at the fire, hands entwined atop his knees. His lips were moving as though he were speaking to himself on another topic altogether.

Lope leaned forward to set the empty skillet on the stove and then turned around again to warm his backside. He kept shivering, as though he could not quite get the storm's chill out of his bones.

"I bet none of you fellas would have handed over your horse like that. Not even to Red Miller. And then wet yourself down your leg!"

"You never know," Francisco said, shrugging and spreading his arms. "A man honestly cannot predict his reactions to some things until he is actually confronted by *those very things*. Do you know what I mean, Hoot? You shouldn't judge yourself so harshly."

"Well, I have. But don't worry. I'm gonna change my opinion of myself real soon. You know why?"

Francisco hunched his shoulders, bunched his lips, widened his eyes, and jerked his head from side to side.

"Because I'm no longer afraid."

"Not even of Red Miller?"

"Not even of Red Miller. You wanna know why?"

"Sure."

Hoot stuck out his right hand, shaping a gun aimed at Francisco. "Miller had me dead to rights. He killed everybody in the saloon. I alone survived. Or so I thought. Then Miller bore down on me with his big, smokin' hogleg. He aimed right at my face and pulled the trigger."

He paused for effect.

Outside, the storm raged. The fire churned in the stove. He felt all eyes on him, even the weird stare of Halcón.

"Ping!" Hoot said, making all three of his guests jerk with starts—even Halcón. "The gun was empty."

"Lucky for you, Hoot!" intoned Francisco, laughing.

"I'll say!" Hoot smiled at the big, bearded man now leaning forward on one thick knee. "But you know what happened in those few seconds while I was waitin' for that bullet?"

"What?"

"I lost my fear."

"*¿Qué?*"

"It was gone, just like that." Hoot snapped his fingers up close to his ear. "Melted right out of my bones. When that hammer dropped, I didn't even blink. And when old Red left me alive, sitting there on the saloon floor behind the bar, I stayed that way. Fearless. And determined."

"Determined?" asked Francisco.

"*Determinado!*" Hoot said, lowering his voice as well

as his chin and punching his chest. "So *determinado,* in fact, that I got no intention of lettin' you boys stop me."

Hoot shot the befuddled Francisco an affable but knowing smile.

Francisco's right brow shot up into his leathery forehead again.

"I seen you on my backtrail before the storm blew in. You followed me out from Sandy Springs where I stopped to water my hoss. You mighta seen the bulge in my shirt pocket—the roll of greenbacks I was paid by the last rancher me an' my former and dearly departed partners worked for.

"We'd come to Tularosa to blow it all on whiskey an' women and likely would have—at least half of it, anyways, me bein' the miserly sort—if Red Miller hadn't come to town."

Hoot narrowed one eye and canted his head to the side. "Sure, you seen that bulge in my pocket and you seen my hoss and you decided to follow me and kill and rob me, steal my money an' my hoss. Because that's what you boys do—now, don't you? Be honest!"

Francisco's broad face shaped a genuinely startled expression, his mustached and bearded mouth forming a near-perfect *O*. He glanced at the other two men.

Lope had turned to stare down at Hoot, his lips shaping a grim smile. Behind him, Halcón had turned his attention to Hoot, as well, but his face was as cold and dead as ever, that wandering eye quivering in place down near the bottom of the socket.

Francisco chuckled then looked at something on the wall behind Hoot. "That your gun, Backtrail?"

"Which one?"

"That one there." Hoot followed Francisco's pointing finger to the big Colt snugged down in the holster hanging from a nail on the wall four feet behind Hoot.

"What about it?" Hoot asked.

"That's a big gun. And *old*. A Walker, is it not?"

"Old cap-'n'-ball horse pistol. That is correct."

"A big gun. A heavy *pistolo*."

"Maybe," Hoot allowed. "For some."

"Do you think you could reach that heavy pistolo before I shot you, Hoot?" Francisco asked, smiling devilishly, his thick arms draped over his thick knees bent before him.

"I reckon, Francisco, there's only one way to find out." Again, Hoot smiled.

Francisco smiled back at him.

Hoot kept his smiling eyes on Francisco but he could feel Lope and Halcón burning brands into him.

He waited. Oh Lord, was he calm!

He'd never known such calm. No fear at all. Part of him basked in the fire's warmth while the other part of him waited for Francisco to make his play. Hoot wasn't sure but he thought his heart was pounding away.

He stared into Francisco's eyes.

As he did, he saw something in those large, watery brown eyes—back behind the smile. What was it?

A touch of apprehension?

Sure enough. Hoot's friendly confidence was nettling Francisco if even a little.

Francisco knew there was no way Hoot, wrapped in his blanket here on the floor by the fire, could reach four feet behind him for the big Walker Colt before Francisco could empty his entire cylinder into him.

Still, there was the faint stain of doubt in Francisco's eyes.

That doubt frustrated him.

Francisco's eyes blazed in sudden anger. He hardened his jaws and gritted his teeth. His right hand moved in a blur of sudden movement to the Colt holstered on his right thigh.

Hoot's left hand pulled the blanket aside as he raised his right hand wrapped around his own Schofield .44, which he'd stowed on the floor in the general vicinity of his unmentionables. He thrust the .44 straight out at Francisco and squeezed the trigger just as Francisco was bringing up his own long-barreled Colt in his gloved hand, bellowing incoherently.

The Schofield blasted a hole through Francisco's forehead.

Hoot heaved himself to his feet, holding the blanket with his left hand, his Schofield in his right hand, and twisted around to face Lope, who howled as the Schofield spoke again, punching a .44-caliber bullet into his guts.

Halcón pushed off the wall behind him, gaining his feet and raising his own revolver. He triggered the piece into his own right foot as Hoot calmly punched the man's ticket with two bullets to Halcón's chest, over his heart.

Halcón screamed and danced along the wall to the door, triggering yet another loud shot into the floor. He bulled the door open with his body, stumbled out into the storm, dropped to his knees, and howled like a gutshot coyote.

Hoot followed the man to the door and drilled one more round into the back of his head. Halcón fell face forward in the mud and kicked his legs as he died.

Hoot turned back to the room. Francisco lay before him, staring up at him, eyes crossed in death. Blood from the hole in the big man's forehead formed a large, shiny bead where the bullet had gone in.

Lope lay to Hoot's left, belly down on the floor near where Halcón had been sitting. Lope was making a soft gurgling sound and quivering.

Hoot shot him again, just to make sure he was dead.

From the stable came a muffled whinny of incredulity from one of the horses.

Hoot dragged both dead men out into the yard where they lay in the rain and mud near Halcón.

Hoot returned to the cabin, wrapped himself in his blanket again, and resumed his position in front of the fire.

He held up his right hand, smiled.

Not a single shake.

"You know," he said, pulling the coffeepot down off the stove and filling a cup with the steaming brew, "I almost feel sorry for Red Miller."

CHAPTER 20

Around the same time but twelve miles south, in Tularosa, Sofia stepped out of the kitchen behind the bar in the San Francisco Peak Saloon carrying two steaming food platters.

"That is a madre of a storm," she said, glancing out over the batwings and through the windows that looked onto the main street that churned like a flooded arroyo.

Stockburn sat back in his chair near a potbelly stove in which he'd lit a fire and blew smoke rings into the air before him. He glanced toward the lightning flashing in the rain-streaked windows. "It is at that."

He frowned at Sofia approaching the table. Her hair was still wet from her bath, which, judging by how long she'd been gone, she must have soaked in for well over an hour.

All she wore was a towel.

"What you got there, honey?" Stockburn asked, glancing at the plates.

"Steak and beans. I found a quarter side of beef in a

keeper shed off the rear of the kitchen, and beans soaking in a crock. I don't know about you, but I'm hungry."

"Well, that's a good sign."

Sofia set one plate on the table in front of Wolf. She set the other on the table three feet to his right. "What is?" she asked, dropping two wood-handled, three-tined forks and two serrated knives onto the table, as well.

"That your appetite's back. Maybe your grief is lifting."

Sofia leaned forward, placing both hands on the table and casting Wolf a sharp, defiant look. "It will never lift until that devil has been sent to hell where he came from!"

The force of the girl's retort pushed the railroad detective farther back in his chair. "All right, honey—I didn't mean . . ."

"It is not lifting. I miss Billy more than I thought I could ever miss anything. I just know that for me to continue riding after his killer, I need to fortify myself with food. And so do you." She shoved Wolf's whiskey bottle aside then slid his plate closer to him. "Don't drink so much. Eat!"

"All right," Wolf said, smiling at the fiery young Mexican. He looked at the thick steak, nicely fat-marbled and drowning in its own bloody juices. The steam rising from it and the beans seasoned with chili peppers made him swoon like a virgin bride. "I can do that, I reckon. I didn't realize how hungry I was."

He dropped his quirley, mashed it out with his boot toe, grabbed his fork and knife, and got down to business. He took the first bite of steak, and the rich, beefy flavor nearly knocked him out of his chair. His head ached dully now, but the arm still grieved him beneath the alcohol glow he was tending. The steak helped.

"Best medicine for an aching man," Stockburn said, chewing.

He was glad to see Sofia going to work on her own steak and beans with nearly as much relish as he was working on his own.

"Si," she said, also chewing. "I will change that bandage for you later."

"No need. The arm's fine."

"It won't be fine unless you keep it clean, the bandage fresh." Sofia narrowed her pretty brown eyes at him. "You should have learned by now that there is no use in arguing with this fiery chili pepper!"

She reached over and gently poked him with her fork.

Stockburn laughed and forked another bite of meat into his mouth. As he chewed, he watched a figure, blurred by the rain, walk along the boardwalk just outside the window. The figure came on down the boardwalk then turned through the batwings.

Lonesome Charlie stood soaked to the gills and dripping wet in front of the doors, rain sluicing off the brim of his hat. The soaked owl feather was pasted to the brim. He just stood there, shivering, staring across the room and into the deep shadows on the room's far side.

"Charlie!" Wolf said, frowning with concern. "You're wetter'n a beaver in a springtime flood!"

Charlie turned his head toward Wolf and Sofia and blinked. He cradled a bottle in the crook of his right arm. "So I am. Don't worry—I'm so drunk I can't feel it."

Stockburn glanced at Sofia, then slid his chair back and rose. While he walked over to stand by Charlie, Sofia rose from her own chair and walked over to the stove.

She paused to glance over her bare shoulder at Charlie then crouched to add more wood to the stove.

"Charlie," Wolf said, giving the soaked sleeve of the old lawman's shirt a gentle tug, "come on over here by the fire an' sit down. You're gonna freeze to death."

"Maybe I will do just that," Charlie said, owning the air of a man walking in his sleep. "Maybe I will . . ."

"You'd better."

Stockburn took the man by his arm and led him over to the table. He kicked out a chair near his own and shoved the old man into it. He took the bottle out of the man's arm and looked at it. Only about an inch of murky amber liquid remained on the bottom.

"I don't say this lightly, because I don't like to hear it myself, Charlie, but you drink too much. Especially for a man in your condition."

When Sofia had the stove stoked to nearly glowing, she strode barefoot into the kitchen. She returned a minute later with a steaming plate of vittles in one hand and a heavy blanket draped over her other arm. She set the steak and beans in front of Charlie, along with a fork and a knife.

Lonesome Charlie watched her with a vaguely curious expression.

Sofia walked around behind the old man and wrapped the blanket around his shoulders. Through the blankets, she ran her hands up and down his arms briskly as though to work the blood into them.

"Silly old man," she hissed in his ear. "Wandering around out in the rain like a *pendejo*! What happened— did you cause a ruckus over at the whorehouse and they kicked you out?"

"Nah, hell." Charlie absently ran a wet hand across his sopping beard, tugging on it. "I didn't raise no ruckus. Hell, I couldn't raise a damn thing."

He glanced at Stockburn standing over him.

"Not a damn thing," he added, a sheen of emotion glazing his eyes.

Wolf and Sofia shared a dubious glance, then Sofia sat back down in her chair and continued eating.

Stockburn squeezed Charlie's shoulder. "Happens to all of us now an' then."

"Damn humiliating. I had me the purtiest two girls in the place and . . . nothin'. They felt so damn sorry for me that I had to leave. If they hadn't made such a big to-do, I'd likely still be over there, sleepin' off my drunk, but I just couldn't take it. My chest got all tight, an' my old ticker was kickin' and pitchin' in my chest till I couldn't breathe. That old crab grabbed ahold, an' . . . I had to get out of there. I took my bottle and I hightailed it!"

"Into the rain," Sofia said, shaking her head as she continued eating her beef and beans. "An old man with a weak heart!"

Charlie turned to the girl, his pale, craggy cheeks behind his soaked beard turning red with anger. "You don't know what it's like. You'll never know what it's like, you harpie bean-eater!"

"No, I'll never know what it's like!" Sofia hissed back at him, narrowing her eyes. "I'll never know what it's like to walk around with so much pride that it's like carrying an anvil on my shoulders, making me weak and small and *stupid*!"

Charlie's face turned redder, eyes blazing. He grabbed the knife Sofia had given him by its handle and, glaring at the girl, pounded the end of his fist holding the knife down several times against the table. He considered her for a long time.

"No," he said finally, pounding his fist holding the knife on the table again, keeping time with a clock behind the bar. "You'll never know what it's like!"

"Eat your food, Charlie," Wolf said. "You'll feel better."

Charlie threw the knife down on the table. It bounced off the table and landed on the floor. "Chili Pepper's right. I'm a damn fool!"

Charlie placed a hand over his face and sobbed. "I couldn't even honor a good friend's last wish!"

"It's all right, Charlie," Wolf said gently. He sat with a hip hiked on the table to Charlie's left, frowning concernedly down at the old man. "You gave it a shot. You tried to honor ol' Hamm's last wish."

"Ah, hell—don't you see?" Charlie's face was in the full, red flower of emotional agony, tears streaming from his red-rimmed eyes. "I'm a used-up old man who has no damn business goin' after Red Miller! I'm *done*!"

With that, he reached down, plucked the badge from his shirt, whipped his arm back and threw the badge with a savage grunt across the room. It slammed against the front of the bar and clattered onto the floor where it spun for several seconds before coming to rest, pin-side down.

The moon-and-star faced upward as though in grinning mockery of the man who'd once donned it.

Sofia stared across the room at the badge on the floor. She chewed her last bite of food then turned toward Charlie. Her brown eyes were large and round. She hardened her jaws and said, "Pick it up."

Charlie scowled at her. "What?"

"Pick it up." Sofia pointed her fork at him. "Get up, go over there, and pick up your badge."

Charlie stared at her, the corner of one incredulous eye twitching.

"Pick it up," Sofia said again, this time with the encouragement of a firm mother who brooked no foolishness. "Go!"

"What?" Charlie looked at Stockburn. "I don't . . ."

Wolf glanced from Charlie to Sofia then back at Charlie again. He smiled.

Charlie turned back to Sofia. "You can't . . . you can't make me . . ."

Sofia rose from her chair and extended her hand to the old man. *"Venga."* Come.

Charlie slid his uncertain eyes toward Stockburn, then returned them to the girl standing before him, extending her hand to him. She snapped her fingers impatiently.

Slowly, Charlie extended his hand to her. She wrapped her young, firm hand around his old, wrinkled one and squeezed.

Charlie winced as he slowly rose from his chair, his old knees popping like twigs under a heavy foot. Sofia led him around the table and over to his badge.

She pointed at it. "Pick it up and pin it back on your shirt."

Charlie looked at her again. He looked down at the badge. His face wore a hangdog, sheepish expression. For several seconds, he just rubbed his hands on his pants as he stared down at the badge.

Slowly, he bent over and with a grunt he scooped the old, tarnished moon-and-star up off the floor. He looked at it in the palm of his hand, as though he were seeing it for the first time, maybe back when it had first been awarded to him two decades ago.

He brushed his thumb across the moon-and-star. He buffed the badge on his shirt and then he pulled the wet garment out away from his chest and pinned the badge to it. He stared down at it there on his shirt for a full minute, then glanced over his shoulder at Stockburn.

Charlie smiled faintly, a little curiously.

He turned to Sofia who stood staring at him with motherly advertence, both brows arched.

Sofia took his hand again. "Come. What you need is a hot bath. And then I am going to heat your food up *one more time*, and only *one more time*. And you are going to eat it, and then I am going to put you to bed upstairs, and you are going to get a good, long night's sleep so you are fresh to strike out on those killers' trail first thing in the morning . . ."

She glanced beyond Charlie at Stockburn. "With Wolf and me. *Compadres*."

"*Compadres?*" Charlie said.

"*Si. Compadres.*"

"I don't got many of them left," Charlie wheezed.

Sofia squeezed his hand, pulled. "Come."

"A bath, huh?" Charlie said, looking down at himself.

"How long has it been since you've had one?" Sofia asked him.

"Hell," Charlie said, pondering. "I . . . I don't recollect . . ."

"Come. Time for a bath." Sofia turned toward the bar and began pulling the old lawman toward the curtained doorway flanking the bar.

Lonesome Charlie stumbled along behind her, glancing

over his shoulder and grumbling, "I'll be damned if she ain't one chili-chompin' holy terror!"

Stockburn smiled and lifted his shot glass in salute to the man.

Charlie followed Sofia through the curtained doorway, and then they were gone.

Stockburn sat back down in his chair and returned his attention to his plate. He took up his fork and knife again and shook his head.

"Go with God, Charlie," he said, cutting the last bite of meat from the bone, chuckling. "Go with God . . ."

CHAPTER 21

"I could get used to this kind of treatment," Stockburn said the next morning. "I purely could."

Sofia smiled, cheeks dimpling, as she set a plate of steak, eggs, and fried potatoes on the table before him. The food's succulent aromas mixed with the smell of the coffee she'd poured for him, and again he nearly tumbled out of his chair.

"What is it about your cooking that tastes so much better than anything else I've ever eaten before in my life?"

Wolf was seated in the chair in which he'd been sitting last night until, after dark as well as after the storm had finally cleared out, he'd drifted upstairs to bed. He assumed the rooms upstairs had once been whores' cribs, though none appeared to have been used recently.

His bed had been comfortable, and, despite the rat still gnawing on his arm, he'd slept uncommonly well. It probably had something to do with the cool, humid night air pushing through his open window and filling his room with the smell of mesquite and piñon pine from the town's fireplaces. Rain had continued to drip from the eaves for a long time after the storm, also lulling him into a deep, dreamless slumber.

"Maybe you are just extra hungry," Sofia said, shoveling a few more potatoes onto his plate. "Being on the trail and all . . ."

Stockburn reached out and grabbed her hand in both his own, gazing up at her with mock beseeching. "Sofia, my dear, I don't suppose, after a reasonable grieving period, you'd do the honor of hitching your star to this old fool's wagon, would you?"

Sofia blushed and was about to respond when a crow-like cackle sounded and Charlie's voice said, "Nope, nope, nope. I won't allow that to happen. I do believe the Spanish princess is gonna be donning this old man's ring."

They both turned to see Lonesome Charlie descending the stairs at the back of the room, clad in only a striped blanket. His thinning, red-brown hair and his shaggy beard were badly mussed, his eyes half-closed as though he were still fending off the sandman.

"Are you forgetting I'm a lowly chili-chomper, Charlie?" Sofia asked pointedly, turning toward him with the pan of potatoes in one hand, a spatula in the other hand.

"I reckon, given the circumstances, I'd be willing to risk putting those concerns aside. Hell, it'd be worth having a stiletto slipped between my ribs or even having my throat cut to have you wash my back the way you done last night *just one more time*." He tipped his head back and howled. "I'll be damned if that weren't heaven!"

"You washed that old man's back for him?" Stockburn asked Sofia, incredulous. "All you did for me was rewrap my arm!"

As Charlie ambled toward the table from the stairs, yawning and scrubbing a gnarled paw through his hair, Sofia said, "He was too stiff and sore to do it himself and

I doubt that leathery old back of his had a good scrubbing in years."

"That makes me jealous enough to shoot him," Stockburn said with mock anger.

"Wait till after I dress." Charlie walked over to where Sofia had draped his clothes over chairs to dry near the potbelly stove, which Sofia had lit again this morning to edge the morning chill from the room as well as to finish drying Charlie's clothes. "Our girl might have shown me the waywardness of my pride but I still got enough left to prefer getting shot with my boots on!"

He cackled out an old man's laugh.

"I've filled your plate, Charlie," Sofia said. "Eat while it's hot."

"Damn, she's bossy," Charlie said to Stockburn. "On second thought, you go ahead an' marry her. Damn, what a harpy!" He put his back to Stockburn and Sofia and glanced over his shoulder, narrowing one commanding eye. "I'm about to drop this blanket and get dressed over here, and I'd appreciate a little privacy."

"Don't worry," Stockburn said, chuckling as he hunkered over his breakfast. "I think we can both resist the temptation."

"I saw enough last night while I was scrubbing his back," Sofia said, heading for the kitchen. She cast Wolf a look of mock revulsion over her shoulder, jerking her shoulders as though shivering.

"Nasty damn chili-chomper," Charlie muttered as he hopped around on his bare feet near the stove, dressing.

* * *

Two days later and a hundred miles southwest, they crossed the border into Mexico.

At least, Stockburn thought they'd probably crossed the border though it was hard to tell because the demarcation was not marked. According to a geological survey map he carried in his saddlebags, they'd crossed into Mexico when they'd crossed an arroyo a mile north of where they were riding now in a devil's playground of sharp-sided dykes, rolling hills studded with rock, sand, a variety of cactus, the occasional rattlesnake and shy coyote, and not much else.

Except sun and heat. Plenty of both.

They knew they were on Red Miller's trail because, as had always been said of the man, he rarely left a cold one. Even after a storm the size of which Stockburn and his two trail partners had endured two nights ago. They'd picked up the man's trail when a couple of miners heading north to look for work in the mountains told Stockburn, Lonesome Charlie, and Sofia that they'd stumbled upon a grisly scene the day before.

They'd ridden onto the compound of a small cattle operation, merely wanting water and a little grain for their horses. They'd found more than they'd bargained for when they'd found five people dead. There'd been a middle-aged man and a middle-aged woman, two boys likely in their teens and early twenties, and a girl. They'd found the girl dead in the barn, likely raped as the miners had found her naked from the waist down, and her blouse torn open.

The miners had found the middle-aged man and the two boys lying dead in the yard outside the barn, two shot-guns and an old Winchester rifle lying near their bodies. The woman had been lying dead on the porch. The miners had figured that whomever had killed the family had likely been holed up the previous night in the barn.

There'd been chickens in a side-shed off the barn; the girl had likely gone into the barn the next morning to gather eggs for breakfast.

It had looked as though the men who'd holed up in the barn had jumped the girl and savaged her. Maybe she'd screamed or maybe her father and brothers had sensed trouble when she'd been gone too long. Whatever had alerted them, they'd apparently tried to intervene and ended up getting turned toe down for their trouble.

"The killers must have had plenty of ammunition," one of the miners remarked, shaking his head darkly. "Because they sure didn't spare any on any o' them poor people."

The woman on the porch had probably run into the yard when she'd heard the shooting, and had staggered back onto the porch after she'd taken several bullets herself.

When the miners had ridden on, heading north, Stockburn and Lonesome Charlie had shared a knowing look and said at the same time, "Miller."

The miners had given them directions to the ranch. They'd continued south from the ranch, now following Miller's well-marked trail. They'd followed that trail around the east side of the White Sands country then south of Las Cruces and Mesilla to the border.

Miller was apparently avoiding settlements of any size, knowing the lawmen they'd likely find in them would have been alerted by telegraph about what had happened in the northern mountains as well as warned to be on the lookout for the notorious killers.

"You know we're bein' followed, right?" Charlie said

now as they rode up a gradual incline toward a series of dead volcanoes in the hazy southern distance.

Stockburn glanced at him sharply, skeptically. "What?" He peered over his left shoulder, seeing nothing.

"No, don't look, for cryin' in Grant's whiskey!" Charlie scolded him. "I don't want 'em to know we're onto 'em. Or . . . at least, that *I'm* onto 'em! I figured that you and your younger eyes and ears already knew."

Wolf glanced at Sofia, who cast her own quick, furtive glance behind her then turned to Wolf again. Scowling, she shrugged a shoulder skeptically.

Stockburn turned back to Charlie riding on his left. "I haven't spotted anybody. I've been checking, too. I always check regular. This close to Mexico . . . or in Mexico, whatever the case may be . . . I check even *more* regular. And even when I don't spot any sign, I usually get a soft humming in my ears. That's what usually tells me I'm being shadowed. I don't hear anything, Charlie."

"They're back there, I tell you," Charlie said with stone-cold certainty, keeping his eyes on the trail ahead. "One, maybe two riders."

"How do you know?"

"I spied a sun flash a couple hours ago when we stopped for water at that spring. Likely a reflection off a bit, mebbe a spur. Besides that, my big toe aches."

"Your big toe aches from arthritis," Sofia said, riding on the other side of Wolf from Charlie.

"Now, don't you start in with your chili pepper sass, chiquita." Charlie narrowed his eyes at her. "I ain't too old to take you over my knee."

Sofia gave a caustic chuff.

"My big toe aches when I got someone on my back-trail." Charlie looked pointedly at Stockburn. "That toe don't lie."

Stockburn cast another quick glance over his shoulder. He saw nothing. There wasn't much but open country behind them for several miles. If someone were behind them, they had to be crawling through the cactus.

Stockburn doubted anyone was shadowing them. Lonesome Charlie had grown feeble, that's all, tragic as it was. But there was no point in getting Charlie's dander up. Even if there wasn't anyone on their backtrail, there was no harm in assuming there was.

"All right, Charlie," Wolf said, keeping his horse moving. "Good to know."

"Me, I'm wonderin' if it might be Miller."

Wolf frowned. "You think he might've circled around behind us?"

"A man like Miller's savvy. He must know by now he's bein' trailed."

"He probably has a big toe as sensitive as Charlie's," Sofia put in with a sarcastic sneer.

"He just might!" Charlie told her, jutting his chin at her. "And his nose probably hurts like hell, since Wolf put a bullet through it. I'm thinkin' he might know Stockburn's on his trail, the man who shot his nose off, and he's itchin' for a little revenge." He grinned at Wolf. "Miller-style!"

Charlie laughed and slapped his thigh.

"Miller style," Sofia muttered.

"As low-down mean an' nasty as a man can get," Stockburn said. "Only lower down an' even meaner, given it's Miller we're talkin about."

"Of course," Sofia said grimly, coldly, staring straight ahead, likely thinking of her dead husband again. "Since it's Miller we're talking about."

Roughly twenty-five miles south of Stockburn, in Old Mexico, Red Miller and the two surviving members of his gang reined their horses to a stop on the outskirts of the little high-desert town of Pequeño Río Azul.

Miller stared curiously down at a little man sitting back against the weathered wooden sign that bore the name of the town in faded red letters. The man was sound asleep, chin dipped toward his chest, softly snoring.

He was an old man with a gray beard and curly gray hair hanging down from his unraveling straw sombrero, the high crown of which was adorned with red, black, and green galloping horses. The old man sat with his arms crossed on his chest, a wine demijohn resting against his right thigh.

His legs, clad in white burlap trousers that time and wear had turned to rags, were extended straight out before him, crossed at the ankles. On his right foot was a rope-soled sandal. The other foot, black with ground-in dirt, the nails like yellow seashells, was bare. Miller saw the other sandal lying off in the cactus and rocks several feet away.

The wind was blowing, making the adobe-colored dust swirl, threatening to blow the old drunk's hat off his head.

About six feet to the left of the old man, a Mojave green rattler was poking its head out from the shelter of a large, mushroom-shaped rock. The forked, black tongue extended out of the diamond-shaped head with its tiny, flat, copper eyes, to test the windy air.

Slowly, the snake extended its head toward the slumbering old man, gradually uncoiling its long, scaled body that was as thick as Miller's forearm.

Miller looked at his trail partners, Harris and Brennan. Grinning, he placed his finger to his lips, and winked.

He returned his attention and well as his devious grin to the snake moving very slowly toward the slumbering old drunk.

CHAPTER 22

The snake moved closer and closer to the sleeping drunk's side.

It seemed to be headed for a patch of tender pale flesh exposed by a tear in the old man's cotton tunic, just up from his hip. The swirling wind and dust must have kept it from sensing Miller and his pards and their mounts.

When the serpent's head was ten inches from the sleeping man's flesh, Miller whipped out his Colt and fired. Even with the rushing wind, the blast was loud.

The old man screamed and, waving his hands in front of his face, sat upright so quickly that his sombrero fell off his head to hang from the neck thong down his back. His mouth and eyes were wide with terror, the loud report likely echoing around inside his head.

"Easy there, old-timer," Miller said in Spanish. "¡Relajarse! ¡Relajarse!" Relax.

Miller wagged his smoking gun at the snake that now lay in two writhing, bloody pieces beside the old man's left hip. The old man looked at the snake. He screamed again and jerked away from it, kicking up sand and gravel, scuttling backward on his butt, eyes still round with shock and terror.

The demijohn fell over on its side; blood-red wine ran out on the red caliche. Not so terrified that he was willing to let good wine go to waste, the old man quickly plucked the basketed bottle up off the ground and held it close against his chest, as though to protect it as well as himself from further peril.

He gazed skeptically at the three obviously hard-bit *norteamericanos* sitting their horses before him.

Miller chuckled. He holstered his hogleg then leaned forward against his saddle horn, smiling behind his dusty spectacles. "You should pick your beds more carefully," he said. "Seems that hollow under that rock is . . . or was . . . home to a most unfriendly serpent—one that didn't particularly like sharing its territory with a drunk old wino."

The old man looked distastefully at the snake once more. Both ragged pieces of the rattler were still writhing but not as violently as before. The old man returned his drink-bleary eyes to Miller, skeptical lines still etched across his leathery forehead.

"Maybe you owe me a favor," Miller said, nudging his glasses high on his nose.

"Favor?"

"Si, si. Favor. In return for saving your life."

The old man canted his head a little to one side and narrowed one watery brown eye.

"Rest assured it's a very easy favor," Miller said. "All you have to do is tell me if Captain Azcona is here in Pequeño Río Azul?"

"Azcona?" The old man's eyes bugged again. He crossed himself. "Si." He didn't seem too happy with the fact.

"Where will I find him?"

The old man rolled his head, giving a fateful sigh. "Oh, Senor . . . no one goes looking for Captain Azcona. He usually goes looking for *you*. Everyone knows that. Even the *norteamericanos* who venture this far south in Chihuahua."

Again, the old man crossed himself then pressed two dirty fingers to his lips, muttering a short prayer. He glanced at Miller again and said, "If you must know"— he glanced around to make sure no one else was near, then said just loudly enough for Miller to hear—"he is at *La Cantina del Pájaro Amarillo.*" He jerked his head to indicate the greater village behind him.

A gun blasted from the direction of the village's heart. The blast, probably a pistol shot, echoed flatly, dwindling quickly.

The old man gasped. "That is probably him now, that devil. He is holding, uh . . . court." Again, the old man crossed himself.

Miller turned to Flipper Harris. "Court, huh?"

Harris smiled. Miller smiled, too.

He dug a coin out of his pocket and flipped it to the old man. The old man grunted as he thrust a hand up to catch the coin but missed. The peso struck him in the forehead and fell to the ground.

The old man winced and rubbed his head.

"That's for a fresh bottle, old one," Miller said, reining his horse back onto the trail. "When you drink it, best make sure there' no snakes around."

He booted his cream on into the village proper, Harris

and Brennan following, Harris on his stolen coyote dun.
Cracked adobe shops and houses lined both sides of the
village's main street. The street was relatively deserted.
The only movement was the dust the wind was kicking up
and splashing against the ancient buildings.

As Miller and the other men rode, another pistol crack
sounded, barely audible beneath the wind. On the heels of
the shot, a man screamed shrilly. His scream was followed
by that of a woman.

A dog came running toward Miller and his partners
from directly ahead, its tail down, ears laid flat against its
head. It swerved to avoid a windblown tumbleweed, then,
seeing the three men riding toward it, swerved sharply to
the right and ran down a gap between two squalid-looking
houses.

Miller and his men followed a gradual curve in the
street. As they did, a long, low adobe building with a brush
ramada running along the front came into view on the
street's left side. The long building sat alone on a broad
lot with a stable, corral, and a privy flanking it. The blowing dust obscured it and the area around it but as Miller
and the other two outlaws drew closer, Miller saw a woman
kneeling beside a lumpy figure lying in the dirt out front
of the place.

"Enrique!" she screamed, sobbing, holding her head
down close to that of the man lying before her. "Enrique!
Oh, Enrique, don't die on me, you fool!" she screamed still
louder in Spanish.

The man did not move.

Miller and the other two men checked their horses
down, casting their gazes between the woman and the
man in the street and the building to the left. Several

horses were tied to the two hitchracks beneath the ramada, their heads down, the wind blowing their tails up under their bellies.

A weathered gray sign hung beneath the gallery's roof, its wind-jostled chains creaking in the wind. Into the wood the words *La Cantina del Pájaro Amarillo* had been burned.

The Yellow Bird Cantina.

To each end of the sign a happy-looking yellow bird with a red beak had been painted. The words and birds must have been given a fresh coat of yellow paint recently, because they fairly glowed in contrast to the weathered gray of the sign they were set against as well as the shabbiness of the ancient adobe set back behind the ramada.

Still crouched over the man lying apparently dead in the street, the woman shot an enraged, tearful look at the cantina behind her and screamed, *"Devil! You dirty devil— I hope you burn in hell for all eternity!"*

Brennan turned to Miller and said with a knowing smile, "Yep—he's holding court, all right."

Miller quirked his own grin. He reached into his coat for the flat blue bottle Dr. Teagarden had given him and sipped. He returned the precious elixir to his pocket then nudged his horse on up to the left hitchrack.

The other two outlaws followed suit. The woman sobbed over the dead man, the wind either drowning her cries or picking them up and throwing them around the street.

Miller and his men swung down from their saddles, tied their horses, then mounted the ramada. Miller pushed through the batwings. The other two followed him inside and flanked him as he stopped a few feet inside the door, and peered into the room before him.

A bar ran along the back wall.

Between the bar and the batwings, a couple dozen villagers of all ages, most in peasants' garb, sat in rickety chairs arranged in neat rows. They all faced a man in the dove-gray uniform of a rurale captain sitting at a table in front of the bar, facing the onlookers.

Captain Azcona was flanked by four rurale privates or corporals standing ramrod straight and holding old-model Springfield rifles at port arms across their chests. Palm leaf sombreros adorned with the silver insignia of the Mexican Rural Police Force partially shaded their faces.

Azcona was a tall, thin, hawk-faced man with a jagged scar running down his right cheek, over his jaw, and down his leathery neck. He was in his early forties, but his coal-black hair and mustache did not show a trace of gray. The captain's comportment was far less soldierly than that of the men flanking him. He slouched back in his chair, his sombrero on the table in front of him.

A young, half-naked senorita with fear-bright eyes straddled his left knee.

Azcona shook that knee absently, causing the girl to shake, as well, as she stared into a corner of the room at nothing. The captain held a long-barreled Smith & Wesson Model 3 revolver in his right hand. His right elbow was casually propped on an arm of the Windsor chair he was sitting in.

The captain turned the Smithy this way and that, fiddling with it, occasionally aiming it at something around the room with a bored air as he appeared to half-listen to the list of transgressions of the accused man standing to his left, also facing the room of onlookers. Another rurale private, plump and baby-faced and with a coal smudge of

a mustache on his thick-lipped mouth, stood behind the
accused man, aiming a rifle at the back of his neck.

The prisoner's hands were cuffed behind his back. The
rurale behind him was half his size.

Clad in peon's soiled pajamas, the accused man was
short and fat and unshaven, and he stood with his heavy
gut hanging down over his dyed hemp sash, the pale,
tonguelike bottom of his belly peeking out from the
bottom of his smock. His thick, square head was thrown
back as he stared fearfully up at the ceiling, rolling beads
of sweat forming runnels through the grime on his face.

Before him, a woman sat with two small girls, all three
crying into their hands, the woman looking up and quietly
urging the captain for leniency. .

The local *policia* stood before the prisoner, reading
from the thin sheath of papers in his hands.

More prisoners were seated in a long line along the wall
to Miller's right—to Azcona's left. They sat tensely, sweating in the Mexican heat, with their hands cuffed uncom-
fortably behind their backs. An armed rurale sergeant sat
to each end of the eight prisoners awaiting sentencing by
Azcona, the head of the local rurale platoon that acted as
a roving band of judges, juries, and executioners, though
Miller knew they were much more than that.

Especially under Captain Nestor Azcona's command,
the rurale platoon were common banditos as well as paid
assassins, stock thieves, kidnappers, and rapists. Azcona
and his band of uniformed desperadoes were well known
in northern Mexico, sanctioned by the current corrupt
government who'd come to power via a recent coup and
who roamed far and wide across Sonora and Chihuahua,

enriching themselves through forced tax payments while tamping down the winds of revolution under the auspices of enforcing the law.

When the local *policia*, a short fat man with a gray walrus mustache and a large, gold star pinned to his wool shirt, finished reading the list of the accused man's transgressions, the room fell quiet.

The *policia* lowered the papers to his side and stood at attention, awaiting Azcona's decision on the accused man's fate.

Miller looked around the room. The onlookers shifted uneasily in their stiff wooden chairs. Some sighed, others cleared their throats, maybe whispered to a neighbor. The accused man's wife and daughters continued to sob quietly into their hands.

Flies buzzed. Somewhere outside, a dog barked. There were the metronomic clangs of a blacksmith hammering an anvil on the east side of the village.

The wind gusted, occasionally groaning like an old man awakening to use the privy, sweeping sand against the adobe walls and closed wooden shutters of the ancient building that served as a saloon, primarily, and, likely once a month or maybe every two months or just when Azcona happened to be in the area, became a courtroom into which the local *policia,* likely in Azcona's pocket, filed his prisoners to await the captain's judgment.

Azcona stared at the ceiling for a time, grimacing. He pointed his top-break, nickel-plated, walnut-gripped Smith & Wesson at the accused man's head, and a collective gasp rose from the crowd.

"No!" cried the accused man's wife.

His daughters screeched.

Apparently seeing the captain aiming the gun at him, the accused man turned to Azcona and wailed, "No, no—please, Captain, don't kill me! As you can see, I have a wife and two daughters. They would starve without me!"

Azcona lowered the pistol, which he'd likely used to shoot the man who now lay dead in the street. He smiled at the accused man, showing his white teeth beneath his black mustache, and said, "I was only fooling with you, Cortez. I don't think any of your offenses, as numerous as they may be, require such severe punishment as that which I had to dish out to Senor Machado. No, no—Machado shot a man's dog. That, to me, is a hanging offense. I am a dog lover, you see? How can a man shoot a dog merely for barking? That is what dogs do. They bark! You shoot one for barking or anything else except possibly attacking crippled children or stealing chickens from a priest, well, then you get a bullet from Captain Azcona!"

He chuckled through his teeth.

"Besides," Azcona added, sobering quickly, curling his upper lip angrily, "I didn't like how Machado looked at me when Senor Amado led him over here. He was thinking something disrespectful about me, I think."

Miller chuckled under his breath.

Azcona said, "To my mind, Senor Cortez, your most severe offense is striking the puta and stealing her money. What hungry man has not stolen a pig a time or two, or wandered drunk and disorderly around a village loudly lamenting the rebuffs of the girl he was keeping on the side and even assaulting her father?"

The captain winked at the man's wife.

The woman sobbed more loudly into her hands. One

of her daughters patted her back, cooing, "Oh, Mama! Oh, Mama!"

Senor Cortez hung his thick head in red-faced shame. The baby-faced rurale standing behind him smirked.

Azcona wrapped both his arms around the frightened girl on his knee, holding his big revolver over her slender left shoulder, and said, "But harming a *puta*? And stealing her hard-earned money?" Azcona clucked and shook his head, nuzzling the girl's neck. "For that I think you must lose a couple of fingers to remind you to keep your remaining fingers out of a puta's sacred poke!"

Azcona grinned, pulled the girl's face down close to his, and sucked her cheek, kissing it loudly, sloppily. The poor girl looked as though she'd be more comfortable in a cage with a rabid mountain lion.

Senor Cortez's wife wailed, "*No, Capitan! No, Capitan! Por favor, no le cortes los dedos a papá!*"

Please, don't cut off Papa's fingers!

"El Capitan—no, por favor!" pleaded Cortez.

Azcona glanced at a rurale flanking him and said, "Private Barrio, do you have your wire cutters on you?"

The tall, red-haired Barrio came to attention, saluting. "*Si, si, el Capitan!*"

"Two fingers of your choosing, Private," Azcona said.

"Si, si, el Capitan!"

Barrio handed his rifle over to the rurale standing to his left then fished the long-handled wire cutters out of his back pocket. As he did, the baby-faced private standing behind Cortez beamed delightedly and slammed the rear stock of his rifle down on the prisoner's left shoulder, driving him to his knees.

Meanwhile, the man's wife and daughters bawled. The

crowd grimaced and shook their heads in disgust, their collective mutters filling the saloon with a low roar.

To Barrio and the baby-faced rurale, Azcona said, "Not in here, *pendejos*! Outside! Do you want to get blood all over the place? Senor Valdez would never forgive me!"

Miller looked at his cohorts; the three outlaws shared a laugh. Miller had never met Azcona before. In fact, on previous visits to Mexico he'd always tried to remain two steps ahead of the man, for it was well known that Azcona did not cotton to americanos and outlaw americanos most of all. Unless they forked over a steep "border tax," that was.

Miller was pleased to see that the rurale captain certainly lived up to his reputation for savagery.

As the baby-faced rurale, Barrio, and two more of Azcona's lackeys grabbed the howling Cortez, Azcona went back to nuzzling the neck of the pretty little senorita on his lap—probably a puta, judging by her skimpy outfit.

He was chuckling devilishly, satisfied with his most recent sentence.

A real lunatic.

Miller laughed again. Being one himself, he could appreciate lunatics. He slipped the bottle out of his coat pocket, took a conservative sip (wanting more but he didn't have much and wanted it to last), swirled it around in his mouth, and swallowed.

God, how he enjoyed the otherworldly, warm feeling the concoction spread throughout him—body and soul. He hadn't felt the torment in his poor, abused nose in days!

Hell, he hadn't felt anything but wonderful in days!

Miller stepped to his right while Harris and Brennan

stepped left, making way for the rurales dragging the howling Senor Cortez toward the batwings. They were followed by the screaming, sobbing wife and two daughters, the daughters screaming, "Papa!" over and over again. "No, Papa! No, Papa!"

All eyes in the room followed them. When the rurales and Cortez had pushed through the batwings and were out in the street fronting the saloon, Miller saw that not only the eyes of the onlookers had followed the rurales and Cortes to the batwings.

Azcona's had, too.

The rurale captain sat staring at Red Miller from his place at the table fronting the bar. The little puta on his knee sat staring unseeing across the room again, eyes wide and blank, tears drying on her cheeks.

The crowd in the saloon/courtroom swiveled their heads back toward the front of the room. They must have seen that Captain Azcona's attention was directed behind them, between them and the batwing doors, beyond which Cortez was now screaming shrilly while his wife and daughters wailed.

"Hold his hand still!" bellowed one of the young rurales in frustration. "Hold his hand still, dammit, or I'm going to take off more than two!"

All eyes in the room were now on the three gringos standing by the batwings.

None of those pairs of eyes was as flinty with recognition as those of Captain Azcona. The captain's eyes widened very gradually, his lower jaw dropping just as slowly, as he matched Red Miller's, Pike Brennan's, and Flipper Harris's likenesses to those sketched on wanted posters being circulated across northern Mexico.

Red knew because he'd seen them. That's why'd he'd come looking for Azcona . . .

Azcona's gaze held on Miller.

Red smiled, eyes glinting behind his dusty spectacles.

Azcona stretched his lips back from his teeth then, extending his Smith & Wesson in his right hand, he hurled the little puta off his lap. The poor girl gave a shrill, indignant scream as she struck the floor and rolled.

Azcona leaped to his feet with such sudden violence that his chair slammed back against the bar behind him with a loud *bang!*

Crouching and extending the big popper out in front of him, Azcona bellowed through a savage smile, "*Red Miller, you wily coyote, now that we meet at last prepare to shake hands with el Diablo in the Hell that spawned you!*"

CHAPTER 23

"Damn, my big toe aches!" Lonesome Charlie complained later that night.

They were in high-desert country, surrounded by ancient stone monoliths that could have been thrown around like giant dice by some lunatic god thousands of years ago, so messily, haphazardly were they arranged.

The night was dark and chill, quiet finally after a fiercely windy day. Charlie had donned his smoke-stained buckskin coat.

He stood now at the edge of the firelight over which Sofia had cooked their meal, staring out into the darkness of the silent desert. He held his Winchester carbine down low along his right leg, not wanting the fire or wan starlight to reflect off it and make him a target.

Stockburn poured himself a cup of coffee, the steam wafting thickly in the cool air. He'd also donned his buckskin mackinaw, which he carried wrapped around his bedroll. He glanced at Sofia sitting on the opposite side of the fire from him. She was running a handful of desert caliche around inside the cast-iron skillet in which she'd cooked their fatback and beans, eyeing Wolf warily.

Charlie had been complaining about his damn toe all day and now well into the night, and he was getting to the girl.

Stockburn sighed as he sat back against his saddle, holding his hot cup against his chest in both his gloved hands. "Charlie, I had a slow walk around the camp. Make that two slow walks around the camp, and a good ways out. I didn't see or hear a thing except pocket mice building nests in the brush. I saw no sign of another fire. Hell, I didn't even hear a hoot owl!"

Wolf blew ripples on his coffee and sipped.

An owl hooted.

It hooted again. Maybe fifty, sixty yards away.

He looked at Sofia again, grinning at the coincidence. The girl looked at him as she continued to clean the pan with the handful of sand, but she didn't smile. Her eyes, coal black in the thick darkness and reflecting the dancing orange flames of the fire, grew slightly larger, warier.

"So, an owl hooted," Wolf said. "That's what owls do. They hoot at night."

A coyote gave a mournful cry. The cry was louder than the owl's hoot, but it came from farther away. The chortling cry continued for another fifteen seconds then dwindled to silence.

Sofia looked off in the direction from which the coyote was likely standing atop one of the giant rocks, some resembling run-aground ships half-buried in sand, some looking like giant houses tipped on their sides, then returned her skeptical gaze to Stockburn.

"And coyotes howl," Wolf said, trying to reassure the girl. "That's what they do. They howl. Owls hoot, coyotes howl."

"Damn," Charlie complained again, turning and walking back toward the fire. No, not walking. The old man was limping, severely favoring his left foot, putting little to no pressure on the tip of the boot. "Now my toe even hurts worse. Look at this." He pointed at his boot. "Swollen up like a child's jawbreaker with a little heart hammering away just beneath the nail!"

He looked at Wolf as though for an explanation.

Sofia stopped scrubbing the pan and sat back on her feet, casting her wary gaze into the darkness, looking around.

"Dammit, Charlie, will you stop frightening that child? What you have is gout. I told you, I . . ."

"You been down here before—ain't you, Wolf?" Charlie had limped over to the edge of the firelight on Stockburn's left. Again, he put his back to the fire as he stared into the darkness to the north of the camp.

"Yeah, I been down here several times, investigating stolen cattle, stolen mail, and even a couple of killers who'd assassinated a territorial senator aboard one of the trains we were guarding, and hightailed it into Mexico. Chester Chavez was the killer's name. I killed him. And, so doing, I got crossways with a nasty rurale captain who sees himself as the biggest cock of the walk down here in Chihuahua and northern Sonora . . . and don't like gringos. Gringo detectives most of all."

"Here I thought it was gringo federal lawmen Captain Azcona hated most of all."

Stockburn turned to Charlie again, one brow arched. "So, you've had the questionable pleasure of meeting Azcona."

"Indeed, and what a *questionable* pleasure it was, too," Charlie said, keeping his voice low as he stared out into the night, turning his head slowly from left to right then just as slowly back again, making a thorough sweep. "First ran into him five, six years ago. My partner and I, Jason Shamblin, followed some reservation-jumpin' Apaches through the Chiricahua Mountains and into Sonora near Nogales.

"Before that, I always made it a habit to stop in at the first rurale outpost I came to, to make it all good with the *comandante,* the man in charge. The man I had been dealin' with was reasonable enough. He made no fuss about us Americans crossing the border to fetch the bad guys. Hell, he even thanked me a time or two! Then I find out that an oily bean-eater named Azcona was somehow in charge.

"Captain Azcona didn't want me an' Jason chasin' Apaches, bronco killers or otherwise, across the border into Mexico unless our government paid five dollars a head for every Injun we captured or killed, because, you see, Azcona had it set up that he and his men were getting the Mexican equivalent of four dollars for every Apache scalp they turned over to the *federalistas.*"

"Scalp hunters," Sofia said, spitting out the words with disdain.

"Si, si—exactly. And I heard it wasn't only the scalps of law-breaking Apaches that Azcona turned over to the federal boys in Mexico City. Any Injun scalp would do. Yucatan. Quintana Roo. Yaqui. Maya. Campeche. Well, you get the drift."

Charlie shot a dark look over his shoulder at Stockburn, still sipping his coffee by the fire.

Charlie turned his head forward again, continuing with: "When we refused to pay for the prisoners we ran down in Mexico, and more or less told Azcona to go to hell, he threw us both in one of his prisons. He turned me loose after two weeks, and sent me back north across the border to fetch bounty money for dear old Jason. I knew our government wouldn't pay any bounty money for what was, officially, an unlawful crossing on my and Jason's part though most deputy U.S. marshals did it, no questions asked. So I swung back after I'd recuperated from the beating he'd given me just before he turned me free, and I figured I'd see about bustin' Jason out of that hellhole my ownself."

Charlie glanced again at Stockburn, mouth corners turned down. "When I rode up to the prison—it was just a couple of old adobes in the middle of nowhere with bars on the doors and windows—it was abandoned. No rurales, no prisoners. Horses and mules were all gone, barn emptied out.

"Only Jason was there. Stripped naked, eyelids cut off, tied to a saguaro cactus at the edge of the compound. Dead. Found a note in his mouth that read more or less: *Cross the border again without due payment and this will be your fate, as well, Deputy Murdock. Signed, Nestor Azcona, Captain, Mexican Rural Police Force.*"

"That son of the devil," Wolf said.

"Yep." Lonesome Charlie turned his head forward again to stare into the darkness. "Damn, my toe aches." He lifted his left foot and gave it a little shake.

In a hushed, fearful voice, Sofia said, "Is it Azcona, Charlie? Do you think Capitan Azcona is out there . . . stalking us?"

"I don't know," Charlie said, just as quietly, his back still facing the fire. "That's what I'm wonderin'. He has spies everywhere that report straight to him when they see

norteamericanos crossing into Mexico. He tried runnin'
me down last time I crossed, but I gave him the slip and
dragged the man I'd been after back north for his murder
trial. Likely really seared that chili-chomper's britches.
"Uh," he added quickly, glancing at Sofia, "I do apologize
for the chili-chomper, remark, senorita."

"Stop apologizing, you old skunk," Sofia said tiredly.
"You're too old to change your stripes."

Stockburn snorted a laugh.

"Well, I'm tryin'," Charlie said. "I do try, at least . . ."

The owl hooted again.

It was followed closely by the coyote's howl.

Sofia gasped. Stockburn sat up straight.

"Hear that?" Charlie said quietly.

"Yeah." Slowly, Wolf set his coffee cup down and gained
his feet. Maybe Charlie and his big toe were onto something. "I heard. Both were closer that time."

"Yep," Charlie said.

Stockburn quickly kicked dirt on the fire, dousing the
flames. He grabbed his Yellowboy and quietly pumped a
cartridge into the action. "And they didn't sound as natural
as before," he said beneath his breath.

"Nope, they sure didn't."

Wolf walked up to stand beside Charlie, dwarfing the
smaller man.

Charlie looked up at him, lifted his left foot, and pointed
at his toe. "Now, you see why my toe's been achin' like a
rabid dog's been chompin' into it?"

"You an' your toe." Stockburn shook his head in amazement. He would have chuckled if he didn't suddenly feel the
dead weight of an imminent threat resting on his shoulders.
"I'll be damned."

"Thought I was old and dried up, didn't ya?" Charlie raked out through a wheezing breath.

"Yep." Wolf glanced behind him, motioned for Sofia to stay here, then started walking slowly forward.

Charlie walked forward, as well, the two men slanting gradually away from each other. Stockburn walked slowly down the rise they were on and through some rocks that offered cover from below. A dry arroyo angled along the base of the rise maybe fifty feet farther down the declivity.

He couldn't see it yet. Too dark. But he could make out the gray jumble of rock that formed its southern bank.

If anyone really was on the lurk out here, and intending to make an assault on Stockburn, Charlie, and Sofia, they'd likely start from the arroyo. The southern side of the rise was too steep—nearly a solid wall of rock jutting nearly straight up and tufted with the deadly cholla, or jumping cactus, as well as rattlesnakes.

Wolf had seen several earlier, when he'd been scouting the area before it had gotten dark. Even in the coolness of the night they'd strike if aroused.

He glanced to his right. He could just barely see Charlie now—a slender, man-shaped silhouette in the darkness, dimly limned by the light of the stars. So far, there was no moon.

Stockburn continued down the slope until the rocks along the arroyo's bank took definite shape before him. Crouching, he stepped up onto one of the rocks, slid up beside another, taller rock, and peered into the arroyo before him.

The arroyo's wending, gravelly floor was maybe fifty feet below and mostly cloaked in darkness though he could see the paleness of the gravel at its bottom and the sides of the rocks rising on the opposite bank.

He could see no shadows sliding around down there.

Still, he felt a cold hand of apprehension splayed across his back, between his shoulder blades. That was his silent warning now, similar to Charlie's aching big toe.

Someone was out here. Someone with evil intent. If not, they would have shown themselves by now.

But where were the stalkers?

Wolf stepped onto another flat rock before him, edging a little close to the lip of the arroyo. If he took another step forward, he'd be descending toward the arroyo's floor.

He dropped to a knee and held the Yellowboy low so the starshine would not find the bluing of the barrel or the brass of the rifle's receiver.

Absolute silence enveloped him.

There were no sounds. Not the owl. Not the coyote. No breeze. Not even the little *snicking* sounds of burrowing critters.

The night was as quiet as the day after the end of the world.

Until Sofia's shrill, horrified scream cleaved it wide open.

CHAPTER 24

Red Miller had drawn his big Colt at the same time Azcona had drawn his Smith & Wesson.

Now the two men stood crouching and aiming their revolvers at each other, Miller yelling, "Hold on, hold on, now, Captain, you chili-chompin' son of Satan! I got you dead to rights! You shoot me, I shoot you an' then where will we be?"

Nearly as fast as Miller, Brennan, and Harris had drawn their own six-shooters and were aiming at the four other rurales remaining in the room. The two sergeants who'd been sitting with the so-called defendants awaiting trial in Azcona's kangaroo court had snapped to life when their captain had, albeit much more nervously, rising from their chairs, fumbling their old-model .45-70 Springfields to their shoulders and uncertainly aiming the cumbersome breechloaders at the gringos.

So, too, had the two rurales remaining behind Azcona. Those two—one young, one old enough to be the younger one's father—now, too, held their Springfields on the gringos at the front of the room, switching their aims between the three as though trying to figure out which was the most imminent threat.

Miller kept his Colt trained on Azcona, knowing that if he wavered for even a second, the captain would send a .44 round through his brain plate. Brennan and Harris slid their pistols right and left and back again, aiming at each of the rurales according to which one appeared closer to firing.

Miller smiled as he pulled a sheaf of greenbacks out of his back pocket. He held the greenbacks up, waved them enticingly. "We come bearing gifts, Captain. You shoot me an' I shoot you—that's the end of what could be a beautiful friendship."

The savage fury in Azcona's eyes softened a little.

He blinked. The skin above the bridge of his hawk's nose wrinkled. "If that is money for the border tax, Senor Miller, well, then, let me tell you that your payment is long past due."

"I been lookin' all over for you," Miller said with a coyote grin.

"Every bartender, stable boy, and pimp between here and Juarez knows where to find Captain Azcona."

"Here you go." Miller tossed the money onto a table before him. "Consider that back payment and a contract."

"A contract for what?"

"Let's you an' me sit somewhere quiet and talk turkey, Captain."

He paused. Still, Azcona said nothing.

The folks present here for the "court" proceedings were now on the floor, where they'd dropped to cower, covering their heads, when the captain and the red-haired, bespectacled gringo had drawn down on each other. Now by ones and twos they were beginning to look up and around, curious but still wary, murmuring amongst themselves.

In Spanish, Azcona shouted, "Everyone out!" He waved his arm. His face flushed angrily, a forked vein bulging in his forehead. "Out! Out—do you hear? *Vamose!*"

While the crowd gained their feet, looking around skeptically before tentatively heading toward the batwing doors at the front, Azcona glanced at the two sergeants standing near the men awaiting trial. "Take them back to the jail. I will deal with them later. Out! Out! Clear the cantina!"

A wave of speculative conversation rose, and boots and shoes drummed on the wooden floor as the crowd headed for the batwings, forming a bottleneck at the front of the room where Miller, Brennan, and Harris still aimed their six-guns, standing still as statues while the court trial crowd did their best to skirt wide of them before scuttling out the batwings.

The prisoners in handcuffs and ankle chains, were hazed through the doors by the two beefy, bearded rurale sergeants casting suspicious glances at the three gringos.

Finally, silence, save for Senor Cortez's wails and his women's sobs dwindling into the distance outside the cantina.

Azcona kept his eyes as well as his aimed Smith & Wesson on Miller for another five seconds, as though trying to read the redheaded gringo's mind. Suddenly, he lowered his pistol to his side, depressing the hammer with a metallic click.

Miller stretched a smile, gave a slow blink behind his

thick glasses, and lowered his Colt. He glanced at Brennan and Harris; they lowered their own six-shooters, as well.

Shadows danced on the floor to Miller's left. He whipped around, raising the Colt again, to see the three rurales who'd led Cortez out of the saloon standing on the stoop, gazing curiously in over the batwings.

Azcona jerked his head, commanding the three rurales to enter. They pushed through the doors, glancing around skeptically at the gringos and then shuttling their gazes to their commander standing between the bar and the table he'd been sitting at. The hands of the tall rurale who'd wielded the wire cutters were dark red with fresh blood.

The little puta must have beat a hasty retreat along with the crowd, because she was nowhere in sight.

Azcona glanced at the young rurale and the old rurale flanking him, then looked at the others who'd just entered, and jerked his chin to his right. "Stand over there and be ready for anything."

As the rurales hurried over to stand against the wall to Miller's left, Red said, "They won't be needed, Captain. This here's a friendly powwow."

"We will see," Azcona said, with a raptorial smile. "Holster your pistols and I will do likewise."

Miller glanced at his two cohorts, hiked a shoulder, then slid his Colt into its holster. He did not, however, secure the keeper thong over the hammer. The shrewd-eyed Captain Azcona saw this and chuckled his understanding.

He extended his hand toward the table on which Miller had tossed the money, and said, "gentlemen, sit down and take a load off. I will bring something you can wet your whistles with."

As Miller, Brennan, and Harris, kicked chairs out from the table and sat down, the chairs creaking beneath their weight, Azcona walked around behind the bar. He whistled to himself as he gathered a bottle and several glasses then walked out from behind the bar, holding the bottle in one hand and cradling four tumblers against his belly with his other hand.

He walked to the table at the front of the room, stopped, and scrutinized each of the three gringos in turn, a bemused smile tugging at the corners of his long, thin-lipped mouth nearly concealed by his thick, black mustache.

As he set the bottle and glasses down on the table, he returned his gaze to Miller, lifted one cheek and narrowed one eye. "Red Miller . . . you old coyote . . . a very slippery old coyote, at that."

He popped the cork on the labeled bottle of tequila and filled Miller's glass as Red said, "That's what's gonna make me such a valuable business partner, amigo."

"Oh?" Azcona glanced at the rurales lined up across the room to his right, maybe twenty feet away, like a firing squad awaiting the order to shoot *revolutionarios* lined up in front of a bullet-pocked adobe wall.

To a man, they chuckled doubtfully. Miller could tell they, as well as Azcona himself, were eager to drop their hammers on him.

Azcona had been after Miller for the past three years, ever since Miller's name and reputation had become so hot north of the border that he'd started delving farther and farther down into Mexico. He'd even been pursuing "business" interests in Chihuahua. By his innate wit and cunning he'd managed to avoid the notorious Mexican thief and killer masquerading as a lawman, himself a raggedy-heeled bastardo son of a puta and a bandit leader—Nestor Azcona.

Azcona so prided himself on keeping the border sealed up tighter than a schoolmarm's corset that Miller knew he had to have been grinding his molars to a fine powder the last few years. He may not have laid eyeballs on Miller's bunch, but he'd known Miller was down here. His many spies would have filled him in long ago, probably even snickering behind the prideful captain's back.

Looking into the man's eyes right now in the Yellow Bird Cantina on a dry, windy day in Chihuahua, Miller knew it was true. The man's pride had taken a beating; it would be no easy task to convince him that he and Miller needed to smoke the peace pipe.

When Azcona had filled his own shot glass, he kicked a chair out and slacked into it, across from Miller. He sat sideways, crossing his long, thin legs, and resting his left arm on the table. He kept his right hand on his right leg, close to the Smith & Wesson tied down on his uniform-clad right leg.

Red noticed that Azcona's own keeper thong hung free of the hammer, making for a fast, easy grab if the situation required. Miller was sure that Azcona was sure the situation would require it.

The captain swept the envelope into his hand and casually riffled through the bills. "Let's see what you have in here." As he ran his thumb across the large-denominational bills, moving his lips, counting under his breath, the frown lines over his nose dug deeper and deeper until the triangle of coffee-brown skin outlined by them rose like a mesa.

He dropped the envelope back down on the table, keeping it close to him, then plucked his shot glass off the table and threw back half the Mexican tarantula juice.

He cast a wary glance across the table at Miller. Red smiled to himself as a bead of sweat bubbled up on the side of the man's face, near the corner of his right eye, and dribbled down . . . down . . . tracing the long scar running down that cheek to his neck and under his collar.

He stared at Miller, not saying anything, apparently waiting for Red to speak.

Glancing at the fat envelope, Miller said, "There's thirty-five thousand dollars in American currency. Let's call it a balm for healin' old wounds. But that's not all I'm of-ferin'."

"What else?"

"A business deal. And . . ." Miller glanced at his pards again, his own sneaky grin giving his lips another work-out. "And the Wells Fargo man trailing us."

"Stockburn." Azcona said the name as though it were an especially nasty profanity. One that even he didn't feel comfortable using.

"As a matter of fact, yes," Red said. "You know Stock-burn, do you, Nestor?"

"Si, si." Azcona's dark face turned darker as another humiliated flush rose in his cheeks. He glanced at his men briefly, self-consciously, the name obviously troubling him. Probably as much as the name Red Miller had trou-bled him.

Damned sneaky gringos . . .

He said it again even more quietly this time: "Stock-burn. Of course, it would be him." He cursed and brushed a sheepish thumb across his nose.

Miller read the man's mind: Stockburn was another

slippery gringo who'd managed to elude him. Red tried not to smile.

Of course, it would be Stockburn.

"Where is he?" Azcona wanted to know.

"Behind us," Flipper Harris said. He, too, was delighting in the affect the name had had on the rurale captain.

"How far?" Azcona asked him.

"Not far," Red said. "An hour, maybe two."

"Are you sure it's him?"

"We never actually glassed him, only spied a curl of dust on our backtrail a few times, both north and south of the border."

"North and south. Hmm."

"It's him." Miller raised his arms. "Who else would it be?"

"Si, si—who else?" Miller tapped the envelope, took a deep, calming breath, and cleared his throat. "*What* else?"

"Girls," Brennan said.

Azcona frowned incredulously. "Girls?"

"There's an orphanage down in Rio Rojo." Miller tapped his thumb down on the table and held Azcona's gaze with a cunning, speculative one of his own. "On our last trip to Mexico, we made a deal with the nuns who run it down there."

"Very bad nuns," said Harris, manufacturing a disgusted look, shaking his head.

"Bad nuns . . ." Azcona said to Miller, speculatively. He grinned and crossed himself.

Red glanced at the envelope. "You know how the Mescins down here like the *norteamericano* girls from *up there*?" He jerked his chin to indicate north. "Well, the gringos *up there* prefer the Mescin girls from *down here* even more. In fact, they're willin' to pay top dollar for 'em. The younger the better. And if you get 'em in the right parlor houses, that is."

"We got us friends who run the right parlor houses," said Flipper Harris, and sipped his drink.

Pike Brennan said, "We're gonna run a wagonload from Rio Rojo north every coupla months."

"Lots of orphans in Mexico," Flipper said.

"To mining camps—Tombstone, Bisbee, Jerome . . . Flagstaff . . ." Miller added, lounging back in his chair, satisfied with the plan. "We're gonna take the first load ourselves. After that, we'll hire men to do it while we sit back and play poker and generally stomp with our tails up . . . right here in grand Old Mexico."

He grinned as he entwined his hands behind his head. "Ain't gettin' any younger," he said. "I figure it's a good way to retire. Take it easy from here on in."

Azcona thought about this, no doubt calculating the amount of money such a transaction would haul in from lonely miners in isolated mining camps, their pockets filled with money and nothing to spend it on—except girls.

The captain nodded slowly. "Hmm." He uncrossed his long legs. "And me?"

"You'll get your cut. Ten percent." Miller blinked slowly behind his glinting glasses. "Every trip will pass right through here—comin' an' goin'. You'll get your estimated cut in advance . . . on the way north. Just so there's no doubt we can trust each other."

Azcona hitched up his trousers and sauntered the ten

feet to the batwings. He stepped halfway through them and turned to gaze north up the windy, dusty street. As he did, he tapped his thumb against the spur of his Colt's hammer.

"Stockburn, eh?" he said, continuing to tap his thumb against his Colt's hammer, faster and faster.

"Stockburn," Miller said. "I'd like to do him myself . . . on account of my poor snout here." He fingered the black, flat tip of his nose. "He gave me this—he sure did. But since it don't grieve me so much anymore, I don't see any reason to hold up our plans by wastin' time on a lowly Wells Fargo man. When there's so darn much money to be made after we reach Rio Rojo. I'll give you Stockburn. I heard you want him. You want him bad. As bad as you wanted me. So . . . he's yours!"

"He's right behind us," Brennan said.

Miller sipped his tequila, sucked the ends of his mustache, and smiled across the table at the captain. "Does that sweeten the pot for you?"

"Pretty girls and bad nuns . . ." said Azcona.

"Pretty girls and bad nuns, Captain!"

"Hmm." Ascona turned and walked back into the room.

He sauntered up to Miller and extended his right hand, smiling, shoving his thick mustache up taut against his nose, slitting his long eyes devilishly. "Twenty percent, and I give you Stockburn free of charge!"

Red slapped the table. "Done!"

"All right, Red—you convinced me. Do you mind if I call you, Red?"

Miller chuckled and slid his eyes to Brennan and Harris.

He returned his gaze to the captain, and extended his own right hand. "Only if I can call you, Nestor."

Both men laughed.

So did the rurales lined up like a firing squad against the wall.

CHAPTER 25

Again, Sofia's scream cut through the otherwise too-silent night.

It was like a bayonet blade rammed through Stockburn's heart.

"Sofia!" he shouted, whipping around and running back up the grade toward their now-dark camp.

A shadow moved on his left, maybe fifty feet away. He cast a quick glance in that direction. Lonesome Charlie was also moving up the grade, on a parallel course with Stockburn, cursing, running in his weak-kneed, shambling fashion, holding his Winchester barrel-up in his right hand. The old man tripped over something, dropped to a knee, cursed again, then heaved himself to his feet and continued running.

"They hurt a hair on that girl's head . . . !" he raked out. "Slimy sonso'devils!"

As Stockburn ambled through the rocks lining their camp, he slowed his pace and held the cocked Yellowboy straight out from his right hip. He was breathing hard from the run up the incline.

He no longer heard anything. The night had gone quiet again. Too damn quiet.

He strode forward, the gray rocks sliding back away from him, the slight clearing in which their fire still smoked opening before him. All that lay around the camp was their gear. The tripod on which they'd hung their coffeepot now stood on only one leg, and the pot lay on its side beside the fire ring, steaming.

He could smell the cedar smoke and the tang of scorched coffee.

Stockburn looked around. He stepped up to the very edge of the camp, knowing he could be walking into a trap.

Quietly, he said, "Sofia?"

No reply. A cold, creeping dread had told him he wouldn't get one.

Lonesome Charlie's raucous spur chings rose on Stockburn's left, and then Wolf saw the old man's slender, bent shadow with his plumed, high-crowned Stetson standing at the edge of the clearing ten feet away from him. Charlie's breath sounded like a quickly pumped bellows. The strained breaths raked in and out of the old man's lungs as he took another stumbling step forward, squeezing his Winchester in both hands, aiming it out before him.

"Stockburn?"

"Here," Wolf said beneath the thudding of his own wary ticker.

"Sofia?"

"Not here."

The detective took another couple of steps forward, looking around. The night around the camp was nearly coal black. One of their horses whickered in the rocks and brush to Wolf's right, where they'd picketed them in a natural, rock-lined corral of sorts.

Charlie cursed fiercely. He swung around to the east, threw his head back on his shoulders, and shouted, *"Chiquita?"* It was no surprise that he was as worried about Sofia as Wolf was. Charlie might have had a fierce bark, but he was a soft touch.

Silence like that of a held breath followed his cry.

A few seconds later:

"Wolf! *Char-leee!*" The girl's strained pleas had come muffled with distance from the southeast.

"That way!" Stockburn swung around, crossed the camp to Charlie's right, and ran through the rocks and cactus on the camp's east side.

He heard Charlie's spur chimes and raking breaths as the old man ran along behind him, cursing under his breath. Stockburn wheezed out his own curse. The old man was going to get them both shot with all the noise he was making. The darkness worked against them in that it was nearly impossible to track Sofia in it, but it worked *for* them in that it concealed them from whoever had her.

At least, it did if their own damn noise didn't betray their moving positions, which it very likely was . . .

The thought had only just passed through Wolf's mind when a rifle cracked loudly twice. The quick orange flashes shone ahead and on Stockburn's right. One bullet curled the air off his left ear while another barked off a rock to his left, just in front of where Charlie was running off his left flank.

"Damn!" Charlie said, throwing himself to the ground.

Stockburn's sentiments exactly. Wolf dove forward and rolled up against a small boulder, losing his hat and gritting his teeth against the sharp-fanged viper clinging to his right arm. He rose to a knee, extended the rifle over the rock before him, and thumbed back the hammer.

He could see nothing but the toothy silhouettes of brush and rocks before him, the faint glitter of stars in the black velvet sky.

He turned his head to yell softly over his left shoulder, "Dammit, Charlie—take your consarned spurs off, for the love of Pete!"

Charlie groaned, spat. He said, "Damn . . . why didn't I think of that?" More quietly and in a voice rife with chagrin, he added, "A few years ago, I would've, gallblastit . . ."

As Wolf started to turn his head back forward, a lance of flames pierced the darkness from ahead and on his right again. He pulled his head down as the bullet plowed into the face of the boulder in front of him. The shot and the ricochet were still echoing as he raised his head and rifle again and sent three angry bullets flying toward where he'd seen the flashes.

A man yelped. There was the clattering thump of a rifle dropping on a rock. It was followed by the heavier, more resolute thud of a body.

"Got the son of a buck!" Stockburn raked out through gritted teeth as he pulled his head and rifle down behind the rock, wary of a shooter aiming at his own flash.

Charlie crabbed up on his left side, doffed his hat, and canted his head to the side, gazing out over the left side of the boulder. "You get one?" he asked through a whisper.

"Uh-huh."

Charlie glanced at him, brows arched. "Good shootin' for a Wells Fargo man. Any sign of the girl?"

Wolf was gazing out around the boulder's right side. "No." He gained a knee. "But we're not gonna find her holed up behind this rock like rabbits hiding from rattlesnakes, either."

"We're not gonna find her if we're both riddled with bullets, neither," Charlie wheezed. "Best wait till morning."

"Whoever's got her could be long gone by then."

"We can track 'em come daylight."

"She'll likely be dead by then." Stockburn rose to a crouch. "Stay here, Charlie. No tellin' who or how many we're dealing with. No point in both of us walking into a whipsaw."

As Wolf began moving forward, hugging the shadows of the larger rocks on his right, he heard Charlie say behind him, "Like hell."

Stockburn moved forward, dropping down the gradual decline. He looked around carefully, set each boot down even more quietly, trying to move with the silence and fluidity of a mountain lion or an Apache. He hadn't been to Mexico in a while, and he'd forgotten until tonight how important it was to move with less sound than a snake through sand.

Trips to Mexico always made a fella conscious of his movements.

He picked his way down the steep embankment of rocks, practically slithering between boulders and holding his rifle very low so the starshine wouldn't catch the barrel or receiver. Finally, he gained the arroyo's sandy floor.

He stepped beneath a dark overhang of rock on the arroyo's far side. He looked around and listened, breathing shallowly, almost silently. He looked at the sandy floor. Several sets of deep scuff marks scored the sand. He

dropped to a knee and placed two fingers against the edge
of the imprint of a man's high-heeled boot, then another.

The prints led off to the southeast.

Two men dragging a third person. The twin furrows
that trailed off nearly unbrokenly along the arroyo, between two sets of men's boot prints, had likely been made
by Sofia's moccasin-clad feet.

Stockburn's heart quickened as he gazed south along
the arroyo. All he could see was the pale ribbon of arroyo
floor foreshortening beyond him between steep, shadowy
walls of rock.

He strode quickly ahead. Too quickly. He couldn't help
but throw caution to the wind. If he didn't catch up soon
to the men who'd grabbed Sofia, they'd kill her.

He followed the arroyo's wending course through the
nearly well-dark cut between high, rocky banks for maybe
a hundred yards before both walls drew inward, forming
a narrow corridor impeded by rocks that had likely fallen
from the banks on either side, and by driftwood and
bleached animal bones likely carried by previous floods
due to springtime melts in the mountains or the yearly
monsoons.

He continued straight ahead, now holding the Yellowboy up high across his chest, his thumb caressing the
cocked hammer. His heart beat slowly, but each beat was
a mule's kick to his ribs.

Never should have agreed to let her ride down here
with him. What a damned fool tinhorn move on his part.
Too damn hard to say no to a pretty, heartbroken girl.

Damn his own lousy judgment.

Stockburn stopped suddenly.

A strangling cry rose from the shadows ahead of him. Cold sweat trickled down his back.

"Sofia?" he called quietly, squeezing the rifle in his hands.

There came the soft, crunching thump of a footstep. A shadow disconnected from the velvet darkness of the arroyo's right wall. The shadow moved haltingly toward Stockburn, who steeled himself, spreading his boots a little more than shoulder-width apart and raised the Yellowboy to his shoulder.

"Sofia?" he called again, a little louder, his heart quickening now, racing.

The shadow moved toward him in a herky-jerky fashion. Too large to be the girl.

Stockburn aimed at the center of the shadow moving closer and closer to him, a man stumbling toward him, and drew his index finger taut against the Yellowboy's trigger.

Sofia's husky, disembodied voice rose from the darkness behind the moving shadow: "Don't let him get away, Wolf. The *bastardo* has my stiletto in his guts!"

Just then the man moving toward Stockburn took shape and definition as he moved into a glimmer of starlight six feet in front of Wolf. The man stopped and stared at the railroad detective. His face was large and round with a shaggy mustache and goat whiskers drooping from his chin. He wore a red serape. A sombrero dangled down his back by a chin thong.

The man's eyes, twin coals set far back in deep, severely chiseled sockets, regarded Stockburn desperately, painfully. The man did not blink. He opened his mouth to speak but there came only a faint trilling sound, as though the Mex was gearing up to yodel. His thick lips stretched back from his teeth a little and then he bowed his head as though in prayer. In reality, Wolf knew, he was looking down at his belly.

Both of his hands were wrapped around the obsidian handle of the knife buried hilt deep in his guts. Oil-dark blood welled up around the blade to glisten in the starlight.

The man looked up at Wolf again. His face crumpled in an anguished expression, deep lines spoking out from his eye corners. He opened his mouth as though to wail but choked out the single word *"Mierda!"* then dropped to his knees.

He fell forward to lie facedown in front of Wolf as though he were praying at the tall railroad detective's boots. He gave a little shiver, broke wind, and lay still.

"Wolf!" Sofia cried from the shadows ahead of Stockburn. "Behind you!"

Stockburn whipped around, raising the Winchester again.

Lonesome Charlie's voice said with off-hand quietness, "Don't get your drawers in a twist, Wells Fargo."

A rifle thundered.

A man yelped. The man-shaped shadow ahead of Wolf and to Wolf's right, jerked back and disappeared against the velvet darkness of the arroyo wall. There was the heavy thud of a body striking the arroyo floor.

"Got him!" said Charlie's disembodied voice along with the metallic rasp of a spent shell being ejected from a rifle's breech, and a live one being seated in the chamber.

Another shadow moved straight ahead of Stockburn. He easily identified Charlie's slump-shouldered frame and the man's halting gait as well as the tall Stetson topping his head. The only sounds of the old man's approach now, however, since he'd removed his spurs, were the crunching of his boots and his wheezing breaths that sounded like sandpaper raked against coarse wood.

Charlie stopped and turned slowly, extending his smoking Winchester out from his right hip. "Any more?" he asked.

"No." Sofia's voice came louder and clearer behind Stockburn.

He turned to see her move toward him from the shadows, her own supple, long-haired figure taking shape in the starlight. She stopped and looked at him wide-eyed then looked down at the man lying dead between them.

"Demonio feo!" she snarled, and gave the body a solid kick in the ribs. Ugly demon! "Take me to the nuns, huh?" She kicked it again. "We'll see who sends who to the nuns, *pendejo!*"

"Nuns?" Wolf said, incredulous.

"Si. They said something about taking me to nuns." Breathing hard with anger, Sofia cursed in Spanish and shrugged.

Nuns. What the hell . . . ?

Stockburn glanced toward where the man coming up behind him now lay unmoving in the darkness. He looked at Charlie, gave a sheepish, lopsided smile. "Nice shootin', old man. And my apologies to your big toe."

Charlie smiled proudly and caressed the still-smoking barrel of his Winchester. "I still got a little left."

Wolf stepped over the dead man and placed his hands on Sofia's shoulders. "Are you all right?"

"Si, I am fine, Wolf."

"Are you sure?"

"Si, si, Wolf—I am fine." She looked down at the dead man at her feet. "This one, though. He's not so fine."

"Are you sure there were only three of 'em?" Charlie asked.

"I saw only three."

Charlie turned to Wolf. "I'm gonna hotfoot it back to camp and check on the horses, just in case there's more where these three curly wolves came from, and they're after our mounts. There ain't a chili-chomper yet born that won't still a hoss!"

Sofia glared down, fists clenched at her sides, at the dead man.

"Good idea," Wolf told Charlie. "We'll be right behind you."

Stockburn turned back to Sofia. She crouched over the dead man, placed one moccasin-clad foot on his shoulder, wrapped both hands around the handle of her stiletto, and gave a grunt as she pulled. The tapering, pin-pointed blade came slowly out of the man's belly, making wet sucking sounds.

Wolf stared at her skeptically, amazed at how much spice this little chili pepper had in her despite her princess-like beauty. She cleaned the blade on the dead Mexican's shirt.

When she'd returned the knife to a sheath concealed beneath her skirt, Stockburn took her hand. "Come on. Let's get back to camp, fer crissakes."

Deep frustration raked him as he led the girl, who could very easily be dead, back the way they'd come. He paused briefly to look for his hat but it was too dark. Deciding to look for the topper again after sunrise, he continued to lead Sofia back to the camp though it wasn't so easy to find on such a dark night.

He and Sofia entered the camp at the same time Charlie did, strolling in from the direction of the horses. "The mounts are fine. If they looked for 'em, which they likely did, they didn't find 'em."

"Good," Wolf said.

He turned back to Sofia. "Are you sure you're all right?"

"Wolf, I am fine!"

"They didn't hurt you a bit?"

"No! Now stop worrying. Mierda, you are worse than an old mother hen!"

Stockburn cursed under his breath, then got to work rebuilding the fire. He intended to keep it small in case other border toughs had heard the shots and decided to investigate.

As he did, Charlie sank back against his saddle and took a pull from a bottle, likely calming his weak old ticker. Sofia filled the coffeepot from a large bladder flask they'd filled with water at a spring they'd come to recently, and then, once the flames were leaping back to life, righted the tripod and hung the coffeepot from it.

Stockburn took a long drink of water from his canteen then sat on a rock at the edge of the firelight, holding his Yellowboy straight up and down between his legs, ready for anything.

He walked over, grabbed Charlie's whiskey bottle. "Give me a nip of that. I don't know about yours, but my nerves are shot."

He took a sip then gave the bottle back to Charlie and sat back down on his rock, far enough from the fire that the light wouldn't compromise his night vision.

"I found that right excitin'," Charlie said, arms crossed on his chest, smiling into the darkness. "It's been so long since I been to Mexico that I'd plum forgot what a good old Mexican dustup was like. I thought for sure chiquita there was a goner and us in the bargain!"

Sofia sat on the other side of the fire from him, arms wrapped around her raised knee. She gave a sidelong smile and said, "If I didn't know better, Charlie, I'd say you were worried about this fiery little chili pepper."

Charlie shrugged. "Only on account of Wolf havin' taken such a shine to you. Me—you know how I feel about Mescins." He grinned across the fire at her. "The purtiest ones most of all." He winked.

Sofia dropped her chin and snorted. "Was your wife pretty, Charlie?"

Charlie widened his eyes in surprise. "Heard about her, did you?"

"Wolf told me."

Charlie stared into the darkness for a time, a long, sad, thoughtful look on his weathered, craggy features. "She was one purty little Mescin firecracker, all right." Charlie lounged back deeper against his saddle and crossed his legs at the ankles. "I don't mind sayin' I miss her."

"I'm sorry, Charlie," Sofia said quietly.

A mist brightened Charlie's eyes. "Ah, hell—a long time ago now. I got her memory." He gave a dreamy smile as he tapped his temple.

He took another pull from the bottle.

They all sat in silence for a time, listening to the coffee come to a boil.

When Sofia had dumped coffee into the pot, let the pot return to a boil, then added a little cool water to settle the grounds, she poured them each a cup. She gave one to Charlie and another one to Wolf.

Wolf reached up to accept the hot mud, and suddenly the dam that had been building in him broke, and he said, "This can't happen again, Sofia."

She frowned down at him, her long hair hanging down both sides of her face. "What can't?"

"You getting taken. If anything happened to you, your mother would never forgive me. And I, I might add, could never forgive myself."

Sofia's frown cut deeper lines across her forehead. "What are you saying?"

"We're dropping you off at the next village we come to. I'm gonna find a nice family to take you in and keep you safe until Charlie and I have finished our mission. When Miller's either dead or in cuffs, we'll return for you and take you on back to your mother in Mesilla."

Sofia stared down at him for nearly a full minute, her wide brown eyes growing flintier and flintier. Finally, she crossed her arms on her chest, cocked one foot out before her, and settled her weight on the opposite hip. "So, that is what you are going to do, eh?"

"That's what I'm gonna do, yes."

"Don't you think I might have something to say about this?"

"Well . . . no. No, I don't. You were damn near killed tonight, and—"

"But I wasn't. I gutted the chili-chomper bastardo who took me, and I will gut any chili-chomper bastardo who ever tries to take me again!"

"Now, look here, sweetheart. I just—"

"No!" Sofia cried, her face swelling and darkening with rage.

She stretched her rich lips back from her white teeth, and, gazing up at her, Stockburn had the uneasy feeling of suddenly finding himself a wildcat's prey. "You look here, Mister Wells Fargo detective. I came along to see Miller killed for murdering my Billy, *and that is exactly what I intend to do.* You can 'sweetheart' me all you want.

"But . . ."

He let his words trail off to silence as she roared off into such rapid-fired Spanish that Stockburn had trouble following. She stood before him, gesturing with her hands and even her feet, bent forward at the waist and even making a lewd gesture by bending her knees and swinging her arm between her legs.

Wolf glanced at Charlie. Charlie winked at him, grinning, as if to say that, having been married to just such a fiery Spanish princess once himself, he'd been through it all before. All you can do is hang on and hope you live to tell the tale.

Wolf looked up at Sofia gesturing wildly before him. As far as he could tell, she was mocking his machismo and berating him for condescending to her because she was female. She was really letting him have it in rapid-fire Spanish, bayonets of pure, unadulterated Hispanic rage flashing in her eyes as she threw her arms up and out and then out again, her hair flying wildly around her face, at times totally hiding it.

Wolf hunkered down against the onslaught, sure the rage would soon ebb. But he soon realized with some apprehension as well as amazement that while her excoriation seemed to reach a crescendo, it was nowhere near abating.

If fact, she was just getting started!

He glanced uneasily at Lonesome Charlie. Lonesome Charlie just lay back against his saddle, gazing up at the enraged female catamount, grinning, his eyes following Sofia around the camp as she gave her castigating tirade its full head of steam.

She kicked rocks and brush clumps, threw her head back, wildly gesticulated with her hands. The castigation continued as she cleaned up around the camp, scrubbing out a pan with sand then shaking out her blankets to rid them of possible black widows or scorpions . . . all the while rattling off the Spanish faster than Wolf had heard it rattled off before, casting him frequent, withering looks.

Stockburn was long past being able to translate. On the other hand, he didn't need to. He suspected it was not only him being nailed to the indignant girl's proverbial cross, but every man who'd lived since the first caveman had dragged the first cavewoman into his cave and started making a family.

He and Charlie sipped their coffee and shared a couple of amazed, schoolboy sheepish glances as the girl continued her diatribe, moving around the camp, straightening gear then preparing her own bedroll and saddle for sleep. The string of epithet-stitched Spanish even continued as she wandered out into the darkness beyond the firelight to perform her ablutions—and even *during* said ablutions.

With a quick glance, Stockburn glimpsed her silhouetted figure squatting and still gesturing with her hands, the harangue continuing beneath the sound of her making water, without surcease.

Wolf turned his eyes away, chuckled his amazement . . . and even admiration . . . at the gauge of the girl's fury—

though he had to admit to feeling a little unsettled, as well, remembering that pig-sticker of hers poking up out of the Mexican's belly—and sipped his coffee.

He and Charlie had yet another cup of coffee while the tirade continued.

Only after they'd all turned into their bedrolls and lay their heads back against the wooly undersides of their saddles, and had let the fire burn down to a mere flicker, did Sofia finally fall silent.

Just like that, she was finished.

She rolled onto her side, drew her knees to her chest, closed her eyes. Her breaths came slow and deep.

Suddenly, it was so quiet that Stockburn, staring straight up at the sky dusted with sequins, thought he could hear the stars burning.

Charlie turned to him from where the older man lay six feet away on his left.

"Ain't that just like a chili pepper?" he raked out quietly and winked. "Always gotta get the last word in."

That set them both off on a bout of uncontrolled laughter.

Finally, they slept.

CHAPTER 26

Stockburn raised the spyglass to his eyes and adjusted the focus.

The village of *Pequeño Río Azul* swam into the sphere of magnified vision—a motley but homey collection of straw- or tile-roofed adobes sprawled across two low, rocky hills and stippled with shade trees including fruit trees, flowering almonds, cottonwoods, and a few Montezuma cypresses. The *pueblito* was brightly splashed here and there with Mexican orchids and dahlias blooming in flower boxes.

The very center of town boasted a square filled with trees and flowers likely fed by the Little Blue River of the town's name and that curved around to the southwest edge of it.

People moved about the square and elsewhere—gray-haired, gray-bearded old men in low-crowned straw sombreros, old women in flowered dresses and rebozos, and peons in their traditional cotton tunics, slacks, and serapes. Wagons pulled by mules or donkeys, and filled with peppers or watermelons harvested from the fields along the river, wended their way through the town's narrow corridors between rows of hunched adobes, as did handcarts filled with straw or firewood.

Two young boys were just then entering the town from the far side carrying cane poles and fighting over a stringer of fresh fish glistening in the midday sunshine, likely pulled up out of a favorite fishing hole.

Two dogs, one large, one very small and yipping, followed close on their heels.

An old desert rat in canvas rags, a corncob pipe drooping from a corner of his mouth, was leading two pack burros toward the village from the northeast. Both burros wore straw sombreros with holes cut for their ears. The old man sang what sounded like some old Spanish ballad as he strolled toward town, likely eager to cash in a fresh poke of gold dust and buy himself a bottle of good tequila and a supple puta.

Wolf trained the glass on a large sign over a nondescript pueblo just south of the central square. "*Cantina Pájaro Amarillo*," he read aloud.

"The Yellow Bird Cantina," Sofia translated unnecessarily. Stockburn had at least that much knowledge of the language. "But you are not supposed to be scouting saloons, Wolf," she gently remonstrated him. "You are supposed to be looking for rurales."

Stockburn gave a wry chuff as he continued to survey the village.

He, she, and Lonesome Charlie were lying on the west side of a hillock maybe a hundred yards from the village's northwest edge. Their horses were ground-reined behind them, at the base of the hill.

It was a clear, mild day, the sky especially clear after the wind of the previous day. When the three had awakened earlier that morning, at the first blush of dawn, no mention was made of the young senorita's tirade of the night before. Since she hadn't brought it up but had merely gone about her chores as she had the previous morning, Stockburn sure as hell wasn't going to bring it up lest he should find himself the target of the girl's wrath once more.

No, sir. That wasn't for him.

He'd fought with guns and fists some of the nastiest, toughest, dirtiest, and downright vilest men on the frontier. But when it came to women with quick tempers—he steered as clear of them as he would a mossy-horned, half-wild Brahma bull straight out of the Texas Brasada country. There was no dealing with a mule-headed, quick-tempered woman, and trying to do so only made a man look foolish. If Sofia was so dead-set against waiting for him and Charlie in the home of a nice family in a quiet village, not unlike *Pequeño Río Azul*—and she obviously was dead-set against it—who was he to make her?

"No rurales as far as I can tell," Stockburn said, finally lowering the glass. He glanced at Charlie smoking a cigarette, one arm draped over one upraised knee. "You know this village, Charlie?"

The old lawman shook his head and blew out a plume of smoke. "Never been this deep in Mexico before. These is Azcona's prime huntin' grounds, though. I've heard he holds kangaroo courts in little villages all across central Sonora and Chihuahua—sorta his way of keeping a stranglehold on both states and tamping down the winds of revolution, which are always threatening to blow up in these parts."

"Yeah, well," Wolf said, "I don't see any gray uniforms. I don't know the village, either, and I'd normally avoid it, but we need supplies for both us and the horses. And there's a good chance Miller and his compatriots are either holed up down here or left some indication of where they're headed. I don't see how we can avoid it."

The wind of the previous day had wiped out Miller's trail. But since it had been leading south, it likely passed through *Pequeño Río Azul*.

"You're right." Charlie stuck his cigarette into his mouth and shucked his Colt .44. He filled the chamber he usually kept empty beneath the hammer then flicked the loading gate closed and spun the cylinder. "It could be our trail ends here."

He grinned hopefully. "Could be ol' Red and his amigos are sound asleep in a hurdy-gurdy house. This is still early for outlaws. We might could take 'em without poppin' a single cap."

"Let's give it a shot, anyway." Wolf grinned as he returned the glass to its leather case. "No pun intended."

Charlie winced as he heaved himself to his feet. He placed a hand on Stockburn's shoulder, leaned in confidentially, and said, "Leave the jokes to me, Wells Fargo. You're not much good at 'em." He glanced at Sofia and winked.

Sofia laughed.

Stockburn grumbled with feigned injury as he followed her and Charlie down the slope to their horses. He'd be damned if he hadn't found himself liking old Lonesome Charlie. What's more, he even admired the old cuss. He was much more than his bluster, Charlie was. Despite a weak heart and an obvious alcohol problem, Charlie could still get the job done and more. The previous night he'd saved both Wolf's and Sofia's lives in that dark arroyo.

That hadn't been lost on the Wells Fargo detective.

Nor the sensitive nature of the old man's big left toe . . .

Without Charlie on the trail with him and the senorita, their trails would have ended in that canyon.

When they'd mounted up, Charlie turned to Stockburn. "Just ride right in, say howdy-do?"

"Why not?" Wolf shrugged. "Skulking around, playin' hide 'n' seek, would only draw attention."

"Not that two old gringos riding into town with one pretty young senorita isn't going to draw attention," Charlie said.

Stockburn sidled Smoke up beside Charlie's buckskin, placed a hand on the man's arm, and leaned confidentially into him. "Make that one old gringo and one gringo in the prime of life."

He winked at Sofia, grinned, then reined Smoke out away from Charlie and the buckskin, and booted him back onto the main trail that straggled off the desert from the north and into the village.

Charlie rode off Wolf's left flank. Sofia rode her own mount off his right flank. As they followed the curving main street into the village, passing through the shade of many trees, the toiling, milling villagers turned toward them, turned away, then quickly returned their gazes to the three unlikely strangers, brows raised with obvious curiosity.

"Yep, you were right, Charlie," Wolf said, leaning forward against his saddle horn. "We are getting the thrice over, all right."

"Yep, we sure are."

They continued through town and across the central square, causing heads to swivel toward them from both sides of the street. Stockburn felt a cool apprehension when a few of those folks giving him and his trail mates the wooly eyeball moved quickly off the street and ducked through doorways, almost as if they thought trouble might be dogging them.

No, not *almost*. They sure enough must be expecting trouble.

Charlie must have spotted the same thing. "Hmmm," he said, giving his left armpit a sniff. "I done even had me a bath night before last, and I'm still gettin' the cold shoulder. What the hell's a fella to do?"

"Si," Sofia said quietly as they continued riding along the narrow, curving main street between shade trees and low adobes hunching behind ramadas and brush arbors, clay pots and ristras hanging from viga poles. "It's as if they've been expecting us."

"Maybe warned about us," Wolf opined, dragging a thumb through the three-day growth of beard stubble on his face.

He glanced at windows and doorways, the shade flanking water barrels and stacked packing crates, looking for concealed riflemen, suddenly wary of an ambush. Miller could be anywhere . . .

Where?

As Wolf and his companions followed a curve in the street, *La Cantina del Pájaro Amarillo* appeared ahead on the street's left side, sitting by itself on a broad, barren lot and on a wide spot in the street. A two-story, wood frame-and-adobe brick livery barn sat a little farther up the street and on the street's right side.

Wolf angled Smoke toward the barn and into a slice of shade angling out from its north wall. He and his two trail pards dismounted, tied the mounts to a hitchrail, and arranged for the barn's hostler—a wizened old bird of an ancient Mex, all bone and sinew concealed by a ragged serape, straw sombrero, and burlap trousers, to feed and water the horses while Stockburn and his compatriots drifted into the Yellow Bird for food and something to cut the trail dust.

"*Si, si, si,*" the old man said, not looking Wolf in the eye but keeping his head down, puffing a cornhusk cigarette dangling from a corner of his mouth.

Stockburn couldn't tell if the man was afraid of him . . . or the trouble he might have brought with him . . . or just shy. Hard to say.

If anyone knew if Red Miller was here, the old man probably would. Wolf elected not to ask. Miller might have hired the old man as a scout, which meant the old man might alert Miller about the two gringos and the chiquita inquiring about him before the two gringos and the chiquita knew about Miller.

Best to wait.

They'd mosey over to the cantina, have a drink and some food, and keep their eyes open, see how things played out around them. If Miller was here, they'd likely know about him soon. Miller was no hothouse flower; he wouldn't stay quiet for long. Stockburn had no doubt that the outlaws knew Wolf was on their trail. They'd been outlaws too long to not know who was shadowing them.

Wolf, Charlie, and Sofia waited for a hay cart and a freight wagon manned by two beefy Mexican mule-skinners to pass, then walked across the street and mounted the steps of the Yellow Bird's front portico. It was a little after noon, and maybe a dozen diners sat at tables, conversing and eating from bowls or plates, tortillas steaming in broad piles on the tables before them. The place smelled of spicy Mexican food, the ristras of drying peppers or garlic bulbs hanging from wood-and-adobe support posts, and tequila.

The tang of tequila was especially strong.

It made Stockburn's mouth water, as did the savory smells of the food being consumed mostly, it appeared by men in business suits though a few thick-set peons, likely farmers or freighters, were indulging in the Yellow Bird's fine fare, as well.

A couple of pretty serving girls were hustling about the tables, too busy to give much notice to the mismatched trio who'd just entered. A balding bartender with a handlebar mustache was hastily filling drink orders behind the bar as well as tending the range on which several pots bubbled and a large cast-iron skillet sizzled. A young boy was helping, just then dipping a wooden spoon into one of the pots, and tasting.

He had to stand on his tiptoes to see into the pot. He muttered to himself then tossed a handful of spice from a pouch beside the range into the pot, and stirred.

Stockburn looked around for Miller and/or his compatriots. As he did, he kept an eye out for rurales in their traditional dove-gray uniforms with red stripes running down the outsides of their trouser legs.

He saw neither. The lack of rurales was a relief. The lack of Miller, Brennan, and Harris was a disappointment. He liked Mexico, but he'd rather retire here than work here. Too damn hot. He was ready to head back north.

Besides, the need to put a bullet through Red Miller's head was a burning desire inside him. He wanted that for Billy Blythe as much as he wanted it for the young man's pretty widow.

Wolf glanced at Charlie and Sofia. Both looked crestfallen.

"Well, let's eat," Charlie said. "My belly's been gettin' way too cozy with my backbone of late. And that tequila smells powerful . . . good." He'd ended that last sentence uncertainly.

Charlie, like Stockburn and Sofia, had suddenly noticed the faces of the diners around them turn to them in much the same fashion as the faces on the street had turned to them. Surprised expressions turned dubious.

Men nudged each other with their elbows, muttered beneath their breaths.

More faces turned to the trio and held.

A heavy silence fell over the room and then by ones, twos, and threes, the diners rose from their chairs, leaving their food and drinks and in some cases even burning cigarettes and cigars, and headed for the door. The room filled with the thunder of chairs scraping across the flagstone floor, men and a few women gaining their feet, grabbing their hats, and hustling to the door so quickly that a bottleneck quickly formed.

There were a few brief skirmishes. Spanish epithets rose in hushed, fearful voices.

Then the crowd was out on the street, dispersing, fleeing in every direction.

Stockburn, Charlie, and Sofia, standing six feet inside the batwings, had turned to watch in grim fascination.

Suddenly the street outside the cantina, previously

bustling with foot, horseback, and wagon traffic, was as deserted as that of a ghost town. Sunlight bled down from the cobalt sky. Dust sifted, swirling.

A sound rose from behind Stockburn. He turned toward the bar, one hand closing over the grips of the big .45 holstered for the cross-draw on his left hip.

The barman was gone. So were the bar girls.

The brown-faced, short-haired little boy who'd been tending the pots stared at Stockburn from behind the bar. Only the boy's face was visible as, chin resting on both his hands laid flat atop the bar, he stared in wide-eyed fascination toward the two gringos and the pretty senorita.

The pots continued bubbling, and the pan continued sizzling atop the range behind him.

A thick arm reached through a curtained doorway behind the bar, grabbed the boy's shoulder, and jerked him back through the doorway and out of sight. The flowered curtain jostled into place until it hung motionless from its rope.

Stockburn returned his gaze to the deserted street. The only things moving out there now were dust being lifted by breeze gusts and the breeze-buffeted leaves of the dusty cottonwoods.

Sofia turned to stare up at Stockburn, her eyes wide with apprehension.

Lonesome Charlie raked his hand across his chin and turned to Wolf, as well. "Do you feel offended, Wells Fargo? I sure do. I feel like that bath was a waste of time."

Sofia turned to the window and gasped, closing a hand over her mouth.

"What is it?" Wolf asked.

The girl pointed with her right arm and index finger.

Stockburn followed her gaze through the window and across the street to a rooftop.

Two men in dove-gray uniforms and holding Springfield rifles stood atop the roof, to either side of a brass-canistered Gatling gun that had been set up on a tripod. A third rurale squatted behind the deadly-looking, mosquito-like machine gun. The third rurale just then rammed a clip into the gun's barrel from the top and wrapped his brown hand around the crank's wooden handle.

He angled the barrel down over the lip of the roof, taking cold aim at the saloon window directly in front of Wolf, Lonesome Charlie, and Sofia.

Stockburn pulled his gaze down from the roof, and his heart kicked a rib.

Captain Nestor Azcona stood in the shade of the gallery beneath the Gatling gun. The hawk-faced rurale smiled as he raised a fat cigar in his beringed right hand and puffed.

As he blew the heavy smoke wreaths out into the sunshine before him, he smiled more broadly and shouted in lightly accented English, "*Come on out of there Senores and Senorita . . . or I will shoot you out of there like rats in a privy!*"

CHAPTER 27

Stockburn stared coldly out the window at the malevolently grinning countenance of Nestor Azcona. He looked at the Gatling gun perched atop the roof above the captain.

The barrel, glistening in the high desert sun, was aimed right at him.

He'd never actually fired a Gatling gun, but he'd heard such a weapon could fire a thousand rounds in a minute. If the Gatling gun didn't take him and his trail pards down as the bullets hurled through the glass of the two large front windows, one on each side of the door, then the Springfields of the other rurales just then spilling out of the breaks between buildings to each side of Azcona and forming a line in the street facing the Yellow Bird, in front of and to each side of Azcona, would.

A quick count told Stockburn he was facing a good twenty men not counting Azcona himself.

Armed with a Gatling gun.

Lonesome Charlie glanced up at Stockburn, narrowing a wary eye. "Somethin' tells me the captain was expectin' us."

Stockburn nodded. "He set a trap and I led us right into it."

"Ah, don't be too hard on yourself, Wells Fargo," Charlie said. "You didn't lead me an' the chiquita nowhere we didn't wanna go."

"Si," Sofia said quietly, casting her own bleak gaze onto the rifle-bristling street before them. "You didn't hear either of us object, Wolf."

"I'm sorry, Sofia. This could be bad."

"I knew it could be bad when I convinced you to let me ride down here with you. Whatever happens, the fault is my own. Not yours."

Stockburn drew a breath.

"We could always try fightin'," Charlie said, gazing pensively out the window.

"We could."

"We might have . . . oh, I don't know . . . a snowball's chance in hell against that Gatling gun."

"It'd cut us to ribbons."

"Might be faster, though," Charlie opined.

"Probably would be."

Stockburn stared through the dusty glass at Azcona, who was just then raising the cigar again to his mouth, taking another couple of puffs as he continued smiling across the street at the trapped gringos and the senorita. Wolf could tell the man was enjoying the conundrum he'd laid out for his quarry.

He was enjoying the impossible, dire situation he'd put them in. Maybe he knew that Stockburn had heard he'd borrowed many torture techniques from the Apache.

Stockburn squeezed the neck of the rifle he held down against his right leg. He considered raising it. As soon as he did, bullets would shred him. They'd shred Sofia standing to his right, and they'd shred Lonesome Charlie.

On the other hand, a quick death might be preferable to what Azcona had in mind for them. Wolf looked at Sofia. Preferable to what he no doubt had in mind for Sofia, too.

Far more preferable.

As though sensing his eyes on her, Sofia turned to him. She gave a faint smile and said, "Let's go out and hear what the man has to say, Wolf." She hiked a shoulder. "I mean, what do we really have to lose?"

Oh, possibly several hours, possibly several days of agonizing torture is all.

He thought as much but didn't say it.

Funny, he vaguely noted. He hadn't thought he feared death. Still, he found himself clinging to every living second like a drowning man to a thrown rope.

He stepped over to a table on his right and set the Yellowboy on top of it. Slowly, gazing out the window at the grinning captain, he unleathered the Colt on his left hip, and set it on the table by the Yellowboy. He did the same with the second Colt and with his bowie knife, as well.

He turned to Charlie. "The girl and I are going out there, Charlie. You comin'?"

Charlie stared at the captain through the window. He grimaced, sighed, then set his own rifle on a table. "Why not? Couldn't hurt too much to hear what he has to say, could it?"

He must have silently answered his own question, because he gave a grim chuckle as he set his old Dragoon on the table, as well.

Stockburn wrapped his right hand around Sofia's

arm as though to reassure her though he was sure of nothing except that they would probably be dead soon. Side by side, he and the girl stepped out through the batwing doors and onto the adobe portico. Charlie walked out behind them and stood beside Sofia.

Azcona stood staring at them through that devilish smile of his, through the smoke webbing in the sunlit air before him. He took a few more puffs, then removed the stogie from his mouth and stepped off the boardwalk beneath the ramada.

He strode across the street, his large Mexican spurs ringing, the heels of his high black boots into which the cuffs of his gray, red-striped trousers were tucked sending up little puffs of adobe-colored dust that were swirled by the gusting breeze.

He stopped about ten feet away from the two gringos and the girl, and gave an official click of his boot heels. "Senores Stockburn and Murdock." His eyes settled on Sofia and turned dark as smoldering coals as they roamed across her fine, nicely curved figure, lingering on the twin mounds testing the fortitude of her calico blouse.

He gave a slant-eyed smile and bowed his head as though greeting royalty. In Spanish he said, "Senorita, I do not believe that I have had the pleasure. If I had, I would surely remember. I am Nestor Azcona, el Capitan of the Mexican Rural Police."

Again, he dipped his chin, let his raptor's eyes rake her brashly once more before turning his oily smile to her face and canted his head slightly to one side in a mock posture of affable deference. He was a subhuman-looking creature, his face long and angular, his nose like a knife, a long scar running down his cheek, over his jaw, and nearly straight down his neck and into his shirt collar.

A machete scar, Stockburn absently thought. At one time or another, the captain must have found himself crossways with a peasant *revolutionario*. The preferred weapon of the peasant was the machete, the best implement for lopping off the heads of the landed gentry as well as those who rode for the corrupt Mexican government, like Azcona himself.

"I am Sofia Ortega."

"And where are you from, my dear?"

"Mesilla in the New Mexico Territory."

"And what are you doing with these two stray dogs?"

"I have ridden down here to seek justice for my husband. He was killed by—"

Stockburn cut her off with: "We're down here on the trail of Red Miller, Captain. A cold-blooded killer north of the border and south of the border, as well."

"Shut up, Stockburn!" Azcona barked, eyes flashing with lunatic rage. "You will speak when spoken to and at no other time, understand? I was conversing with the senorita."

Lonesome Charlie stepped forward, raising his hands palms out and giving an affable smile. "Now look, Captain. Surely we can work things—"

The captain rammed his right, gloved fist into the old man's belly.

Charlie jackknifed and dropped to his knees, clamping his arms over his midsection, his hat tumbling from his head to land crown down in the street beside him. His face was a red mask of agony.

He grunted and groaned, making strangling sounds as

he tried to draw a breath into his lungs though his damaged stomach muscles, clenched like a fist, were having none of it.

Raw fury exploded inside Stockburn. He clenched his right fist, took two steps forward. Azcona widened his eyes in total disbelief at the gringo's brazen attack. Wolf buried his fist in the captain's belly. When Azcona bent forward, grabbing his own bruised middle, the big detective drove his right knee up, slamming it resolutely into the rurale captain's face.

"Achh!" Azcona cried, the blow knocking his head up and back.

He staggered backward, blood spurting from his broken nose. He dropped his cigar as he threw his arms out for a balance he did not attain. He tripped over his own spurs and struck the ground hard on his back.

As he did, the Gatling gunner rattled off a half-dozen shots, the bullets pluming dust in front of Stockburn before Azcona raised one hand, palm out. "Stop! Stop! *Don't you dare kill him!*" He clutched his hand to his bloody nose and rolled onto his side, straining to get a breath into his lungs, just as Charlie still was.

"Not yet!" he fumed, spitting blood from his lips. *"No—not yet!"*

Stockburn stood tensely, fists still raised, boots spread, rage still a wildfire inside him. He'd been as shocked by his assault on the rurale captain as Azcona himself was, but there was no taking it back. His heart thudded angrily; he was a teased bull pawing the ground, ready to fight.

Sofia was on both knees beside Charlie, one hand on his back, the other on his shoulder, consoling him. Charlie looked up, his face still a red mask of agony. But he looked from Azcona lying on the ground ten feet away from him, and then to Stockburn, and managed a smile and a wink.

"Aún no!" Azcona repeated. "Not yet!"

The other rurales on the street had taken one or two offensive steps forward, aiming their old Springfields straight out from their shoulders. The two rurales standing on the roof also aimed their rifles at Wolf, while the young rurale manning the Gatling gun smiled eagerly down the barrel.

Azcona heaved himself onto his left shoulder and hip. He spoke in a high, nasal twang as he said, "You arrogant son of a three-peso, toothless, diseased puta! How dare you ride into my country and assault me!" He spat more blood as, eyes crossed to either side of his beaklike nose, he screeched, "Don't you realize you just committed suicide, *pendejo*?"

A fresh wave of fury washed through Stockburn. He narrowed his eyes at Azcona, hardened his jaws, and shouted, "Who you tryin' to fool, Azcona? You intended on killin' us, anyway! Stop your infernal caterwauling and do what you're gonna do, you low-down greaser scum!"

The captain stared up at him. A smile spread across his lips over which blood from his broken nose trickled in twin rivulets. A girlish-sounding chuckle issued through those fluttering lips as he pushed himself into a sitting position.

He kept his eyes on Stockburn as he said, "Corporal Monterosso? Are you here, Hombrecito?"

The rurale standing on the roof to the right of the Gatling, lowered his rifle slightly and shifted his gaze to Azcona. "Si, si, El Capitan! I am here!"

"Get down here," Azcona said in Spanish.

"Si, si, *jefe!*"

Monterosso lowered his rifle, taking it in one hand, then stepped down the pitched roof to his left. He made his way, taking mincing steps on the cracked red tiles, to the building's right front corner. He shifted his rifle to his left hand, then, throwing out his left arm as though it were a wing, he leaped off the roof to the ground, striking the street flat-footed and bending his knees.

Stockburn judged it must have been a good thirty-foot drop. But Monterosso, or "Hombrecito," as Azcona had called him, endured it without so much as a flinch or even the pop or creak of a bone. In fact, as the man straightened his legs, a smile spread across his broad, round, black-bearded face.

Stockburn immediately saw why the man had made the plunge look so easy. Monterosso's legs were as broad as poplar boles but likely as hard as oak, with knees as stout as the hubs of ore drays.

The moniker, *Hombrecito*, or, "Little Man," as Azcona had addressed him, was a joke, of course. Monterosso was no *hombrecito*. While he didn't appear much over six feet, he was built like a Brahma bull.

Muscles bulged in his shoulders, upper arms, forearms, and thighs. He was so muscular that he resembled nothing so much as Greek statues Stockburn had seen in pictures. Only, this statue had the face of an ape—an ape with a single, heavy black brow mantling his large, round eyes. His face behind his black beard was Indian-dark, and his thick, angular arms hanging down from his yoke-like shoulders were so long that his hamlike hands drooped nearly to his knees.

His gray slacks were too short for him, the cuffs stopping well above the rope-soled sandals he wore. The gray tunic appeared two, to three sizes too tight, for the shoulder seams were unraveling, showing the grimy paleness of an unwashed, sweat-stained undershirt also trying to contain the bulging muscles.

He wore a buckskin pouch—or was it a *human skin* pouch?—around his neck from a length of hemp. It dangled over the twin cartridge bandoliers crisscrossed on his chest.

Azcona heaved himself to his feet with a grunt. He brushed his fist across his broken nose, glared at Stockburn, and cursed.

"Step forward, *por favor,* Monterosso," the captain said, keeping his malign gaze on Stockburn. "Your services are required."

"Si, si, el Capitan!"

Monterosso spread his legs slightly, hiking one hip, and broke wind to the chuckling amusement of the other rurales around him. A couple of them elbowed each other and wagged their heads. Good old Hombrecito! The smile in place on his ape-like face, Monterosso came ambling forward with all the grace of an aged cow, his sandals flapping against the heels of his feet that were easily the size of serving platters.

They were as hairy as the feet of a primate, Stockburn noted with an inward grimace.

The other rurales had turned their attention to the big man as soon as Azcona had called him, and they kept their attention on him now, smiling delightedly as he approached Azcona and Stockburn standing just beyond the fallen rurale captain.

In every large association of men, there is always one who stands out. He is usually a small, extroverted man gifted with a singular personality or a big, reckless man, taciturn perhaps but also gifted with a singular temperament. For the mere reason that he stands out among the other men in his group, he is the source of great amusement in an otherwise humorless endeavor. For his entertainment value alone, he has earned the love and respect of his peers and is given abnormal sway by his superiors, who value him for the same reason his peers do.

Because no matter what you did, you could never make him fit in. But at the same time, he is inextricably a part of the group. In fact, he is the improbable glue that holds the group together.

The great bull snake at the heart of a writhing nest.

"Si, si, el Capitan," barked Monterosso, in guttural, heavily accented English. "Hombrecito is at your service."

Azcona's smile, still directed at Stockburn, grew foxier. "Senore Stockburn," he said, "Meet Jorge Monterosso. Or 'Hombrecito,' as we call him with great affection."

"Hi, Hombrecito," Wolf said, scowling at the man. "How you doin', old son?"

Monterosso only glowered at him.

"Monterosso is a fighter," Azcona informed Stockburn.

"You don't say."

"A bare-knuckle fighter. He has made me and his amigos"—he glanced at the rurales flanking him, all smiling in eager delight—"much money when we have pitted him against the best fighters in the other rurale platoons throughout Mexico. He has fought many of our rurale amigos, even Diego Cataño, the one known as "Samson" . . . and he's never lost. In fact, he's never come *close* to losing."

"Samson is now a babbling idiot who wets himself," said one of the rurales flanking the captain.

The others laughed.

Monterosso smiled, showing two broken upper front teeth.

Azcona chuckled, keeping his mouth closed but jerking his shoulders and arms.

Stockburn took the big man's measure again with his gaze. His jaw ached just looking at the hulking punisher. Swallowing a dry knot of dread in his throat, he turned back to Azcona.

"And, of course," he said with a grim smile, "you want me to fight him."

CHAPTER 28

"Fight him?" Azcona said, chuckling through his teeth. "*Fight* Hombrecito? No, no, Senor." He wagged a chastising finger. "You give yourself far too much credit, Senor Stockburn. Now, you might have been able to catch me off-guard and sucker punch me in traditional, cowardly gringo fashion. But do not call yourself a fighter. For compared to Hombrecito, you are nothing but a disease-carrying bug in need of squashing."

The other rurales chuckled.

Monterosso just stared at Stockburn, his dark eyes as flat and glassy as those of a bear. Stockburn was having remembered visions of Whip Larimore in the Athenaeum Saloon in Ruidoso.

"Don't get me wrong, Senor Stockburn," Azcona added quickly. "You are *going* to fight him. You *have* to fight him."

"What's in it for me?" Wolf asked.

"Here is what is in it for you. You see, if you fight him . . . and somehow manage to knock him down before he knocks *you* down . . . I will free you and the old man and the chiquita. You can go about your business. As long as that business takes you out of Mexico, you understand?"

Wolf glanced at Lonesome Charlie, who'd managed to sit back on the heels of his boots and appeared to be breathing regularly again. At least, as regularly as Charlie could manage these days. Charlie returned Stockburn's glance with a fateful one of his own.

Sofia sat beside Charlie, looking at Wolf, terror in her wide brown eyes. She glanced at the hulking Monterosso, returned her gaze to Stockburn, and shook her head slowly.

Turning back to Azcona, Stockburn said, "Just knock him down?"

"Si, si. If you knock him down before he knocks you down, I will stop the . . . uh . . . *fight*, if you wish to call it that . . . and allow you and your amigos to leave." Azcona grinned, shrugged, as though he'd just offered Stockburn the deal of the century.

"All right," Wolf said, shrugging out of his coat.

"Don't do it, Wolf," Charlie said, his voice still tight from the damage of the captain's unexpected attack. "Look at him. He'll turn you inside out and tear you apart. Besides, everyone knows the captain is *not* a man of his word."

Azcona glared at him, then looked at Stockburn. "You have my promise, Senor. I assure you." He placed a hand on his belly and gave a courtly bow.

"Come on, Charlie," Wolf said, dropping his coat on the ground. "Give us both a little credit, the captain an' me." He was rolling up his shirtsleeves. "I can take him." He looked at the glowering bruin again before him, and winced. "Leastways . . . we'll never know till I try."

As he rolled up his left shirtsleeve, one of the other rurales came up to take Monterosso's hat, bandoliers, rifle, and tunic. The big man kicked out of his sandals. Once unencumbered, he shoved the sleeves of his undershirt up his bulging arms then jogged backward, swinging his firsts, beckoning Stockburn to join him in the middle of the street.

He jogged in place, swinging his fists, feinting, ducking, pulling his head back, warming up.

He wasn't very light on his feet, Stockburn saw. On the other hand, a fighter built like that didn't need to be. He could probably stand there and take all the punishment Wolf could dish out to him then flatten the rail detective with one right cross.

Monterosso kept thumping his chest at Stockburn, challenging, beckoning, glowering, his single brow, which was the same texture and color of his tight cap of coarse, curly hair, formed a single, heavy line over both bulging eyes.

"Don't do it, Wolf," Sofia pleaded, standing beside Charlie now, sobbing.

Charlie had his arm around her as he gazed at Wolf darkly.

"Don't worry, darlin'," Wolf said, trying to sound encouraging. "We'll be out of here in two jerks of a donkey's tail."

"That is right," Azcona mocked him, smiling at Sofia. "Two jerks of a donkey's tail!"

He threw his head back and laughed.

So did the other rurales. Excepting Hombrecito. The big man was jumping in place and thumbing his chest with his roast-sized fists, taunting Stockburn in Spanish, daring him to come over and join the fun. *"No se preocupe, ¡esto no llevará mucho tiempo!"* Don't worry—this won't take long!

The others laughed.

Stockburn gave a heavy sigh. He was already feeling his eyes swell shut, and he hadn't taken a single punch yet.

He stopped and glanced over his shoulder at Captain Azcona. "We know what happens if he goes down first." He narrowed one eye in dreadful speculation. "What happens on the off chance *I* go down first?"

Azcona unsheathed the Smith & Wesson .44 holstered for the cross-draw on his left hip. He clicked the hammer back and aimed it at Lonesome Charlie's head. "Your friend dies. And the girl?" His smile broadened. "She becomes the spoils of war!"

The other rurales cheered.

Hombrecito looked at the pretty senorita, and he smiled for the first time, fairly slathering, though his eyes remained as dark and flat as a mindless bruin's.

Sofia merely hardened her jaws and flared her nostrils as she glared at the captain.

"Had a feelin' it would be somethin' like that," Stockburn muttered as he walked toward the big bruin jogging in place before him. Monterosso kicked his heels high, swinging his fists broadly now, grimacing with each false punch, making the wind in front of him whoosh.

And making Wolf's jaws ache with anticipated punishment . . .

"All right," Wolf said, crouching and raising his own fists. "You asked for it, Hombrecito. Don't say I didn't warn you."

Monterosso smiled finally and glanced at the rurales lined up behind him including the two on the roof, one still crouched menacingly behind the Gatling gun aimed down into the street.

Wolf walked to within six feet of his hulking opponent and stopped. The man might have been a few inches shorter than him, but he was twice Stockburn's width. He probably outweighed him in muscle alone by fifty pounds.

Hombrecito drew his head down, grinning his hideous smile with those two broken front teeth and that single brow, and touched his right index finger to that cheek, mocking him with his eyes as well as his words. "Come on, gringo. Go ahead. I give you the first one. *Vamos*— give me all you got!"

"All right." If the man was going to give him an open shot at him, he was going to take it. The stakes were too high not to.

Stockburn clenched his own fists and, crouching, stepped first left then right, then swung his right fist toward the big man's granitelike head. He stopped the blow suddenly, smiling inside, satisfied with his tactical deceit, wanting to take the man off his guard, then rammed his left fist squarely against Monterosso's doorstop nose.

With a savage grunt, he hammered a right uppercut against the man's left jaw.

He delivered both blows with all the strength he had in each arm. He'd connected well. But as far as he could tell, Hombrecito's head hadn't moved a bit. Delivering those blows truly had been like punching a big lump of fixed granite.

The man's nose was fine. Just fine. Not a single drop of blood shone in either nostril!

Stockburn stepped back, crestfallen, fists aching.

The rurales laughed. Wolf could hear Azcona chuckling through his teeth behind him.

"Oh boy," Charlie said.

He took the words right out of Wolf's head.

He stepped back, dread a hot, throbbing coal in his belly.

Hombrecito moved toward him, smiling, crouching, the big muscles at the back of his neck rising like a rabid cur's hackles. Suddenly, he lurched forward and sideways, swinging a right haymaker.

Wolf managed to dodge it but then the man's left connected glancingly with his forehead. Even that graze slammed his head back and caused bells to toll in his ears.

He crouched low and hammered two quick jabs against his opponent's hard belly. Hombrecito didn't even grunt. He just moved toward Stockburn, kicking up dust around his bare feet, and rammed his left fist and then his right fist against Wolf's mouth, splitting his lips.

Stockburn stumbled violently backward, spitting blood and shaking his head to clear it.

Somewhere to his right, Charlie sucked a sharp breath through his teeth. Sofia gasped.

Wolf tried desperately to get his boots set beneath him. He nearly went down, tripping over his own left boot heel before, by sheer force of will, he got both set relatively firmly down in the dust, his weight again centered.

He had no time to revel in his ability to remain upright against such an onslaught. Monterosso was on him in the next second, the man's face set hard, eyes implacable. He swung a right cross that kissed Wolf's chin as Wolf drew his head back quickly. His big opponent tried to smash his already bloody mouth again with a hard left jab.

That fist brushed across Stockburn's right shoulder as Wolf lurched to his right, swinging around to the bigger man's left side and hammering two firm punches to the man's ear. Continuing around behind the man, Stockburn slammed both his fists against the back of the big man's head.

Finally, he got a reaction!

Hombrecito bent his head forward then turned to glare over his left shoulder at his taller, lither opponent. The man's ear wasn't bleeding, but it turned pale and then crimson, and one eye briefly watered.

Wolf smiled. He'd hurt him. At least, he'd hurt him.

Encouraged, Wolf continued to shuffle around the man, landing one blow after another . . . until Hombrecito turned to face him, squared his shoulders, and cut through Stockburn's own punches with two of his own.

Again, Wolf stumbled backward, trying desperately to keep his feet.

Again, Sofia gasped. Charlie sucked air through his teeth.

When Stockburn had caught his balance again, Monterosso was before him again, crouching, shuffling, glowering up at him from beneath that long, heavy brow. The man thrust a jab at Wolf. Wolf deflected it with his left fist then hammered the man's mouth with his right.

Astonishingly, he cut Hombrecito's upper lip.

The other rurales muttered their surprise.

No one looked more astonished than the big man

himself. He licked his lip then flared his nostrils at his opponent.

Stockburn couldn't relent. He'd hurt Monterosso and while the man was rocked back if only metaphorically on his heels, Wolf had to keep at him.

He thrust two more sharp jabs at the man's face, wanting to keep working on his mouth. Hombrecito deflected both blows with his big fists then landed his own glancing blow across Stockburn's chin.

Wolf shook away the cobwebs and lurched forward so fast that he caught his opponent by surprise. He brought a haymaker up from his right knee and landed it square on Hombrecito's mouth, deepening the cut in his upper lip.

Monterosso took two stumbling steps backward, eyelids fluttering.

Again, the rurales muttered their collective exclamations of surprise.

Encouraged, Stockburn shuffled forward and landed two more blows before Monterosso could get his hands back up, deflecting a third. Now Wolf had cut the right side of the man's brow.

Monterosso brushed his fist across his brow, scowling and shaking his giant head. As he did, he laid his other eye open, and Wolf, gritting his teeth and grinning, landed a left cross, opening up a gash along the other side of the massive brow.

Monterosso stumbled sideways, blinking and shaking his head. He grabbed at the ground with his bare feet, trying to steady himself. Fear shone in his eyes.

Stockburn wasn't going to let him get settled. He followed the man, smiling eagerly, punching, deflecting

Hombrecito's own blows, which did not bear the force that they had a few seconds ago.

Wolf hammered the man's hard belly, evoking a grunt from his opponent.

When Monterosso lowered his arms to deflect another blow to his midsection, Wolf went to work on the man's lips and eyes again, landing blow after blow. The man raised his hands to deflect the blows, but Wolf worked around them, hammering his cheeks and even landing two good jabs against his right ear, cutting it just above the thumb-sized lobe.

When Hombrecito squealed out *"Mierda!"* from behind his raised fists, Wolf knew he had him.

The man was in shock. Maybe even afraid. Stockburn was working faster than his big opponent was accustomed to. Likely, Monterosso had always fought men as big as himself. Probably as slow as himself, as well.

Now he was fighting a man taller and faster, and one who had nothing to lose but everything to gain in taking every advantage he could find.

Wolf hammered the big man's face blow after blow after blow, following Monterosso in a broad circle as the man backpedaled, fists raised to shield his face, lowering them to shield his belly, which was also suffering from the rail detective's savage attack.

Beneath the caterwauling of his own desperate rage in his ears, Wolf could hear the rurales shouting encouragement to their fighter. In the periphery of his visions, he could see them waving their fists as they stumbled forward, closing around the two warring bruins.

Stockburn smacked Hombrecito's mouth, his left eye, his right eye then moved around him to smash his left ear with two quick jabs. He shuffled to the man's other side and smashed his mouth again.

As Monterosso stumbled backward, his eyes rolling back in his head, Wolf followed him, savagely assaulting the man's face with left and right crosses and thundering jabs, making a gooey red paste of his opponent's mouth.

Somehow, while Monterosso appeared to be weakening, he wouldn't go down.

He stumbled backward and to each side, his eyes rolling around in their sockets like washed-out marbles, but the man would not go down.

Stockburn himself was nearly out of steam.

Suddenly, he could no longer raise his arms. Each weighed as much as an anvil.

He stopped, looked down at his fists. They looked like freshly ground beef.

A shadow moved toward him across the ground. Hombrecito's big ape feet came into view before him.

Dread flooded Wolf's belly like a gallon of rattlesnake venom.

Weakly, he raised his head. Monterosso stood before him. The man's face was in little better condition than Stockburn's fists.

Suddenly, the rurales gathered closely around them stopped shouting and wildly gesturing. Silence fell over them as their previous optimistic smiles played over their sun-seared faces again.

"Ah, hell," Wolf heard Lonesome Charlie say.

"Mios dio," he heard Sofia say.

Before him, Monterosso smiled through the bloody mask of his face.

Then the big man raised his right fist, pulled the arm

back, and thrust the fist forward. Stockburn wanted to deflect or dodge it, but he could do neither.

The fist grew larger and larger before him before becoming a blur as it hammered his left cheek. He was only vaguely aware of leaving his feet . . . then of striking the ground on his right shoulder and hip and rolling, dust roiling around him in thick, sunlit tendrils.

CHAPTER 29

Sofia sobbed and ran over to Stockburn. "Wolf!"

He blinked through the wafting dust as Sofia dropped to both knees beside him, lowering her head to his chest, wailing.

Stockburn tried to raise his right hand. The hand was numb and the arm still weighed as much as a yoke. Still, a little strength ebbed back into him. He raised his hand and set it on the back of the girl's head.

"S-sorry . . . sweetheart," he raked out between cracked and bloody lips.

Suddenly, Captain Azcona, his nose caked with dried blood and both eyes swelling and darkening, was standing over him. The captain reached down and pulled Sofia up by her hair.

The girl yelped as Azcona held her by her hair and one arm. He grinned down at Stockburn and then turned to Monterosso standing nearby, and yelled, "To the victor go the spoils!"

Azcona lowered his hand to the collar of Sofia's blouse, and ripped it straight down the back. He ripped the chemise beneath it, too, and tossed both garments to the ground.

Sofia's slender, brown shoulders looked painfully vulnerable in the sunlight as did her tender brown bosoms poking out from behind the screen of her coal-black hair.

She screamed and closed her hands over her breasts.

Azcona laughed. "Here you go, Hombrecito! Take the gringo-loving chiquita inside and show her a real good time!"

He gave Sofia a savage shove right into the waiting arms of the lusty-eyed Hombrecito.

"When you're done, we'll pass her around to the others!"

The other rurales, standing in a ragged half-circle around Azcona, Stockburn, Sofia, and Monterosso, laughed and cheered and thumped their chests. Some yapped like coyotes, raising their chins to the sky.

Hombrecito crouched, picked the wailing Sofia up in his thick, muscular arms and threw her over his shoulder as though she were a light sack of feed corn. He trundled forward, the girl screaming, wailing, kicking, and pummeling his back with her fists.

"No!" Lonesome Charlie cried, lunging toward the big man, who shrugged him off as though he were no more than a pesky fly.

Charlie hit the ground and rolled, groaning, clutching his left arm. With all the stress, his ticker must have been kicking like a wild mule in his chest again.

Monterosso stepped through the saloon's portico and disappeared through the swing doors. Sofia's screams echoed around inside the stout adobe building, issuing over the batwings, making Wolf's own heart leap and twist.

He glared up at Azcona gazing down at him. "You rotten devil."

Azcona blinked slowly and smiled. He raised his

revolver, angling it down toward Wolf's face. He clicked the hammer back and narrowed one eye as he aimed down the barrel, drawing a bead on the railroad detective's forehead.

Ah, hell, Wolf thought. He closed his eyes. *Just get it over with, you stinking devil.*

He couldn't stand another second of Sofia's agonized screams.

All at once they stopped.

Stockburn opened his eyes. Azcona was still grinning down at him, aiming the Smith & Wesson .44 at his head. But now the skin wrinkled incredulously above the bridge of the man's blood-crusty nose.

From inside the cantina came a loud roar of male misery.

Monterosso cursed in Spanish.

Frowning, Azcona lowered the pistol to his side and turned his head to peer toward the saloon's portico. Stockburn turned his own aching head to stare in the same direction.

The rurales behind him muttered uncertainly amongst themselves.

Lonesome Charlie, on the ground ten feet to Wolf's left, shot Stockburn a questioning glance then directed his own gaze toward the saloon.

Another roar sounded from inside, echoing. It sounded like the indignant exclamation of an enraged bear.

The thunder of heavy footsteps grew louder.

A shadow moved behind the swing doors. Monterosso pushed through the doors and staggered out through the portico. He stopped at the edge of the boardwalk. He stood stiffly, ramrod straight, blood trickling from the many cuts and abrasions on his large, round face.

His dark eyes were bright with agony.

He raised a hand high as though trying to reach around behind his head. He couldn't do it. The arm flopped back down to his side.

Hombrecito lifted his chin and shouted, *"¡La puta me ha matado!"*

The whore has killed me!

His eyes rolled back into their sockets, dark brown gophers retreating to their holes. He fell straight forward, like a felled tree, and hit the street in front of the boardwalk without even raising a hand to break his fall.

Dust billowed around him.

Stockburn felt a smile quirk his mouth corners as he studied the big, unmoving body.

Sofia's stiletto jutted from the back of Monterosso's neck. Only the handle was visible. She'd thrust it hilt deep.

Stockburn had only a second to revel in the chiquita's handiwork. Azcona turned toward him again, the man's eyes blazing with fury. He aimed the Smith & Wesson at him again, and again he ratcheted back the hammer. *"Die*, you . . ."

A large, round hole appeared in the middle of his forehead. The blood and white brain tissue geysered out the back of the man's head, across the body of Monterosso lying behind him, and onto the boardwalk beyond the big man.

The thundering *rat-a-tat-tat* of what could only be the Gatling gun broke the heavy silence. Suddenly, men were screaming and cursing. Wolf looked up in confusion to see the rurales who'd formed a semicircle around him being shredded with the .45-caliber rounds.

What the hell . . . ?

They didn't have time to raise their Springfields or to even cut and run before the bullets hammered into them, opening gaping bloody wounds and staining the dirt around them with blood and viscera.

Again, Wolf asked himself: *What the hell?*

The only conclusion he could come to in the few seconds following the onslaught of the blasting reports was that the young man operating the Gatling gun didn't know what he was doing. He didn't know how to handle the big gun, so that when he started firing, the gun simply got away from him and he was accidentally cutting down his own platoon.

What other explanation could there be?

Soon, the rurale would discover his mistake and bring the machine gun to bear on his intended targets.

Stockburn lowered his head and covered his ears, awaiting the inevitable bullets.

The shooting stopped.

He frowned, staring down at the dust and finely churned straw of the street an inch before his eye.

A man groaned.

The Gatling gun spat out a couple more bullets, ending the groan.

Stockburn wasn't sure he should move. Maybe the Gatling gunner thought he was dead . . . ?

Curiosity got the best of him. He lifted his head and rolled onto his back, sitting up. He glanced behind him. Lonesome Charlie was sitting up now, as well, his sweaty hair and beard coated with the dust of the street. He looked pale and badly rumpled but generally unharmed.

At least, he didn't appear to be sporting any bullet wounds. He looked as surprised as Wolf did in that regard.

Both men turned their curious gazes toward the top of the tile-roofed building across the street. Two rurales lay dead in the street before the place. Stockburn recognized one as the Gatling gunner. The other was the rurale who'd been standing beside the Gatling gun, wielding a Springfield.

What the hell . . . ?

Wolf lifted his even more curious gaze to the roof again. The person rising from a crouch behind the smoking Gatling gun was not a rurale. In fact, the person rising from a crouch behind the smoking Gatling gun was a woman.

Stockburn shook his head, blinked his eyes to clear them.

No. Couldn't be. He'd taken a worse beating than he'd thought. His brains were scrambled.

Again, he looked up at the roof of the building across the street.

No, it was not a woman standing there in a black cowhide vest with nothing else beneath it except her own lovely wares. She wore black leather slacks with flared cuffs and adorned with silver conchos down the outsides of the legs. A concho-studded belt encircled her lean waist, and from this belt a matched set of ivory-gripped revolvers bristled on her hips, each with its handle angled forward, cross-draw fashion.

On her head was a black, silver-stitched, steeple-crowned sombrero. The hat's broad brim half-shaded a face that only a god in love with the idea of "woman," especially "exotic Hispanic woman," could have crafted slowly but surely and only bequeathed to the Earth when he was sure he'd gotten her right . . . her face, her thick curling hair, and her voluptuous body, as well . . . and was sure that she would melt the knees of any man lucky enough to lay eyes on her.

Stockburn chuckled, shook his head.

He'd been beaten senseless, that was all. His mind was playing tricks on him. It was probably some ugly, pot-gutted hombre up there but his mind, in its addled state, wanted to see a woman, so it made one up.

"Hey, what are you two gringos looking at?" came a husky female voice, lightly accented in the rich, exotic, rolling vowels and dahlia-soft consonants of Spanish.

Stockburn looked up at the roof again. By God, she was still there.

Wolf glanced over his right shoulder at Lonesome Charlie. Charlie was staring up at the roof with much the same, droopy-eyed, hang-jawed expression.

"Haven't you ever seen a woman before?" the husky voice came again in all its exotic Spanish splendor.

Wolf shuttled his gaze back to the roof. If ever a voice matched a face and a body . . .

He spat dust from his lips and cleared his throat. "Who're you?"

The lovely creature shook her hair back behind her bare shoulders, planted her fists on her hips, and gave a crooked grin. "Elaina de la Cruz."

She gave a throaty chuckle, then stepped around the Gatling gun to the roof's right side. She stuck two fingers to her lips and whistled. A cream-colored horse rode up from the rear of the building to stand at the front corner. It tossed its fine Arabian head, pawed the ground, and whinnied.

The woman chuckled then stepped off the edge of the roof. She dropped gracefully onto the cream Arab's black leather saddle, grabbed the reins from the horn, and booted the horse into a spanking trot over to Stockburn. She swung lithely down, the rich curls of her dark brown hair flying about her shoulders and glistening like copper in the Mexican sunshine.

Stockburn found the woman's appearance energizing. Enough so that he managed to summon enough strength back into his abused countenance to heave himself to his feet, albeit with a weary grunt. He glanced back to see Lonesome Charlie do the same thing. Apparently the loggy-hearted lawman didn't want to be lounging around on the ground like an old dog in the shade any more than Stockburn did in the presence of such a beguiling creature as that standing before them now.

Charlie grunted, groaned, his old bones popping, sinews creaking, but somehow managed to right himself and get his boots squared beneath him. He even crouched down to retrieve his hat and set it on his head. That was more than Wolf himself was up for.

The woman strode up to him, smiling, long, chocolate-brown eyes lit as though by an inner fire. Silver hoop rings dangled from her ears.

She stopped in front of Wolf, only two feet away, and gazed up at him, smiling as though at a secret joke. "Who are you?"

"Me—I'm, uh . . . uh . . ."

He'd be damned if he hadn't suddenly become a

tongue-tied schoolboy finding himself confronted alone in the cloakroom by the prettiest girl in the class. No. By the very real manifestation of his most haunting and lascivious dreams.

"Sí"—the dream manifestation raised her right hand and poked his chin with her index finger—"you."

"Wolf Stockburn," Charlie answered for him, walking up from behind to stand beside him, smiling bashfully at the woman who was not real, couldn't be real, though Wolf's brain hadn't gotten the message yet.

Vaguely, he wondered if she might have been caused by sun stroke on top of the beating he'd taken.

"Me—I'm Charlie Murdock. Lonesome Charlie, they call me." Charlie brushed his thumb across the sun-and-moon badge on his shirt. "I'm a deputy United States marshal, don't ya know." He chuckled as he rose up and down on the toes of his boots. "Stockburn here's one o' them fancy-Dan Wells Fargo detectives. I let him tag along with me down here to Old Mexico though he ain't been nothin' but trouble so far. We're trackin' owlhoots, don't ya know."

Stockburn looked the woman up and down. He couldn't help himself. What man could? She must be somewhere in her mid to late-twenties though she carried herself with a rarefied maturity and aplomb—and what woman wouldn't who looked like her?

His eyes lingered of their own accord and with shameless abandon on the leather vest that pushed up her bosoms enticingly, forming a deep dark V of cleavage. Her skin was as smooth as a baby's rump, and tanned to a deep, golden coffee color. It contrasted beautifully with the black of the leather she wore. Her shoulders were so well formed and alluring that Wolf wanted to caress each one.

The woman chuckled then nudged Stockburn's chin up with her finger and said, "Hey, amigo, you don't look so good. You took a bad braining, eh? By that big lecherous bull, Monterosso—Hombrecito." She smiled, showing a perfect set of healthy white teeth, her long eyes rising beguilingly at the corners. "You almost had him, though. One, maybe two more punches and—plop!—he'd have hit the ground. The first time any man has laid him out. You were so close! I wanted to intervene earlier but I had to wait and see how it turned out."

Stockburn scowled at her, incredulous. It was starting to sink in that she was, in fact, real. Not just a figment of his battered, feverish brain. "What'd you say your name was?"

Sofia's voice, hushed with shock, came from behind Stockburn and Charlie. "Elaina de la Cruz."

Holding her hands over her bare breasts, the senorita stepped off the boardwalk and crouched to retrieve her blouse and chemise. Holding them up in front of her, covering herself with the torn garments, she turned her gaze back to the strangely alluring woman, and said, "*El gato montés de Chihuahua.*"

She glanced at Stockburn and Lonesome Charlie, and translated: "The Wildcat of Chihuahua."

CHAPTER 30

Lightning forked the pregnant bellies of black clouds set against a stormy, periwinkle sky.

Thunder rumbled and cracked, sometimes booming so loud and violent that the ground trembled.

"How much farther?" Pike Brennan yelled above the storm, galloping his horse behind Red Miller.

Miller glanced back at the man, blinking against the cold rain slanting against his face. "Should be just beyond that next ridge!" He grinned with mockery. "What's the matter, Pike? A little rain gettin' your neck in a hump, is it?"

The rain hammered the outlaw leader, but his tarred poncho kept him dry.

Brennan wore a cowhide poncho. It kept him as dry as Miller's poncho did. Still, he was cold, and his face was wet. Yes, he was uncomfortable. Any man would be uncomfortable in this storm. Miller would have been uncomfortable, too, if not for the blue bottle he kept taking pulls from. The elixir the prissy doctor had given him seemed to build a bastion inside him against the slightest discomfort.

The heavy-lidded smile on Miller's face told Brennan

the man was not only tolerating the rain, he was enjoying it. Maybe seeing it as somehow magical, the way a dreamy kid might.

Brennan would love to have a sip of the stuff. He'd love to have the chill driven out of his bones, the bite taken out of the storm, relieve his worry that the trail they were on was going to get washed out or flooded and leave them stranded out here in the storm, possibly under threat of drowning. They were in mountains now, very rugged country, and every arroyo they crossed was flooded.

If the rain kept coming down as hard as it was, they would no doubt come to an arroyo they couldn't cross.

On the other hand, Brennan wasn't sure he wanted the strange, abrupt mood changes that went along with Teagarden's elixir. After a few sips from that blue bottle, Miller's face acquired a lazy, dreamy look. A totally relaxed look. As though snakes couldn't bite him and bullets wouldn't tear his flesh. As though everything was just fine and dandy, and always would be. Better than dandy.

Beautiful and even amazing!

Birds, leaves, the sunshine, horse apples . . . a crooked wooden sign pointing the way to an outlying village, the Catholic shrines along the trail—all just amazing and worth staring at for minutes at a time.

But those lazy, dreamy moods of Miller's had broken a few times, and left the man even more irritable and arbitrary than normal. The night before, he'd threatened to shoot Brennan for nudging Miller's foot with his own when Pike had reached for the coffeepot steaming on the iron spider they'd set over their campfire.

The evil glint in Red's eyes, and the way the man had held his Colt so steadily and certainly, had told Brennan he was about to be a dead man. He'd seen Miller's right index finger draw back against the trigger. Pike didn't know what had stopped him from firing, but Red finally responded to Brennan's as well as Flipper Harris's pleas to stand down by slackening his trigger finger.

He'd given a cold smile, his eyes hard as granite, as he'd suppressed the hammer and returned the revolver to its holster. Brennan had heaved a heavy sigh, realizing his back was bathed in cold sweat. He'd shuttled his incredulous, terrified gaze to Harris.

Flipper had shrugged, shaken his head, and given a nervous laugh, knowing that the target of Miller's wrath could just as easily have been him. That it might very well *still be* him. All it would take is the slightest misstep or the wrong glance.

Miller turned his head back forward, chuckling. He opened his mouth to the rain, let the heavy drops patter against his tongue. He drew his tongue into his mouth and took his time, savoring the taste of the cool rain.

Odd how a man never really thinks to taste the rain . . .

He was thinking about that, finding himself lost in the thought, a little sad, a little amazed, a little amused, as he followed the old trading trail down toward another shallow canyon.

Just off his right flank, Flipper Harris's horse whinnied shrilly at a bright lightning flash. The horse stopped, curveted, and reared, throwing its front foot high. Flipper gave an indignant curse and, dropping his reins, went hurling over the coyote dun's right hip. He hit the muddy trail with a splash.

Miller checked down his own mount, laughing. For some reason, he'd found the horse's sudden pitch and

Flipper's unceremonious dismount amusing. Something in the way it had taken poor one-armed Flipper so totally by surprise.

Brennan stopped his own mount behind Miller and turned to where Harris was just then shoving himself up off the muddy ground with one arm, glaring furiously at the horse whose reins Miller reached out and grabbed before the dun could hightail it.

"Whoah, now!" Red said. "Whoah! Whoo-ahhh, there, big feller!" He laughed again.

"What the hell's so funny?" Harris said, switching his glare from the horse to Miller. He crouched to retrieve his hat but kept his angry gaze on Red. "That's the second time he's done that!"

"It was just the lightnin'," Red said, tipping his face to the storm, opening his mouth and his eyes, letting the rain hammer him at will, enjoying it.

"That damn broomtail is not afraid of lightnin'!" Harris bellowed. "He just used it as an excuse to buck me off again 'cause he don't like me!"

Harris walked up to the wet, muddy horse, and unsheathed his pistol from beneath the flap of his yellow rain slicker. "Cursed beast!" he bellowed, slamming the barrel against the horse's long snout.

The horse whickered and jerked its head up, rattling the bit in its teeth.

"Whoa, now!" Red said, holding tight to the dun's reins. "That's no way to treat your hoss, there, Flipper. He's a good mount, all-in-all. You're just an unfamiliar rider. He'll get used to you! You'll get used to him!"

"Maybe I'll just shoot the cussed beast!" Harris raised the pistol, aimed at the horse, and cocked the hammer.

Miller lashed Flipper with the dun's reins. "Stand down, now, dammit, Flipper! You shoot that hoss, you sure as hell are not ridin' with me!"

"You're not ridin' with me, neither," Brennan put in, shouting above the storm. "Red's right, Flipper. Put the damn gun away, and climb back up onto that horse. We'll be out of the storm soon!"

Flipper cursed the horse again and shoved his pistol back into its holster. He took the reins from Red and swung back into the leather. He whipped the horse's left wither with the reins and yelled, "Damn broomtail hates me!"

"He ain't no broomtail!" Red said, chuckling his amusement. Brennan was glad he was amused, because he just easily could be aiming his six-shooter at Flipper's head. "He's a good horse, but he just takes some gettin' used to. Now, come on—maybe them nuns'll whip us up a hot meal!"

Miller booted his cream down the decline. The arroyo at the bottom had some water running through it but not enough to prove a hazard. The three outlaws crossed it without difficulty and climbed the long, steep grade beyond. As they did, Miller could see the massive masonry structure of *Convento de Cuilapam de Guerrero* take shape before them.

Sitting on a high ledge against a towering mountain wall, the old convent looked especially forbidding on such a dark and stormy afternoon. Since the sky was nearly as dark as night, the convent was a hulking black silhouette until lightning flashed, revealing the red tile-roofed turrets and towers and the heavy, pale stone walls of the cloisters and dome-roofed cathedral that flanked the place.

Miller and the two other outlaws followed the climbing, twisting and turning trail up the mountain between walls of rock or wind- and rain-battered tall trees and low shrubs. One canyon closed on their left while another canyon opened on their right, an open, black mouth threatening to suck the riders off the perilously narrow trail.

Rain pocked the narrow trace, the large drops splashing like bullets fired into a lake. Mud flew up from the horses' galloping hooves. Lightning flashed, intermittently illuminating the trail. Thunder crashed like cymbals. The smell of brimstone peppered the riders' noses.

Enjoying the smell and the storm in general, Red Miller grinned.

Above the men, the formidable-looking convent, built hundreds of years ago and named after some chili-chomper *revolutionario* general, shifted to and fro, disappearing from view at times then disappearing altogether as the riders made the last leg of the steep climb. As they rode up through a corridor of large boulders and crested the broad ledge that thrust itself out from the side of the mountain, the convent lay before them in all its grim, dark glory, its many deeply recessed windows glowing amber with the light of burning lamps.

A long, pale, brush-roofed adobe barn lay off to the right of the hulking structure. The barn was flanked by a large, fenced-in paddock. As Miller and the other two outlaws galloped into the convent's muddy yard, which was lit an eerie gunmetal blue by the frequent lightning flashes, two beefy, bearded men wearing greased hide ponchos, sombreros, and high-topped boots jogged out from the barn.

Neither said a word as Miller, Harris, and Brennan dismounted. Miller grabbed his saddlebags off the cream's back, and slung them over his left shoulder. Both hostlers merely led the horses toward two large, open double doors and on inside the barn, where Miller was sure they would be well-tended.

Sister Lucia Morales's "Convento," as the place was known—though most God-fearing folks saw the retainment of the name as a great sacrilege, given what the convent really was in its present manifestation—had a good reputation for satisfying not only the men who visited, but those men's mounts, as well.

The outlaws shifted their gun rigs on their waists as they strode, walking abreast, toward the high, stone front steps of the massive nunnery. As they did, they could hear the sawing of a fiddle and the strumming of a mandolin. In the window right of the large, oak front doors topping the stone steps, two shadows moved together—likely a man and woman dancing.

"I hope the deal's still on," Pike Brennan said. "Wouldn't want to have ridden all this way for nothin'."

Miller laughed as he patted his saddlebags. "I don't think we have to worry none about that. The deal we made with the sis is one she can't best. Not down here she can't. A thousand dollars a head? No, sir! She can't beat that even with that bumper crop she has waitin' fer us!"

He led the others up the steps and used one of the heavy, iron cross knockers to knock on one of the tall, broad, steel-banded oak doors. Both doors opened immediately and three armed men walked out onto the steps on a wave of warm air from within scented with the enticing aromas of liquor, perfume, opium, candles, and the fresh-cut hay aroma of marijuana. The sister was known to cultivate the best marijuana in Mexico, which in and of itself lured many men to *Convento de Cuilapam de Guerrero.*

One of the three men confronting Miller now had a short, fat cigar clamped in a corner of his mouth. All three were dressed as peasants but two wielded new-model Winchesters while a third handled a sawed-off, ten-gauge Richards shotgun. Cartridge bandoliers crisscrossed their chests. Hanging down over the bandoliers of each man was a gold cross.

The cross in combination with the bandoliers made Miller smile.

He smiled as two of the men frisked him, Harris, and Brennan, taking their revolvers and knives. Miller was not miffed. No guns were allowed in the Convento, and there were no exceptions—except for Sister Morales's henchmen, that was. As he remembered from his last visit, there were three or four. Not many. But enough.

They were big, capable, well-armed men who brooked no trouble. They were likely common bandits or former revolutionaries who'd sworn an oath of loyalty to Sister Morales.

They kept the big, sprawling hurdy-gurdy house buttoned down. Any form of violence would not only be met with violence but with death. On previous visits, Miller had wakened in one of the *convento*'s many cribs beside a slumbering puta to see a man or men dragged outside and shot on one of the several tiled patios or flower gardens ringing the old convent.

Red had assumed the doomed men had been caught fighting or beating one of the sister's girls—definitely a capital offence—and were simply paying the piper for their foolishness. The sister did not suffer fools. The joke was that she let St. Peter decide their fates.

When Miller and his partners had been relieved of their guns, the three silent henchmen stepped back into the convent, closing the doors behind them. A few seconds passed during which Red could hear the low roar of regulated revelry coming from within—singing, laughing, dancing, jovial conversing. Occasionally a woman's especially loud, bawdy laughter vaulted above the more sedate, general din before quickly settling back into the generalized din again.

The doors opened again suddenly and Sister Morales herself stood before Miller, Harris, and Brennan. She was a round woman only a little over five feet tall. In her traditional nun's white habit and black veil, with a hemp rope knotted around her portly waist, all that was visible of her body was her round, pudgy face. Her otherwise pale cheeks were always apple red while her small brown, slightly bulging eyes had never, at least in Red's experience, betrayed the slightest emotion. Her nose was like a small white lump of dough left on a baker's table.

Red thought she could be anywhere from thirty to seventy. It was that hard to tell. Just as she seemed ageless, she was one of those women who seemed sexless, as well. She gave off the aura of neutered asceticism and even a sullen contemptuousness toward coitus, her strange disdain none the less obvious despite its irony given her occupation as the madam of one of the most storied whorehouses in all of Mexico.

You had the sense around Sister Lucia Morales, whom it was said had been raised here as an orphan herself, that since all men and women were sinners who made whoopee, she might as well profit from it.

Red smiled broadly as Teagarden's tonic continued to course blithely through his veins, and dipped his chin to the woman. "Sister Morales, how wonderful it is to—"

"Do you have it—the amount we agreed to?" the sister asked, abruptly cutting him off. She spoke with only a faint trace of a Spanish accent.

Again, Miller smiled and patted the lumpy bags. "Si, si."

The woman stepped back and to one side. *"Entrar."*

CHAPTER 31

Miller and his cohorts stepped into the nunnery, the heady aromas wafting in the dim, smoky air, nearly taking Red's breath away.

Sister Lucia Morales closed the doors behind them, then stepped up beside Miller and poked his shoulder. He glanced at her, one brow arched. She poked the saddlebag pouch hanging down in front of him.

"Oh," Red said. "Sure, sure."

He glanced at the other two men, chuckled, then unbuckled the flap of the pouch hanging down over his chest. He lifted the flap. Sister Morales peeked inside. She looked up at him, arched her brows, bunched her lips, and gave a single approving nod.

"Come." She swung around, the black skirt of her gown billowing out around her short legs, and started forward.

The three Americans followed in single-file—first Red, then Flipper Harris, then Pike Brennan. As they moved through the vast room, which was like a scene out of a painting of Hell, all three men looked around, eyes wide, lower jaws hanging. Through the haze of smoke from tobacco and other substances, men and women moved together intimately, sitting or dancing or cavorting behind room partitions that did not entirely conceal them nor the intimate sounds they were making.

The room was ringed by a second-floor balcony, and more men and women cavorted atop the balcony or climbed the steps hand in hand from the main floor to the balcony then slipped through one of the dozen or so doors up there. Some of those women—no, many of those women, in fact—were entirely nude save a pair of earrings or a pearl necklace. Even some of the men were naked save maybe a hat or a cigar.

It was as though the men and women mixing in the giant, masonry-walled room, were mimicking the scenes depicted in the enormous oil paintings that hung on the walls, and which portrayed some of the lewdest goings-on Miller and his two Amercan partners had ever seen. At least, outside of *Convento de Cuilapam de Guerrero.*

Ahead of Miller, Sister Lucia Morales fairly floated through the smoke haze, wending her way between singing and dancing couples, past men and women cavorting at the room's enormous, glistening wooden bar flanked by a mirrored backbar that shone like polished diamonds. Several bartenders dressed in silk shirts, bow ties, and short, red velvet waistcoats hustled to fill empty glasses or draw beers from several spigots.

Miller would be damned if, as he followed the sister passed two folks "cavorting" on a green plush sofa ringed by grinning spectators, she didn't so much as give the scene even a passing glance but continued on to the other end of the room and through a velvet-curtained doorway.

Miller himself grinned at the brazen lascivious display then turned to wink at his two amigos following close on his heels, also taking in the spectacle with big, amazed grins even on their jaded, outlaw faces.

Visiting *Convento de Cuilapam de Guerrero* was a rare treat indeed!

The outlaws followed the silent nun up two flights of cracked flagstone stairs and down a broad hall between walls of endless rows of ancient wooden doors. The sister had pulled a guttering lantern off a wall peg just beyond the drinking hall. Now she held it high as she walked, shoving the shadows of the dark corridors and stairwells forward and to both sides.

Lightning flashed in the occasional, rain-streaked window. The thunder sounded like muffled coughs beyond the stout masonry walls and high ceiling.

Occasionally a frightened peeping sound followed the scuttling of little rat feet. Tiny eyes glowed in the shadows near the floor.

Miller looked around. They must be in the old orphanage section of the nunnery now, for old wooden toys and parts of dolls could be seen here and there on the floor. Cracked, half-ruined statues of patron saints stood here and there about the hall, some holding babies or infants.

Finally, the nun stopped in front of two stout wooden doors.

She rapped twice with the end of her fist.

Shortly, there came the scraping sound of a key in the lock. The door scraped open, hinges squawking. The head of a wizened old crone in a nun's habit and veil appeared in the partly open door.

"They're here," said Sister Morales.

The old crone, who looked more dog than human, pulled her head back and, shuffling arthritically, drew the door wide. She muttered in raspy, rapid-fire Spanish, "They had play-time in the cemetery before the storm, and took their baths early. They are darning clothes now. We were about to take them down to supper."

"Wait," said Sister Morales crisply as she stepped through the door the crone held open.

Miller followed her into what he assumed was once a small chapel and that now served as a girl's dormitory. Twenty or so cots were arranged along the walls before him, awash in the wavering light of many candles and several hurricane lamps arranged here and there about the room. At the far end of the room stood a pale altar on a dais flanked by a large stained-glass window. Statues of saints gazed out from niches in the walls surrounding the room.

On the edge of each cot sat a girl holding an article of clothing and needle and thread. There was a girl for each cot. All the girls were dressed alike—in plain sack dresses and sandals. Their hair was still wet from the baths the crone had mentioned.

Another old nun—not as old and wizened as the crone still holding the door open—sat in a brocade armchair at the base of the dais. She, too, held some piece of clothing; she continued to repair the cotton pantaloons with needle and thread as she gazed from her chair at the room's far end toward Sister Morales and the three unshaven male visitors in dripping ponchos and Stetsons flanking her.

Sister Morales stepped back and held out her arm to indicate the girls the way a farmer would display a barn full of milk cows. "Take a look. They are the cream of the crop. We've fed them well. They will weather the journey north and sell to the highest bidder."

Miller stepped forward, grinning as he cast his gaze at the young female faces regarding him warily from around the room.

"No sickness?" he asked.

"I don't take in the sickly. If they get sick here, they are quarantined in the infirmary or they are weeded out."

Miller glanced back at the grave, humorless woman, absently wondering what "weeded out" entailed. Judging by the cold, hard look in the woman's eyes, back where she stood between Harris and Brennan, the top of her head barely rising to the men's shoulders, Miller had a pretty good idea what "weeded out" entailed, all right.

He smiled again as he continued strolling forward. The woman's cold-bloodedness amused him no end. The devil in a nun's habit, which she wore totally without shame.

Amazing!

"Any, uh . . . troublemakers?" Miller asked as he moved slowly into the room, a general inspecting his troops.

"Troublemakers learn not to make trouble fast at *Convento de Cuilapam de Guerrero*," the sister said crisply.

None of the girls reacted. Likely, none understood English. They were all Hispanic, some with some Indio blood, judging by the darkness of their skin and eyes. They probably came from deep within Mexico. Likely peasant fare. Farm stock. Some were probably genuine orphans. Others might have been sold to the convent to bring extra money in for a family that had grown too large to sustain itself.

Others, of course, had been taken by less legitimate means by bounty hunters, and then sold to the sister for a tidy sum depending on the value of the flesh they'd brought her.

Miller knew how things were run here at the so-called *convento*. It was not a secret. Everyone in Chihuahua and likely most of Mexico was well aware of Sister Morales's *laissez-faire* methods of turning a peso. Not to mention the obvious heresy of having converted a nunnery into a brothel. That wouldn't normally go over well in a country as Catholic as Mexico, but it was said that the sister had friends in high places.

As high as Mexico City.

In fact, her grand, heretical parlor house was quite the exotically forbidden destination for more than a few of the most powerful politicians in the country. Those men so enjoyed the pleasures they found here that they made sure that Sister Morales was never interfered with. Neither were the bounty hunters who hunted down the best female flesh in Mexico for the diabolical nun—almost always poor peon girls from families powerless to intervene on the girls' behalf.

Miller walked through the room, inspecting the faces gazing up at him, dark eyes reflecting flickering candle-light. The girls' ages ran anywhere from twelve to twenty, as far as he could tell. Miller did not doubt that Sister Morales kept the true cream of the crop for herself. In fact, he'd seen quite a few raving young beauties as he'd passed through the main drinking hall a few minutes ago.

But the girls around him now would do. In fact, a few were quite the lookers. But they didn't need to be all that attractive. The gringo miners in Arizona and New Mexico just wanted them young and unspoiled.

He stopped and gazed down at a pretty young girl in her mid-teenage years. He cradled her chin between thumb and index finger and lifted her chin, taking a good long look at her. The reflection of a single candle burned in her coal-dark eyes.

Red's heart beat faster, his blood warmed.

No, no, he told himself. Off-limits. They must remain pure to retain their value.

The girl gazed up at him, fear gradually darkening her long, almond-shaped eyes. A sheen of tears closed over them and she turned toward Sister Morales and gave a little chirping sob deep in her throat.

Sister Morales silenced the girl with a sharp gesture.

The girl lowered her head and squeezed her eyes closed, her black hair falling down to hide her face. Miller gazed down at her, his heart thudding. He could practically smell her fear; it touched something very deep and predatorial in him. A hot, inexplicable fury grew inside him. He was only vaguely aware of clenching his fists at his sides.

"Come on, Miller," the sister called. "You've seen enough. I don't want you to get them all worked up. They are about to be taken downstairs to supper, and then to mass. They will be ready to go first thing in the morning. As we agreed, and which was included in my compensation, I have prepared three wagons for the transport as well as food. Seven girls per wagon. I have hired three drivers and two outriders—all men who know the dangers of travel in this country."

The chill gleam in the woman's right eye told Miller she'd hired good Mexican gunmen. Likely, *pistoleros*. The sister knew the best bad men in the country. They were likely downstairs now, enjoying themselves on the eve of their northward trek to the border.

His heart slowing, his anger diminishing, Miller turned

toward the woman and smiled. "You are nothing if not prepared, Sister Morales." He walked to her, stood smiling down at her rosy-cheeked, dark-eyed, expressionless face eerily lit by the lamp she held low against her side. "I like that in my nuns."

"Talk is cheap." The sister turned and stepped out into the hall. When Miller, Brennan, and Harris joined her, she held out her hand to Red, palm up. "Pay up."

"Now, now, now," Miller said, digging a half-smoked cheroot out of his shirt pocket and sticking it into his mouth. "After the girls are loaded." He smiled as he snapped a match to life on his thumbnail.

Sister Morales widened her eyes. The apples in her cheeks grew slightly redder. "You don't trust me, Senor Miller?"

"Nothin' personal, Senora," Miller said, touching the lucifer's flame to the end of his cigar. "But when it comes to Mexico, I wouldn't trust Madre Maria herself."

He flipped the match away and crossed himself mockingly, grinning through his smoke at the nun.

"Fair enough." Sister Morales swung around and, raising the lamp, started retracing her steps down the long, dark hall. "The price for the festivities of which you will be partaking this evening . . . downstairs . . . will be included in the final tally."

"Wouldn't have it any other way," Miller said as he and Brennan and Harris followed her back down the hall.

Suddenly, the woman stopped and turned back around, one brow arched with schoolmarm-like admonishment. "May I remind you to be on your best behavior? As you'll remember, I do not put up with any, uh, *nonsense*. Your behavior last time was less than commendable, Senor.

It almost ruined our business relationship and got you kicked out of here."

"Ah, hell." Miller felt his cheeks warm as he smiled sheepishly. "I was just a little drunk is all, sweet sis. I promise to be on my best behavior this evenin'. I've already ordered my two lieutenants here to watch me like a hawk. If I get out of line, they're to see that I get back in it pronto or to give me a good tap with a pistol butt."

He glanced at Brennan and Harris. "Haven't I, fellas?"

They both assured Sister Morales that he had.

"See that you do," Sister Morales said, giving each man a stern look of warning.

She swung around and continued on down the hall.

Red continued forward, as well, puffing on his cigar. To his left, Pike Brennan snickered and elbowed him.

All three chuckled.

Miller reached into his pocket and took another swig of Teagarden's elixir.

Damn, he couldn't seem to get enough of that stuff!

CHAPTER 32

"El gato montés de Chihuahua." Wolf Stockburn raised the quirley to his lips and drew the peppery Mexican tobacco deep into his lungs as he gazed out the front window of *La Cantina del Pájaro Amarillo* in the pueblito of *Pequeño Río Azul.* "Wildcat of Chihuahua."

He said the words slowly as he exhaled the smoke through his nostrils, as though savoring the vision of the woman dancing in the street before him with the peasants, as well as the flavor of the spicy, south-of-the-border tobacco. The two went together well, he silently opined.

"Don't stare so hard." Sofia plucked the cigarette from between his fingers and set it carefully on the edge of the table, so that the coal lay over the edge, the smoke curling up in the shadowy air of the Yellow Bird Saloon. "You're going to burn a hole right through her."

She glanced at Lonesome Charlie sitting on the other side of the table from Stockburn, also staring out the window at Elaina de la Cruz, the lovely young Spanish vixen who'd saved their lives only a few minutes ago.

"You, too, old man," Sofia scolded Charlie as she propped Stockburn's right arm on the table before her and started to wrap the torn, swollen knuckles with long swatches of felt. "Remember your ticker."

"Hard to remember anything," Charlie drawled with a dreamy expression on his craggy face, "with her dancin' out there . . . like that."

Stockburn smiled as he watched the Wildcat of Chihuahua dance with the men and women of the village out on the street before the cantina. A four-piece band had formed from seemingly out of nowhere, and the three men and one young woman were playing their hearts out while the villagers danced.

Elaina de la Cruz danced at the heart of the dancing crowd, with several young men and with several old men, as well, flapping her arms and twirling on the tips of her boot toes, her hair flying in a lovely black mass around her head, hoop rings flashing in the light of the fast-fading sunlight. Just then as Wolf watched, fully captivated, the Wildcat flung herself into the arms of a little, gray-bearded old-timer in a striped serape and straw sombrero. She brushed his hat from his head, ran her hands through his hair, tugged on his ears, and planted an affectionate kiss on his forehead.

When she spun away from him, the old-timer beamed, flushing brightly, and stumbling backward as though about to faint. The others around him steadied him and clapped and laughed at the old man's good fortune.

Wolf smiled as Sofia continued wrapping the cloth around his hand.

He hadn't had time to thank Miss de la Cruz for saving his, Sofia's, and Charlie's bacon with the rurales' Gatling gun before the villagers had emerged from where they'd sought sanctuary after the rurales had shone themselves.

The smoke and dust hadn't settled before the villagers converged on the apparently much-admired Wildcat of Chihuahua, shaking her hand and hugging her as though she were a saint come down from Heaven to save and bless them.

The band—a mandolin, a trumpet, a fiddle, and an accordion—had formed on a boardwalk under a brush ramada. Demijohns of wine and platters of food were laid out on tables, and the dancing began. It was a spontaneous festival with a guest of great honor at its heart—none other than Elaina de la Cruz herself, *El gato montés de Chihuahua* who had single-handedly cut down the vile Captain Nestor Azcona and his platoon of much-reviled bandito rurales.

As for the dead rurales, they'd been laid out on boards leaning up against an adobe wall across the street from the cantina. As the singers and dancers paraded past them, they paused in their revelry to spit on the carcasses. Some kicked dirt on them or threw rocks. Dogs raised their legs on the dead men, anointing them in their own special fashion.

Business had returned in grand fashion to the cantina itself. The big man and the boy were back behind the bar, cooking and splashing tequila, wine, and sangria into wooden cups, which were passed through the crowd to the buyer after said buyer had tossed coins into the small, brown hand of the little boy, who had gotten good at snatching the coins out of the air. Each time he caught a coin, the crowd roared its praise.

A liver-colored tomcat sat atop the bar, staring with no particular interest through the smoky, dimly lit room and out at the raucously dancing and cavorting revelers beyond. It hooked its tail around itself and lifted the white tip each time it blinked its gold-green eyes.

Stockburn blew another smoke plume into the air then gazed out through the window again. The Wildcat of Chihuahua was just then dancing with a little girl in a flowered cotton dress. A crowd gathered around them, clapping. Several wooden buckets with dippers and likely filled with wine or sangria were being passed around the crowd.

"She is beautiful, though, isn't she?" Sofia, too, was now gazing through the window. She'd cut the felt, which the little boy behind the bar had supplied for bandaging the gray-haired *hombre grande* who'd come very close to snuffing Hombrecito's wick. "I'd always heard she was but suspected it was an exaggeration, the way most legends are exaggerated."

Charlie turned to Sofia. "How did you know about this gal, chiquita? This Wildcat of Chihuahua?"

"All the peasants in Mexico and along the border know about Elaina de la Cruz," Sofia said, sipping from the small glass of sangria she'd accepted free of charge from the big man who ran the place with his son, whose name Stockburn had learned was Miquel.

Wolf and Charlie were sharing an unlabeled but very good bottle of tequila, which was taking the edge off both men's aches and pains. Charlie had washed a nitro tablet down with the stuff, and he'd found the combination to be right soothing. He was getting a good bit of satisfaction from the cigar he'd lit, as well.

"I grew up hearing stories about *El gato montés de Chihuahua,* as most boys and girls my age did." A very famous *revolutionaria*. She was raised in a poor peasant family south of Durango. Her family was killed by government troops. She was kidnapped and raped and forced to live with and satisfy the goatish pleasures of a fat javelina of a *federale* general until she cut the old drunkard's throat and escaped.

"She formed her own band of *revolutionarios* and declared war on the Mexican government. She's been killing rurales and federales ever since, and robbing the government-supported banks and gold shipments to support her small army of loyal followers. A true legend, as savage as she is beautiful, riding her cream Arab stallion in her feverish quest to kill all of the fat, corrupt land-owners who enslave the peons, and to turn the government over to the peasants whom it rightly belongs!"

Wolf and Lonesome Charlie looked at the silver-tongued chili pepper with brows arched in surprise.

Sofia smirked. "That's what the Mexican newspapers say about her, anyway. We get one in Mesilla, and I have followed *El Gato Montés de Chihuahua*'s exploits most religiously." She smirked again and took another sip of her sangria.

"Well, that tears it—I'm gonna go get to know the Wildcat of Chihuahua, by damn!" Wolf slapped his right hand down on the table and instantly realized his mistake.

His swollen knuckles burned as though acid had been poured over them. He sucked air through his teeth and cradled the appendage against his chest.

"Stupid gringo!" Sofia castigated him.

"Best tread easy, Wells Fargo," Lonesome Charlie counseled. "That pretty firecracker's already got you hurting yourself over her." He snickered a devilish laugh.

Stockburn set his hat on his head, shouldered his

Winchester, and rose from his chair. He looked out the window. The Wildcat was just then dancing up the street to the north with a couple of young boys, two dogs barking circles around them.

Wolf glanced at Sofia then winked at Charlie. "Look after the senorita here, but don't wait up for me."

"Rogue!" Sofia condemned him.

Wolf chuckled then strode across the room, glad to have regained his land legs after his savage dustup with Hombrecito, who now lay sprawled across two planks, the Wildcat having nearly shredded the big man. He saw the ravishing *revolutionaria* again, dancing on up the street, singing and laughing, spinning young girls and boys, taking time to dance a few steps with an old man or one of the young ones falling all over themselves to be the next to join flesh with the legendary young woman.

As Stockburn approached her, she cast him a quick glance then turned away and continued dancing up the street through the reveling crowd.

Wolf frowned. He was sure she'd seen him approaching her, but she'd spun quickly away, heading in the opposite direction.

He continued forward several paces.

Again, she glanced over her shoulder at him, laughed, then kissed the cheek of a fat man in a derby hat and smoking a big cigar and continued dancing up the street.

Again, Wolf stopped, perplexed. What the hell was she doing?

She glanced over her shoulder at him again as she strode on up the street and out of the now-thinning crowd. Again, she laughed and turned her head quickly forward, hair flying about her shoulders.

Was she egging him on? Daring him to follow her?

Intrigued, Stockburn continued walking north, following a bend in the now nearly dark street. She was roughly fifty yards ahead of him; he could barely see her retreating silhouette now where no oil pots or torches had been lit. The festival now lay behind him, the jubilant roar of the crowd and the raucous music of the four-piece band dwindling quickly.

Here, the night was quiet and dark save for the yammering of coyotes just beyond the town's ragged edges. The savvy brush wolves were likely waiting for the revelers to revel themselves out so the pack could venture into town and pick over the villagers' leavings.

Wolf stopped.

He could no longer see the woman's silhouette nor hear her heels clacking on the worn cobbles.

Slowly, he moved forward.

Faint laughter sounded from a narrow alley mouth on the street's right side. A woman's vaguely taunting laughter.

There she is!

Stockburn hurried forward. He swung right into the alley and headed east, stumbling over bits of trash and a pile of stacked packing crates. The crates nearly took him to the ground. As he regained his balance, the woman laughed again from somewhere ahead.

Stockburn cursed, suddenly feeling as though he were the butt of the woman's joke. He had a mind to turn around and go back to the Yellow Bird. As if reading his mind and knowing he could no more turn away from the beguiling creature before him than he could stop breathing right here and now, the woman laughed again, her taunting voice echoing off the adobe walls around him.

Against his will, Wolf continued forward for another fifty feet. He stopped suddenly.

He'd come to a dead end. A tall, narrow, three-story hotel stood before him across a small courtyard of potted flowers and citrus trees. The ancient, tile-roofed building was abutted on both sides by towering almond trees in full blossom. The blossoms perfumed the cool evening air. He associated the enticing aroma with the woman herself— the one he was chasing like some panting dog with his tongue hanging out.

The hotel's front windows shone with faint yellow lamplight behind thin curtains.

Don't go in there, a voice far back in his mind told him. *Danger there, amigo. That wildcat has lured you out to this raggedy-heeled edge of town for a reason. That reason can't be good.*

Ignoring the voice in his head, Stockburn strode forward.

She's a kill-crazy *revolutionaria*. Probably hates gringos every bit as much as she hates *hacendados* and rurales.

Stockburn strode up the hotel's ancient stone steps. He pushed through a wooden door and into a small, cool, tile-floored lobby. A lamp burned on the desk to the right, under a clock tick-tocking on the adobe wall.

"Hello?" Wolf called.

He tightened his jaws, half-expecting a bullet. Or for the beautiful *revolutionaria*, silent as a panther, to step up behind him and run a knife across his throat. The thought itself caused the hair at the back of his neck to prick.

He glanced behind him. There was only a potted palm standing in the corner by the door. A trapped fly struggled in the cobweb dangling down from the tip of one green leaf.

The fly touched him with foreboding.

Still, instead of retreating, he called again, "Hello?"

No response.

He glanced at the desk. The open register book was turned toward him. A pencil lay on the open page, as though recently used. The book was urging him to look at it.

He did.

The last name written on the page was his own: *Wolf Stockburn*.

It was written in blue-black ink in a flowing feminine hand.

CHAPTER 33

Another chill ran up Stockburn's spine. Again, the hair beneath his collar rose.

"Hmm." He placed a finger on his written name and slid it to the numeral 8 scribbled beside it.

He glanced at the dark mouth of the narrow stairs running up between two adobe walls just beyond the desk. He pricked his ears listening.

The building was totally silent. If there was anyone else in it, Stockburn had a feeling they were hiding, holding their breaths. Very faintly, he could hear the music and low roar of the festival continuing near the Yellow Bird cantina.

Feeling as trapped as the fly, squeezing his Winchester's receiver in his right hand, the detective moved to the stairs and started climbing. His boots clacked quietly on the masonry steps. At the top, he turned to stare back along the dark hall toward the window at the front of the building.

Nothing moved in the sour murk.

He walked along the hall, squinting at the numbers on the doors.

1 . . . 2 . . . 3 . . . 4 . . . 5 . . . 6 . . . 7 . . .

He stopped at room 8. He tapped lightly on the door with the backs of his knuckles.

"Come in and take a load off, amigo," came a sultry, Spanish-accented voice from behind the door.

Stockburn twisted the knob, shoved the door open. He took one step inside the room, tightening the muscles in the severe Scottish chiseling of his face with its high, broad cheekbones surmounted by deep-set, dark Scottish eyes. Those eyes were as dark and chilly as the stormy North Sea now as he took one more step and then stood three feet inside the room, gazing at the woman. She was seated at a cloth-draped table before him, abutting the far wall adorned with a colorful Mexican painting of fields and a river and a boy fishing with a cane pole, and the obligatory crucifix.

A window shutter flanking her was open. The smoke from her long, slender black cheroot was a gray streamer rising and slithering through it and out into the dark night, dispersing against the crisp glow of the stars. She'd removed her sombrero and hung it on a peg protruding from the wall behind her.

She lounged back in a hide-bottom chair, facing Stockburn, one elbow on the table. She'd taken her boots off; her feet were bare. One bare foot was crossed over one leather-clad knee. An uncorked tequila bottle, a half-filled glass, an empty glass, and one black, pearl-gripped Colt Navy .44 lay on the table near the ashtray in which she absently flicked ashes as she regarded her visitor with fascination.

Stockburn returned the favor.

"So . . . the Wolf of the Rails . . ."

Stockburn frowned, curious. "*El Gato Montés de Chihuahua* . . . how do you know me?"

"I overheard Azcona announce your name, Wolf Stockburn. I know who you are." Elaina de la Cruz took a drag off the cheroot and blew the smoke into the air toward Stockburn. "Your reputation precedes you."

"I didn't realize it preceded me this far."

"Unlike you Americans regarding Mexico, I try to keep abreast of what is happening in your country." She added with a thin, shrewd smile, "And who is doing what. You are a famous railroad detective. Formerly the Wolf of Wichita."

Stockburn walked slowly over to the table. "And you are a famous *revolutionaria*. One who saved this famous railroad detective's life a couple of hours ago. I haven't had a chance to thank you."

"Well, you do now."

"Muchas gracias."

"Sit." With the hand holding the smoldering cheroot, she filled the second glass with tequila from the bottle and slid it over toward the chair on the opposite side of the table from her. "Put the long gun down. Take a load off."

"Don't mind if I do."

Wolf leaned his rifle against the wall, pegged his hat, ran a hand through his thick thatch of roached gray hair, and sat in the chair. He set his left elbow on the table, lifted the glass, and looked across the table at the young woman still studying him closely. She didn't look as young as she had in the lens-clear Chihuahua light on the street. Very fine crows' feet stretched from her eye corners.

Mentally, he revised her age to be nearer thirty than twenty. It was in her eyes, too. On the street, she'd swaggered with youthful bravado. Now he thought he detected a note of weariness in those deep, inky brown orbs behind the tequila shine.

Stockburn sipped the tequila and smacked his lips. "Not bad. I should be buying drinks for you, though."

"You have done me the bigger favor, *hombre grande*." She flicked a bemused smile at him. "How big are you?"

"Six-four."

"A big man. You almost felled that oversized privy snake, Hombrecito. No man has ever gotten as far with him as you did."

"I got the sore hands and mouth to prove it." He gently fingered his split lips, which Sofia had cleaned up as well as she could. He probably needed stitches, but he didn't have time to bother. He'd have a few more scars to add to his collection.

"It was something to see."

Stockburn gave a dry chuckle. "Glad you enjoyed it."

"Who's the girl? Should I be jealous?"

"Sofia? Friend of mine."

"*Friend?*"

"She's old enough to be my daughter, Elaina. Do you mind if I call you Elaina?"

The Wildcat hiked a bare shoulder that the candlelight caressed bewitchingly. It shone like honey on polished oak. "Some men like them young, Wolf. Azcona did."

"I take it you've run into him before."

"Si. Many times. The first time, I was very young. It didn't go well for me. I have waited many years to butcher that ugly coyote—the spawn of Hell if any man has ever been."

"Glad I could distract him for you."

Elaina laughed throatily and threw back the rest of the tequila in her glass. She refilled it then topped off Wolf's glass, set the bottle down, and reached across the table to place her hand on his. "What are you doing down here, amigo? Do you mind if I call you amigo? I have very few of those left."

"I'd be proud to call myself your friend, Elaina."

Her eyes glistened more than before. Stockburn frowned, curious. Was the Wildcat of Chihuahua getting drunk and sentimental?

"I'd think a lady such as yourself . . ." He couldn't help dropping his gaze momentarily to enjoy the seasoned but untrammeled beauty of such a wild, ravishing creature. ". . . would have plenty of amigos."

"No. I have plenty of *enemies*. As for *friends . . . lovers* . . . they are few and far between." She took another sip from her glass, took another equally quick drag from the cheroot. Blowing out the smoke, she said, "In fact, I lost the last of those earlier this year."

"Dead?"

She pooched out her lips, nodded slowly, slitting her eyes. "Si, many have died. Over the years. By ones and twos and threes and fours. Others replaced them. There seemed to be no end to those who were eager to strap on guns and fight beside me. Then they too died . . . or grew old and weary, seeing nothing but futility in the fight that never seemed to end . . . just as the evil . . . the corruption never seems to end."

She took another puff from the cheroot, blew the

smoke at the ceiling. "The last of my loyal armada grew old. Some in body, some in mind. They wearied of the fight. They went back to where they came from so long ago . . . to what they were doing before they took up arms to fight the good fight along with *El Gato Montés de Chihuahua* against the fat cats and the corrupt politicians they own. One morning . . . months ago now . . . I woke up in a musty *establo* of a *campesino* . . . and I was alone."

"I'm sorry."

"You know what this tough brush warrior did then, Wolf? I had a good cry. Si!" She laughed raucously. "Then I paid the campesino to ride into the nearest village and buy a couple demijohns of cheap wine. I spent the rest of that day getting drunk and crying and wandering alone in the desert around the *granja* . . . while the campesino and his family watched me from their fields . . . wondering what in holy hell had happened to the mighty *El Gato Montés de Chihuahua!*"

She laughed again but this time without humor.

Again, she refilled both empty glasses and set the bottle down so hard that some of the precious tequila splashed up out of the mouth.

"I couldn't bear their looks anymore, so I saddled my horse and finished getting drunk alone. And good and drunk I got, too! And do you know what I decided the next morning . . . after I woke with a splitting headache and a mouth that tasted like the bottom of a long-dry well in the desert?"

"What'd you do, Elaina?"

"I vowed I would never feel sorry for myself again. I vowed that I would kill Azcona any way I could find even if I had to do it alone . . . and I would go to America and start a new life for myself."

Stockburn smiled across the table at her. He threw back half his tequila, which had filled him with a delicious warmth that dulled even the severest of his aches and pains. "That was one tall order. Looks like the hard part is done."

"What about you? What are you doing in Mexico, amigo?"

"Chasing owlhoots."

"Well, we have plenty of those."

"I'm after three in particular. Red Miller, Flipper Harris, and Pike Brennan."

She blinked slowly, smiling her catlike smile. "I suspected as much."

"You know about them?"

"I've been in the village awhile . . . keeping tabs on Azcona . . . waiting for an opportunity to take him out. I was outside *La Cantina del Pájaro Amarillo* when he was making a business deal with Miller."

"A business deal?"

Elaina flared her nostrils distastefully. "A lucrative one involving selling Mexican girls into whoredom north of the border."

"Nasty."

"Si. It involves a nasty old nun I've been wanting to kill for almost as long as I've wanted to kill Azcona. I almost forgot about her . . . until I overheard that rabid coyote Azcona talking to Red Miller. Now I have revised my plans to include the lopping off the head of Sister Lucia Morales before I start that new life for myself in your country."

Stockburn plucked her cheroot from between her fingers and used it to light the quirley he'd rolled for himself while he'd been listening to her speak. Puffing smoke and returning the cheroot to the beautiful *revolutionaria,* he said, "I take it you know where to find her."

"Si."

"I take it when we find her, we'll likely find Miller."

She blinked again slowly, peering at him devilishly through the haze of tobacco smoke between them. "Si." She glanced at the window in which lightning flashed.

It was only then that he realized that while he'd been listening to this intoxicating creature before him that a storm had rolled in—another monsoon gully-washer though this one starting later than usual—silencing the festival and likely shepherding all the villagers to shelter.

Thunder rumbled and banged, making the floor beneath Stockburn's boots shake.

Elaina refilled their glasses then clinked hers against his. "Drink up," she said. "It looks like we're in for a wild, stormy night together, *mi nuevo amigo!*"

CHAPTER 34

In a dream, Stockburn opened his eyes to see Lonesome Charlie and Sofia Ortega staring down at him and the Wildcat of Chihuahua as they slumbered in the hotel room's soft, lumpy but somehow comfortable bed.

He blinked, frowned up at the two—Charlie grinning, Sofia giving him her customary schoolmarm's scowl. Then he realized that he wasn't dreaming.

The Wildcat of Chihuahua realized the same thing at the same time Wolf did.

"Ach!" Elaina sat up suddenly, drawing the sheets to her chin. "*Dios mio,* Wolf—did we really let an old man and a little girl steal into our room as we slept?"

Charlie's grin faded. *"Old man?"*

Sofia's scowl deepened. *"Little girl?"*

Stockburn cursed and sat up, too, pulling the sheet up over his privates. It was chilly in the room after last night's storm, but he and the Wildcat had so exhausted themselves neither apparently had awakened enough to draw up the covers. Instead, they'd sought warmth by entangling their arms and legs.

"How in the hell did you two get in here?" Stockburn wheezed out phlegmily.

Charlie smiled. A burning cigarette dangled from a corner of his mouth, dripping ashes. "Wasn't too hard since the door wasn't locked."

"How did you find us?"

"Senor Flores from the livery barn told us where the Senora de la Cruz usually stays when she comes to *Pequeño Río Azul*," Sofia informed with a sneer. She glanced at Wolf and added tartly, "You work fast."

Holding the sheets taut across her bosoms, Elaina looked at Wolf. "I thought you said you two were only friends."

"We are."

Elaina glanced at Sofia then turned to Wolf again. "She's jealous."

Sofia gave a caustic chuff then looked away, a flush rising in her cheeks.

"Up and at 'em, pard," Charlie said. He lifted a burlap sack in one hand and held up a corked crockery jug ensconced in straw in his other hand. "Brought burritos and coffee. No time for a sit-down breakfast. We're burnin' daylight!"

Elaina sniffed the spicy aromas emanating from Charlie's bag, then reached for it. "I'm starving. You are a lifesaver, old one!"

As she grabbed the bag out of Charlie's hand and began rummaging around inside, Charlie's craggy features acquired another hurt look. "I'd appreciate it if you'd come up with another moniker for me, Senora. I mean, I realize you're the infamous Wildcat of Chihuahua an' all, an' you could probably cut my tongue out of my mouth before I even saw the knife in your hand, but I'm a deputy U.S. marshal, doggoneit"—he brushed his thumb across the badge on his vest—"and I'll thank you for a modicum of well-earned respect!"

Elaina pulled two burritos wrapped in corn husks from the bag. She gave one to Stockburn, asking, "Does he always talk this much? I don't know if I can travel with him."

"'Travel with him'?" Sofia had opened the sack she was carrying, and set four small wooden bowls on the table. She looked inquiringly at Stockburn and asked, "She's riding with us?"

Stockburn nodded as he tore into the burrito, mindless of his cut and swollen lips. He hadn't realized how hungry he was until he'd smelled the spicy burritos of goat meat, beans, rice, and chili peppers. Chewing, he said, "She knows where Miller's heading."

Charlie was filling the four bowls from the crockery jug, adding the aromatic steam from the coffee to that rising from the burritos. "Where's he heading?"

"*Convento de Cuilapam de Guerrero*," said the Wildcat of Chihuahua, sitting up, leaning against her knees and eating as hungrily as Stockburn was. She accepted one of the two coffee bowls Charlie had brought over to the bed. Wolf accepted the second one, and sipped the hot, black Mexican mud.

"A *convento*?" asked Sofia. "What would Red Miller want with a *convento*?"

"This isn't just any *convento*, Senorita," Elaina said. "It is an orphanage of sorts, run by a very bad nun named Lucia Morales. A witch from hell, I assure you."

"What do you mean an orphanage *of sorts*?" Charlie

wanted to know. He brushed some spilled beans and rice from his bearded chin.

He and Sofia were sitting at the table at which Wolf and Elaina had sat the night before and were going to work on their own steaming burritos and coffee.

"She raises young women there . . . and whores them."

Sofia stopped eating to stare at the beautiful *revolutionaria* who continued eating and drinking her coffee. Sofia's eyes shone with disbelief.

"Si, it is true. Sister Morales was raised there herself. It is said that she and several other girls turned on the nuns. They slit the nun's throats as they slept, and turned the place into a brothel, all the girls who lived there into whores."

"Dios," Sofia muttered in shock.

"Believe me, Senorita," Elaina said, brushing her hand across her chin. "No God lives at *Convento de Cuilapam de Guerrero.*" She curled her upper lip and flared her nostrils. "Only the devil's own puta! I have wanted to kill her for years but have always been too busy killing corrupt *men*. But now it is time."

Elaina hardened her jaws and nodded slowly.

Charlie had stopped eating his own burrito to listen in mute fascination at the woman's story. Now he took another bite of his burrito and, chewing, asked, "How far away is that wicked perdition?"

"A day and a half ride southeast."

"Are you sure Miller and his two owlhoot pards are headin' there?"

"She overheard them talking to Azcona," Wolf explained.

"Si," Elaina said. "They padded the captain's pockets and assured him there was more where that money came from. Miller intends to take a shipment of young women across the border into Arizona . . ."

"And sell them to brothels in mining towns," Wolf added.

Sofia sucked air through her teeth and shook her head, eyes blazing. "That's where those three banditos who attacked us the other night intended to take *me*. To the *nun*!"

"Sounds about right," Wolf said, nodding.

Charlie said, "If Miller and his pards are gonna roll back north with slave girls, they'll likely roll right through *Pequeño Río Azul*."

"Si," Elaina said.

Charlie looked at Wolf. "Why not wait for him right here? When he rides into town, take him down."

Wolf said, "Elaina wants to shut the nun down for good. I'm all over that myself. Sofia came damn close to ending up there. In fact, if it hadn't been for your big toe, she would have!"

"See?" Charlie said, smiling proudly.

Elaina cast Stockburn a dubious look. "His big *toe*?"

"A story for another time," Wolf said. "She sounds every bit as nasty as Red Miller himself. I say we ride down there and kill both him and her and Harris and Brennan. If we meet Miller and his pards between here and there, then we'll go ahead and take 'em down. After we've snuffed their wicks, we'll continue down to the so-called convent and shut Sister Morales down for good."

Charlie set his empty corn husk on the table and scratched his beard, pensive. "Sounds risky. She's gotta have men on her dole. Guards for her convent-whorehouse. Who knows how many?"

He glanced at Elaina.

She nodded as she sucked from between two upper front teeth. "Si. She likely has guards." She glanced speculatively at Stockburn and said with a not-so-subtle jeering air: "If you two gringos are afraid . . . well . . ."

"I'm not!" Sofia said, her pretty cheeks flushing with rage.

"Hell, I'm not, either!" Charlie threw in. "I was just mentionin' it—you know, so we ain't caught with our pants down."

Elaina turned to Stockburn. Wolf had finished his burrito and coffee and was leaning back against the bed's brass headboard, thoughtfully rolling a smoke.

"How about you, Hombre Grande?" She reached over and ran a hand through his thick thatch of prematurely gray hair. "Are you afraid?"

Wolf smiled at her. "Yes, I am. Scared as hell. But I already told you I was all over it, *mi amore*." He took her hand and kissed it.

Elaina leaned farther toward him and kissed him on the mouth. As she did, the sheet slipped down revealingly. Charlie watched the sheet's descent, riveted. The old man's lower jaw sagged. His bulbous nose as well as his cheeks behind his silky gray beard turned bright red.

Wolf pulled the sheet up to cover his lover of the previous night. "Careful, there, Wildcat. The old man over there's got a weak ticker."

Elaina turned to Charlie and smiled.

Charlie fumbled his tablet box out of one coat pocket and a tequila bottle out of another coat pocket. Quickly, he opened the box, stuck a tablet on his tongue, and washed it down with several deep pulls from the bottle.

* * *

They'd been on the trail for about four hours and were riding through a stretch of flat, rocky desert, ragged hills blotting out the horizon in all directions, when Lonesome Charlie, riding at the rear of the four-person pack, said, "I'll be hanged if my big toe ain't achin' again!"

Riding point with Sofia walking her own horse just off his right stirrup, Stockburn glanced over his right shoulder and said, "That tears it—my back itches!" He reined Smoke to a stop and curveted the mount, casting his gaze far back beyond Charlie.

Elaina checked down her sleek cream Arabian, and frowned at Charlie and then at Wolf. "I don't understand. What is the significance of the old man's big toe and your itchy back?"

"They both mean we're being shadowed." Not seeing anything but rocks, cactus, and creosote shrubs beyond Charlie, Stockburn peered eastward.

Nothing there, either.

"Si," Elaina said, turning her head slowly to give the middle-distance a thorough scout. "I have had a ringing in my ears for almost an hour now. That usually means I'm being stalked. Usually by rurales. In this case, given the condition of Azcona and his men back in *Pequeño Río Azul*"—she gave a hearty chuckle—"it must be someone else. Bounty hunters, perhaps."

She pulled a Winchester carbine from her saddle scabbard, cocked it one-handed, and rested it across her saddlebow as she continued scouring their backtrail.

"You're all looking behind us," Sofia said, staring ahead

along the trail and to the east, shading her eyes with her hand. "What if it's someone watching from ahead of us?"

Wolf, Elaina, and Lonesome Charlie turned toward her, frowning.

"Why do you say that?" Charlie asked.

Sofia kept staring ahead and to the east of the thin cart trail they'd been following south from Blue River. "Just a few seconds ago, I saw a sun flash from those rocks over there."

Just as Stockburn followed the girl's gaze to a long, sun-washed dyke about a hundred yards away and which looked like a clipper ship half-swallowed by the desert, an angry whine rose in his ears. The bullet crashed into a rock to the right of the trail. All four horses jerked. Sofia's mount reared; Sofia gave a clipped cry as she flew back over the horse's left hip, striking the ground with a hard thump.

"Ambush!" Wolf shouted, shucking his own Winchester as he leaped from his saddle.

Elaina sprang from her Arab's back a half-second later. Wolf slapped Smoke's hip with his open palm, and the horse went buck-kicking off the trail to the west. Elaina's Arab followed, both horses swinging their heads indignantly.

Wolf ran forward and dropped to a knee beside Sofia. "You all right, honey?"

She sat up, leaving her hat on the trail, and reached for her lower left leg. "I think I twisted my ankle."

Another angry whine. Stockburn flinched as a second bullet plowed into a rock to his left.

"Come on—we have to get to cover!" Wolf rose, pulled

Sofia up beside him, then looped her arm around his neck. "Lean on me!"

The girl groaned as he led her limping off the trail's right side and over to a low, long pile of rocks and cactus. Elaina hustled up to the same rock pile, to Wolf's left. The *revolutionaria* dropped to a knee, doffed her hat, and gazed over the top of the pile toward the direction the shooter had fired from.

Wolf turned to gaze back at Charlie. Charlie's horse was running back along the trail to the north. Charlie must have had a rather unceremonious unsaddling. He was down on one knee, disheveled and dusty, his hat in the dirt beside him. He unsheathed his big Dragoon and looked around warily.

Stockburn beckoned. "Come on, Charlie. You're a sitting duck out there!"

"Here I come!" The oldster heaved himself to his feet and came running at a crouch.

Another bullet sawed through the air to pock the dust to the side of Charlie's left boot. Charlie cursed and kept running, if you could call it running. It was more of a chug. Finally, he reached the rock pile and crouched down on the other side of Sofia from Stockburn.

"That was close!" he wheezed out, breathless.

"Yeah." Wolf looked at Elaina. "See anything, chiquita?"

"I see nothing, *Hombre Grande*. The bastardo has pulled himself back down out of sight behind that ridge there."

Stockburn set his sombrero on the ground and lifted a look over the crest of the rock pile before him, ready to pull his head back down in a hurry if he spied movement atop that far ridge. For a time, there was only the slanting face of the sandstone dyke that shone like a new penny in the desert light.

Cicadas buzzed a monotonous rhythm. The sun seemed to throb where it hovered about halfway down in the west, beginning to push shadows eastward.

Then something moved over there. A rifle barrel rose above the dyke. It was followed by a hatted head. The head and the rifle moved very close together and held still.

"Get down!" Stockburn yelled at Elaina.

A half-second later, another bullet blasted into the face of the rock pile just below where Stockburn's head had been a moment before. The pinging whine of the ricochet was followed by the rifle's flat belch.

Elaina rested her rifle atop the rock pile and returned fire—three quick, angry rounds. *"Mierda!"* she yelled in frustration as the last shot still echoed. "Whoever he is, he's a wily coyote! Keeping himself out of sight."

"Let's go introduce ourselves, honey."

Elaina turned to Stockburn, who was smiling at her. She returned the smile. "Took the thought right out of my head."

"And what a pretty head it is, too!"

"Get your mind away from last night, amigo." Elaina cackled out a bawdy laugh. "We're being shot at!"

"Si, we're being shot at," Sofia scolded Stockburn. "Get your mind off last night, Wolf."

Kneeling beside Sofia who sat with her back against the rocks, one leg extended straight out before her, the injured ankle curled inward, Charlie chuckled. "I think he likes Mexico."

Sofia shot a cool look at Elaina, and flared a nostril. "I wonder what he likes about it."

Stockburn kissed the girl's cheek. "You'll always have my heart, chiquita." He nudged her chin. "We'll be right back."

"Don't hurry on my account," Sofia grumbled, squeezing her injured ankle.

"Stay with her, Charlie." Wolf turned to Elaina. "Let's work around him. Ready?"

"I was born ready, *Hombre Grande!*"

"Let's go!"

CHAPTER 35

Stockburn ran out from the rock pile's right, western side as Elaina ran out from the opposite side.

They ran crouching, each triggering a shot toward the dyke to pin the shooter down. Wolf ran wide around the dyke to the southwest, weaving through rocks. A bullet plowed the coarse red caliche near his left boot and he hurled himself forward, rolling up behind a slant-topped boulder roughly half the size of a ranch wagon.

The crack of the shooter's rifle reached Stockburn's ear, dwindling quickly.

Stockburn fired around the right side of his covering rock then took off running again, weaving around rocks and cactus and tufts of wiry brown desert scrub. Occasionally he glanced to the east to see Elaina moving covertly, as well, running at a crouch, dropping behind cover, slinging a shot at the dyke, then running again.

Quickly, they both narrowed the gap between them and the dyke. Stockburn worked his way around it, then slowed his pace as he came up on it from behind. He weaved his way through the rocks. Approaching the backside of the dyke, he heard a man cursing under his breath, and spurs chinging. He took two more steps, moving around the left side of a barrel cactus and stopped, raising the Yellowboy to his shoulder.

A sandy-haired man in dusty trail garb was just then trying to mount a horse that wanted no part of it. The man clung to the horn with his right hand, holding the reins with his left hand, and, in a desperate attempt to toe the stirrup, he hop-skipped along beside the horse that was trying to run away to the south.

"Dammit—hold still, you broomtailed peckerwood!"

Orange dust rose behind horse and would-be rider.

Stockburn fired two shots into the gravel around the cowboy's boots. The man yelped, fell, and rolled. The horse whinnied, ripped its reins from the cowboy's hands, and galloped away, shaking its head and buck-kicking.

Elaina poked her head up from the rise beyond the cowboy, bringing her own Winchester to her shoulder. Stockburn waved her off then strode toward where the cowboy rolled onto his back and sat up, reaching for the old hogleg holstered on his right hip.

"Don't try it, kid!"

He may not have been technically a kid, but he sure acted like one. Wolf was surprised to find that a fellow gringo had been slinging lead at him.

As he walked up to the young man squinting up through his and the horse's still-sifting dust, Wolf said, "Give me one good reason why I shouldn't drill you a third eye."

The young man had lost his hat in his tumble. His longish sandy, sweaty hair hung in his eyes, which were baby blue. A scar ran from his upper lip to his nose; a two- or three-day growth of blond beard stubble fuzzed his sunburned cheeks. His undershot boots, silver spurs, and brush-scarred and fringed chapparreras marked him as a range rider, all right.

But a north-of-the-border one. Not a Mexican.

The young man—he was maybe twenty-five, still young to the forty-year-old Stockburn—stared up at Wolf, his own gaze acquiring a curious cast. He glanced at Elaina who was coming down the rise to his right then returned his eyes to Stockburn.

"Who're you?"

"Get your hand off that hogleg."

The young man removed his hand from the Schofield's grips.

"The name's Stockburn. Who are you?"

The young bushwhacker leaned forward and rested his arms on his slightly bent knees. He brushed gravel from his chin with his fist. "Hoot Gibbons."

"Why in the hell were you shooting at us, Hoot Gibbons?" Elaina asked him, striding up while extending her carbine one-handed from her right hip.

Her narrowed brown eyes flared like those of an angry cat.

Hoot Gibbons shrugged a little sheepishly. "I thought . . . I thought you was followin' me. I thought you were after my horse. You know—banditos. I had a run-in with some before a few nights back."

Stockburn glowered incredulously at the young saddle tramp. "So you decided to shoot us off your trail?"

"Hell, no—I wasn't tryin' to *shoot* you. Hell, I'm a better shot than that!" He grinned as he bragged. "If I wanted to shoot you, hell, you'd all be coyote bait. I was just tryin' to scare you off my trail. You know—let you know that just 'cause I was a gringo well off his own beaten path, I wasn't gonna be an easy tap."

He turned to Elaina. "I always heard Mescins play the odds. I wanted to show you the odds were steep. That's all." He shrugged again. "I do apologize." He turned his head to stare over his shoulder to the south. "Say, you didn't see where my hoss went, did you? I tell you, that's the most mulish damn broomtail I ever rode, and I rode a few. I sure am gonna be one happy cow puncher to get Rowdy back!"

Elaina shouldered up to Wolf and said, "I think we should shoot him for his own good. He's obviously touched. Maybe sunstroke."

"You might be right." Stockburn shouldered his own rifle then walked up to Hoot and hunkered down on his haunches, studying the disheveled young man curiously. "Hoot, what are you doing down here? You do realize you're in Mexico, don't you?"

"Hell, of course I realize I'm in Mexico. I ain't simple!" Hoot cocked his head to one side and narrowed one baby blue eye shrewdly. "What're you doing down here?"

"I asked you first."

Hoot chewed his lower lip, scowling suspiciously. "I ain't sure I should tell you."

"Why not?"

"Why do you want to know?"

"Just curious is all."

"Are you an outlaw?"

"Nope."

Hoot glanced at Elaina. "What about her?"

"Bandita?" Elaina said, smiling her disdain for the question. "Hah!" She held out her arms and glanced down at her own ample, scarcely concealed wares. "Have you ever seen a bandita who looks like this, cowboy?"

Hoot studied her as he nibbled his lip again. As his eyes traced her opulent curves, a red flush mottled his flour-white forehead, smooth as a baby's ass where his hat concealed it from the sun and weather. "Good point."

"Oh, fer chrissakes." Stockburn straightened and gazed down at the young man impatiently. "I'm a railroad detective from north of the border. I'm down here hunting a passel of badmen led by Red Miller. You better be a little more certain about who you're taking pot shots at, you damn idiot, or . . ."

Hoot cut him off with: "Miller?" His eyes widened with sudden interest, and he sat up straighter. "You're after Red Miller?"

Again, Wolf's gaze grew dubious. "You know Miller?"

"Well, we ain't amigos or anything like that—I can tell you that much!" Hoot grabbed his hat and climbed to his feet, studying Wolf closely, a boyish optimism stretching his sunburned lips. "But I'm on his trail, all right. He stole my horse, Rowdy."

Stockburn and Elaina shared a glance.

"Rowdy?" Wolf asked.

"Yeah. They took him in Tularosa." Hoot's cheeks flushed again, and he glanced down as though suddenly plagued by dark thoughts. He kicked a rock, lifted his hat, ran his hand through his hair, grabbing at it as though trying to hurt himself. He set the hat back on his head and cast Wolf a hard, determined gaze. His baby blues were suddenly all grown-up business. "I aim to get him back, all right. And I'm gonna drill a bullet through Red's head. Right here."

He planted his right index finger to the center of his forehead, just below his hat.

"You're gonna have some competition, kid," Wolf said.

"Compe . . ." Hoot let the words die on his lips when a raspy, old-man's voice said, "All clear down there?"

Stockburn turned to see Lonesome Charlie poking his head up above the stone dyke's far side. The old man had regained his hat and rifle, which meant he must have retrieved his horse, as well.

"So far, so good."

Charlie pulled his head back behind the dyke. He reappeared a minute later with Sofia, both trotting their respective mounts out from behind the formation. Charlie was leading Wolf's stallion; Sofia was leading Elaina's Arab. Old man and girl looked a little worse for wear but only by a little. Sofia, seasoned by rough travel over the past many days, was as tough as the old man.

"Who's this?" Sofia asked in a tight, hard voice, casting her acrimonious gaze down at Gibbons.

The cowboy smiled and pinched his hat brim, his blue eyes sparkling in appreciation of the Spanish cameo pin vision seated on the horse before him. "Hoot Gibbons at your service, senorita." He glanced at Stockburn. "You ever ride with any plain-faced women, Mr. Stockburn?"

"Were you the one shooting at us?" Sofia asked crisply, having none of the young man's fool male fawning.

"He made a mistake," Wolf said.

"Yeah? I make mistakes, too." Lonesome Charlie angled the barrel of his Winchester out from his right thigh and down, aiming at the cowboy's belly. "Sometimes my trigger finger twitches. An old-man problem. Probably the palsy. When it twitches and I got my finger on this old

Winchester's trigger and a hot one in the breech, it can make an awful mess."

Hoot looked at the maw of Charlie's rifle and smiled. He glanced at the badge on Charlie's vest then turned to Wolf again and frowned. "The old man's a lawdog?"

"You can call me Marshal Murdock, you lame-brained toehead," Charlie bit out, keeping the Winchester aimed at Hoot's midsection. "Your mistake was mighty hard on my backside, and that rankles me. It purely does. Bein' bushwhacked by some tinhorn saddle tramp tends to do that to me. Always has."

Elaina looked up at Charlie. Impressed by the old man's anger, she chuckled but said, "Stand-down, amigo. Hoot here's a silly gringo frightened by shadows so far away from home here in Mexico. He thought we were banditos out to steal his horse."

Hoot turned to her, his mild smile in place though his eyes were cool. "You're part right, Senora de la Cruz. I lack experience down here in Mexico, and I've never claimed to be the sharpest tool in the shed. I mistook you for banditos out to steal my horse. It was silly on my part. I should have scouted you better before I started throwing lead. For that I apologize."

The cowboy's smile thinned noticeably as he added, "But I'm not afraid of one damn thing. And I intend to get my horse back from Miller. After I kill him."

The smile broadened again as he pressed his index finger again to a faint freckle on his forehead.

Wolf and his trail mates shared curious, vaguely incredulous glances.

Charlie said, "You're after Miller, *too*?"

"That's right." Hoot reached up and carefully adjusted

the set of his hat on his head. "He stole my horse and my honor, and I intend to get both back." He glanced at Stockburn. "Mind if I ride along with you folks?"

"Go back north where you came from, you stupid pup," said Lonesome Charlie, still rankled.

"I can't do that, Marshal Murdock."

Charlie glanced at Wolf, scowling suspiciously.

Was this pilgrim off his nut?

Stockburn glanced at Elaina and then at Sofia. Neither woman appeared to have an opinion on the subject of Hoot Gibbons's company. Since the cowboy was heading in the same direction they were, he might as well tag along with them. At least they could keep their eyes on him.

A puzzling character, though—Wolf would give the kid that. Especially his saying he wasn't afraid of anything. Not only him saying it but *how* he said it. With such cold-blooded certainty. It hadn't sounded like mere bluster, either.

Damned particular.

Yeah, maybe it's best they keep their eyes on him.

"You best fetch your hoss," Wolf told Hoot, glancing at the sky, which was suddenly turning stormy again. The wind was tossing the women's hair and the horses' manes. "Looks like we got another monsoon rain dogging our heels."

CHAPTER 36

Stockburn was lucky this time. He and the others gained shelter before the storm unleashed the full force of its wrath on them.

Led by the Wildcat of Chihuahua, who'd grown up in this wild, forbidden country, they'd continued south into rugged, mountainous terrain. As the first drops of the cold rain began spitting, they'd sought shelter in a cave above an arroyo.

They'd picketed their horses in a rock corral of sorts to the north of the cave and the steep ridge it had been chiseled out of by the natural forces of wind, water, and time. Those forces must have finished the bulk of their work a good long time ago.

A whole heap of time so long he couldn't imagine it.

Maybe another eon or two after those forces had done their business, people had started occupying the shelter. Probably wandering bands of native hunters. They'd left their marks in the form of many brightly colored paintings that adorned the walls like the gaudy paper you found in high-end hurdy-gurdy houses.

Some of the pictures were just as ribald as the paintings

the parlor gals hung on their walls, too. Some had to be the drunken exaggerations of the brashest hunters in the pack, or Wolf missed his guess.

When they'd tended the horses, they'd quickly gathered sun-bleached driftwood from the arroyo and hauled it all up to the cave. The wood hadn't quite dried out from the previous night's storm, so it took some coaxing on both Wolf's and Hoot's part to get a fire going, over which Stockburn erected his tripod for the coffeepot he'd wait to fill with rainwater. They'd found the *tinajas,* or natural water tanks, out here to be few and far between. There was no water to spare for the luxury of fresh-brewed Arbuckles.

When the storm unleashed its wolf, so to speak, Stockburn set the coffeepot outside. The runoff from the ridge above filled it in less than a minute. He made coffee while Elaina boiled frijoles and fried tortillas. They ate sitting back from the hot fire, staring out into the gray gauze of the storm, lightning flashing like diamonds on a ball gown.

It was not a cold rain. The air was soft and silky as it pushed into the cave, which was roughly the size of a modest-sized hotel room. The roar was too loud for conversation, but somehow the steady rush of rain, the intermittent lightning flashes, and the distant drumming of the thunder lulled Stockburn, Elaina, and Lonesome Charlie into deep slumbers. Charlie lay his head back against the underside of his saddle, snoring loudly.

Stockburn and Elaina sat close together, shoulders touching, heads tilted toward each other, chest rising and falling slowly, almost in time with each other.

Hoot finished the last of his beans then set his plate and fork outside to let the rain clean them. He turned to where Sofia sat near the cave entrance, resting leisurely back against the cave wall. She'd taken her left moccasin off and curled that leg inward. Only the tips of her brown toes peaked out from the folds of her calico skirt. She had her head turned so that she stared out into the storm, a vaguely forlorn cast to her pensive gaze.

Hoot rummaged in his saddlebags and pulled out a small, unlabeled tin of salve. He crawled over to sit down near Sofia and extended the tin to her.

"Here—put some of this on your ankle. It'll take the swelling down and the sting plum out of it." Hoot winked at the pretty senorita. "Guaranteed or you can run this snake oil salesman out of town on a greased rail."

Sofia turned her head toward him, frowning distastefully. She shook her head. "No."

She turned her head to stare out into the storm again.

Hoot frowned back at her. "Why not?"

"Go away. I don't know you. It's because of you I twisted it."

"I know. That's why I'd like to help." Hoot shook the hand holding the tin pressingly. "Go ahead. Rub some on. Can't hurt and I won't look. I promise."

He turned his head away while continuing to hold the tin out to the girl.

He didn't think she was going to take it. When he felt her fingers close over the tin and lift it out of his hand, he was pleasantly surprised.

"Don't look," she said tartly, the storm's roar nearly drowning her out.

"I won't."

He continued staring off to his right, toward that front corner of the cavern and at the gray sheet of the rain billowing over it, until he felt her set the tin on his left knee.

He turned back to her. She had closed her skirt over the ankle and was gently massaging it through the cloth.

After a minute or two, she looked up at him, mild surprise showing in her eyes. "It feels better."

"See?"

"I think the swelling might even be going down."

"See—I'm not a snake oil salesman, after all."

She wrinkled her nose as she stared down at her ankle hidden by her skirt. "Stinks something awful." She turned her questioning gaze to Hoot. "What's in it?"

"You don't wanna know," the cowboy said with a chuckle. "But don't worry—it's safe. I've used it many times myself. An old ranch cook gave me the recipe a few years ago, after I'd twisted my own ankle helping a momma cow and her calf out of a mud wallow. He said a Confederate medico raised in the Smoky Mountains had given him the recipe during the war. Took the soreness away and the swelling down in a few minutes. I was back on both feet later that day. Just movin' a little slow was all."

Hoot set the salve tin down beside Sofia. "Go ahead and take it. I can make more."

Sofia studied him, shook her head, and slid the tin back over to him. "No."

"All right, but you let me know when you want some more. It's best to keep it rubbed in for a coupla days, till it's all healed."

Sofia turned her expressionless gaze back to the storm.

Hoot sipped his coffee and rolled his eyes toward the girl. He liked her. She was pretty. He'd been alone for a while now, and he felt like talking.

He took another sip of his coffee, swallowed, and said,

"How come you're here, Miss . . . I mean, Senorita . . . Ortega? On the trail of Miller, I mean."

At first, he didn't think she'd heard him above the storm's steady roar punctuated with intermittent thunder. Then she slowly turned her face toward him again and said in a dull, toneless voice, "He murdered my husband."

"I'm very sorry to hear that. *Lo siento.*"

Sofia turned back to the storm. She wanted to sit here alone and in silence, but she felt this gringo cowboy's eyes on her. She also sensed his loneliness, maybe even his desperation. He wanted to talk. She supposed she could oblige him for a minute or two.

She turned back to him. "How did he get your horse?"

Hoot winced, sighed. He took another sip of his coffee and gazed straight out into the storm. He didn't want to talk about it. On the other hand, maybe it was best to confront the demons in his head. Trying to ignore them somehow seemed to make them stronger.

"I gave ol' Rowdy to him. Just turned him right over and even thanked him for taking him from me." Hoot blinked a sheen of emotion from his eyes. "My good, loyal horse, Rowdy, who I raised from a colt and broke myself." He shook his head in bitter disbelief. "I turned him right over without any objection whatsoever."

"Why did you do that?"

"Because he was Red Miller. I knew the man's reputation. As soon as I realized it was Red Miller I was facing, demanding my horse for one of his men who didn't have one, my blood ran cold. I won't tell you what else ran cold, since I'm in the presence of a lady, but it ran cold, all right."

Hoot took another bracing sip of his coffee then turned

to see Sofia still gazing at him, as though inviting him to continue.

"Fear," he said. "Just plain, bone-chillin', tooth splinterin', razor-sharp fear. Never felt it before. Not like that, and I once had to hold a pack of wolves off one night with burnin' sticks when my hoss went lame and set me afoot in the Cimarron River country." He shook his head again slowly. "Nope. Never felt nothin' like that before. Turned Rowdy right over to the son of the devil. Best horse I ever had!"

"How did you lose it? Your fear."

"He come for me later. Maybe an hour later. He was in a saloon in Tularosa. I was in the other saloon. Red an' his pards killed everybody in their saloon and then came over to kill everybody in the saloon I was in. I practically leaped out of my boots flying over the bar. A minute later I look up and there he is, standing on the bar, staring down at me with those great big fish eyes of his behind those thick spectacles. He held his big pistol on me, sorta smilin' the way a coyote smiles when it smells a rabbit near. Know what I mean?"

Sofia dipped her chin, nodding, her heart breaking as she wondered if it had happened like that with her Billy, too. Had Miller smiled that evil coyote smile at Billy before he killed him?

"Go on," Sofia said. "What happened?"

"He dropped the hammer on me. *Ping!*"

Sofia jerked with a start and a slight gasp.

"Sorry," Hoot said, "but that's how it happened. The gun was empty. That seemed to amuse ol' Red. Just scarin' the crap . . . er, sorry, I mean *stuffing* . . . out of me must have been enough. He sorta grinned, called me lucky, and rode away with my hoss."

"And your fear . . . ?"

"It was gone. Just before that hammer dropped, it melted out of my bones like butter in a skillet. Staring back at the ugly face of death like that just seemed to take away my fear of it." Hoot paused, sipped his coffee, looked out at the storm, then turned to Sofia again. "You know what I did then?"

"What?"

"I begged him to come back and kill me. You know— so I wouldn't have to live with my cowardice, knowin' what I did to Rowdy."

"But now you have decided to confront the devil head-on."

"That's right."

"And get your horse back."

Hoot smiled at her. "Yep."

Sofia returned his smile with a bitter one of her own. "Good for you, Hoot ."

"Thank you, Senorita."

"But I intend to kill him."

Hoot smiled as he sipped his coffee again. "We'll see about that, Miss Sofia. We'll just have to see about that."

Behind them, Stockburn studied the pair with hooded eyes. Their soft voices had awakened him; he'd heard every word of their conversation. He hadn't meant to eavesdrop but he was glad he had.

It's always good to know what's at stake for everyone in your party. They each had a stake for his or her own reason. Except for the Wildcat, that was. She was after the evil nun.

Stockburn hoped she got her just as he hoped either Sofia or Hoot Gibbons got Red. He himself didn't care who killed the man. As long as when the smoke cleared, Red was dead.

Wolf tilted his head against Elaina's and drifted back into a restful slumber.

CHAPTER 37

"How we gonna play it?" Lonesome Charlie asked early the next morning.

"I'm open to suggestions," Wolf said, keeping his voice down.

"I'm fresh out. That's a big-ass building, and we don't even know if Miller's in it or not."

Hoot Gibbons said, "Want me to go in and take a look around? I could say I was an early customer."

"No, you don't," Sofia said, casting the cowboy a defiant glare. She thumbed her chest. "I've got first dibs on Miller. He only took your horse. He murdered my husband."

To Stockburn's right, Elaina chuckled and tipped her head to Wolf to mutter, "Just by looking at them, you wouldn't think butter would melt in either one's mouth."

Wolf smiled.

"I didn't say I was gonna kill him," Hoot said. "Only see if he was in there. As soon as I find out, I'll come back out." He smiled at Sofia. "I promise. If you're so determined to shoot him first—well, then, go ahead. But let me punch one into him before he expires."

"Pull your horns in, both of you," Wolf said, sliding

the spyglass this way and that, carefully scrutinizing the hulking building. "Give me a minute to think it through. It's early and I'm still squishy in my thinker box."

They'd left the cavern well before the dawn's first blush. While the storm had had some venom in it, it had howled itself out just before sunset. By the time Wolf, Charlie, Sofia, and Hoot Gibbons had struck out on the southern trail behind the Wildcat of Chihuahua, the flood-waters had receded from the arroyos.

Now, after only another ninety-minute ride, they were hunkered atop a low, rocky ridge overlooking the compound of *Convento de Cuilapam de Guerrero*. From the southeast, they faced the sprawling, forbidden old masonry building with its four corner towers and the red-tile, arched roof of the cathedral flanking the main building. Early dawn shadows clung to the former *convento,* but its roof was dappled salmon and orange with the sun rising into notches between the tall ridges flanking Stockburn's party.

As Stockburn gazed through his glasses at the compound, he saw the shadows gradually thinning and retreating.

A large adobe barn fronted the nunnery/whorehouse to Stockburn's left. An old man in canvas tunic and baggy, rope-belted trousers had clomped out of the barn in sandals a few minutes ago, yawning and scratching the back of his bald head.

He'd opened the door of the adobe chicken coop that sat beside the barn, freeing twenty or so chickens of various sizes and plumages. He'd fed the chickens, calling out their names, then stowed the feed sack in a bin beside the coop and walked out in front of the barn to stare toward the convent looming large before him.

He'd filled a corncob pipe, lit it, stood leisurely puffing the pipe and gazing toward the convento as though waiting for someone to emerge.

The evil nun, perhaps? Wolf silently opined.

Wouldn't that be sweet?

What about Miller, Harris, and Brennan?

Charlie was right. There was no way to tell if they were here. There was a chance they'd come, picked up their virgin cargo, and headed north on a different trail from the one Stockburn's party had taken to get here. If they were hauling the girls in wagons, which would make sense, they'd likely need a wagon road of some kind. It would be possible to drive wagons on the trail Stockburn had taken, but it wouldn't be easy.

Definitely, it would be slow. Especially with the monsoon rains coming every evening. But in wagons they'd be easy to track . . . and relatively easy to overtake.

First things first. Stockburn had to find out if they were still here at the so-called convento.

"The kid's right."

Charlie, bellied up to the slope on Wolf's left, looked at him. "What?"

"The kid's right."

"Si," Elaina said, to Wolf's right. "The only way to know if they are here is to go on inside. We can't stay out here and call for them."

"I told you!" Hoot said.

"Only, I want you to stay out here," Wolf told Hoot, belly-down against the slope on the other side of Sofia, who lay prone on the other side of Charlie. "Charlie and I will do-si-do in the front door of the place."

"I can walk in a lot more inconspicuous than you two can," Hoot pointed out. "I mean, no offense . . . but an old . . . er, I mean . . . a *middle-aged* gringo and a big tall gray-headed drink of water? You two'll stand out where I'd blend in."

Stockburn shook his head. "I want you to stay out here and cover us with your carbine if we come out shootin'." He gave the cowboy a pointed look. "Most likely, we're gonna come out shootin'. And most likely men are gonna follow us out of there shootin'."

He silently wished they'd taken Azcona's Gatling gun. He'd considered it but had thought it would slow them down, which it most likely would have. It would be nice to have it now but they didn't.

Rifles and six-shooters were going to have to do the trick.

"All right," Hoot said. "I reckon you will need somebody out here. But let me give Miller the finishin' shot, will you?"

Before Stockburn could answer the cowboy's question, Elaina turned to Wolf. "I'll slip around the back of the place. There must be a rear entrance. If not, I will make one."

Stockburn opened his mouth to object but Elaina hurried to cut him off: "You are going to need help in there, *Hombre Grande*! Help on your flank. It's suicide to go in there alone, with no one backing your play. There is no telling how many armed men Sister Morales has working for her. And, then, there's Miller and his two devils, as well."

"What about me?" Sofia asked.

Elaina looked over Stockburn and Lonesome Charlie at the pretty young senorita. "I like your spirit. You will come with me."

"Wait, now," Stockburn said.

But before he could say anything more, the two women rose and hurried off down the backside of the slope together, an air of female excitement rising around them, like two debutantes on the eve of their coming-out balls.

"Damn women!" Wolf said, biting it out sharply, adding another epithet to the mix. "Riding with one was bad enough. But then you get two together and a fella loses all control!"

Lonesome Charlie nudged him with his elbow. "When it comes to Spanish women, no man ever really has control, Wells Fargo. Take it from me." He winked.

Stockburn chuckled in spite of himself. He picked up his spyglass and gave the convento one last lingering look. The only man he could see anywhere around the place was the old stableman. He was repacking his pipe and talking in sweet, dulcet tones to the chickens pecking the fresh feed around his feet.

No one was manning the front door.

Stockburn hoped that the sister's guard would be down this early in the morning, and that most of her men were still asleep. On the other hand, there was a chance the front door was locked, and that she didn't let anyone in till later in the day.

Only one way to find out . . .

Wolf returned his spyglass to its pouch. "Let's get a move on, Charlie." He turned to Hoot. "Keep an eye on that door for us, kid. And keep your trigger finger loose. You'll likely be usin' it soon."

"I'll be here," Hoot said, keeping his eyes on the door.

When Stockburn and Lonesome Charlie had crabbed down the ridge toward where they'd left their horses, Hoot shifted his gaze slowly to the big adobe livery barn near the base of the ridge he was on, to his left. Several horses stood in the rear paddock, munching hay from a crib.

One in particular caught Hoot's attention. He must have caught the horse's attention, as well. The rangy, sleek-lined coyote dun was chewing and staring up the ridge toward Hoot. In the clean, cool, quiet air of early morning, Hoot heard a familiar whicker.

The cowboy shaped a delighted smile. "Rowdy!"

Stockburn and Lonesome Charlie put their horses up and around the last bend in the steep trail and into the yard fronting the massive, foreboding *Convento de Cuilapam de Guerrero*.

The sun was an exploding lemon drop in an inverted V-notch of a far southeastern ridge, sending a sheen of dazzling golden light over the convent. It winked off the deep-set windows and caused the red tiles of the roof to glow like fresh blood.

Wolf and Charlie rode their horses on past the barn and up to one of the three hitchracks arranged near the base of the convent's front stone steps. They feigned a leisurely air—just two gringo saddle tramps who, having found themselves in the area this heavenly Chihuahua morning, had decided to see what all the fuss regarding *Convento de Cuilapam de Guerrero* was about.

Wolf dismounted, tied the reins to the hitchrack, and walked around to Smoke's right side. He reached automatically for his rifle then lowered his hand and turned to Charlie, who stood frowning a question at him.

Charlie said, "If we go in there loaded for bear . . ."

"We'll attract attention. Our hoglegs will have to do."

He patted Smoke's wither, said, "Stay boy. Hopefully, this won't take long."

He and Charlie shared a fateful look then mounted the stone steps and confronted the heavy, steel-banded oak doors. Stockburn tripped the steel latch, opened the door, and stepped inside. Charlie came in behind him, pulled the door closed.

Wolf and Charlie stood side by side, looking around the large, high-ceilinged, cavelike room. It appeared to have once been a worship area, or maybe where the nuns prayed or meditated in the morning. It was longer than it was wide. A second-floor balcony ringed the room, flanked by varnished doors with brass knobs behind which, Stockburn assumed, were whores' cribs.

There were five doors on each of the balcony's four sides. A total of fifteen rooms up there. There was only one person up there—a redheaded, full-bodied gal maybe in her midthirties and dressed entirely in white cotton underclothes and black silk stockings. Her thick, curly red hair hung down to the small of her back, some of it spilling invitingly forward.

Her face paint was smeared, and her chocolate-brown eyes looked tired as she gazed expressionlessly down at Stockburn and Lonesome Charlie. She leaned against the balcony rail to their right, roughly fifty feet above them, smoking and blowing the smoke down toward the main floor.

There was a vague question in her otherwise weary eyes.

Stockburn smiled up at her. She didn't return the smile but only took another puff from her cigarette.

Wolf cast his gaze across the room before him. It was lit by several windows, but the shafts of bright sunlight were broken by heavy velvet shadows. Smoke hazed the room in which twenty or thirty men milled, sitting at tables playing poker, or eating breakfast and partaking in desultory conversation. The room was broken up by gaudy dividers behind which Stockburn saw shadows move intimately.

All around the room's perimeters were velvet sofas and chairs and fainting couches, most of them occupied—men sitting with women in quiet, vaguely flirtatious conversations, or women sitting by themselves, talking desultorily or not at all. On one short blue velvet sofa, a young woman, as scantily or alluringly clad as all the others, was brushing out the hair of another young woman—this one a blonde though Stockburn had a feeling the blonde was from a bottle for the girl herself had deep, dark, Mexican skin and almond-shaped eyes that blinked slowly, luxuriously as the other girl slowly brushed her hair.

A bar ran along the far wall, to Stockburn's right. No one stood at the bar—either in front of it or behind it. Drinks were apparently still being served, though, for several of the male customers were drinking hard stuff or beer. Some drank coffee to go along with their breakfast that, judging the aromas, were eggs with chili peppers, grilled goat meat, big helpings of beans, and corn tortillas.

A short man in a white apron was just then serving up two large, steaming platters to two men playing cards with a half-dozen others, maybe twenty feet away. All of the card players wore three-piece suits with silk shirts, foulard ties, and short wool jackets with gaudy Spanish embroidering.

Wealthy businessmen. Where from? As far as Wolf knew, there was only one near village, but a small one. These men must be wealthy landowners who'd come from far and wide to enjoy the illicit pleasures of Sister Morales's evil convento.

The short man with the apron bowed and smiled to the diners then grabbed a couple of empty glasses and bottles from the table and hustled back in the direction of the bar.

The smell of the food made Wolf's mouth water.

He heard a wheezing, raking sound on his right. He turned to Charlie, frowning. Charlie nudged his arm then canted his head to indicate a big man sitting in a chair against the wall about six feet away from the front doors flanking the two newcomers. The man was a thick-set Mexican in a short black waistcoat, red pantaloons, and a ribbon tie. He wore a big, garish black sombrero with silver stitching.

His chair was tilted back against the wall. The toes of his high-topped black boots were suspended several inches above the floor.

The man was sound asleep, his bearded chin dipped to his chest, deeply snoring. His thick, dark, freckled hands were wrapped around a double-barrel, sawed-off twelve-gauge shotgun resting across his thick thighs. His right index finger was curled over the savage gut-shredder's eyelash triggers.

Again, Charlie nudged Wolf's right arm. He canted his head to indicate a small room opening on his left. Over the door a sign read: SALA DE ARMAS.

Weapon Room.

To each side of the door was a long, vertical sign warning in no uncertain terms:

SIN AMRAS EN CONVENTO! ¡DEPÓSELOS AQUÍ!

No weapons in the convent. Deposit them here.

The room had a counter running its width just beyond the open door. All manner of gun and knife lay on a table or hung from pegs in the wall flanking the counter. A large book, like a hotel register, lay open on the counter. Likely, the gun room was usually manned. Probably in the off-hours, when there was little new business, it was manned by the man who also pulled guard duty.

That man sat here behind Wolf and Charlie, dead asleep. Albeit with a wicked-looking twelve-gauge on his lap . . .

Stockburn and the old lawman shared a dubious look.

Absently, Stockburn tapped his right thumb across the big Colt Peacemaker holstered on his right thigh. He'd be damned if he was going to turn in his weapons while he was on the prowl for Red Miller. If he had to, he would. But the guard was asleep.

Everyone in the room looked three sheets to the wind. Even the gamblers. Besides, they were all too involved in their own affairs to notice the guns on the two newcomers.

Or so Wolf hoped . . .

"Come on, Marshal," Wolf said, strolling forward,

keeping his voice low, not wanting to draw attention to him and Charlie. "I'll buy you a drink."

As he wended his way through the smoky room cluttered with men, women, and furniture, he scanned the crowd for his quarry. He kept his right hand close to his right-hand .45. If Miller was in the room—and it was damned hard to tell with all the bright sunlight contrasting the heavy shadows, dust motes as big as 'dobe dollars, and smoke haze—as soon as the outlaw recognized Wolf, he'd leap to his feet and open fire.

There was no doubt about that.

Stockburn had to find Red before Red found him.

CHAPTER 38

Looking around the room as he sauntered toward the bar, Wolf lost track of his feet. He kicked a chair leg.

The man sitting in the chair, a dapper Mex with a girl on his knee, gave an indignant grunt and looked abruptly up at Stockburn. The man wore a red silk shirt and black silk string tie, and he had a cigar sticking out of his mouth. Thick, curly black hair capped his head; black muttonchop sideburns framed his long, hook-nosed face.

He gazed up at the tall detective, frowning curiously. His large, dark tan eyes were rheumy from drink.

Inwardly, Wolf cursed. He hadn't wanted to draw unwanted attention to himself and Charlie. He'd known that would be easy. His height alone made him stand out in a crowd; in a crowd of customarily shorter Mexicans even more so. His thatch of gray hair and his gray mustache didn't make him stand out any less. Then, there was the fact that he was a stranger in a strange land.

He became very conscious of the ivory-gripped Peacemakers thonged on his right thigh and holstered for the cross-draw on his left hip. The girl looked up at him, too, wonderingly. The man and the girl both looked at Charlie who had stopped to Wolf's left.

Two gringos are a long way from home.

Stockburn and Lonesome Charlie shared an uneasy look.

Finally, the Mexican staring up at him narrowed an eye and wrinkled a nostril, ashes dribbling from the burning end of his cigar, and he said, *"¡Mira a dónde vas la próxima vez, torpe patán!"* Watch where you're going next time, you clumsy oaf!

He returned his fawning attention to the girl; hers to him.

Inwardly, Stockburn gave a relieved sigh.

He and Charlie continued walking to the bar. The man in the apron was hustling another round of breakfast platters and tequila to another table, and there was nobody currently manning the bar. Wolf and Charlie gave their backs to the deserted bar, and continued to study the room, squinting through the sunlight, shadows, and the smoke haze so thick it was like ground fog. The peppery Mexican tobacco mixing with the spicy smells emanating from the breakfast platters made Wolf's eyes water and his stomach grumble.

He could do with a plate of eggs and spicy beans, a few freshly fried tortillas . . .

The kitchen must have been through a curtained doorway on the far side of the room, he silently opined. That was where the apron-clad barman was hustling the platters in and out of.

Again, Wolf scanned the room slowly.

"I don't see hide nor hair of him," Charlie said, standing

on his right now, casually rolling a smoke in his arthritic fingers. "I got me a feelin' he and them other two ring-tailed catamounts done pulled foot on us, an' we wasted a trip down here just to kill a nun."

He paused and glanced incredulously up at the taller Wells Fargo man. "Wait—did I just say what I think I said? Did we come down here to kill a nun?"

Stockburn chuckled and hiked a shoulder. "It's Mexico, Charlie."

"Si, Senor," Charlie said, keeping his voice low though the hum of conversation in the room was loud enough to drown their voices. "Only in Mexico will a man find a woman purty enough . . . and crazy enough . . . to convince him to help her kill a nun."

"Speaking of whom," Wolf said, casting his gaze to a curtained doorway at the cavelike room's rear, "where do you suppose she and Sofia are?"

"God only knows an' He ain't tellin'." Charlie struck a match to life on the bar behind him. "Er, maybe given the devilish caliber of this perdition, it's the devil his ownself."

"Can I help you, Senores?"

The question spoken in nearly perfect English and in a female voice caused Wolf to give a little start. The voice had come from behind him. He turned now to see a pretty, round-faced Mexican girl, as scantily clad as the others in the room, and with glinting stygian eyes, place her hands on the bar and lean forward.

"Ah, si, si, Senorita." Wolf smiled at the girl affably, and removed his hat. "My partner and I are dying of thirst."

"Hermono is busy, as you can see. I am helping out."

"Your English is near perfect, young lady," remarked Charlie.

The girl glanced around the room with a quick, furtive air. She returned her gaze to Wolf and Charlie and said, "I am not from here. I am from across the border, in the Arizona Territory."

Again, she looked quickly about the room, her eyes now owning a fearful, secretive cast.

She returned that gaze again to the two gringos, "What are you drinking?" she asked. She grabbed a bottle and two glasses, hastily filled one of the glasses. "Hurry. You need to have something to drink so you don't stand out the way you are standing out now. They are waiting for you. Don't you understand? *She* is waiting for you!"

Stockburn glanced at Charlie, frowning.

"Who is waiting for us, darlin'?" Wolf asked.

"Fools!" With quivering hands, the girl slid the glasses toward the gringos. "I had hoped you would save me. Free me from this place! Take me back to my family in Arizona. Don't you see—her bounty hunters took me! I have been waiting for you . . . or for men like you for two years . . . but now you have come and walked right into her trap!"

"Whose trap?" Wolf said, his right hand straying toward the grips of the Colt on that thigh.

"Hers!" the girl hissed, leaning forward, her eyes wide and round with urgency and terror. "And his! Miller knew you would come! He warned her! She has spies everywhere. You need to go . . . and come back with an *army!*"

Stockburn and Charlie shared another uneasy glance.

Then Stockburn turned to face the room once more. So did Charlie.

Both men froze. The puta behind the bar gasped.

Stockburn stared straight across the room. A woman in a nun's habit and flowing black robe stood just outside the door that Wolf figured led to the kitchen. She was a short, squat woman with a face like that of a baby bulldog.

Her pale cheeks were apple red. Her shallow eyes were not cold and calculating, as Stockburn would have expected from a woman with Sister Lucia Morales's reputation, but flat and indifferent. The beaded rosary that dangled from her right sleeve cuff caught the gold light of a near window and appeared to catch fire, extending the blaze into the nun's flat brown eyes.

Two big men in serapes and straw sombreros stood to each side of her, wielding Winchester rifles. She glanced to her right. Wolf followed her gaze to the Mexican who'd been sound asleep by the door.

He stood in front of the doors now, smiling. He held the savage twelve-gauge barrel down along his right leg.

Of course, no hired gun of Sister Morales would be asleep on the job. He'd been feigning sleep under the sister's orders to let the two gringos on the trail of Red Miller all the way into her trap. She didn't want Stockburn or Lonesome Charlie to suspect they'd been expected.

Sister Morales fingered the beaded rosary as she strode through the crowd toward where Stockburn and Charlie stood in front of the bar. The two big Mexicans accompanied her, having to slow their steps a little to stay in stride with the much smaller woman with her short legs concealed by the billowing robe.

As she and her two henchmen came through the crowd, the drinking and cavorting hall became very quiet. Faces turned toward the sister and the two big rifle-wielding gunmen, and then toward the objects of her attention.

"Well, Wells Fargo," Charlie said out the corner of his mouth, "how do you want to play this one?"

"Only one way to play it, Charlie."

"Yeah. I know." Charlie's tone was grim. "When you say . . ."

"Now!" Wolf said, reaching across his belly for the Colt on his left hip.

He'd just closed his hand over the revolver's ivory grips when a girl's scream cut through the now-silent hall. It was a ripping, terrified wail that echoed, making Stockburn's ears ring.

The scream froze everyone in the room, including Charlie, who stood to Wolf's right, his hand wrapped around the butt of his still-holstered Dragoon. As did everyone else in the room, Stockburn turned his gaze to the balcony straightaway and above him, where a stocky man with long, almost femininely pretty red hair shuffled out an open crib door. He shoved a girl out ahead of him, aiming a cocked pistol at the back of the puta's head.

The gun thundered. The girl's head jerked sharply backward. Her body followed her head over the balcony rail to turn another backward somersault before landing on the table at which six men were playing poker. Cards, coins, glasses, and blood flew in all directions.

The gamblers scrambled to their feet, stumbling and cursing and gazing down in shock at the dead girl on the table before them.

Red Miller stepped up to the balcony rail. He stretched his lips back from his teeth and, spectacles glinting fire in the bright red rays of the morning sun, gave a bellowing wail of untethered lunacy.

Five minutes earlier, Red woke slowly, enduring a violent disorientation as though pinwheeling through fog.

He heard a high-pitched squealing. It was so close to his ears that the din almost sounded as though it were coming from inside his own head. All he knew for sure was that at the same time he was waking, he was wrestling with a four-legged, ring-tailed demon that had stolen into his room to strangle him as he slept.

Horror gripped him as cold sweat bathed him. He had his hands around the green-eyed demon's scaly neck, and he was doing his best to squeeze the life out of the wretched thing. The demon stared up at him, laughing as it choked, the long, pointed horns protruding from its temples slashing dangerously close to Red's eyes. Its cloven hooves flailed wildly. The demon was very slowly—too slowly—growing weak from lack of air.

The demon's long, craggy face—a warlock's face if Red had ever imagined one—was swollen and red, several blue veins bulging in its forehead. It kept laughing as it choked. This was a growing frustration for Red, who needed to kill the beast before it killed him and dragged his soul off to hell.

Suddenly, another scream joined the first.

This second scream jolted Red from his lingering slumber, and he opened his eyes finally. He stared down in shock through his thick spectacles. Not a demon but a girl lay beneath him on a brass-framed bed from which most of the bedding had been ripped. Red's hands were wrapped around the girl's neck. She lay still and limp as an empty grain sack. She stared up past him at the ceiling, her light brown eyes swollen and blood-red from burst veins.

Her face was a queer mix of pasty white and robin's egg blue.

Her long, light brown hair hung slack about her shoulders. Her pale, freckled arms sagged at her sides. There was no kick in her legs. Her chest was not rising or falling.

She'd been dead a good long time.

Just as the knowledge that Red had strangled the girl in his sleep penetrated his thick, hazy consciousness, he realized that the first set of screams sounded as though they were coming from inside his own head because they were.

He was the first screamer.

He turned to see that the second screamer was the girl who'd opened the crib door just now. She must have been walking past the room to head downstairs; having heard Red's own caterwauling, she'd opened the door to find Red strangling the blue-faced corpse.

Red's heart thudded, raced.

Suddenly self-conscious, he stopped his own infernal caterwauling. He released the dead girl's broken neck and, reaching for the .44 on the table beside the bed, knocked over the bottle of Tilden's India Extract that the prissy sawbones, Teagarden, had given him. Nothing spilled from the bottle. It was empty.

And it was—or *had been*—his second full bottle.

He realized now in the back of his mind as he grabbed the revolver that he maybe should have taken the fancy-dan pill-roller's advice and gone easy on the stuff. His mind was no longer his own. The demons as well as the snakes and bugs he'd seen crawling the walls of the so-called convent the past three days, while he and Harris and Brennan had been turning their wolves loose before starting the long trip back north with the virgins, had probably not been real.

He vaguely remembered shaking a blanket out the previous night, after he'd come to the crib with the pretty little puta he'd now killed. She'd laughed at him, telling him there were no bugs in the bed, silly gringo.

Now he wheeled toward the puta clad in only her underwear, a pink cotton wrap, and black ankle boots standing in the open doorway, sandwiching her face in her hands and screaming in horror at the dead puta on the bed.

Miller leaped from the bed, spry as a kitten. Everything looked lens clear even in the bright light and thick shadows of morning. Even the bugs crawling over the screaming girl's face, slipping in and out of her open mouth and her wide eyes.

She looked at the gun in Red's hand, screamed even more shrilly then stumbled back out of the room. As she leaned back against the balcony rail, Red squeezed the Colt's trigger and watched the girl spread black wings and become a crow before taking flight and winging out over the drinking hall below, climbing . . . climbing . . . climbing to a high window.

He lurched out the door and turned the wild animal free inside him, raising a coyote-like yammering howl. He peered down into the drinking room below him and was mildly surprised to see the girl lying belly up on a table surrounded by cursing men scrambling to their feet, some with drinks and/or cigars or cigarettes in their hands.

"Miller!" came a woman's piercing screech.

He followed the sound to its source. Sister Lucia Morales stood near the bar, maybe fifty feet away from Miller's perch on the balcony. Her dark eyes blazed as she thrust an arm and pointing finger at him. "How did you get your hands on a gun, you fool?"

Miller grinned, raised his right hand, and rubbed his thumb and index finger together. The sister's beefy henchmen were not above a bribe offered for a weapon. Miller was not fool enough to let himself go unheeled in *Convento de Cuilapam de Guerrero*. Not with poisonous snakes slithering everywhere—across tables and under chairs and up the walls to hang from gas chandeliers.

Even when he half-suspected they weren't real.

The sister stomped her foot in fury. "The deal is off! No virgins!" She turned to the two henchmen standing to each side of her. "*Sacarlo! Sacarlo! ¡Mátalo!*"

Take him out! Take him out! Kill him!

The henchmen had only started to raise their rifles and shotguns when Miller grinned and extended his still-smoking Colt over the rail. He angled it down to aim at the dead-center of the sister's forehead, just beneath the white cotton habit. He narrowed an eye as he clicked the hammer back.

"Lower your weapons, *pendejos*, or I blow Sister Morales's brains out! You'll be out jobs and back in the gutters where you came from!" He laughed his lunatic laugh.

The sister's eyes widened in shock. She moved her small, little-girl's round mouth but no words issued.

"Pike?" Miller shouted. "Flipper?"

"Here, Red!"

Pike Brennan stood on the balcony across the room from Miller and to Miller's left. An open crib door flanked him. Inside the crib, a puta cowered on a bed. Brennan cast Red a wary look as he aimed his Smith & Wesson over the balcony rail and down into the drinking hall.

"To your left, Red," said Flipper Harris, standing outside a door two cribs down on Miller's left. He held a cocked hogleg over the balcony rail. Both men were disheveled and half-dressed but as alert as wolves. They'd ridden with Miller long enough to know to always expect trouble. Even when they least expected it.

Harris glanced at Miller, his own eyes uncertain. "What the hell happened?"

"Minor indiscretion," Red said, still aiming down the barrel of his Colt at the sister's head. "Time to pull our picket pines."

"I see that."

"Sister!" Red barked warningly.

Staring up at the maw of Miller's cocked Colt bearing down on her, the man's eyes unblinking behind his glinting glasses, Sister Morales said, *"¡Retirarse!"*

Stand down!

Stockburn watched the two beefy gents standing before him now, their backs to him as they gazed up at Miller on the balcony rail, follow the sister's orders. They lowered their rifles. The man with the shotgun lowered the twelve-gauge. Miller had not spied Stockburn yet. He must be too intent on the nun though the big rail detective stood only about seven feet behind her, beside Lonesome Charlie.

The two men turned their heads slowly to share a dubious glance.

Interesting turn of events.

CHAPTER 39

Miller looked at Harris and Brennan in turn, and nodded toward the smoky drinking hall below.

Both men kept their pistols aimed over the rail as they made their way in opposite directions along the balcony to separate sets of stairs. Harris made his way down the stairs at the back of the room, to Miller's left, while Brennan strode down the stairs at the front of the room, to Miller's right.

They left the stairs and walked into the hall and stopped, aiming their revolvers warningly. They had the sister and the sister's henchmen in a whipsaw.

Aiming his Colt at the sister's head, Miller gave a grim smile and said, "Send them two big Mescins for the virgins. Bring 'em out here pronto! Parade them right through this room and out the front door! Try anything funny, and the sister buys the farm!"

The sister's eyes widened, blazing.

Miller held his own menacing gaze and the barrel of his .44 on the nun's face.

Her eyes, cast with a cold apprehension, flicked from

Miller's lunatic gaze to the barrel of his .44 and back again. "*Vamos!*" she screeched at the two men beside her.

The men jerked to life. They glanced at each other in silent conference then wheeled away from the nun and trundled away, rifles on their shoulders, to the curtained doorway at the rear of the room.

When they were gone, the clomping of their boots and sandals receding, a heavy silence fell over the room until Miller glanced at Brennan and said, "Have that old hostler bring up the wagons from the barn, Pike."

Brennan nodded, swung around, and pushed out through the heavy oak doors.

Silence settled once more.

Stockburn glanced up at Miller, keeping his chin lowered just enough that the brim of his sombrero hid his eyes. He thought he had that and the sunlight and shadows in his favor. And the fact that Miller's crazy attention was on the nun.

She hadn't mentioned Stockburn.

In all the fuss, had she forgotten?

Or maybe he and Charlie were a pair of aces she'd hold until she needed them . . .

Maybe she was just scared.

Standing behind her, Wolf saw a single bead of sweat ooze from a pore high on her left cheek and dribble down the apple-red skin to her jaw.

All the customers and the whores stood or sat frozen in place, staring and blinking but otherwise not moving.

To Wolf's right, Flipper Harris stood aiming his revolver straight out in his right arm at the big man with the shotgun standing nearly in the middle of the room to Wolf's left, maybe fifty feet away.

Tobacco smoke billowed softly.

Golden dust motes danced in the gradually sliding shafts of morning sunshine while the shadows grew less dense, lightening with the growing day.

Wolf glanced up at Red again. He considered pulling his hogleg and blasting the man out of the balcony. The problem was a shaft of sunlight obscured Red, making it a tough shot. When he fired, he couldn't miss. And then he had to take out Harris on his right, also a murky figure in the sunlight and shadows.

There was also the problem of the man with the shotgun standing fifty feet away on his left.

Too risky. He and Charlie were in a whipsaw. He'd wait and try to take them outside where he and Charlie would have Hoot Gibbons's help.

No, that wouldn't work.

Now he saw that the problem was the girls. *They'd* be caught in a whipsaw. He had to take Miller in here, after the girls had gone outside.

Nasty situation. It wouldn't end well for any of them. He just had a feeling.

But, then, that was Mexico for you.

Absently, he wondered where the Wildcat and Sofia were.

Beyond the curtain, quick footsteps sounded. Men barked orders in Spanish, their voices echoing. There came a low roar of frightened female exclamations and cries also echoing off the masonry walls.

Presently, the curtain parted and one of the beefy henchmen entered the drinking hall, holding his Winchester up high across his chest. A small nun entered the drinking hall behind him. Wolf couldn't see the nun's face for she walked with her head down, eyes cast toward the floor. She held a rosary in both small hands as she strode forward behind the lumbering henchman.

The girls appeared behind her, coming through the curtain by twos and threes. Some sobbed. Several embraced as they walked, bawling quietly. Others stumbled forward as though in a trancelike state, following the nun into the room, the procession moving quietly toward Wolf and Charlie.

A second nun brought up the rear of the group of girls. Walking slowly with her head down, habit concealing her face, she was dogged by the second beefy, bearded henchman also wielding his Winchester.

The girls were clad in simple sack dresses and sandals. The sandals made quiet slapping sounds against the stone flags of the floor.

Stockburn glanced at Charlie. Charlie returned the wary, confounded look.

Stockburn's heart thudded.

Let them get outside, he silently urged the nun standing with her back to him. *Let the girls get clear.*

As though having heard his wise counsel, and deciding to defy it, she glanced over her shoulder at Stockburn. A cold smile shaped her lips. She turned her head forward again and screeched, "Senor Miller, your friend Senor Stockburn is here!"

She lurched forward, ducking and reaching for one of the girls just then walking past her.

At the same time, Stockburn ripped the Peacemaker from the holster on his left hip. Clicking the hammer back, he lifted the gun as well as his hat brim, and took quick, cool aim at Red Miller.

In Spanish, Sister Lucia screeched, *"¡Mátalos a todos!"*
Kill them all!

Stockburn drew a breath and centered his sights on Miller's chest. Miller's gaze had just found Stockburn. His eyes widened behind the glinting lenses. Cold fury shaped itself on his raptorlike features framed in all that red, womanish hair.

Miller slid his own Colt toward Wolf.

Wolf's Colt barked first but just as the sister threw one of the girls into him, forcing him back and to one side and nudging his shot into the balcony rail in front of Miller.

Miller howled as the bullet caromed off the rail and into his right side as he triggered his own revolver. The bullet barked into the floor a foot to Wolf's left.

"I got him!" Charlie shouted, bringing up his old Dragoon and triggering two quick rounds at the balcony.

But the howling Miller had turned and run back into the crib. Charlie's bullets tore into the crib's front wall and the edge of the door, missing Miller by inches. A moment later came the crash of shattering glass as the outlaw must have leaped out a window.

"Damn!" Charlie bellowed. "Missed that son of Satan!"

"Get down, Charlie!" Wolf shouted as the big henchman with the shotgun cut loose on him and Charlie with the twelve-gauge.

Several things happened at once as Wolf threw himself to the floor, on top of the young girl the sister had thrown into him.

Buckshot whined wickedly as it flew over him, Charlie, and the girl to pummel the front of the bar behind them. As Wolf aimed his Colt at the shotgunner and fired, he saw out of the corner of his right eye the nun who'd been dogging the virgin girls wheel suddenly toward Sister Lucia, who'd dropped to her knees and poked her fingers into her ears against the fusillade.

Only, the nun who'd been dogging the girls was no nun. Elaina, the Wildcat of Chihuahua herself, ripped the habit from her head and shook out her thick, dark brown tresses. She brought up one of her pretty, pearl-gripped, silver-chased Colts from a fold in her robes, aimed at the sister's head, and bellowed in Spanish, "Go back to the devil that spawned you, daughter of el Diablo!"

Sister Lucia's eyes widened in terror.

A second later, she was sporting a third eye about two inches above the bridge of her nose. The blast of Elaina's Colt rocketed around the room, keeping time with the echoes of Wolf's own Colt as his bullet tore into the chest of the big henchman with the shotgun. Stumbling backward, the big man fired the shotgun's second barrel toward the balcony above him.

Meanwhile, Lonesome Charlie howled crazily as he fired on Flipper Harris, who stared dumbly, apparently frozen with befuddlement at the quick, violent turn of events, unable to comprehend the fact of the nun drilling Sister Lucia that third eye. As the sister flopped back flat onto the flagstone floor, quivering as though struck by lightning, Charlie's slugs picked up Harris and threw him straight back onto a table behind which several customers were cowering, fingers in their ears.

Only about five seconds had passed since the start of the proverbial dance.

Wolf shifted his attention to the third and sole-surviving

henchman who'd been standing up near where all of the virgin girls cowered on their hands and knees on the floor, against the far wall. Wolf frowned curiously, held his fire.

His intended target lay belly-down on the floor, wailing and bleeding from his neck. He'd dropped his rifle and was trying to grab the back of his neck from which blood geysered and a knife handle protruded. The smaller of the two nuns who'd led the girls into the room just then planted one moccasin-clad foot on the bellowing man's shoulder and used both her hands to remove the obsidian-handled stiletto from the man's neck.

Sofia used the knife to cut the man's throat then straightened, snarling down at the henchman expiring at her feet.

She looked through the smoky, shadowy, sunlit air of the room, and her eyes found Wolf. She smiled.

"I'll be damned." Wolf looked around quickly, ready for another offensive.

None came.

The wicked sister was dead. Her three henchmen were likely dogging her heels through hell's smoking gates.

Charlie was on one knee to Stockburn's right, also looking around, his smoking Dragoon in his hand.

The two "nuns"—Sisters Elaina and Sofia—stood nearby, also looking around for trouble. They both ripped off their robes and habits.

The only other living souls in the room now were the cowering, unheeled customers and the virgin girls, who knelt in one big, quivering, bawling group between Sofia and Elaina.

The girls' sobs were the only sounds.

Stockburn turned to Charlie. "Miller and Brennan!"

He leaped to his feet and ran toward the front door.

Outside, guns crackled. A man screamed.

Another howled as though in victory. A horse's whinny pealed.

Hoof thuds rose just beyond the door. They grew louder as did the victorious yammering.

Wolf stopped in the middle of the room. Outside, a horse and rider climbed the stone steps. Hoot Gibbons rode a rangy claybank horse through the big, double-front doors, ducking his head but not low enough that the top of the door didn't rake his hat from his head.

Mindless of the dislodged topper, Hoot galloped the horse into the room, the shod hooves clacking on the flags. A man stumbled in behind the horse and rider. The man was bound with a rope. Hoot had the other end of the rope in his hands. He led the man into the room, stopped, and curveted the horse.

"*Whoah, Rowdy! Whoahhh!*"

Red Miller dropped to his knees about ten feet in front of the doors.

Hoot raised an arm and lifted another raucous, victorious yell at the ceiling, "Folks, let me introduce you to my new pard—that horse-thievin', cold-blooded murderin' old polecat *Red Miller!*"

Miller looked around dully. He'd lost his glasses. His head wobbled on his shoulders. Blood oozed from Stockburn's bullet in his left side. More blood oozed from a shoulder wound. He had a split lip, and one eye was swelling up.

"Hoot, you crazy loon!" bellowed Charlie, laughing.

Hoot looked down at Sofia, who stood just off his horse's right wither.

He smiled and dipped his chin nobly at the girl. He was a white knight bringing the princess her enemy's severed head. "Just for you, Senorita. I knew you wanted the honor of sending Red Miller to his reward."

Sofia smiled up at him. She looked at Miller and then at the crazy cowboy again. She stepped up close to Hoot's right stirrup, crooked her finger at him. When Hoot leaned down, Sofia planted a tender kiss on his cheek.

Then she went to work with her stiletto.

While Miller's screams caromed around the so-called convent, Stockburn, Charlie, and Elaina shepherded the sobbing virgin girls outside. Three barred wagons had been pulled up before the front steps. Pike Brennan lay near the wagons, twisted and bloody and dead.

Elaina herded the girls far away from the wagons and into the shade of the barn. When she'd gotten them settled down with her reassuring words, she strode over to where Stockburn, Lonesome Charlie, and Hoot Gibbons leaned against one of the savage jail wagons, which no longer had a use here at *Convento de Cuilapam de Guerrero*.

Meanwhile, the customers stumbled out of the convent's front doors looking dazed. They regarded Wolf, Charlie, Hoot, and the comely Elaina warily as they hurried to the barn for their horses.

Inside, Miller was still screaming beneath Sofia's religious chants delivered in some semblance of Spanish mixed with what was probably some Indian tongue. She was setting free her beloved Billy Blythe.

Stockburn turned to Elaina, frowning curiously. "Where on earth did those robes come from?"

"Sofia and I stumbled onto the room where the virgins

were being kept. They were guarded by two evil old crones."
She dragged her finger across her throat and smiled devilishly. "The habits hid our faces from the two pigs that
came for the girls just as we were about to squirrel them
outside. They were too intent on the girls to bother with
either of us crones."

"Hell of a thing for those poor girls to go through,"
Charlie said as he slowly rolled a quirley, glancing at the
frightened girls.

"Don't worry," Elaina said. "I will see that each is returned to her home."

Wolf glanced at her.

She shrugged. "What else do I have to do?"

"I thought you were going to head north and find a rich
husband."

"I think I am needed more here in Mexico." Elaina
turned to the girls milling in the shade of the barn, pulling
themselves together. She smiled, nodded, and turned back
to Wolf. "Si. This is my home. I will stay here where I am
needed." She curled her upper lip. "There are more devils
here in Mexico where Sister Morales came from."

"Indeed," Wolf said. "I reckon I'll be heading back to
the border to track the vermin north of it."

"I'll ride with you," said Lonesome Charlie, patting
Wolf's shoulder. "Wouldn't want you gettin' lost along the
way, Wells Fargo."

Stockburn snorted a laugh. He spied movement behind
him and turned to see the young puta who'd been behind the
bar when he and Charlie had entered the convent. The one
who'd been taken from Arizona. Wolf smiled and pinched
his sombrero brim to her.

"I got a feelin' there's gonna be quite a few of us headin'

north." Turning back to Charlie, he asked, "How you feelin', you old devil?"

Charlie frowned, drew a breath, and raised his left arm. He gave a happy though slightly puzzled smile. "Damn fine. In fact, I don't know when last I felt so good!"

Hoot Gibbons was leaning over the wagon's front wheel, also rolling a smoke. He cast Wolf a bashful glance. "I reckon Miss Sofia will be riding back north with you, too—won't she?"

"Yes, she will." Wolf glanced at Charlie, hooking a wry smile. "Why do you ask, young man?"

"Oh, I don't know." Hoot closed the quirley and shaped his bashful, slightly sheepish smile again. "I was wonderin' if I could ride with you all. I mean, since I'm alone. Just me an' Rowdy."

Charlie snorted.

Stockburn smiled at Hoot. "Sure. Why not? I don't think Sofia would mind. In fact, I think you just got on her good side for good."

Hoot blushed then glanced at the convent's open doors through which Red Miller's dwindling cries still issued. "That's good." He winced, shook his head. "I'd sure hate to be on her bad side!"

Wolf, Charlie, and Elaina laughed.

Keep reading for a special excerpt!

HELL'S JAW PASS
Wolf Stockburn, Railroad Detective

The building of the transcontinental railroad is the story of America itself. Full of great dreams— and greater dangers—it required bold vision, backbreaking work, and one brave man to stop the baddest of the bad men every step of the way. His name is Wolf Stockburn, railroad detective . . .

The killers are organized—and ruthless. One by one, they slaughter a railroad crew at Hell's Jaw Pass in Wyoming Territory. No survivors. No mercy. To ensure the rail line's completion, Wells Fargo sends their best detective, Wolf Stockburn, to the nearby mining town of Wild Horse. It's a rowdy little outpost full of miners, outlaws, and downright killers smack in the middle of two of the largest ranches in the territory. It's also as close to the pit of hell as Stockburn has ever been . . .

Train holdups, ranch wars, slaughter—this little boomtown's got it all. Stockburn's not sure he can trust anyone here, even the deputy's daughter. This pretty gal isn't just flirting with Wolf, she's flirting with disaster. And that disaster comes with a hail of bullets, and— before it's all over—a lot of blood on the tracks . . .

**Look for
HELL'S JAW PASS
everywhere books are sold.**

CHAPTER 1

Spotting trouble, Wolf Stockburn reached across his belly with his right hand and unsnapped the keeper thong from over the hammer of the .45 Colt Peacemaker holstered for the cross-draw on his left hip.

He loosened the big popper in the oiled scabbard.

Just as casually, riding along in the Union Pacific passenger coach at maybe twenty miles an hour through the desert scrub of central Wyoming, he unsnapped the thong from over the hammer of the Colt residing in the holster tied down on his right thigh. He glanced again at the source of his alarm—a man riding four rows ahead of him, facing the front of the car, on the right side of the aisle.

He was in the aisle seat. An old couple in their late sixties, early seventies, sat beside him, the old man against the wall and idly reading a newspaper. The old woman, wearing a red scarf over her gray head, appeared to be knitting. Occasionally, Stockburn could see the tips of the needles as she tiredly toiled, sucking her dentures.

Most folks would have seen nothing out of kilter about the man in the aisle seat. He was young and dressed in a cheap suit—maybe attire he'd purchased secondhand from a mercantile. The left shoulder seam was a little frayed and both shoulders were coppered from sunlight.

The young man wore round, steel-framed spectacles and a soot-smudge mustache. Stockburn had gotten a good look at him when the kid had boarded at the last water stop, roughly fifteen minutes ago. Something had seemed a little off about the lad as soon as Stockburn had seen him. Wolf wasn't sure exactly what that had been, but his seasoned rail detective's suspicions had been activated.

Maybe it was the pasty, nervous look in the kid's eyes, the moistness of his pale forehead beneath the brim of his shabby bowler hat. He'd been nervous. Downright apprehensive. Scared.

Now, the iron horse was still new to the frontier West. So the kid's fear could be attributed to the mere fact that this was his first time riding on a big iron contraption powered by burning coal and boiling steam, and moving along two slender iron rails at an unheard-of clip—sometimes getting up to thirty, thirty-five miles an hour. Forty on a steep downgrade!

That could have been what had the kid, who was somewhere in his early twenties, streaking his drawers. On the other hand, Stockburn had spotted a telltale bulge in the cracked leather valise the kid was carrying, pressed up taut against his chest, like a new mother holding her baby.

Adding to Stockburn's caution, a minute ago the young man had leaned forward over the valise he'd been riding with on his lap. The kid had reached a hand into the valise. At least, Stockburn thought he had, though of course he didn't have a full-frontal view of the kid, since he was sitting behind him. But he had a modest view over the kid's left shoulder, and he was sure the kid had shoved his hand into the grip.

As the kid had done so, he'd turned his head to peer suspiciously over his left shoulder, his long, unattractive face pale, his eyes wide and moist. He'd looked like a kid who'd walked into a mercantile on a dare from his school-yard pals to steal a pocketful of rock candy.

He'd run his gaze across the dozen or so passengers riding in the car, the train's sole passenger car for this stretch of rail, between the town of Buffalo Gap and Wild Horse. His eyes appeared so opaque with furtive anxiety that Stockburn doubted the lad would have noticed if he, Stockburn—a big man—had been standing in the aisle aiming both of his big Colts at the boy. Wolf didn't think the kid even noticed him now, sitting four rows back, in an aisle seat, staring right at him.

Stockburn's imposing size wasn't the only thing distinctive about him. He also had a distinct shock of prematurely gray hair, which he wore roached, like a horse's mane. It stood out in sharp contrast to the deep bronze of his ruggedly chiseled face. He wore a carefully trimmed mustache of the same color. He wasn't currently wearing his black sombrero; it sat to his left, atop his canvas war bag, which the barrel of his leaning .44-caliber Winchester Yellowboy repeating rifle rested against. His head was bare.

When the kid's quick survey of the coach was complete, he turned back around to face the front of the car, his shoulders a little too square, his back too straight, the back of his neck too red.

He was up to something.

Stockburn started to look away from the back of the kid's head then slid his gaze forward and across the aisle to his more immediate right, frowning curiously. A pretty young woman was staring at him, smiling. She sat two rows up from Wolf, in a seat against the other side of the car. The two plush-covered seats beside her were empty.

She was maybe nineteen or twenty, wearing a burnt-orange traveling frock with a ruffled shirtwaist and burnt-orange waistcoat and a matching felt hat, a little larger than Wolf's open hand, pinned to the top of her piled, chestnut hair. Jade stones encased in gold dangled from her small, porcelain pale ears.

She was as lovely as a Victorian maiden cameo pin carved in ivory. Her deep brown eyes glittered in the bright, lens-clear western light angling through the passenger coach's soot-streaked windows.

Stockburn smiled and looked away, the way you do when you first notice someone staring at you. It makes you at first uncomfortable, self-conscious, wondering if you're really the one being stared at so frankly. Certainly, you're mistaken. Wolf's gaze compelled him to look the girl's way again.

Her gaze did not waver. She remained staring at him, arousing his curiosity even further.

Did she know, or think she knew, him?

Or, possibly, she did know him but he didn't recognize her . . . ?

He smiled more broadly, holding her gaze now with a frank one of his own, one that was tempered ever so slightly with an incredulous wrinkle of the skin above his long, broad nose. That made her blush as she turned timid.

Cheeks coloring slightly, she looked down and then turned her head back forward.

But the smile remained on her rich, full lips, which were the color of ripe peaches . . . and probably just as cool and soft, Stockburn couldn't help imagining. They probably tasted like peaches, as well.

He chuckled ironically to himself. Get your mind out of the gutter, you old dog, he admonished himself. This girl probably still wears her hair in pigtails at home, and you're old enough to be her father—a disquieting notion despite its being more and more true of late.

Stockburn returned his attention to the back of the shabby-suited lad's head. He looked around the car—a quick, furtive glance. He thought he probably saw more in that second and a half gander than the suited lad had in his prolonged one.

Wolf counted fifteen other passengers. Five were women, all older than the chestnut-haired cameo pin gal. A young woman, likely a farmer's wife, sat directly in front of Wolf, rocking a baby he guessed wasn't more than a few months old. She and the child were likely en route to their young husband and father who'd maybe staked a mining or homesteading claim somewhere farther west.

A couple of men dressed like cow punchers sat nearly directly behind Stockburn, three rows back, at the very rear of the car. An old gent with a gray bib beard was nodding off on the other side of the aisle to his right. The rest of the men included a preacher and several men dressed in the checked suits of drummers.

One could have been a card sharp, because he was dressed a little more nattily than the drummers, but he probably wasn't much good with the pasteboards. You could tell the good ones by the way they carried themselves—straight and proud, usually smiling like they knew a secret about you and wouldn't you just love to know what it was?

This fellow, around Stockburn's age, with some gray in his sideburns, was turned sideways and laying out a game of cards, furling his brow and moving his lips, counseling himself, as though he were still learning the trade. Like his suit, his pinky ring had likely come from a Montgomery Ward wish book.

He wasn't a train robber. Stockburn knew his own trade, and he could usually pick a train robber out of a crowd. At least, seven times out of ten he could.

The two men behind him might be in with the lad near the front. He couldn't tell about the others, including the old couple. Just being an old, harmless-looking married pair didn't disqualify them from holding up a train. Stockburn had arrested Jed and Ella Parker, married fifty-three years, who'd preyed on passenger coaches for two and a half years before Wolf had finally run them down.

They'd enlisted the help of their forty-three-year-old son, Kenny. Kenny had been soft in his thinker box, as the saying went, but he, Ma, and Pa had gotten the job done, stealing timepieces and jewelry and gold pokes as well as pocket jingle from innocent pilgrims.

The Parkers had lost their Kansas farm to a railroad and had decided to exact revenge while entrepreneuring an alternative family business. Jed and Kenny had been as polite as church deacons. Ella, on the other hand, had cursed a blue streak, jumping up and down and hissing like a devil, as Stockburn had locked the bracelets around her wrists. If the detective business did one thing for you, it taught you that you never really knew about people. Even when you thought you did.

Hell, the cameo pin gal might even be in cahoots with the lad with the lumpy valise. Maybe she'd smiled at Wolf earlier because she suspected what line of work he was in, and she'd been trying to disarm him, so to speak. Stockburn didn't think she was a train robber, but he'd been surprised before, and it had nearly gotten him a bullet for his carelessness. He wasn't going to turn his back on this pretty little gal, which wouldn't be hard, as easy on the eyes as she was.

When the train slowed suddenly—so suddenly that Stockburn and everybody else in the passenger coach became human jackknives, collapsing forward—Stockburn was not surprised. His heart didn't even start beating much faster than it had been when he'd just been riding along, staring out at the sage and prickly pear, going over the assignment he had ahead of him—running down the killers who'd massacred a crew of track layers working for a spur line near the Wind River Mountains.

Wolf could tell by the violent abruptness of the stop that the engineer must have locked up the brakes. That meant there was trouble ahead. Maybe blown rails or an obstacle of some kind—a tree or a telegraph pole felled across the tracks.

The brakes kicked up a shrill shrieking that caused Stockburn to grind his teeth against it. Gravity pushed him up hard against the forward seat in which the young mother had slipped out of her own seat and fallen to the floor.

The baby was red-faced, wailing, and the mother was sobbing, staring up at Wolf with holy terror in her eyes.

The train continued slowing, bucking, shuddering, squealing, throwing Wolf forward and partway over the seat before him. He felt as though a big man were pressing down hard against him from behind, one arm rammed down taut against his shoulders, the other clamped across the back of his neck. He wanted like hell to reach for one of his Colts in preparation for what he knew was coming, but at the moment gravity overwhelmed him.

"Oh my God—what's happening?" the young mother screamed.

The young mother and the child were a nettling distraction. Stockburn's attention was torn between them and the young lad near the front of the train. That danger was bored home a moment later as the train finally stopped, and the big bully, gravity, finally released its iron-like grip on Wolf's back and shoulders. While Wolf stepped into the aisle, moving around the seat before him to help the young mother and the baby, the lad whom Wolf suspected of chicanery bounded up out of his own seat.

He, too, stepped into the aisle but without chivalrous intent.

He raised an old Schofield revolver and tossed away the valise he'd carried it in. He fired a round into the ceiling and bellowed in a high, reedy voice, "This is a holdup! Do what you're told and you won't be sent to hell in a hail of hot lead!"

At the same time his words reverberated around the car, evoking screams from the ladies and curses from the male passengers, another man—this one sitting at the front of the coach and on the same side of the aisle as Wolf—leaped to his feet and swung around, giving a coyote yell as he pumped a round into his old-model Winchester rifle. He was a scrawny coyote of a kid with a pinched-up face and devilishly slitted eyes.

Stockburn hadn't seen him before because he was so short that Wolf hadn't been able to see him over the other passengers. He doubted the kid was much taller than your average ten-year-old. He wore a badger coat and a bowler hat, and between his thin, stretched-back lips shone one nearly black, badly crooked front tooth.

"Do what he says and shut that baby up back there!" the human coyote caterwauled at Stockburn. He couldn't see the baby nor the mother, but the baby's screams no doubt assailed the ears of everyone on the coach, because they sure were assailing Stockburn's. "Shut that kid up or I'll blow its head off!"

Instantly, Stockburn's twin Colts were in his hands. He aimed one at the coyote-faced younker and one at the taller, bespectacled youth with the Schofield. "Drop those guns, you devils! Wolf Stockburn, Wells Fargo!"

Both youths flinched and shuffled backward a bit. They hadn't been expecting such brash resistance.

"S-Stockburn?" said the bespectacled younker in the shabby suit. He was aiming the Schofield at the rail detective but Wolf saw the hesitation in the kid's eyes. That same hesitation was in the coyote-faced kid's eyes, as well. They might have leveled their sights on him, but he had the upper hand.

For now . . .

"Wells . . . Wells Fargo . . . ?" continued the bespectacled youth, incredulous, crestfallen. One of his clear blue eyes twitched behind his glasses, and his long, pale face was mottled red.

The coyote-faced youth swallowed down his own apprehension and glowered down the barrel of his cocked carbine at the big rail detective. "I don't give a good two cents who you are, Mister Stockburn, sir. If you don't drop them two purty hoglegs of your'n, we're gonna kill you and ever'body else aboard this consarned train—includin' the screamin' sprout!"

CHAPTER 2

The passengers had settled down. Most had, anyway.

A few women sobbed, and the baby, still on the floor with the mother to Stockburn's left, was still wailing. The other passengers were in their seats and merely casting frightened glances between the two gunmen at the front of the coach and Stockburn standing near the feet of the mother with the crying baby, in roughly the center of the car.

Stockburn kept his two silver-chased Colts aimed at the two firebrands bearing down on him with a rifle and a hogleg, respectively.

"Children," Stockburn said tightly but loudly enough to be heard above the baby's wails, "you got three seconds to live . . . less'n you lower those guns and raise your hands shoulder-high, palms out."

Sliding his gaze between the two would-be train robbers, on the scout for a deadly change in their eyes, knowing these two were too green-behind-the-ears not to telegraph when they were about to squeeze their triggers, Wolf stretched his mustached lips back from his large, white teeth and barked, "One . . .!"

Both younkers flinched. Fear passed over their features. Their hands holding their guns on Wolf shook slightly.

"Two . . . !" Stockburn barked.

Again, they flinched. Both men's faces were pale, their eyes wide. No, they hadn't expected this. They hadn't expected this at all. They'd expected to come in here and fleece these defenseless passengers as easily as sheering sheep, then they'd be on their way to the nearest town to stomp with their tails up. "Apron, set down a bottle of your best labeled stuff and send in your purtiest doxie!"

Stockburn shaped his lips to form the word "Three" but did not get the word out before the coyote-faced lad slid his enervated gaze past Stockburn toward the rear of the car, shouting, "Willie! Roy! Take him!"

A black worm flipflopped in Stockburn's belly when he saw the two men dressed as drovers behind him lurch up out of their seats, cocking the hammers of their hoglegs.

Ah, hell . . .

Like any experienced predator, human or otherwise, when the chips were down, all bets placed, Wolf let his instincts take over. What he had here was a bad situation, and all he could do was play the odds and hope none of the passengers took a bullet.

He squeezed the triggers of both his Peacemakers, watching in satisfaction as the bespectacled youth, who triggered his Schofield at nearly the same time, screamed as he flew back against the coach's front wall. The coyote-faced lad screamed, as well, but merely fired his rifle into the ceiling before dropping it like a hot potato and falling back against the front wall, shielding his face with his arms, screaming, "Kill him! Kill him!"

As the guns behind Wolf roared loudly, he dropped to

a knee in the aisle, wheeling hard to his right, facing the rear of the train now as the two "cow punchers" triggered lead through the air where his head had been a heartbeat before. All the passengers were yelling and screaming again, and the baby was wailing even louder, if that were possible.

Stockburn intended to take the two men at the rear of the car down as fast as possible, before a passenger took a bullet. He shot one of them with the second round out of his right-hand Colt. The man jerked back, acquiring a startled expression on his thinly bearded, red-pimpled face, as he triggered one more round in the air over Wolf's head before collapsing, Wolf's bullet instantly turning the bib front of the shooter's poplin shirt red.

Wolf shot the second "puncher" with the third round out of his left-hand gun, for that kid—they were all wet-behind-the-ears, snot-nosed brats, it appeared—ducked and ran for the back door, triggering his own gun wildly. Fortunately, that bullet only hammered the cold wood stove in the middle of the car before ricocheting harm-lessly through a window on the car's north side, evoking a scream from the girl with the cameo pin face but other-wise leaving her unharmed—so far.

Straightening, Stockburn aimed both Colts at the kid running out the rear door as the kid twisted back toward him, raising one of his own two hoglegs again. Wolf hurled two more rounds at the kid, his Peacemakers buck-ing and roaring fiercely, smoke and flames lapping from the barrels.

The kid yowled and cursed as, dropping to his butt on the coach's rear vestibule, he swung to his left and leaped to the ground, out of sight. A gun barked in the direction from which he'd disappeared. The bullet punched a hole through the back of the car and pinged through a window to Stockburn's right.

Cursing, Wolf ran out onto the vestibule. Swinging right, he saw the kid running, hunched over as though he'd taken a bullet, toward where three other men sat three horses about fifty feet out from the rail bed. Those men were holding the reins of four saddled horses.

Apparently, those were the men who'd blown the rails. They were trailing the horses of the four robbers in the coach. Or the four *who'd been in* the coach.

Three still were though they were likely dead or headed that way. These three out here didn't look any older or brighter than the four Wolf had swapped lead with. They appeared startled by the dustup they'd been hearing in the passenger car, and their horses were skitter-stepping nervously. One man was having trouble getting his mount settled down and was whipping the horse's wither with a quirt.

They were all yelling and so was the kid who was run-limping toward them, tripping over the toes of his boots.

"What in the bloody tarnation happened?" one of the horseback riders yelled at the wounded kid running toward him.

"Wells . . . *Fargo!*" the run-limping younker screeched.

Another horseback rider pointed toward Wolf. "Look!"

The run-limping kid stopped and glanced warily back over his shoulder toward Stockburn standing on the rear corner of the vestibule, aiming his right-hand Colt toward the bunch while holding the other pretty hogleg straight down in his left hand. Stockburn shaped a cold grin and was about to finish the limping varmint when a girl screamed shrilly from inside the coach.

Stockburn's heart leaped.

He'd forgotten that he'd left that sandy-haired little devil with that dead front tooth still alive.

He lowered his right-hand Peacemaker and ran back into the car, stepping to his right so the open door wouldn't backlight him. Good thing old habits die hard or Wolf would have been the one dying hard.

A gun thundered near the front of the coach. The bullet screeched a cat's whisker's width away from Stockburn's right cheek before thumping into the front of the freight car trailing the passenger coach.

Stockburn raised his Colt but held fire.

The nasty little sandy-haired devil with the dead front tooth held the pretty cameo pin girl before him, his left arm wrapped around her pale neck. He held his carbine in his right hand. Just then he jacked it one-handed and aimed it at Stockburn, spitting as he bellowed, "I'm takin' the girl, big man! You come after me, she's gonna be wolf bait!"

The kid backed up, pulling the girl along with him toward the coach's front door, keeping her in front of him. She stared in wide-eyed horror at Stockburn standing at the other end of the car.

Her hat was drooping down the side of her head, clinging to her mussed hair, which had partway fallen from its bun, by a single pin. A red welt rose on her left cheek. The sandy-haired devil had slapped her. Her mouth was open, but she didn't say anything. She was too scared for words.

Rage burned through Stockburn.

As the kid pulled the girl out the coach's front door and

then dragged her down off the vestibule, Wolf hurried forward, yelling, "Everybody stay down!"

He holstered both Colts and grabbed his Winchester rifle from where it now lay on the floor in front of the seat he'd been sitting in. He was glad to see that the young woman with the baby appeared relatively unharmed. She sat crouched back against the coach's left wall, against the window, rocking the still-crying baby in her arms, singing softly to the terrified infant while tears dribbled down her cheeks.

Stockburn pumped a cartridge into the brass-breeched Winchester Yellowboy's action, strode down the central aisle. The passengers were muttering darkly among themselves while another child cried and the old lady with the old man wept, the old man patting her shoulder consolingly.

Once they were all out of the carriage, the sandy-haired little devil started running toward the three men on horseback, pulling the pretty gal along behind him. The young robber Stockburn had drilled was toeing a stirrup and hopping on his opposite foot, trying unsuccessfully to gain his saddle and sobbing with the effort, demanding help from the others.

"Look out, Riley!" one of the men on horseback shouted, pointing at Wolf.

Riley stopped and swung back around. He pulled the girl violently up against him and narrowed his mean little eyes at Stockburn, showing that dead front tooth as he spat out, "I told you I'd kill her, an' I will if you don't—*owww*!" the kid howled.

The girl had spun to face him and stomped one of her high-heeled, black half-boots down on the toe of his own right boot. The kid squeezed his eyes shut and hopped up and down on his good foot before snapping his eyes open once more and then smashing the back of his right hand against the girl's left cheek.

There was the sharp smack of hand to flesh.

The girl screamed, spun, and fell with a violent swirl of her burnt-orange gown.

"I'll kill you for that," Riley bellowed, raising his Winchester, his face wildfire red with fury. "I'll fill you so full of holes your rich old daddy won't even recognize you, you McCrae whore!"

"Don't do it, you little son of Satan!" Wolf narrowed one eye as he aimed down the Yellowboy at the kid. In his indignation at having been assaulted by the girl he'd been trying to kidnap, the little devil seemed to have forgotten his more formidable opponent with the Winchester. "Raise that carbine one eyelash higher, and I'll send you back to the devil that spawned you!"

Riley snapped his gaze back to Stockburn, eyes narrowed to slits. A slow, malevolent smile spread his lips. "My father is Kreg Hennessey. Yeah, Hennessey. Get it? Understand now?"

The kid bobbed his head twice as though Stockburn should recognize the name. "If you shoot me, you're gonna have holy hell come down on you, mister. Like a whole herd of wild hosses!" He turned his slitted demon's eyes back to the girl, who stared up at him fearfully. "This little witch just struck me. Thinks she's so much 'cause she's a McCrae! You just struck a Hennessey, and you're about to see what happens when even an uppity McCrae strikes a—"

Stockburn squeezed the Yellowboy's trigger. He had no

choice. There was no way in hell the kid was not going to kill the girl. The little snake was not only cow-stupid, he was poison mean. And out of control.

The Yellowboy bucked and roared.

The bullet tore through the kid's shoulder and whipped him around to face Stockburn directly. The kid triggered his carbine wide of the girl, the bullet pluming dust beyond her. She gasped and lowered her head, clamping her hands over her ears.

The kid held the rifle out to one side, angled down. He held his other arm out to the other side as though for balance. The kid glanced at the blood bubbling up from his shoulder as he stumbled backward, rocks and little puffs of dust kicked up by his badly worn boots.

A look of total shock swept over his face, his lower jaw sagging, mouth forming a wide, nearly perfect "O."

Still on one knee, Stockburn ejected the spent cartridge from the Yellowboy's breech. Wolf pumped a fresh round into the breech and lined up the sights on the kid's chest as gray smoke curled from the barrel.

"Drop it," he ordered. "Or the next one's for keeps."

Riley stared back at him. The kid glanced at his shoulder once more, then looked at Stockburn again. The shock on his face gradually faded, replaced by his previous expression of malevolent rage. Jaws hard, he gave a dark laugh as he said, "You're a dead man, mister!"

He cocked the carbine one-handed then took it in both hands, crouching over it, aiming the barrel at Wolf, who pumped two more .44 rounds into the kid's chest. The rounds picked the scrawny kid up and threw him two feet back through the air to land on his back.

The girl screamed.

The kid writhed like a bug on a pin, arching his back, grinding his boot heels into the dirt and gravel. He hissed like a dying viper. He snapped his jaws like a trapped coyote. He lifted his head to look at Wolf, and he cursed shrilly, his oaths growing less and less violent as the blood leaked out of him to pool on the rocks and sage beneath him.

Finally, his head sagged back against the ground.

"Dead man," he rasped, chest rising and falling sharply. "Oh . . . you're a . . . dead man . . ."

His bloody chest fell still.

His head turned slowly to one side.

His body relaxed against the gravel and sage.